THE ELDER

THE ELDER

A NOVEL BY

Cris Freddi

Alfred A. Knopf ✸ New York 1985

THIS IS A BORZOI BOOK
PUBLISHED BY ALFRED A. KNOPF, INC.

Library of Congress Cataloging in Publication Data

Freddi, Cris.
The elder.

I. Title.
PS3556.R367E4   1985   813'.54   85-40119
ISBN 0-394-53914-1

Manufactured in the United States of America
FIRST EDITION

for Les Milkins again

THE ELDER

The Glen

HIGH IN THE MOUNTAINS, in the keep of a castle hewn out of a cliff, a small cowled figure looked down from a window over the valley far below.

The cowl and the man's sacking robes were white as a bone. In that overcast place, in the hour before dawn, they were the only hint of light.

The hooded figure stood without moving, propped against the sill, and looked into the valley as if—even from that steepling height, even in the dark—nothing was hidden from him.

In daylight, the entire glen was clearly visible from the keep. A spring, gushing from some obscure grotto in the hills below the castle, tumbled into a big strong healthy river that flowed along the length of the valley and spilled into the coastal waters at the western cliffs. On both sides of the river, the country reached out flat and rich with silt, divided into broad open fields by a cross-work of woven hawthorn hedges—or crowded with deep ancient oakwoods, the land eventually rising into high slopes of grass and sapling woods, ribbed with long, undulating drystone walls and split in the steepest places by thin deep coombs cut in the hillside by sharp little waterfalls. These in turn became streams that hurried into the main river at all angles and urged it through enormous banks of reeds and rushes, past endless poplars in single file, through to the sea.

Beyond the sea, and beyond the vast upland moors above the glen on either side, there was nothing at all.

Back at the other end, the thin end of the V-shaped valley,

a set of hunchbacked hills squatted against the first cliff of the huge mountain range. The castle, built on the very highest hill with the cliff behind it, was cut out of the mountainside itself, so that its back wall was also part of the cliff face. The other three walls were high and massively thick—as deep as the height of six men—and bolstered with turrets that reached from the ground to high above the battlements. Each tower was blank, grey and windowless, the only gaps in the stone cylinders being a series of slits for archers, cut in the shape of crosses to fit bows and crossbows.

The single gateway, with its barbican that also served as a belltower, had been built in the centre of the front wall. The vast gate-door, like most other constructions in the valley, was dark and oak. It opened onto a steep path leading down to the lower hills and the river spring.

Inside the fortress, a cobbled courtyard sloped up away from the gate to the cliff wall—to the keep, the tallest round-tower, built right up against the wall, far higher than the rest of the castle —reaching up, it seemed, into the giant peaks themselves.

The mountains were of iron-grey granite, the oldest and hardest stone, veined black with basalt. As they stood there, dark and silent and utterly still, it was hard to imagine they'd been formed by huge upheavals of land—that once, millions of years before, they'd boiled and lifted and thrust up from the ocean floor, violently molten. Millions of years before. Not now.

The castle, made from the same stone, had a similar forbidding look to it. Stern and cold, blown by endless high winds, it overshadowed the countryside from its grim rocky fastness. A stronghold not a place to live.

It stood so high above the valley that on a clear day someone looking down from the keep could have seen all the way to the distant shoreline, beyond the chalk cliffs of the firth to some of the sea—and, to left or right, the first stretches of high moorland.

On a clear day. Not now, surely, in the early hours, with the entire glen and surrounding heaths lost in darkness. And yet the man in the cowl stood looking down from his window for over an hour, turning his head at intervals or leaning out as if to examine things more closely. The room behind him was unheated and sometimes he shuddered.

First light came up behind the mountains, first touching the coastal stretches, then seeping slowly back along the valley towards the hills and the grey citadel. The man in the white robes leaned out of the window and made a feeble gesture with his hand. Almost at once, the barbican door swung open at the start of the day. The man watched the first soldiers ride down into the valley, then turned away from the window and limped across the room.

It was a small square chamber, bare and always dark, the walls thick as the very oldest tree, the floor a single stone slab. There was nothing in it besides a disused iron torch-clasp on one wall and a skinny steel mirror next to the only door.

The hooded man stood in front of the mirror. For a while he did no more than that, standing with his hands together in his big sleeves in front of him.

He made no sound and there was nothing from outside— while the only, faint movement was under his robes, where his thin ribs were jostling for breath.

The dawn, having spread its way over the valley and border-ing hills, came in through the window, and the stone room was in some kind of half-light by the time the man in white unclasped his hands. When he drew the cowl back from his head, his face, in the mirror, was easy to see.

The features had slackened with old age, and it was mostly skin and bone. There was no hair on the head, a wrinkled dewlap under the chin. The eyes were wet.

Just the face of an old man, then. Any old man. Nondescript, even anonymous. It was the face of the oldest and so the most exalted man or woman in the glen—and he seemed to like the look of it. The lipless mouth opened a fraction, closed, and he pulled the hood back over his head, shrouding the face in shadow.

Again he stood still for a time, as if the minimal effort had exhausted him. Then he shuffled across to the door and lifted the latch. The oak panels had been made purposely thin and the whole thing was no higher than a small man, but he struggled to open then pull it shut behind him.

There was a ledge outside, unlit and very narrow, a tightly spiral stairway at the end of it. The man padded his way down the steps and his sandalled feet were noiseless on the stones as he vanished into some dark unknown recess of the fort.

The early morning outside was autumn chilled, with mists that rose from the light ground frost and drifted in from the sea to swathe the knees of the oak forests and cloud the hillsides—and gasp through the shanties where the valley dwellers lived, the bizarre townships that cluttered vast areas of every slope in the glen, like giant wooden boxes piled one on top of the other. Thousands upon thousands of them.

Somewhere in the mist, a madcap cockerel woke up late and crowed all morning till someone finally kicked it quiet.

THE BOY

The Stag

BY THE TIME HE WAS FOURTEEN, Jeo hated his grandmother more than anything. He hated the rest of the family too—his father, sister and four brothers—but he wasn't afraid of them and he didn't hate them as much. Not nearly as much.

Jeo lived with the family in one of the great sprawling shanty towns, on the southern slope above the river. The shanties were all made of wood—oak from the deep forests—and they were enormous, some of them more than thirty storeys high, none of them less than twenty, and all at least a dozen rooms deep, so that each block was like some huge wooden warren, with thousands of corridors between the crammed box-rooms.

If the construction was rudimentary, the design was no better. In fact, there was no real design, no architecture. As more peasants were born, when a new family needed housing, another set of planks was pegged together to form a rough cube, and added to the tenement wherever there was space: perched on the highest storey or squeezed between two existing rooms or fixed with rude stakes in the ground.

Each tenement was founded on the lower slopes, never on the valuable farmland of the valley floor, so that every ramshackle block soon reached a height where it touched the steeper upper slopes, and many of the rooms pressed their backs against the hillside.

The older quarters, usually at the base of each building, were darker, often black—and the more recent additions didn't stay fresh and tawny for long. Those not already stained green or dark brown while the oak was still growing were soon discoloured by smoke and refuse and the weather. Or covered in a thick mattress of moss, or studded with fungus. Warped and split, in time. In these colossal shambles, fires were frequent, structural collapse a daily hazard, thieving and covert violence as common as rats.

Jeo and the family lived in one of the upper storeys, deep in the middle of their block, enclosed on all sides by other similar dwellings. They lived in two rooms: old mother Cromarty in the larger garret, the others all together downstairs. Throughout the glen, it was a system bound in time, inviolate—and no one, least of all in Jeo's family, seriously questioned it. Except Jeo. It was one of the reasons he hated his grandmother.

It was quite cold and still dark when Jeo woke from his usual semi-sleep. He was lying outside the family quarters, curled into a very narrow space between two rooms across the corridor. He slept here almost every night, tucked deep in the shadows, hidden from the passageway by the darkness and a big wooden board propped across the alcove. There wasn't much room in this tight little gap, but it was a better place to sleep than the single room overcrowded by the rest of the family. At least he was left alone here.

He got up as soon as he was awake. The gap was narrow but it was quite high, so he was able to stand upright and stretch himself, arms above his head. He yawned, tugged his tunic and kilt into place, then bent to look under the heather-filled sack that served as his bedding. He found a small cloth pouch attached to a very long coil of rope which he wrapped twice around his waist and tied in a knot so that the pouch hung down in front of him. Another yawn as he stood up and did nothing for a moment, just listening. Then he slid the oak board to one side and stepped out into the passage.

Here the darkness was more grey than black. The corridor, like the rest of the tenement, was never truly silent, but in the very early morning it did have a kind of restless quiet. Jeo glanced along it, left and right, seeing next to nothing in the dark, listening as much as looking. His hearing was very good. He caught the sound of some small rodent rustling along a beam. Someone was snoring in an overhead room. Old wood grunted behind him, muffled in the distance. A fly made its noise somewhere else. Jeo crossed to the family room and pushed the makeshift door ajar, only slightly open.

Blackness, so for a time he couldn't see a thing. As usual, he noticed the smells in the room. Warm unwashed bodies asleep, heather and hanging onions, a latrine bucket. And charcoal, the great smell of the tenements.

There should have been any number of different wooden odours in the shanty towns. Fresh new-cut planks, old joists and rafters pimpled with fungi, landings and disused stairways deep in lichen, soft damp wood, very dry wood, old oak and sapling furniture. All this wood—but it had no smells. They were all masked, hidden deep under the reek of charcoal—of the part-burnt fuel itself, of things cooked over it, of smoke. Even the darkness of the apartments was due in part to interior walls being black with the soot.

Jeo sniffed and slid his thin little body through the half-open door and stepped quickly round the first bunk. His father lay sleeping face down, his snores losing themselves in the rag pillow. Jeo moved across the bare floor, between the beds of his brothers, past the oak trestle-table, the benches and the charcoal burner, to the far side of the room.

Here, in one corner, a slope of charcoal reached almost to the ceiling. In the other, Jeo picked an armful of bullrushes from the tight pile fenced in against the wall. He carried them under his arm to the adjacent wall, where a clumsy wood ladder led up to a trapdoor in the ceiling. In the short bunk beside the ladder, his sister Sharn rolled in her sleep and made wet noises with her mouth. Jeo scowled at her in the darkness before climbing the ladder, pulling himself up with his free hand.

At the top he pressed the trapdoor open with his palm, threw the rushes through the gap, hauled himself up after them. Then he got up and stood in his bare feet in the common blackness of his grandmother's room. He didn't shut the trapdoor.

He couldn't see, so he smelled things. The retch of dirty reeds and rushes and stale foods, of the slop bucket and piss on the wood floor, of charcoal, of course—and the sickly, rather sweet smell peculiar to old people who weren't washed, the one Jeo always noticed first. Other children grew accustomed to it.

Jeo stood where he was for a while. He left the bunch of rushes on the floor and fiddled with his fingers as he stared in the direction of the big bed across the room, listening for sounds of breathing.

He stood like that every morning, block-still and breathless, listening for sounds, wondering if someone was watching him from the shadows of the bed he couldn't see.

He bent and groped for the rushes, gathered them in both arms, always staring towards the bed. He put the rushes down on a bench by a wall, took a twig broom from where it leaned on the same bench, crossed the room—a sudden movement on the bed crackled the dry heather in its mattress, and Jeo took an involuntary step backwards, eyes wide in the dark.

Nothing else happened, no more sound. Jeo crossed the room in silence, away from the bed, reached a corner and began sweeping the floor, blindly bustling the soiled rushes towards the trapdoor. He worked hurriedly and as quietly as he could, hoping to finish the chore without waking anyone.

He cleaned nearly all the room and held the broom in one hand at arm's length to garner the last remaining rushes from somewhere near the bed—and there was another, heavier movement on the mattress.

This time Jeo stood absolutely still. He knew from the very thin grunting breathing that his grandmother was awake. There was a short twitching hiatus, then he made some small helpless noise and the old woman realised someone was in her room.

"What now? What's that?" The voice, half-asleep, was

hoarse and damp—the phrases meaningless, as they often were. Jeo was used to them.

"It's me," he said in a low voice. "Jeo. I'm cleaning."

The old woman coughed in the dark. She said something but it was lost in the cough. Jeo waited and she cleared her throat and said a single word but he didn't hear it clearly.

"What?" he said, his voice louder with impatience.

"Senior," she repeated angrily in a higher tone. "Senior, boy. Use the word when you speak to me."

"Senior," muttered Jeo with feigned humility. The word was a term of reverence. The young were expected to use it whenever they addressed their elders. Jeo used it as little as he could get away with.

"What are you doing, child? What?" Jeo frowned. The old hag knew he came to her room to clean it. What else would he be doing there? Why did she ask the same questions every time? He hated her stupidity.

"Cleaning," he said again.

"Speak out, boy. How can I hear if you whisper?"

Jeo was sure she only pretended to be hard of hearing. "I'm cleaning," he spoke up.

"Senior!"

"Senior."

"Cleaning? In the dark, lad? Why always in the filthy dark? Make a light. How can you see?"

Jeo had been dreading this more than anything. Sometimes, when he was lucky, the old woman didn't wake up at all. At other times, she woke up and was content to lie there in the dark as she scolded him. And sometimes, rarely, she wanted a light in the room.

He was shuddering as he turned to look for one. His eyes were almost used to the darkness by now. A few grey beams straggled in through gaps in the plank walls. But the boy had no need of them. There wasn't much in the room and he knew where it all was.

When he reached for the tinderbox on a table, he fumbled because he was afraid. He didn't want to look at his grandmother. He hoped the tinder would be damp. It often was.

It was dry and he lit it with his first blow of the flint. He touched the flame to a candlewick and stood the candle upright in its iron stick.

Turning away from the table and facing towards the bed, he kept his eyes down—but then the old woman made an incontinent noise in her throat and he glanced up, still holding the broom handle hard in his small fist.

The dirty crate of a room was auburn in the candlelight. Larger than the family room downstairs but equally Spartan. Just the four walls, without tapestries or carpets, or glass to let in light. Blotched with black shadows, the coarse blankets on the bed a bundle of browns. Old Cromarty was sitting up in the bed, her back against a wall, her hands pulling at her hair.

She had extremely long hair. It was thin and off-white and hung loose to her waist, where she could pick at it with her brittle fingers.

Her face frightened him so he gave it no more than a glance, but he saw it all too clearly. He knew it from memory.

Her features were nearly lost in folds of old skin. A jutting nose dominated the face, above the very thin tight mouth pursed by wrinkles. Even as a young girl she'd had an obvious nose. It was the feature of her face. Now, as the skin had stretched on the bone, it was more prominent than ever.

Her eyebrows, either through her own attentions or in the natural way of her face, were very thin and arched—and, together with the lines on her brow, highlighted her eyes and gave her a fixed malignant look. Even her rare smiles, which Jeo had never seen, seemed vicious.

Jeo hated and feared the very sight of her. Not because she was ugly or always angry or feeble-minded or horribly crippled —though she was all of that—but because she was old. He wished she'd go and live with others of her own age.

For some reason she didn't speak to him any more as he went on sweeping her room, and for that he was grateful. But all the same he sensed her eyes on him as he went about his work in the half-light.

The floor was thick with the soiled rushes and he swept them into a heap beside the trapdoor, making a bad job of it in his haste. He replaced them with fresh ones, scattering them on the bare boards, found the wooden slop pail and filled it with the old rushes, then took the bucket and broom in one hand and used the other to help himself down onto the first rungs of the ladder.

Only his head and scant little torso were still in the room when Cromarty made a sound halfway between a laugh and a growl, and Jeo jerked his head round towards her.

She was still sitting up and her hands were working her hair in front of her, but now she was leaning further forward from the waist and looking up from under her brow, staring hard in her grandson's direction. In the candlelight her crone face gleamed like puckered fat. Jeo could see both the bones in her forearm, the topknot of skin at her elbow. He tried to hide his blench of revulsion.

"That boy," she mumbled. "The look in his eyes. Won't say Senior not at all and been the same since he was a bairn. That look in his eyes. Have to cut it out if we can. Have to."

She didn't seem to be talking to him at all, but there was no doubt where her eyes were looking. Jeo almost fell down the steps of the ladder in his haste to escape from the room.

The crude oak door swung inwards on its hinge pegs and Jeo stepped carefully out into the corridor.

The passageway was still empty, but rather brighter than before. Bits and pieces of daylight had found their way into it, through cracks and splits in the timber roof and walls. The boy put the broom away in his own sleeping den, then walked quietly along the passage with the bucket in his hand.

The corridor seemed to go on forever and was still dark, but Jeo was quite visible from the far end. His white arms and legs and face leered in the darkness.

He was visible, but there was no one to see him. It was very early morning on the one rest day of the week and the gallery was empty. Jeo was glad of that. The tenements were never entirely safe, especially for a small skinny boy. There was often someone waiting round a corner or in a rough alcove or moving along the corridors, alone or in a gang, with sticks or a stolen knife. Jeo had pressed a piece of bread and a sausage in his pouch. He wasn't going to eat them. If he were attacked in the passageways, the food would be taken from him and he might be left unhurt. He kept his eyes open as he went.

He passed a hundred shadows along the walls, passing slowly, ready to run fast if he had to, his eyes always moving. The angles of wall and ceiling were soft with veils of cobweb, some broad as blankets. Long heavy planks, their surfaces disfigured by knots like walnuts, leaned upright against walls and across doorways. Thin blades of wood poked riskily through splices in the timber. Once or twice Jeo's face was briefly lit by a wedge of light angling up between floorboards. His feet made little sound in the dust and sawdust. They were bare but hard as boots, and splinters didn't bother him. He passed any number of doors—heard a chandler's family rising in one, old Coreach the stonemason relieving himself in another. Something creaked in the floor above his head. Someone coughed or groaned behind a wall or a door. And always the thick smell of charcoal, and charcoal smoke where early morning braziers were lit.

Jeo carried the bucket to the end of the corridor, turned the corner, went down another passageway—there was a sudden noise behind him and he jumped round to face it.

There was just a small dog in the corridor. A cairn terrier with its ears pricked up, its oatmeal colouring blending with the surrounding wood, even in the shadows. Just a dog, one of the hundreds that infested the shanties, living off pilfered scraps and sleeping where they could until someone caught and killed them.

Jeo, when he'd recovered from the fright, smiled at the terrier. He took one of the rushes from the bucket and held the lank thing out, offering it to the dog as he crouched towards it. The little scavenger backed away and snarled at him. So he scowled and threw the contents of the bucket at it. The terrier ran away with a yelp, disappearing down some thin old hole in the wall.

The boy stood for a moment to examine the inside of the pail. He'd been meaning to take it down to the river, to empty the mess in the water and collect a bundle of fresh rushes. But now he decided not to bother.

He didn't want to carry the bucket with him, but he couldn't leave it lying around to be stolen, so he looked around for a place to hide it, and found one. He walked away down yet another long passageway, leaving the slops uncleaned behind him. The rushes would soon be eaten by a dog or a ferret or a small child, and the rest would stink for a while. Then the charcoal would take over.

He moved on, with all his usual nervy stealth, on the balls of his feet, putting his head round corners before turning them. He went away from the centre of the tenement, out to where the walls were thicker and the wider corridors were empty with echoes and criss-crossed by broad shafts of dusty light that sliced the darkness and sent a quick fulvous glow across his face and limbs as he passed through.

He blinked when the light hit him, and squeezed his eyes almost shut when at last he came out of the shanty onto a broken porch in the brash morning sunshine.

He was facing east. The sun crashed down along the valley from behind the giant peaks directly ahead of him. It was still quite low on the sky, pouring its rays between the mountains rather than beaming over the top. Jeo shielded his eyes with a hand as he looked around him.

The porch he was standing on was some twenty floors up. From there he could see much of the eastern half of the glen. The striated flank and roofing of another tenement block in front of him, lower on the slope. A long way down to his right, the daylight springing about on the river. Nothing very different on the other bank.

He stepped off the clumsy platform onto an old broken stairway, picked his way down the steps, and stood for a while in the grass at the bottom.

Again he looked around, and still he didn't see anyone. He turned his back on the river and after a quick frown into the sun in the direction of the castle he set off up the slope on his left.

On the other side of the river, a man on a horse saw him climb the hillside.

As the sun went up towards noon, the shadow cast by the mountains was pulled back into the foothills like something shrinking from the light. And as the sun climbed, Jeo went up the long south slope.

The hillside was cut by a number of simple dirt paths, bordered with thin grasses and very yellow ox-eye daisies—but Jeo didn't use the paths. He walked barefoot in the grass, which was still damp and in places long enough to tickle his knees so he had to stop and scratch. In other parts it was cropped short, especially in the narrow green-lanes between any two of the drystone walls.

Jeo stood up on one of the walls, a few feet off the ground, and strolled along it. It was a clever piece of construction, made without mortar—so the top stones were loose and not for walking on. But Jeo found it easy enough. He skipped along the wall with practised balance, arms slack by his sides, whistling badly to himself. Soon he jumped down. There was no challenge in it any more, and there were quicker ways to travel, especially now that the slope was abruptly steeper.

Not for the first time he looked back down the hill behind him. Yet again nobody there, and he wasn't surprised. No one, almost no one, was allowed out on the rest day. It was precisely that, a day of enforced repose, in preparation for the next week's work. Only the old people and the guardsmen who policed the glen could leave the shanty towns and go where they pleased. Jeo, the son of a bondsman and only fourteen years old, could not.

But sometimes, like this day, he simply had to get out. He would be caught eventually and his father would beat him as he always did, but Jeo didn't care. It was worth a beating to be out here, out of the introverted slum in the bright, cold sunlight with dew on his legs and a day's ramble ahead of him. It was one of the few pleasures. He wouldn't give it up easily.

He walked on, more slowly, forced to push with his legs on the steeper ground. He glanced ahead more than once, at the crest of the hill, in places russet and blurred with heather. He saw, high on his right, a cloud of morning flies bustling in the air, above what he knew to be one of the Shrieking Pits. He turned his eyes away from them and went further up the hill.

There was hidden stamina in his spare little body, so he didn't stop along the way until he came to a point where one of the sheep walls was very thick and rounded in the form of a small shrine.

Jeo approached it slowly. He stood in front of it with his hands by his sides, and looked inside. It was a shrine like any of the others dotted around the valley hills. Just a simple stonework alcove, with a small flat slab as a ledge jutting out of the back wall. On the ledge, a grey stone statuette made without skill in the shape of a cowled figure in robes.

Jeo took two steps into the shrine, enough to bring him within easy touching distance of the statue. He had another of his frowns on his face.

The figurine had been sculpted so that the hood hid the face. Jeo wanted to smash the thing. It was small and dry and old, chipped in places, easy to break in many pieces. He left it alone. If he broke it, it would be found and he would be blamed, he was sure of that. They would take him to one of the Pits.

He left the image alone, without so much as spitting on it, and hurried out of the shade back into the sun, to stride up the hill without a backward glance. Quite near the top of the hill he took a small knife out of the pouch at his waist and toyed with it as he went.

A last look behind him and he caught sight of a henge of standing stones on the very top of the far slope across the river. They were gigantic sarsens, far bigger than any house, but from that great distance they were like small conical stacks, shadowy in the mist. Jeo turned away and threw his knife ahead of him.

Jeo loved the knife, one of the very few things he didn't hate. It was a beautiful, crafted piece of work, a short, slender dirk with a bone handle and a clean two-pronged iron blade. A very old, almost ancient knife, the only old thing he was fond of—though he liked it because, in a way, it was no longer old. He'd scraped the rust and field mud from it, rubbed a shine into the blade, cleaned every trace of dirt out of the bone—till he felt he'd wiped all the age off it. He also loved it because he owned it. He had no other possessions.

As he walked he played with the dirk in any number of ways: throwing it any distance to land, always blade-first, in the ground; throwing it fast or slow; tossing it spinning in the air to catch the tips of the blade as it came down, snatching the sharp metal in just two fingers. He threw it out of the back of his hand, or fast and carelessly from hand to hand, or hand to mouth, trying to catch it with his teeth. He threw it at things and was annoyed if he missed. He had something like mastery over the knife—and no fear of it, which was unusual; he was a boy who was afraid of many things.

Near the crest of the slope he heard sounds and hastily pushed the dirk back in the pouch, hiding it in the cloth folds at the bottom. Two sheep appeared on the skyline and trotted down the hill in his general direction.

Jeo stood and watched as they wandered down past him—on their way, he knew, to their fold at the base of the hill, away from the open fields as winter came near. They were ugly scrawny creatures, small blackface hill sheep, their hides still bearing the marks of the shearing knife. Another sheep came over the rise, then a few more . . . slowly, the rest of the flock. Jeo watched them amble down the hill. Several had their rumps dyed in various bold colours. Some had rough brown wool like sackcloth. One wore a small bell round its neck, jangling as it went.

The distant bark of a dog turned his eyes back up to the hillcrest—and he was startled to find someone else suddenly standing there ahead of him, in the low mist on the brow of the slope.

She was a strange looking girl, wild and ragged and staring at Jeo with something fierce in her face. He made fists of his hands and though she wasn't close to him he took a sideways step.

On such high ground, with so little cover, there should have been a wind, above all now in autumn. But there wasn't. Not so much as a whisper. The mist was undisturbed. And yet the girl's hair had a draggled windswept look to it, bunched and jostling on her shoulders, almost hiding the wide bands of bronze she wore as earrings. It was brown hair, but tinged with something like purple, the colour of fresh heather. Her face, unlike Jeo's, was tanned. The curves of her body, under the yellow spun tunic, were all muscle.

Jeo noted all this and didn't speak. They stood and looked at each other in silence. Jeo said nothing because every time he saw this girl she made him very nervous. Though she was no more than a year older, she made him feel like a child. The girl didn't speak because she was mute.

She stared at him with big eyes, not looking at his meagre little limbs and sprawling black hair or the small owlish nose on his very flat, wide, white face. She looked only at his eyes, and stared at him as if she—and perhaps only she—could see that though his face was saturnine, underneath it all he smouldered. She came down the hill to stand closer to him and he took another stupid step away.

At this point, Jeo felt he ought perhaps to speak or something. He felt awkward saying things to her because he knew she couldn't talk back. So he put a small silly grin on his mouth and gave her a nod.

She grinned back at him, but it was an altogether different expression. He could see her tongue between her teeth. He looked away from her face. Her tunic was short and rough, very dirty but bright yellow with dye from gorse petals. She moved her hands deliberately over the front of it, still grinning.

He tried not to look at the gesture, stared instead over her shoulder, up towards the top of the slope, at nothing in particular, wondering what to do next. Someone else appeared and caught his eye, and the girl turned to follow his gaze, taking the smile from her face.

A shepherd in dark clothes came over the rise and stood there, utterly still as he looked at the two youngsters below. Jeo looked back at him, timidly. The shepherd didn't move, and Jeo could see all too clearly why his kind were known as Lookers in the valley. They could stand or sit motionless for hours, scanning the hillsides and open moors for predators or a stray lamb, and seeing what went on in the glen, watching people as well as sheep. Quiet and patient as herons. Just looking. Always looking. A big border collie, trotting a few paces behind the shepherd, came and sat down and waited beside him, its mouth half open.

Jeo and the girl stood still. Jeo wanted to run away. The shepherd came striding towards them down the hill, holding a short willow crook in one hand, the collie at his heels.

He was a short wiry man, older than middle aged, with a hard weathered face tanned a kind of grey. Jeo saw at once that unlike most other valley men he had no beard. Indeed, his face was altogether hairless, as if winds and the rain had worn it smooth. He wore a thick olive green smock above a black kilt, a grubby white plaid slung over one shoulder crossing his chest down to where a broad shearing knife hung from his belt.

Jeo glanced at the stub of rolled tobacco that was always on the man's lower lip, and saw it was unlit. He glanced too at the metallic brown hair under the flat tweed cap, at the single iron earring—and back into the shepherd's hard stare. He had to look away. The old man moved his eyes briefly from Jeo to the girl.

Jeo knew he kept her in his house, though she was no relative, and was harshly jealous of her. His name was Gara.

"This is the rest day, boy. You know that. You shouldn't be out here." The voice was coarse-grained and strong. Jeo couldn't think of anything to say so he nodded his head.

"What are you doing up here?" the shepherd went on. He glanced again at the girl and scowled. "Come to see my Rhosarran, is that it? If you have, boy, I'll beat all the skin off you and leave you to the hawks."

He moved a pace nearer to the boy, who retreated shaking his head. The girl also shook her head, and stepped in front of the old man, putting her hand on his arm to restrain him. Gara pushed her aside and she staggered down the hill. Jeo watched and did nothing.

The shepherd spat on the grass. "Touch me again, you young slut, and I'll break my crook across your back. Now get you away and take the beasts down. Wait for me there."

For a moment, Rhosarran stood defiantly still, and clenched her fists. Gara lunged at her with his crook and she ran down the hill, following the flock to the fold at the bottom.

Gara stared after her, then turned sharply to Jeo, who was still standing there with his mouth open. The shepherd reached out and slipped the curve of the crook round the boy's neck. Jeo didn't try to escape it. He allowed himself to be pulled a couple of paces across the grass.

The shepherd had the same old-people smell Jeo had breathed in Cromarty's attic, but it wasn't as strong. He smelt more of hircin and rough old tobacco and chiefly of new sweat.

"Now, boy." Jeo stared up into the brown, grampian face, very close to his own. He made a move to draw his head back but the crook held him in place. "If you've not come to stare at my housegirl, tell me what you're doing here, rest day and all. Tell me quickly."

Jeo licked the ceiling of his mouth. "Going for a walk," he said weakly. The shepherd punched him on the forehead and pulled him back with the crook to stop him falling, holding him closer.

"Senior," he said quietly.

"Senior," mumbled the boy. There was a pain in his head and his legs didn't feel strong.

"Going for a walk," said Gara. "Going for a bloody walk, on the rest day." He frowned deeply in Jeo's face. "Listen to me, my lad. Look at me. You go for too many walks. I've seen you. I'm not the only one. I don't want to see you taking a walk, boy —not on the rest day. Understand me?"

Jeo nodded. "Yes, Senior."

"I don't want to see you at all, not up here in the hills. You stay in the wooden places, boy. Work in the fields. Keep your nose clean. People are watching you. Any more walks and they won't just watch, understand? No more walks. Say it."

"No more walks," said Jeo glumly. The shepherd hit him again, this time on the cheek with his open hand. The hand was hard as leather and Jeo nearly fell again. Gara gripped the shoulder of his tunic to keep him upright, took the crook away and poked him in the chest with it.

"Senior," he said grimly. "When will you learn, boy?"

"Senior," said Jeo.

"No more walks."

"No more walks, Senior."

"Not on the rest day."

"No, Senior."

The shepherd nodded. Jeo hung his head. He couldn't stop the tears so he tried to hide them.

From somewhere down the hill, the sound of a small bell. Gara recognised it at once and jerked his head round. It was the sound of his bell-wether, the old ewe with the bell at her throat, and the sudden clanging noise told him she was moving faster than usual, perhaps because the flock was in danger, running from a predator or a thief. He cursed under his breath, turned back to the boy and spoke faster than before.

"Don't walk any more today." The voice was still stern but seemed far away. Jeo wasn't listening any more. "Go back to sleep. That's what you do on the rest day. Lie down, sleep, stay inside. Like the Elder wants you to do. Now piss off and don't let me see you again."

He tugged the boy's tunic, spun him round, and sent him stumbling down the slope with a hard prod from the crook. Jeo recovered his step and walked slowly away down the hill.

He turned to face the old dalesman and looked at him, just for a moment, before turning back to sprint off into the distance, running across the slope rather than straight down it.

Gara scowled again as he watched him go. The boy had said nothing to him when he turned. Just a look, that was all. But it was enough to make the shepherd think. He didn't see that kind of look very often in the children of the glen. His girl Rhosarran had it, and he could do nothing about it, though he sometimes beat her and kept her without food. She only had it in her eyes when she was anywhere near this Jeo brat. He'd noticed that, and it dug at him inside, angered him.

He tapped the tip of the crook on his teeth. So what was it? A rebellious glance, shared—or the expression of something carnal. Either way, it troubled him.

The sheep bell jangled insistently in the valley, clattering across the shepherd's thoughts. He paused just long enough to watch Jeo disappear over a distant wall, then hurried away down the hill, moving as quickly and sure-footedly as one of his own rams.

It was the middle of the morning and Jeo had no intention of going back to spend the rest of the day in the dark tenement. He swarmed over a wall and crouched behind it, peering between the topstones as he watched the old man stride off down the hill. Then he got to his feet and set off up the slope towards the skyline.

The early chill was gone from the air, warmed by the

stronger sun. The sort of day Jeo liked. He walked with a brisk step, feeling the sun on his neck rather than the pink bruise on his cheek, whistling out loud.

He looked one last time behind him into the valley, and again saw no one watching him. Just animals out to pasture and scare-crows. He looked up in the air and shut his eyes at the sun, lifting his arms straight above his head as he stood on tiptoe and stretched his body in the warmth.

He turned his back on the glen and was about to move up further south when he glanced at the mountains far away to the right.

He saw them every day. They were part of the scenery. Big and bright now in the rising sun. Tawny, for the most part. Grey, white, shadows everywhere. They were good to look at, usually. Now, truant that he was, he could almost believe they were threatening.

He looked at the high grey castle. His eyesight was very good and in the sunlight he could see the whole thing well. Wall turrets and battlements and tiny windows, but no faces—and yet it was said that anyone in the glen could be seen from the fortress. He remembered what old Gara had told him. How he, the shepherd, wasn't the only one watching him. But could he really be spied from so high up, so very far away? It didn't seem possible. But then Jeo couldn't be sure. He'd never been in the castle. He didn't want to be sent there.

He stared for a time at the great central keep. Like everyone else in the valley, he himself had seen the Elder more than once, when the old man leaned from the high window at dawn and ordered the central gate-door to be opened—with a motion of his white-sleeved arm. With just a small movement of his arm, Jeo reflected. To have such power. . . .

A picture appeared in his mind, of himself in an old man's white robes.

He turned quickly away and marched off through the first broad patch of bracken, crossed an acre of ugly long grass, climbed a small knoll and found himself looking out over a spread of countryside totally different from the valley and its hills. A vast tract of moorland, miles and miles of it, reaching as far as he could see ahead of him. Jeo hugged himself as he stood and stared at it.

It didn't look anything to get excited about. There were peat bogs everywhere. Great raised bogs the size of basilica domes. Others no bigger than hummocks. Drowsy with cotton grass and bristling with sedge. Deep black scars and furrows showed where the glen people had exercised their turbary rights by digging the peat for fuel.

But the bogs, big though they were, were merely dotted around the scape. They didn't dominate. Their browns and blacks and lichen greens seemed no more than dark worn patches in a huge rug of ling heather.

It stretched to the horizon in a great monotony of endless purple, scarcely interrupted by gorse bushes, trees, the odd straggling brook, the bogs. Where the heather had been scorched to make room for game birds, the reaches of purple were punctuated by burnt black squares, the whole expanse laid out in an enormous tartan in front of the skinny boy who stared at it all with wide eyes.

Jeo didn't think the moors were beautiful to look at. But he hugged himself because they were broad and open and empty, quite unlike the tenements and the valley hills. He could get away from things out here, away from the glen people. And besides, who could know what was beyond these great heaths? Somewhere else perhaps. A place where you didn't have to be old to do the things you wanted. He took his knife out of its pouch and played with it as he walked on.

In places, the ground was hard and stony, with few bushes and some short grass. In others, it was soft and deep, wet as a sponge. One minute Jeo found he was squelching through a bog with the damp peat reaching over his knees, or struggling waist-deep in fells of heather, where he could slice off a dozen bell-like flowers with one slash of his knife. Just a few paces on, he was

treading bare granite flats or a bed of gravel that almost hurt his
feet. Once, he pushed through a bank of deer sedge and came across
a thin shallow beck hurrying splashily over its stony bed to some
distant coomb or another, wider stream.

The bridge across the beck was cut from the same stone as
the surrounding banks, and but for the row of keystones on the
lower rim would have looked like a form of natural arch. Jeo
didn't think about it. He knew the bridge from earlier rambles. It
was just a bridge. He stood on it and spat in the brook, watched
as the water swallowed his spit and carried it briskly away,
watched till he couldn't see it any more, then ran over to the far
bank and scampered off over the next spread of moor, throwing
the dirk high ahead of him and running to catch it by the handle
as it fell. Before long he came to a wide dip of grassland on the
edge of a spinney—a deep corrie bristling with short trees.

Being a hollow, it still had a mist, on the ground and up
between the trees. Jeo wasn't interested in the place and would have
moved on—then, from somewhere deep in the fog, a sound that
stopped him in his tracks. The loud coarse bellow of something
heavy and inhuman, booming out twice through the mist. Jeo
stood still and something loomed out of the fog between the two
nearest trees.

At first the boy could see no more than a shape, no taller than
himself. He thought it was a guardsman and he was afraid. It came
closer and he saw it was a deer.

There was another right behind it. Two short slender hinds
with very dark grey bodies and long faces. Utterly harmless. Jeo
knew at once that neither of them could have made those loud
roars. He stared behind them into the mist, waiting for another
bellow. There was silence for a time, so he turned back to the hinds
and took a couple of steps towards them. They took several stiff
paces back. He moved a little closer and they bolted back into the
hollow, deep into the thicket of fog.

Jeo noticed that they hadn't seemed at all frightened by the
great roaring sounds, as if they were used to them. Perhaps they

might lead him to where the sounds came from. More curious than afraid, he followed the deer down the slight slope, almost crouching as he walked, the knife held out in front of him in both hands in an exaggerated pose.

It was a patchy fog, thick at the base of the hollow, very faint near the top of the far slope where Jeo found the rest of the herd huddling in and around a small compendium of hybrid trees.

Some were browsing in the misty heather, searching with their lips for toadstools and bilberries, others nosing at the bark of the trees themselves, or standing around doing nothing. The moment they caught sight of the boy, some distance away, they lifted their heads to him and stood very still and staring. They all seemed to have things in their mouths, chewing over and over, always at the same regular pace. Most were small—young or female—though a pair of junior stags moved to the front of the group to face him. They made no sound as they stood there, and in the silence, for no reason at all, Jeo caught the distant cry of a curlew.

He wondered what to do. He looked hard at each of the stags, trying to decide if either or both could have made those loud noises. They looked back at him, wary and ruminative, wondering what he would do.

From somewhere beyond the herd, another great bellowing call, louder this time because it was nearer. Jeo had been half-expecting it but he was scared all the same. The deer pricked up their ears at the sound, one or two moved their heads, but otherwise they seemed to take no notice. The two young stags glanced behind them, just for a moment, then turned back to go on watching the strange young boy.

Jeo adjusted the grip on his knife, then set off in the direction of the sound, circling left to skirt the herd. They moved only their heads to follow him with their eyes, watching as if impassively. He quickened his step, left them behind in their hazy netherworld, and was back on the open moor, where the breezes had largely swept all mists away.

A long slope stretched away ahead of him, nothing but bog

grass and a few stemless thistles on it. It reached up as far as a small shaw of mountain ash knee-deep in strange undergrowth. Jeo couldn't see beyond the trees.

Another hoarse cry, from behind the ash thicket ahead. Not so loud this time, more of an after-grunt. The boy hesitated when he heard it, but only for a moment. He padded up the rise and pushed his way, timorously and as quietly as possible, through the undergrowth.

The long low hill reached almost to the sky before levelling out into the rest of the moorland. All pea-green grass with the sun all over it. Near the crest of the slope, very dark against the light sky and snorting to itself as though in a rage, stood the oldest and by far the biggest highland stag Jeo had ever seen.

He knelt in the shadow of a tree and gaped at the huge thing as it paced the ground and made noises in its nose and throat, biting the grass as it pawed the earth with a hoof and threw its head right back to open its mouth wide and roar at the air. As if completely demented.

Jeo had an idea the herd's breeding season was at hand, and the great beast was blurting its defiance to any other stag which might dare to challenge its monopoly of the hinds. He stared at the sheer size of the animal, at the span of its antlers and the depth of its chest. It was big as an elk, very deep brown with a great black ruff of neck hair like a bearskin on its shoulders. The antlers were like big bunches of kindling, with a countless number of points —so the stag was very old as well as very big. Jeo had never seen anything so impressive, or so terrible. His pulse was so hard it shook his teeth.

The huge animal lurched its head back again and let out another of its great belling calls. This time, quite unexpectedly, it was answered by a similar noise from somewhere down to the right, Jeo's left. At first the boy thought it was an echo but when he looked quickly to one side he saw a second, much smaller stag cantering into view over the crest of a hump of peat.

It was a younger beast. Much younger. Bright brown, small

antlers, an awkwardness in its movements. Barely full grown. The boy, who was already on edge, had a sudden wild pang at the sight of it.

The big stag saw the arrival at the same time—and it stood abruptly still and straight as if taking a very deep breath, pushing out that massive chest. It was suddenly silent too—though it threatened a roar with the continuous twitching of its deciduous old muzzle.

The newcomer came closer, slowing to a walk, passing the bunch of ash trees—and Jeo saw for the first time just how small it was in contrast to the old monster on the brow of the slope. Shorter than a man, it had absurdly thin legs and a tight, spare body, no shoulders to speak of. Gracile and well built for speed —but it seemed to have no place out here in the shadow of the laird of the herd. Jeo felt he ought to stand up and do something —he didn't know what—but then the two stags moved towards each other and he had no time to think.

They lowered their heads simultaneously and advanced, quickening their stride as they closed on each other, snorting through their noses. The younger circled to the right, looking to outflank its enemy and snatch the advantage of the upper ground —but the old stag crabbed to one side to block the move, dipping his head even lower to present the full array of his antlers to his rival, who was forced to back off.

They stood still and looked at each other, just for a second, then the smaller deer made a run straight towards the other, antlers aimed at his chest. The giant stag stood his ground and the rush came to a halt. It had only been a mock assault, an attempt to draw its elder into a charge of his own so the young stag could dart past and gain the top of the hill.

The older beast knew his challenger had no other tactic. There was no hope of resisting the big stag if he attacked with all his weight down the slope, so it had to somehow move above him to stand any chance at all. It was still moving, sideways, when the old giant decided to end the skirmishing and threw himself into a full-blooded gallop down the hill, nose brushing the grass and those immense antlers bristling like a thornbush.

The young deer was taken by surprise, not least by the speed of the attack. It jumped to one side, but a little too late. It couldn't escape the assault and had to drop its head very fast to avoid taking those great horns full in the face.

Their antlers met with a sound like a clash of sticks and the new stag was rushed several helpless paces down the hill. Its hindquarters gave way and it slipped on the grass, collapsing with a grunt and rolling over on its side.

The chief stag overbalanced and had to twist and jump sideways to avoid tripping over the fallen body—but he turned back very quickly and put in another vicious thrust that again the smaller deer could only counter with a desperate show of antlers.

They locked horns a second time—and the contest, such as it was, ended almost at once. There was a brief, ludicrous trial by strength, then the thin young stag slumped to its knees with a groan that made Jeo clamp his teeth. The vast antlers went on pushing till their victim had been forced into a buckled heap a small distance down the hill.

The young animal got to its feet, slowly, grunting for breath, and stood for a while facing back up the hill. But it kept its head bent, its eyes down. There was blood on its nose. After no more than a few seconds it turned tail to limp hurriedly away back along the hummock of peat and out of sight.

The senior stag hadn't broken sweat and was still breathing evenly. He drew himself up to his full height and opened his throat to throw out yet another raucous bellow, this time in triumph as well as defiance—but before he had time to make a sound, there was a sudden brusque movement on his left and he turned his head to see a very pale skinny boy coming out of the nearby scrub with a knife in his hand.

Jeo didn't want to be out there facing the huge thing. He was completely petrified and felt even smaller and more puny than he was. But he was there just the same. Another warm moorland silence. A bird almost overhead made a small sound, but neither of them heard it.

The king stag was quite still again. He lowered his head, tipping the antlers forward. There was no sign of fear on him. He knew men, had grown to know they wouldn't harm him. And yet this scrawny little boy . . .

Before the stag could do anything at all, Jeo put all his courage into one fast action, drew back his arm and in a whiplash of forearm and wrist threw his knife at the great beast, aiming for the big, long neck and its mat of black hair.

He was too close to miss. The dagger, moving with the speed of excellent timing, slashed into the muscled neck and dived in to the hilt, checking the stag's roar of shock and pain so that all it could do was gasp and stand strangely still and stare at the boy.

Jeo had thrown the knife at live animals before. Small ones. Frogs and rabbits and birds in flight. But never at anything remotely so big. He was interested to see it stick in the deer's throat as it did in trees and granary doors, with much the same kind of sound.

The stag took a single tottering step forward, its eyes bulging, mouth wide open as it groaned for breath. Then it turned and staggered away across the moor hill, away from its attacker, head thrown back so far that the antlers lay along each of its flanks.

Jeo, now that he'd carried out the act, was numbed by it, couldn't believe it was his doing. He knew it was forbidden to kill the highland deer. Venison was exclusively for the old people, culling of the herd a responsibility of the middle-aged. And no one ever killed the old stags or hinds. For a moment he stood and fretted with his lip. Then he started to run back towards the distant valley. Then he stopped. He remembered something.

His knife. It was in the stag's neck. Someone would find it. Someone would have seen him leave the tenement that morning —someone always did—and the old shepherd had seen him in the hills. When the knife was discovered, it would only be a matter of time before he was caught and punished. For killing a deer, an

old one, that would mean the Shrieking Pits. Jeo dashed back across
the hill, tracking the stag to a thick coppice of birch trees at the
foot of yet another drab dome of peat.

There weren't many trees in the group but they were so close
together and there was such a tousled undergrowth that it was
actually dark in the thicket. The boy moved slowly and fearfully
through it, peering at the shadows. Something blocked his path and
he flinched from it. Just a big ivy-throttled log, dim lit. He stepped
across it.

He didn't have far to go to find his victim. The stag was lying
in a nettle bed, half on its back, half on its side, one leg half in
the air, the head propped against a root or something—so that one
eye was staring at the boy when he stepped slowly closer.

He stopped and stood there and looked at the enormous dark
carcass, the hide mottled with sunlight flushing its way in through
the creepers. The deer was breathing with difficulty, the great chest
thrusting, the breath itself a series of long, laboured rasping sounds,
as if all the air were passing not between the half-open lips but
through the wound in the neck.

Jeo, more terrified than ever, couldn't look at the stag's face.
He didn't want to see that eye looking back at him. Gathering
what was left of his thoughts and courage he stepped forward to
retrieve his knife.

He had to feel for it in the semi-darkness—and there was
blood on his hands, a lot of it, when he finally found the hilt and
heaved it from the body. It made no difference to the stag's
breathing, which was rough and slow as before.

It occurred to the boy that he ought to finish the animal off,
with a stick or a stone if he could find one, with the knife. The
stag was clearly in its last pain. But he didn't have any nerve left
for that.

He ran back towards the glen, ran till he was exhausted, then
ran on till he fell and lay where he fell in a bank of low heather.
He stayed there in a heavy faint while the sun moved to its

mid-day height, drying the blood on his fingers as it went on down into afternoon.

As Jeo lay senseless on the ground, a man on a horse rode up over the crown of the hillside and onto the moors. The same rider who'd seen the boy leave his tenement earlier that morning. He wore a hauberk of black chain mail and had a sword. Below his helmet his face was heavily bearded. He watched as he went, searching the moors for a sign of movement. Seeing nothing out of the ordinary, he soon returned to the base of the valley and didn't pass close to where Jeo was lying.

Halfway down the long hillside Gara caught up with his flock and found them all quite safe. The bell round the old ewe's neck had jangled because she'd had to run faster down a steep part of the hill. Nothing more serious than that. The shepherd cursed the animal and shouted at the heather-haired girl to carry on taking the sheep down the hill, watching as she went. He made her stay close to the flock at all times, which left him free to roam the glen, looking—and meant he always knew where she was. He watched her go, then made his way across the slope to a point somewhere above the level of the highest tenements, to a stone fort with high walls and a small gateway.

It was a simple round broch with grey rubblestone walls four times the height of a man enclosing a courtyard in the middle of which reared a round-tower surrounded by crude domed huts like granite hives.

The moment the shepherd reached the gatehouse, two guardsmen stepped out and stood in front of him, levelling long, heavy infantry lances at him. When they saw who he was they took the lances away and touched their foreheads with their hands. He said something to them and one ran across the yard to the tower.

Before long he came back accompanying another guardsman, who was buckling on a belt and who spoke to Gara without first touching his brow.

He was older than his subordinates. A stocky, almost burly, bearded man of middle age. Unlike the others he wore no helmet, just the hood of the grey cotton tunic under his sleeveless leather jerkin. Unlike the others he carried no weapon apart from the knife in a sheath in his belt. He stood, feet apart, and listened to what the shepherd had to say, following the old man's gestures with a glance every time Gara pointed towards the top of the hill. He nodded sometimes but said nothing and the old man finished talking and walked away to rejoin his sheep.

The chief guardsman strode across the courtyard, barking a command as he went. Two more soldiers appeared from one of the huts and he said things to them before disappearing back into the grey tower.

The two guardsmen went out through the gateway and turned to march up the hill. One of them unhooked a long black shillelagh from his belt and swung it as he walked, using the slim club to snap off the heads of flowers and hit the branches of young trees.

When Jeo woke and saw where the sun was, he jumped to his feet and dashed away down the hillside. He ran not because he was late —he would be punished when he got back, late or early—but because he was afraid and wanted to get away from the moors as fast as he could. Above all, he had to find somewhere to wash the blood from his hands.

There was a stream not far away, a quick little brook plashing its way directly down the hill, lined with alders and saugh trees. He knelt in the mud of the bank and dipped each arm in the water, up to the elbow, rubbing it hastily with the other hand. He lay face down and put his head under the water to drink and wash his face.

When he stood up he examined his tunic and found no trace of blood. His knife was back in the depths of his sporran. As he followed the stream downhill he glanced around, expecting to see some tenement elder or an armed guardsman coming towards him from behind every tree or wall he looked at.

He was glad to see no one at all—and after a while he began to feel less fear. The old stag wouldn't be found for a long time —he convinced himself of that—and anyway the weasels and hawks would soon scent the wound and go to eat the meat. And no one could have seen the act of death itself. Not even, surely, from the castle.

He looked around at things in the distance to see exactly where he was and to plot a slow way home. There were buildings on the lowest slopes down ahead of him to the left, huge communal byres with adjoining cow pens packed with long-horned highland cattle with shaggy winter coats and high bony shoulders, more like oxen than cattle. Closer to the river, a single vast grey sty in a field with big razorback pigs. And three large tithe barns overfilled with grain and textiles and metals and foodstuffs ready for transportation to the castle. In the far distance across the main river, short stocky dale ponies did nothing in small groups.

On the boy's right, close by, an orchard with low walls. He climbed in and helped himself to a few fat costards from a short tree, held one in his teeth and put two others in his pouch. Eating the apple, he carried on down the slope, still following the stream.

All of a sudden a kingfisher dashed down from a willow branch and fell in a flash of harlequin to the water surface where it stabbed some thin fish which had wandered up in search of alderflies—then it was gone in an instant, but Jeo had caught his glimpse of it—and he smiled, not so much for its bright halcyon colours but for its keen beak as slick as a knife and the unhesitating thrust of its kill, for its act of death which no one would ever discover. He walked away, eating his apple.

He was quite close to the first of the shanty buildings, walking down a familiar lane between two hill walls, when he turned one of the corner bends and saw two tall guardsmen striding towards him with clubs in their hands.

They saw him at the same time and instead of coming towards him they stood perfectly still, arms and legs straight as swords, the long clubs pointing at the ground by their feet.

They knew as well as Jeo did that there was no point in his trying to run away. They would catch him and hit him with their sticks. So he did what they expected from him. He put his hands down by his sides and walked towards them. He made fists of his fingers.

They said nothing for a time, didn't even threaten to speak, while he stood in front of them staring at their shadows on the grass. Then one made a movement with his club and as Jeo edged slightly to one side away from the weapon the other stabbed him hard under the breastbone with his own stick. The boy fell to his knees like a foal breaking its legs and stayed where he fell, coughing for breath that wouldn't come. He couldn't get up on his own, so the guardsmen had to pick him off the ground and he stood there again, crying this time and keeping his head down to try and hide the tears. An apple fell out of his pouch.

One of the soldiers picked it up and tossed it in his palm before pushing it somewhere in the chest of his tunic. The other opened the boy's sporran. He threw away the bread and the sausage and kept the other apple.

"You know the rules. Half of these go to the Elder," he said in an attempt at humour. Jeo wasn't surprised when they took both the apples. He was glad they didn't look further and find his knife.

The other guardsman lifted the boy's chin with the tip of his club. Jeo, forced to look at them, saw how their hoods made them look very much the same. He saw too how young they both were, their faces unlined and scarcely bearded. As young as his own brothers—yet with the privileges of older men because they'd been chosen as guardsmen. Jeo hated them for that, as much as he hated the old people—and for a moment it must have showed in his face, because one of the soldiers poked him in the shoulder with his club.

"You can get that look off your face for a start, you little shit. And dry your eyes. Big boys don't cry, remember?"

Jeo's eyes flashed. "I'm not crying," he snapped—but then wished he hadn't opened his mouth, as they both hit him hard with their sticks, one on the pad of his shoulder, the other cripplingly on the knee. He squealed and fell again, squirming on the grass as he reached for his knee with both hands and jerked with the pain. The guardsmen were expressionless.

"Maybe that'll teach you how to talk to your elders and betters," said one. "And remember to say Senior next time, or we'll have to break your legs a bit, won't we?"

Jeo didn't say anything at all as they picked him up again and took him half-dragging half-limping along the green-lane and across the slope, walking for what seemed nearly an hour before they were back at the gateway of their broch.

They had to hold the boy by the arms to stop him falling again. The pains were gone from his body but everything ached and he still hadn't recovered from the blow to his chest. His breath came in quick noises.

The soldiers hauled him through the gatehouse and across the courtyard, the metal heels of their boots clipping harshly on the cobbles. When they stopped, Jeo lifted his head and found himself facing the same short, bulky guardsman whom old Gara had come to see earlier.

The boy forgot his discomfort and stood upright at once. This wasn't just any common garrison captain. It was Meagher, one of the very highest commanders of the glen, second in rank only to the Guardian himself. Jeo's lips were dry and he wanted to lick them but was worried it might be seen as a gesture of disrespect.

The soldier's face was broad and rather flat and the heavy trimmed beard was greying. The eyebrows were very thick, like the stone-grey hair. He was on the short side for a guardsman, but heavily built. The face was ageing but still hard. Jeo looked him in the eyes. Eyes like a guard dog.

"How old are you, boy?"

Jeo looked away. "Fourteen," he said.

"You look younger." Jeo was glad. "What were you doing in the hills?" The question was predictable and the boy had been expecting it, but he had no easy lies at hand. He shrugged.

"Nothing—" the guardsmen, in unison, kicked the legs from under him, holding his arms tight to keep him on his feet as his body sagged like a sack. Meagher held the boy's chin very firmly in his fingers, lifting the flat white face so he could see it better.

"What," he repeated, more slowly, "were you doing in the hills?"

Jeo shook his head in the hard leather grip. He tried to put the sight of the dead stag out of his mind. "Walking," he mumbled. "Going for a walk. Fresh air."

One of the guardsmen pressed the butt of his stick against the boy's cheek but Meagher waved it aside. He looked hard at the youngster's upturned face, frowning at the big round eyes. Going for a walk, for fresh air? The same thing he'd told Gara. The captain worked his lips. Going for a walk? It was possible. What else could a scrap of boy like this be doing? There was nothing in the hills.

"You don't go for walks on the rest day, boy. You don't need me to tell you that. This isn't the first time. You've been out before, other rest days. Haven't you?"

The same line of questioning as the shepherd. Jeo gave a clumsy nod. Meagher leaned forward so their faces were almost touching. He was a short man, not very much taller than Jeo, who was small for his age—but the grip on the lad's chin and cheek was not that of a boy. It forced Jeo's mouth open.

"I said: this isn't the first time, is it? Am I right?"

"Yes," muttered Jeo. The man brought his face even closer.

"Senior," he said quietly.

"Yes, Senior."

"It's not the first time, as I say—but it's the last. If you're ever seen out again on the rest day, or find yourself going for a walk, you'll not only get the thrashing of your life, you'll be sent to work in the castle—or even to the Shrieking Pits. So you'll stay inside, won't you? You'll stay in the glen."

"Yes, Senior." And at that moment he meant it. The Shrieking Pits were the greatest fear of anyone in the valley. The guardsman dropped his hand from the boy's face. He made a gesture of some kind and the two soldiers took Jeo away.

Meagher watched them go, then returned to the central tower. That boy, he was thinking. That stubborn edge to everything he did. The expression in his eyes that no amount of hard knocks could remove. The captain had seen that look before in other youngsters. The anger of the young against their elders. Very tiresome. He'd had those youngsters watched, and the look had always died with the years. How many were there this time? Just the two of them, the boy and the mute girl? Even the old shepherd, who knew everything worth knowing, had no idea as yet. Still— Meagher shrugged—they were only children, after all. They would surely change, as children did. He climbed a set of stairs and was lost in big shadows.

When night came into the giant tenements it was enormous and totally blind. A complete and utter thing with not even a dot of light, no filtering moon or starlight, all charcoal fires forbidden. In his small narrow alcove Jeo lay on his back and stared into the black space above him. He had no idea what time of night it was. There had been no curfew bell because it never rang on the rest day. He couldn't know if he lay awake for two hours or half the night, hardly feeling the aches of the day.

He had bruises from all the blows, from the old shepherd, the two guardsmen, his father. But he also had a big smile on his face. He was excited, not afraid any more, about his killing of the stag.

It was already more like a dream than a memory, and he found it hard to really believe he'd killed the huge beast. He alone with his own little knife. He'd never dared to do anything like that before, to strike out against something old. Seeing how the young stag had dared, that had made him do it. Perhaps—and he grinned in the darkness—perhaps one day he might do it again. Next time kill an old man or even a guardsman. Maybe, just possibly, even Meagher himself. Yes, he would like that. Meagher himself. He closed his eyes at the thought and later fell asleep.

Before dawn broke on the hushed valley, a man on a horse rode along the hilltops to the castle. He turned back in the saddle and took one last look down and around the glen . . . then went on and entered the fortress by the central door.

Soon another man, a white hooded figure, appeared at the highest window of the castle keep and stayed there for an hour, watching over. The first of the early birds made the tiniest of noises in the oakwoods and the hooded man moved his head as though to listen.

The Guardian

EVERYTHING IN THE GLEN—its rule and government, its day-to-day life, allocation of work and privilege, its hierarchy—was rooted in one thing. The law of Age. The oldest person in the valley was always its overlord, the Elder; the new-born baby its least inhabitant.

The very old people who lived in the castle or the best of the cottages, the elders in their white hooded robes—they were the ruling caste, and their rights were absolute. To reach their standing, a valley dweller simply had to stay alive long enough to join their age group, moving up from one level to the next.

A child of six, say, had no rights at all and had to carry out all the small dirty unwanted chores of the day. A young boy or girl of ten had the same chores but was granted a small measure of responsibility, perhaps the feeding of a goat or the kneading of dough. Adolescents were thralls who worked in the fields or held semi-skilled jobs in the flour mills and forests, had an hour's free time every day, and bullied their juniors. A young woman in her twenties, though allowed no possessions, had some freedom of movement and the right to choose her own friends, unless forbidden by an elder. Even in middle age, a man was still a bondsman tied to the plough and a skinny strip of land in the work fields. He still lived deep in a tenement, still stayed inside on the rest day, owned little more than the clothes on his back. His immediate seniors, those in early old age, were heads of their households. They did no work, had their own rooms, ate the best food on the table, drank spirits and wine as well as beer. Within their families, their word was law. They apportioned chores and arranged marriages. When they were old enough they moved from the shanties to live in their own stone cottages, alone or with other elders, with their own choice of young servants, their own cornfields and orchards and herds of livestock—and, in time, their own white robes and their place in the castle. When the Elder died in the stronghold, the oldest living habitant was elevated at once. There was always an Elder.

It was an ancient state of order, surviving by its simplicity as much as anything. Age was the only criterion. A handicapped girl would work in the ploughlands while her able-bodied father might stay at home and rest. A twenty-year-old of high intelligence would do the bidding of the subnormal middle-aged. The Elder had been a woman as often as a man. Nothing but age made any sort of difference. If you were old enough, you were good enough. No one doubted it. No one fought against it. And it applied its hard simple code to everyone.

Only the guardsmen were, to an extent, exempt. The cadets did not carry slop buckets and the junior officers never turned the soil. They were all free to go anywhere in the glen, at any time, as their duties led them. Their captains were not ranked by age. They were different, too, in having no women in their ranks. Guardsmen were men.

One of their captains made his way up the highest reaches of the southern slope, then turned right and walked along the ridge towards the western end of the valley as the sun went down.

Sunsets were often spectacular in the glen, the sky splashed with reds, the kind of sunsets found over an ocean. On this day, this late evening, the sea sky was dull with clouds and the captain didn't have to narrow his eyes as he moved towards it.

The very distant snort of a horse made him turn and look behind him, to see a group of elders moving through the hills under the castle. Riding in carts, with armed escorts, the dreary white of their sackclothes showing against the black surrounding stone. He stood and watched. He liked seeing the castle there. It gave a sense of massive solidity, a security unshaken by time or the spites of the weather. It was a huge constant. A guardsman could go about his work with ease of mind, knowing the fortress was at his back. It had always been there. Meagher went on along the hillcrest, looking down into the valley on his right.

He walked with a good step. He wasn't tired. It was very early spring, so the days were still quite short, with no great heat to sap a working man. He strode firmly through the heather. Near the end of the ridge, near the sea, he looked ahead and saw a man on a big horse waiting for him on a low rise of land.

He was still some distance away, so Meagher couldn't see if the Guardian was looking at him. He quickened his pace. Soon he was close enough to see the other's face.

He was younger than Meagher. The captain didn't resent the fact. He was glad a guardsman's rank wasn't decided solely by his years. Old soldiers weren't fit to command. And he had a deal of respect for this Guardian. He was a little afraid of him too, which he saw as a good thing.

He reached the top of the small incline and stood beside the horse. The Guardian had placed himself this far to the west so he could watch most of the valley with the low sun at his back not in his eyes. As a result, Meagher had to face west to look at him, and he could see little of the man's face.

"Quiet day," said the Guardian. A fact not a question.

"Patch of trouble near the eastern mills," said Meagher. He didn't say Senior. The Guardian didn't notice. Guardsmen of almost equal rank were lax about a thing like that.

"What kind of trouble?"

"Rape. Girl called Abhail. Some young farmer's lout attacked her going down to the river. We're keeping him overnight in one of the brochs."

The Guardian nodded. Meagher saw the black dome of his helmet move. "Is she older than him?"

"No, three years younger. What do you want done with him?"

The Guardian stared away towards the coast, looking at nothing so he could think. Simple rape, he was thinking—but complicated because the victim was younger, and not *much* younger. Had she been a child and the attacker an elder, there could be no thought of punishment. And even in this case the lad could hardly be thrown in a Shrieking Pit. He was, after all, her senior. Had he been younger than her, he would have already been put to death.

Still, rape was an aggravated crime. A man could steal from his juniors with impunity. He could beat them and make them do his work. But he couldn't kill them or rape their bodies. They were acts that undermined the *order* of the glen, the well-being and efficacy of its workforce. Acts that were usually punished. But what punishment in this case? The girl was younger. A beating would be more than enough.

"Warn him," said the Guardian, turning to face the captain. "Let him know if it happens again he'll get a flogging—from a guardsman, not his grandmother. Give the girl a rest day tomorrow."

Meagher nodded. He shrugged. "Apart from that, nothing worth a report," he said. "Like you said, a quiet day. I sent two men to watch the coast this morning."

"To watch Sligo?"

"Yes. Nothing there either. All he does is fish all day. How long's he been out there?"

"Six years," said the Guardian. "Nearly seven."

"That's a long time at his age. I'm still surprised he wasn't thrown in a Pit."

"He's an elder."

"I know. But even so. Think he'll ever be allowed back?"

"Not while I'm here."

They put the man called Sligo out of their minds and looked into the valley, keeping one last watch. They were turned partly away from the sunset, which was to their left. The glen was in grades of darkness down away to the right. No firelights. Peasants moved like small black things in a herd, out of the great grey fields on either side of the river. Meagher looked at them but his thoughts were on the man alongside him. He didn't know him very well. He'd been the Guardian only two years. Meagher gave him a glance. The man was a loner, but a Guardian was meant to be. Most of the soldiers were. They were required to associate with one another according to rank, not age, and since most of them found that difficult they tended to go their own ways. It was normal.

"Tell me more about this boy Jeo."

The captain sniffed. "There's not much to tell. He's done nothing wrong. Does his work, stays inside, keeps himself to himself. Back to normal, it looks like."

"Are you sure?"

"Not yet. That's why I'm still keeping an eye on him. But it looks that way. Another month, then I think we can ease off him. We need the men for other things—and there's always Gara to watch him."

"That's true," said the Guardian. "Is he still worried the boy is after that girl of his?"

"Yes. Still."

"Old man, young girl. Always trouble. Is *she* being watched?"

"Gara hardly lets her out of his sight."

"Of course. But have them watched anyway. All three of them for a while. There may still be trouble there."

Meagher agreed in silence.

"The easy thing," the Guardian went on, "would be for one of the elders to take this Jeo as a houseboy. That would keep him out of the way for good."

The captain cracked a short laugh. "I've thought of that," he said. "But none of the elders will have him. They don't want him anywhere near them. His grandmother can't stand the sight of him, I hear."

A pause before the Guardian made a reply, though whether

he was smiling at the thought, or frowning, or nothing at all, Meagher couldn't tell.

"Keep on him a while longer, then. Let me know when you're sure he's safe."

It was dark now, almost night. Just a strip of pale light down on the horizon's edge, on the ocean. They couldn't see each other. The valley noises seemed louder. Meagher went away.

"Don't come to report tomorrow," called the Guardian. "I've got things to look into." He ran his hand down the horse's neck and it moved its head.

There was no need for lights in the valley. No one moved around after dark. For the young it was forbidden, for the elders a waste of time—there was nothing to see. So no one used the night—but no one was afraid of it. There were no superstitions in the valley. No myths, gods or devils. No teaching of any kind. Just work and rest and getting older, with few distractions. No geography, no mathematics, no astronomy or alchemy or medicine. There were no decorations to daily life—no carpets or tapestries, no houseflowers, no pets. No music or songs, no paint or poetry, no written word. No history except the distorted stories handed down by word of mouth. Now, at the start of a night, no lights.

Not that the Guardian was thinking about such things. They had never existed. Nor did he cast his mind over the question of young Jeo. That would sort itself out. He was thinking, rather whimsically, about his own name. For two years nobody had used it when talking to him, and nobody would ever use it again. That happened to every Guardian, he knew. It was meant to imply that nothing changed, that each Guardian—like every Elder—was no different from the one before, that the old order would be maintained. Even after two years he wasn't quite used to it.

He listened and caught the flutter of trees in a lowland breeze, the faint wash of the sea on its rocks. In the blackness, the valley had its kind of peace, and the Guardian could believe it was undisturbed under the cover of the night, that the tenements were not seething. He reined the horse's head round and went back towards the castle. The animal seemed to know its own way even in the dark.

The Children

"Is THAT ALL YOU CAN think of doing?" asked the eldest boy. "Nothing else—just sit there and get older?"

"We can't stop ourselves getting older, Rea."

"Very funny," he said. The others laughed.

There were four others beside Rea, who was a squat boy of fifteen: two twin brothers, younger than him, a very small very ugly girl of his own age and—lying on the grass slightly apart from the rest—Jeo, eating a piece of black bread.

It was a working day like any other. The sun was at its height and the five of them were taking their mid-day meal under a spreading willow at the side of a field. They'd been working since dawn, working together, sowing dung on the ploughland. They were hot and very dirty but too tired and hungry to notice. They were more interested in their food than the shade of the tree.

"Anyway," said one of the twins, "what else can we do except wait to get older?"

"There must be something more than that," said Rea.

"You can try become a guardsman," said the twin. His brother agreed.

"That's right. They don't have the same rules about young and old. Be good to be a guardsman. You get more what you want." They both grinned.

"I hate them," said Rea. "They keep everything the way it is. I'd never be one of them."

Jeo stared at him. It was like listening to himself.

"It's a better life than we got now," one of the brothers persisted.

"Course it is," said the other. "I don't know why you talk like that, Rea. What do you expect us to do? We're too young. We got no say."

The older boy moved his hair from his eyes and pushed it behind his ears. His face was wide and a first growth of hair blurred his cheeks.

"We could try not doing what we're told," he said. "For a start, we could stop saying Senior."

"If you don't say Senior, they half-kill you," said a twin. "You can't be serious, Rea."

"I am. We ought to do something. What's the use of just waiting to get old? You have to wait years to get what you want —and you might die before you get old enough."

"But we don't just wait, do we? We don't really lie around waiting to get old. There's too many other things to think about."

"Like what? It's all work and doing what we're told—"

The twins openly disagreed. "There's running and wrestling and going down to the river. And food and girls."

"Speak for yourself," said the girl, sitting against the tree. The boys didn't look at her.

"Shut your hole, Smithereen," said a twin.

"You come and fucking shut it for me," she said.

"Sorry, Smithereen."

"You will be, if you don't use my proper name."

"Yes, Smithereen."

"It's Siobhan. Don't fucking forget it."

"No, Smithereen."

She threw a hand of loose dirt at him and they left each other alone. They all went back to eating their bread and their sugar beets. The girl turned her attention to Rea.

"They're right," she said. "There's nothing we can do. If we step out of line, they break their black clubs on us."

Jeo looked across at her. She was small. Very thin, and short as a dwarf, though she didn't have a dwarf's face. It was an ugly face, but Jeo still wanted her, as he wanted any girl. He knew she didn't want him. The ugliest girl in the glen, and she wouldn't touch him. It did nothing for his state of mind.

"So you think the same, do you?" Rea asked her. "All we can do is wait to get old like everybody else? Do what we're told?"

"I don't like it," she said. "No one who's young likes it. But what can we do?"

"What do you think about it, Jeo?" said Rea.

Jeo looked up from the water in his iron mug and saw the boy looking hard at him. He didn't know what to tell him. He'd been listening, and wanting very much to say what he was thinking —but he couldn't. He couldn't let himself trust them. The valley was thick with informers of all ages. Some were well known to everyone. Most weren't known at all. Any of the youngsters under the tree might have been one of them. Perhaps they all were.

"I don't know," said Jeo.

"What does that mean?" said the girl. "Do you think we should do something or not?"

"Oh, leave him alone," said a twin. "He doesn't care either way. All he wants to do is go walking by hisself in the hills."

"Bloody daydreamer," said his brother.

"He might go and tell someone what we said," frowned the girl.

"You must be bloody joking. The guardsmen hate the sight of him. Forget about him."

She shrugged and looked away and Jeo took another drink from his mug.

"I know what we can do," said Rea. "We could stop working. If we don't work, they'd have to listen to us. They need us to do the work."

"No," said Smithereen. "The guardsmen would do it. Everyone else would work twice as hard. They'd keep things going for a while. Long enough, anyway. They'd throw some of us in the Shrieking Pits and starve the rest of us till we was so hungry we'd go back to work. You're not the only one who's thought of that, Rea."

"It might work," he said, but he was less sure of himself.

Smithereen wasn't listening to him. "Keep the noise down," she said. "There's someone hanging around out there."

They were all quiet now as they looked through the curtain of drooping willow branches, all sunlight and leafwork.

"I can't see anything."

"I can," said Jeo. The girl looked at him again.

The branches were brushed aside and a man came into the shade under the tree, frowning when he saw the youngsters. He was much older, with a beard. There was a thick moment's pause.

"Hake," said Rea, and the others groaned.

"Fuck off, Hake," said the girl. The man stood very still and stared at her. He was tall and very wide and his tunic was green and very dirty. His legs were bare and dusty and his boots were broken. He had a rake in his hand. He was adult yet the children addressed him without respect and no fear.

"What are you doing with that rake?" asked Rea.

"Nothing."

The twins chuckled.

"I don't mean what are you doing now. Where are you going with it?"

"Going home." The speech was slow, the eyes permanently wide as if with bewilderment.

"What work have you been doing?" asked Rea patiently.

"Been raking," said Hake. He nodded several times over. "Done old Rhiodha's gardens."

It wasn't a job for a man of his age. None of his contemporaries would ever touch a field tool. But Hake was very different. He did odd chores around the glen—often the meanest chores—even though he was old enough to do as little work as he cared to. He did the jobs because he wanted to, and no one could stop him— he had the right. He worked, he said, because he liked to meet people. He wanted to be friends, but didn't have any. Everyone of his own age shunned him because they regarded his like of work as degrading, and because he spent so much of his time with children. It wasn't normal. The children themselves were unkind to him because he was simple and slow—and the only person older than themselves they could ill-treat with impunity.

"Been working all day," he told them.

"You worked yesterday too," said one of the brothers. "I saw you. Working on the rest day."

"I don't need rest."

"Nobody says you got to need it. You got to do it anyway. That's why it's called the rest day, fucksake."

"Done any other good jobs today?" said Rea. "Cleaned any stables out, have you? Scraped the shit off a guardsman's boots?"

The big man looked from one boy to the other. "No," he said uncertainly. "Done none of that. Been to the sea last week. Been fishing."

"What, with Sligo again," said a twin with distaste.

"Sligo's my friend."

"He's mad as you are."

Hake frowned again. "He's my friend. Careful how you talk about him."

"Who's Sligo?" said Smithereen.

"One of the elders," said Rea. "He used to be, anyway. Lives by the sea now. Never leaves it. They sent him there because he went soft in the head."

"No," said the big man. "He's alright. He's good. Lets me help him fishing."

"Only because nobody else will work with him," said someone. "The one job nobody wants."

Hake looked angry but said nothing.

"What are you doing here anyway?" Smithereen questioned him. The big man tapped his ear.

"Heard noises," he told her. "Outside, and I heard noises so I come in under here. What you all doing?"

"Talking, that's all," said one of the boys. Hake smiled. His teeth were bad.

"I can talk with you," he said, nodding.

"Fuck, I think it's time to go," said Rea, getting to his feet. The others agreed. They shuffled across to the hanging branches, kicking dust and dead leaves. They pushed past the man.

Jeo was last of all. Hake touched him on the head, with timid gentleness. Hardly a touch at all.

"Sligo's alright," he said.

Jeo gave a very small frown. "I don't know anything about him," he said—and moved away, off along the field with the others, back to work.

As Jeo walked across to join the others, Gara the shepherd watched him from the darkness of a small copse, camouflaged like a buff-tip moth against the bark of a birch.

The old man had come down into the valley because the boy hadn't been seen in the hills. He hadn't put a foot wrong for months. Here in the fields, with children of the same age, Gara hoped to catch him in an unguarded moment—a loose word or a flash of temper, anything to incriminate him. There was something between Jeo and his own girl Rhosarran, he was still sure of it—and the thought gnawed at him. So far, the boy had given nothing away. But he would, sometime. He was that kind.

The old shepherd had seen him with the other children, but he didn't care about them. They had nothing to do with Rhosarran. Still, one of them was the girl they called Smithereen, once a known troublemaker. It might be as well to mention her to one of the captains.

The day after, she was sent to work in the castle and Jeo never saw her again.

Alone in his little sleeping den, he lay on his back and was thinking as always. Maybe it was true there was nothing he could do till he was much older. Until then, what? No others of his own age would help him. They might scowl at elders and guardsmen behind their backs, steal a few apples from an old man's yard, swear undying hatred for all things old—but it was nothing. Puppy revolt, no more. It died in everyone.

Would he always have to go on pretending he was dutiful like the rest? It was very difficult. He didn't know how much longer he could do it.

Smithereen came to mind. Her bony little body. And the mute shepherd girl, much more vivid. Though he didn't masturbate, he thought about her for a time before going to sleep.

The Girl

IN THE EVENING AT THE end of a long, sluggish day, a dark-haired girl in a yellow tunic was walking through a young beechwood on a slope just above the valley floor. She was only just inside the wood, hidden from view by the outermost line of trees and undergrowth, and she could see everything that was happening on her side of the river.

It was early spring and she saw that the vast fields below were still nothing but spreads of dark ploughland separated by hedgerows, with people working in them. The girl made her way across the slope, taking care to stay behind the last rank of trees, and watched the work going on as she passed.

It all seemed much the same from one field to the next. Mostly small groups of peasants with an ox-drawn plough. The usual springtime work. The usual crops. Fields roughly divided into threes. Wheat, barley, the third left fallow or covered with nettles and couchgrass. A few smaller fields for root crops, peas and beans. A simple open-field rotation system. The same from year to year, unchanged as long as anyone could remember.

Since it was evening the work was drawing to a close. Some of the peasant groups unshackled their oxen and prepared to go home, and the girl stopped at times to watch them. In among the workers she saw scarecrows scattered around, draped in rags like little children—and statues of cowled elders, half-hidden in hedges or looming beside high wooden gates.

The day was nearly over and the light quite bad by the time Rhosarran came to a halt behind one of the beech trees and looked

out at a band of young men working the edge of the adjacent field.
Five of them, with a pair of oxen and a donkey. Four of them tall
and heavily built—but she stared only at the fifth, the smallest boy,
who was walking a few paces behind the others.

She shook some of her ling-coloured hair from her face and
frowned pensively in the direction of the boy. He looked much
the same as he always did—dishevelled and dirty and very thin—
and he didn't seem to have grown at all since she'd last seen him
close, in the hills the previous autumn. He looked so small out
there with his big brothers. Small and very young. Thrillingly
young.

She was frowning because she couldn't understand why she'd
hardly ever seen him through all the winter months. He seemed
to have suddenly become like all the other children in the glen,
quite prepared to do no more than work in the fields and get on
with his chores, and otherwise stay inside in his tenement room like
everyone else.

She found it hard to accept the change. She was sure he wasn't
like the other children. And yet for the last few months . . . she
was suddenly angry at the way things were, the old laws that kept
him from her. She wanted to run down the hill and touch him,
to take him away from the field, where he looked so thin and tired
as he laboured. She wanted to speak to him, with her hands and
face, to ask him what was wrong, to help. She couldn't. She was
an elder's girl, owned by the shepherd.

She cast a look around the open fields. The work was hard
and the workers were gaunt. Mostly young, she saw. Girls as well
as boys. Children doing a man's work. They didn't keep all the
crops they raised. Half went to the tithe barns, to be used by the
Elder. Rhosarran looked at Jeo again. His brothers had dark skins,
an outdoor colour, almost tanned—but his own body was sickly
white as ever. She wanted his small white body against her, his
fierce young hands instead of the touch of the old shepherd. She
made expressive faces as she watched him.

Jeo, for his part, kept his eyes on his work and his thoughts to himself. He'd spent the entire day out in the same field treading the same interminable soil with very little food and not enough to drink and he was glad it was almost time to finish.

Up ahead of him his four brothers went about their appointed tasks. The tallest and strongest held the ploughshare and pushed as the oxen pulled it in front of him. The two animals were led by another brother—while a third, further back, guided the donkey which dragged the harrow. The eldest brother, even further behind, took handfuls of seed from the pocket of his leather apron and threw them broadcast in all directions, glancing occasionally over his shoulder to swear at Jeo, who lagged some distance behind the rest of the team.

He was too small and altogether too puny to do any of the pushing and pulling jobs, and not old enough to be allowed the high office of sowing seeds. So he brought up the rear and threw stones to keep the rooks away.

It was a dull job and most children of Jeo's age couldn't wait to grow out of it. But he was quite happy with the arrangement. It meant he was left alone with his own thoughts, and throwing the stones was practice for throwing his knife. He hurled the blunt pebbles to good effect, accurately and surprisingly hard.

It was almost dark—the sky was dirty red over the western coast—when the brothers unhitched their animals and led them towards the giant sheds nearby, taking the plough and harrow with them. As usual at this time Jeo was sent into a nearby stonefield to pick a bunch of nettles for supper.

This was a job he really didn't like. It was bad enough to go in and wade through the thick stinging weeds with no hose on his legs and no shoes on his feet, but on top of that he had to tear up the nettles with his bare hands—and since they grew to a height well above his chest, his whole body would itch with pain by the time he left the field every night. Some of the plants even stung him through his tunic.

They were useful things, nettles. Jeo knew that. The family used them to make tea and beer or cooked them to eat as a vegetable. The cattle were fed on them and his sister made sacks and rough blankets from the spun stems. Jeo knew all this, but he couldn't see why he alone should have to pick them. Just because he was the youngest.

He cursed as he always did in the nettlepatch and snarled sometimes. But he got on with it just the same—and soon he was overladen with nettles, holding them in both hands pressed against the front of his body and keeping his head well back to avoid brushing his face with the top leaves.

As he was about to leave the field a group of children appeared from behind the bordering hedge and stood in front of him, not far ahead, blocking his way. Four boys and a girl.

Jeo bit his lip when he saw them, but otherwise his face did nothing. He'd learned over the past winter not to put any expression on it. He knew the children and knew they didn't like him. They were all bigger than him—one of them, a fat boy called Ouse, seemed twice his size, though only a couple of years older. All the boys had small scrub beards. Jeo held the nettles tight to his body. He wanted to run away but he didn't.

"Good to see you again, Jeo," said one of the boys and Jeo looked at him while the others chuckled.

The smallest boy had spoken, a wiry fair-haired youth with freckles and the face of a sand lizard. He was chewing a stem of grass, his name was Kyrie and he was Jeo's age, old enough to have been chosen as a very junior guardsman in charge of his own small gang. Jeo knew this and loathed him for it.

"Not talking tonight, then? Mind you, been quiet for some time, haven't you? No more walks in the hills, either. What's the matter, Jeo—don't like the fresh air any more?"

They all laughed together. The girl made faces at him. Jeo waited and hoped they'd go away.

"Well now," Kyrie went on, "this is no fun. Come on, Jeo. Put those things down and talk to us."

"Put the nettles down, Jeo," said another boy. "Talk to us."

Jeo saw he was one of the twins from under the willow tree, weeks before. His brother wasn't with him.

Jeo clung to the nettles with both arms as though they were precious. The fat boy picked up a pebble and lobbed it at him.

"Come on—drop the bloody things, Jeo."

"Put them down, Jeo. Tell us a few things."

He bowed his head to avoid being hit in the face by a small piece of flint and it scraped the crown of his head. The big fat boy threw several stones hard and one hit him under the knee. He gasped and moved one of his hands, loosing his grip on the nettles so some of them fell to the ground. The children cheered. He bent to regather them but they threw more stones and he had to stand up and back away, still clutching the remains of his bundle.

He saw out of the side of his eye that Kyrie wasn't throwing anything. He hadn't joined in the jeering and was standing apart from the others, arms folded across his chest, his face quizzical.

"Don't talk to us, then," said the girl. "Just call us Senior and we'll leave you alone."

"Senior, Jeo," said the others. "Say it for us."

They threw more stones and some rocks and forced him to retreat further, holding his arms with the nettles in front of his face. One large piece of shale cracked against his fingers and he dug his teeth into his cheeks to stop himself crying out. His tormenters chanted the word Senior. More pebbles hit his legs and chest and he half-turned to run away—suddenly the girl let out a sharp cry and held her elbow.

The others turned to look at her. Kyrie frowned. One of the boys hissed as something struck him on the back of the leg. All of a sudden the air was cut by stones and the noise they made. The children jumped round to see behind them and Jeo looked up the slope to the edge of the beech forest.

The heather-haired girl was standing there, legs firmly apart, her face set and expressionless, calmly taking a clutch of heavy stones from one hand and flinging them down with the other.

She was very strong and she was throwing downhill so when she hit someone she hit hard. The youths cried out and cursed and put their hands up to their faces and skipped aside to dodge her missiles. They tried throwing back but she was uphill and out of range. The fat boy Ouse ran up the slope towards her, but she stood her ground and pelted him with rocks, splitting his chin, drawing blood. He staggered back down the rise.

She went on throwing till Kyrie himself was hit on the ribs and hurried out of the field and away to the left, leading his little mob in the direction of the nearest tenement. He turned, very briefly, and gave Jeo a last quick look before disappearing in the gathering dusk.

Jeo watched him leave, then looked up the hill. Rhosarran returned his gaze but only with a glance and she turned away almost at once to stride back into the wood.

Jeo picked more nettles and took them away. He took the long way back to his shanty to be sure of avoiding Kyrie's gang. He hardly felt the pain from his bruises and the nettle stings.

A hot day in the summer, though for once it was dry, not humid. No breezes, not a bluff of wind, so when evening came slowly down the clouds stayed where they were on the brick-dust sky. No breezes, no air to cool the bodies of men working in the fields.

All day all along the edge of the widest pasture close to the river they were repairing the hawthorn hedges. Gangs of young men tearing away the swarming weeds and grasses and carrying bundles of branches which their fathers cut into stakes under the eye of the old master woodcutters. It was a task usually carried out in early winter.

Sweat slipped down Jeo's bare back and itched his skin but he couldn't scratch at it. His hands were full. He carried the big clay water gourd past the line of workers and they took the ladle to drink, saying nothing to him.

His arms and shoulders were hurting now and his feet were

very hot and swollen, black with dust between the toes. He'd been out there all day with the others, with very little rest and no shade at all, and he was very tired. He took a small drink from the gourd and trudged back along the dirt road to fetch wood for the fences.

A stack of branches stood heaped at the corner of the field and Jeo put the clay jar down beside it. Other boys his own age milled round the stack and pulled wood from it. One or two stopped for a drink from pitchers of their own. They pushed and shoved one another for the smallest lightest branches to carry, for the last dregs of water—but they did it all quietly, in a muted way, too weary to bother very much. Jeo cradled a bale of branches and stood for a moment before carrying them away, looking along the row of workers as they went about their duties.

Close to the big stack, a gang of about a dozen men were using hatchets to cut the twigs off hedge-tree branches, chopping one end of each into a sharp point before tossing it on the heap. Towards the end of the line, far ahead, more of these same branches were being hammered into the ground wherever the hedge needed rebuilding. Nearer by, in various places, men were cutting and shaping strips of hazel with bill-hooks before handing them to others, older men and women who wove them horizontally between the stakes as binders. All around the workers, the younger men and boys and girls were doing the odd jobs. Holding the stakes to be planted. Clearing away the hedge debris. Ladling the drinking water. Fetching and carrying. Flies everywhere, scenting the sweat.

Some of the children, some younger than Jeo, were bruised on the face and body where their family elders had battered them. They were the ones who appeared most sullen, the most withdrawn and watchful, the ones Jeo knew to be violent at times. They didn't smile much. Yet they wore their weals like badges of guilt, as if they were beaten for doing something wrong. There were few of them here working by the ditch. There were many in the glen. When he saw them, Jeo didn't know whether he was more angry with the elders who'd hurt them—or with the chil-

dren themselves, for thinking it was somehow right they should
be punished. He stopped looking at them and got on with his
work.

He'd been doing his menial chores since early morning, and
though he was the smallest there, he was treated as anything but
the nestle-cock of the crew. They worked him hard.

He looked to the sky and wished it would be dark soon. The
clouds were puce. He looked away. One of the labourers was
staring at him. The fat boy Ouse, standing threading a switch of
hazel between the tall poles, eyes fixed on Jeo while he went on
with his work with dextrous hands, ignoring the flies. His face was
redder than ever, with exertion and sun, his russet hair dark with
sweat. There was sweat on his pudgy chest, tracks of sweat like tear
stains on his dusty face and back, and sweat in his sparse ginger
beard. His eyes were just looking at Jeo. Not openly malevolent.
Just staring. Jeo looked away.

"Don't just stand there, fucksake. You'll get us both in trouble."

His brother gave him a push on the back and they walked
off together carrying their stakes to a distant work gang, road dust
puffing at their ankles.

Ouse watched him go, then turned away for something else
to look at while he worked. Hake was there, nearby, further back
down the line, cutting branches into stakes, hardly looking up as
he carved at the wood. He seemed to find the task awkward, but
worked very hard, as if glad to do it. His beard twinkled with
sweat.

Ouse didn't give him a second glance. He saw the rest of his
own gang, doing small things. All of them were there except their
leader Kyrie who was doubtless away wandering the hills. Ouse
didn't like that. He was older than Kyrie, yet had to spend most
days in the fields. He didn't mind the work. It was a duty and he
did it willingly. But he was angry that someone younger than
himself had the right to avoid the hardest labours, just because he
was a cub guardsman. The fat boy wanted to be a guardsman

himself, but he didn't agree with soldiers being exempt from the age laws—

"Too slow, boy. Move your fat arse." The old carpenter slapped him and walked on.

"Senior," said Ouse, and he worked faster, threading the hazel stems with sweaty eagerness. A girl walked past, offering water from a jug, but he swore at her and she went on her way.

Further along the work line, Jeo glanced at his brother. The boy was the youngest of the others, just a few years older than himself. Like the others, he looked different from Jeo. Square bully face and a brutal haircut. Jeo hated him like he hated the rest of them. But not very much. They were, after all, much the same age.

They walked on in silence for a way, Jeo glancing around at the work going on and the young women gleaning in the fields and the raiding parties of dung-coloured starlings, his brother staring straight ahead. Jeo looked at the men, young and old, and saw they all had beards of some sort. He didn't have one and didn't care.

"Is it good being older?" he asked. His brother was surprised to hear him speak. They rarely said a word to each other though they had to work together most days. He gave Jeo a frown and looked away.

"How should I know?" he shrugged. "I'm not older."

"You're older than me. You can do some things they won't let me do."

"So?"

"Do you feel good about it?"

The boy stopped to wipe his brow on the branches in his arms. He sniffed and walked on. "Not much," he said. "I'm still too young."

"When do you think you'll feel good? When you're old as him?" He nodded at a young albino of twenty or so.

"I suppose so."

"Do you think he feels good?"

"Ask him."

Jeo shook his head to keep the flies away. "Maybe he thinks *he's* too young. I wonder when you start to feel good."

"You ask too many questions," said his brother and Jeo didn't ask any more. They walked on in the usual silence and were close to where their armfuls of sticks were needed when sounds on the road behind them made them look back.

A cart was running along the dirt path, a simple loading wagon with two seats at the front, drawn by a big young gelding whipped to a very quick pace.

"Get off the road," snapped Jeo's brother—and he took some hasty steps into the low ditch across the road from all the fence workers. Jeo followed him at once but in his haste he lost his balance on the crumbled surface and the bundle of sticks wavered in his arms. As he struggled to hang on to it all, the cart was upon him. He looked up—a brief wild glance—and the driver lashed at him with the whip, catching his shoulder and neck with pain. Jeo fell into the dry ditch, the branches showering around him, and the wheels of the speeding wain threw dust at him.

Even through the pain that streaked his shoulders he noticed everything. He saw the two faces on the cart. The driver with the whip, a girl of fifteen or so. And a fat little old man with very black hair. Both laughing at him, and he boiled inside when he saw them—at the girl more than the old man.

The elder turned away and Jeo had no more than a quick sight of his flabby old face. Puckered wrinkles around the mouth, a moment of brown gums in a smile. Then nothing but the back of the head, the hair impossibly black on one so old, as the cart galloped away, taking another large half-share of food to the castle.

Then Jeo felt all the pain of the lash. He didn't show it. He didn't reach to his neck with his hand. Some of the men were laughing at him but most had turned back to their work. Trivial incident. His brother swore at him and went on his way, leaving him to stoop in the dust to gather the spilled branches.

He stood again, still squeezing his teeth against the tears—

and found he was facing back from where he came. As he turned to go on, he saw something across the field, away from the workmen, where the land began its first rise up the hill.

In among the few low trees he saw the dark shepherd girl hiding. Far away, but he saw for sure that she was looking hard at him. When she knew he'd seen her, she tilted her head back proudly and squared her shoulders—and he mimed her gesture, his mouth in a small defiant pout. He didn't want to cry any more. She gave him only the glimpse of a smile but he noticed it. He could even see the look in her eyes.

Across the road, ahead of him, Ouse was staring at him again —and followed his gaze over the field to the small copse. But he saw no one there. He waved flies from his face and looked again, but the girl was quite gone. He glanced back to Jeo but the boy was now hustling off along the road with his stock of wood, the welt from the horsewhip already showing very red across the pallor of his shoulders.

When his grandmother had no chores for him, when his brothers didn't want him in the fields, Jeo was sent to work for any of the elders who might have some small use for him.

One hot afternoon, he was standing alone in the yard of a big cottage on the valley flats, tossing handfuls of grain to a brood of fat tethered hens. It was his last task of the day and it was more tiresome than taxing. He stopped from time to time to look idly about him, looking at nothing in particular.

The cottage itself had boulder walls, no mortar, made as skillfully as the weighted reed-thatch roof. It stood in a little pict of very dry land, a small farmyard with hen coops and barrels and a lean-to shed, patches of grass and insipid yellow flowers. Altogether not much to it and Jeo didn't look at it for long. He gazed away across the nearby fields that went to the horizon directly west. All he saw there was the sky. He took another fistful of grain and threw it on the chickens. The farmyard gate opened and he saw the two old women who lived in the cottage, returned from their afternoon walk.

They came into the yard and crossed it without a word, without looking at Jeo. The little boy at their heels opened the door to the low building and they went inside.

Jeo didn't think about the old women, but about the small boy. They kept him for their small daily tasks. They used him in bed. Sometimes other children too, sometimes younger. It happened all over the glen. The little boy was nine years old. Jeo looked down at the hens at his feet. None of the elders had ever wanted him that way, in their beds, and he was glad. Some day it might happen. He put the thought away.

He was very thirsty and looked around for something to drink but there was nothing outside the cottage. He glanced up to the flabby sun, still quite high but dulled. He didn't have to squint. The cottage door opened and one of the women came out. This time he looked at her, and watched as she shambled across the yard, vaguely in his direction, croodling to herself like a wood pigeon.

She was Uehag, the younger of the two. Jeo's face lightened a little. She was quite a pretty old woman, he thought. Small head and cheeky face. Though there were many lines at her mouth and neck, the flesh didn't droop from her bones and her eyes were bright and nut brown. Neat not skinny, chirpy, robes two shades of brown—there was much of the female sparrow about her. She passed close to Jeo and stopped beside him and he smelled her old-people smell.

He thought she was going to say something to him, probably to scold him or tell him what to do next, so he stood and waited. But she wasn't even looking at him. He saw she was staring into space. She was wringing her hands in a curiously jolly way. He didn't know why she'd come out into the yard.

Then she looked at him, with quite a sharp turn of her head, and he saw an unusual expression in her eyes, something not unlike the look he remembered on the shepherd girl's face. Not a common expression for an elder. He stared at her and now he *wanted* her to speak. That look in her eye made him feel it was safe to talk to her. All she did was look through him.

"Is it good being old?" It was all he said because she gave no answer and turned from him almost at once—though she smiled at him widely before she turned. As she walked across the yard she laughed loudly to herself and shook her head.

Jeo didn't understand but he had no time to dwell on it. The other old woman heard the laughter and came out of the cottage and he looked at her.

She was Chacmagh, bigger than Uehag. Heavy legs and hips, a full bag of bosom under the simple grey robe. Hair grey like iron and the face was stern, the brow low over her eyes, small grey whiskers around her mouth. When she opened her mouth to shout to Uehag, Jeo saw her single tooth jutting down from her upper jaw. He would never dream of asking *her* anything, or speaking at all unless she spoke to him. She shuffled across the farmyard like some fearsome old baboon, took Uehag by the arm and appeared to scold her.

Jeo went on throwing grain and stole glances at the two women as they talked in loud voices. Chacmagh gave him a fierce look and he looked away. He thought she might come and hit him as she often did. But she took Uehag's arm and they walked off together, the sparrow and the baboon, and went into their cottage.

The boy let the grain run between his outspread fingers as he looked away, away from the building so no one could see from the windows that he wasn't keeping his eye on the chickens. He looked at the countryside ahead of him and reflected that these two old women owned it all, at least the league or so he could see. They lived in their little house in a mere rood of dirt land, but they weren't just simple cottars with a small roof over their heads. They were old enough to own freehold the many acres all around them, with all the huts and fields and livestock, the giant orchard. Jeo saw a huge half-timbered tithe barn looming above the trees far to the left. They owned that too.

The local rooster came strutting past him and he watched as
it went on its way, all penis and swagger, across its yard, ignoring
the hens. Jeo threw more grain and thought about nothing but his
thirst. The sun was going down slowly.

In answer to his needs, a long, hard-skinned comice pear
rolled a few feet through the dust and stopped close to his feet.
He stared at it almost comically, then bent quickly to snatch it
from under the beak of an eager pullet.

He kept his back to the cottage so no one would see him eat,
and looked into the nearest field. There were no pear trees in the
field, but he wasn't looking to find any. Nor was he searching to
see who'd thrown the fruit. He knew that already. He was looking
to find the shepherd girl and perhaps nod his thanks. But he saw
no one. There was a small movement in the undergrowth around
one of the patchwork plane trees nearby, but it was brief and gone
and might have been anything. He sucked the juice from the pear
and it was so good it made his mouth glands ache.

Near dusk the old women sent him away and he trotted back
to his tenement through the edge of a thin forest. Somewhere up
the hill he caught sight of the freckled boy Kyrie and his gang and
he hid in the grey bushes. They passed close by and he thought
they must see him but they went on their way and he waited a
while then dashed away to his shanty.

Further down the slope Ouse turned to glance over his
shoulder. "He was there," he said again. "You bloody saw him
yourself."

"Yes," said Kyrie.

"We should have picked him up there and then, the little
runt. I owe him one."

"Forget it."

"Why—because you say so?"

"Yes. We've got other things to do."

Ouse kicked a block of moss out of his path. "Few months
ago, you couldn't talk to me like that. You had to call me Senior."

"A few months ago, I wasn't any kind of guardsman. Do what you're told—leave him alone."

"I owe him one."

"He can wait."

"Why?" snapped the fat boy. But no one was listening to him.

The Forest

AS JEO'S FAMILY SAT DOWN to a very late supper, there was a shout in the upstairs room and they all looked up. Another shout, and the sound of something falling on the ceiling.

"Poor Jeo," grinned one of the brothers.

"He's most likely spilled everything," said his sister.

"Maybe the old mother she don't like your cooking, Sharn."

She turned on him. "Maybe you won't get any at all," she said. He gave a big shrug and toyed with his spoon.

Another noise, but this time just the trapdoor opening. Jeo made his way down the ladder and turned to face them. The boys all laughed at once. His tunic was dark where it had been splashed by soup. In the dim light of the charcoal burner, the patches were black and easy to see. The empty bowl, wood spoon and a plate of mutton were in his hands. He looked more miserable than ever.

His eldest brother chuckled. "You can't go pouring it over yourself, Jeo. Drink it instead."

"Not old enough to drink it without spilling," said another boy, grinning.

Jeo stood and waited for them to finish, looking from one to the other. He was still in pain from the hot soup on his front, but didn't let them know. They would only laugh even more.

"What happened up there?" His sister said it simply but her face was severe. Jeo hesitated before answering.

"She threw it at me," he said in a small voice. The brothers laughed again. His father hid a smile in his beard.

"Didn't she like it?" said the oldest boy, trying to keep a straight face. Sharn glared at him.

"She said I didn't serve it right," said Jeo. "I didn't bow when I gave it to her. She didn't eat the meat either."

"Did you say Senior?" queried his sister.

"Yes."

"Little liar," she said.

"Is she alright? Does she need anything up there?" His father was half-frowning.

"Said she doesn't want to eat now. She wants to be left alone."

"We'd best keep the noise down, then. She might want to sleep." He motioned with his hand. "Come and sit, Jeo. Before you do any more damage." The brothers had one last chortle.

"No, don't sit." Sharn pointed to the charcoal burner. "Give the soup out first."

As he went past the table, she took the dish of mutton from him and put it in front of her father. He ate while the boys watched him.

Jeo put the bowl and spoon in a pail of cold water near a wall. It was brighter here, in the corner where the burner stood, and he found a piece of sacking without having to look very hard. He soaked it in the water bucket and wrung it, then wrapped it around the bare handle of the copper pot squatting on the bright-hot coals. He found a black iron ladle.

"Come on, Jeo. We haven't ate all day."

"You might not be hungry but we bloody are."

He carried the pot around the table and put soup in their flat wood bowls—his father first, then Sharn, then the others.

"Careful with that, Jeo. Your hand's shaking."

"Yeh, pour it over yourself if you want—I like it in the bowl."

"Don't talk to him like that when he's got that soup in his hand. He's deadly with hot soup."

It was cheerful, heavy-handed teasing, nothing more than that. Jeo hated them for it.

"Sit down, lad," said his father. "Eat something. You need to fill out. You don't look strong enough to lift that thing."

Jeo put the pot in the middle of the table and sat on one of the two benches, at the end of it. He spooned the soup to his mouth in hectic little movements, almost digging at the bowl—but no quicker than any of his brothers. They fed like ravening men— and they were quiet, for once. This was serious business. They emptied their bowls almost immediately, then sat silently looking at their father while he finished his own. He didn't want any more soup—nor did Sharn—so they fell on it and drained the pot, leaving Jeo a spoonful or two at the end.

"Is the soup good?" It was the girl who asked. Her brothers paused very briefly in their feeding and looked blankly at her.

"We're eating it, aren't we?"

"You'd eat each other if you had a spoon in your hands. Is it good?"

"Yeh, yeh, it's good, Sharn." They nodded and plunged back into their bowls. She looked across the table at Jeo. He dropped his gaze. The remains of the soup were down in front of him. A weak broth, padded with nettles, few beans, too much salt. He felt her eyes on him. What did she want from him? It was only soup.

"It's good," he said plainly. He glanced at her but only for a second. In the low light, her expression was even sterner than usual. She looked like old Cromarty in that light. Otherwise her face was like that of her brothers, though the nose was sharper. It was a good face. It could have been attractive, but she never brightened it with a smile, and her hair was cut austerely short.

Her skin was white, like Jeo's, never tanned by the sun because she didn't work in the fields. She was old enough to stay inside and cook, which wasn't a menial task in the glen. It had an element of skill and only an eldest child—boy or girl—was allowed to do it. She was still staring at her youngest brother when he looked up again. He tried to keep his face humble.

"It's good," he repeated, nodding this time. His brothers made themselves heard again.

"Fuck, Jeo—you've said it once already."

"Yeh, we heard you the first time."

"Leave him be," said their father. "He's just showing respect. More than the rest of you do, most times."

"That's right—he's very nice and polite now, isn't he?" said the second eldest. "Not like he was, few months back. What's come over him, I wonder?"

They looked at Jeo, whose flat face was white like wax in the half-gloom. He looked back at them with nothing but mild surprise on his face.

"I've not done anything wrong," he said.

"That's the bloody point," gruffed the same boy. "You used to do *everything* wrong. What's happened?"

"He's just changed, that's all," said his father, chewing the last piece of mutton. He put his knife down. "Just going through the change, he is. Everybody does the wrong things when they're young, thinks everything's unfair. Everybody changes."

"Not everybody's like that when they're young."

"Aye, everybody. You too, I remember."

"Not me, Senior."

"Yes, you was," said the youngest brother. "You used to say everything ought to be changed, why did we have to be old to get anything. You used to make a lot of noise about it."

"I remember that too."

"No, I wasn't never like that."

"You was," said the father—and his son didn't protest any more. He scraped in his empty bowl with a mote of bread.

"Well, if I was, I don't remember," he muttered. "Anyway, I grown out of it now."

"No, you haven't," smirked the oldest boy. "You're still a big baby."

"No, I grown out of it." He looked to his father, who nodded over the table at him.

"You have. Everybody has. That's what Jeo's doing now."

"Well done, Jeo," mocked the third son.

"Yeh, well done. Welcome back."

They made faces at him, waving their tongues and grinning, but there was no cruelty in any of it. He pretended to look sheepish, even raised a small smile. How he hated them all.

"More food," said the father, and Jeo got up to fetch some. He came back to the table with a plate of potatoes and another of boiled nettles, then an iron pan of long haddock and sprats.

"Fish," said one of the brothers without enthusiasm, edging his nose over the pan then quickly back. "Always the fucking same. Can't we get nothing else?"

"Yeah, what about some meat sometime?"

"You don't do enough work to earn meat," said Sharn.

"What are you talking about? We work plenty."

"Your sister's right," said their father. "You know how it is. Half the work you do is for the Elder, half for us. Do enough work and our half gets paid back in meat as well as bread and beans."

"We done enough work. We work bloody hard all day."

"Aye, you may work hard—nobody's denying it. But you don't do *enough*. You don't cover enough ground out there. So if we want something other than bread and greens, we have to go to the sea and fish for it. We keep all the fish. Elder don't want it."

"I still say we work enough to get some meat."

"You still say wrong then. You want meat, you work hard."

"We bloody do," the young man raised his voice. His father cut him short by pointing at him with his knife.

"You say Senior, boy. Don't let nothing make you forget that."

"Senior," he said resignedly.

"And eat your fish," his father added. "Eat plenty of it. Have the bread too. Give you the strength to work harder tomorrow. To earn meat."

Why? Jeo asked himself. Any scraps of meat they might be

given would go to old Cromarty—and if she refused them, to their father. Why work any harder? Why couldn't they all have meat?

"I don't know what you're moaning about," said the third brother. "You only have to eat the fish, same as the rest of us. It's me has to go and catch it."

The others didn't care. One of them used his breadknife to stab the eye on the haddock on his plate. "All the fucking fish we eat, surprising there's any left out there. Must be a bloody big sea."

Everybody laughed except Jeo and his sister.

"It's bad enough for us—think what old Sligo has to eat."

"He must be made of fish."

Not for the first time, Jeo wondered about Sligo—but no one mentioned him any more and the talking went its own way, leaving Jeo out of it. He looked at nothing much as he ate, bolting the thin fishes and the black bread and wishing there were more of it. From time to time he glanced from one of his family to the next. But never for long, never thinking about them.

Except his sister, for a moment. He knew she didn't like him. Nor did his brothers—but whereas they thought of him as just the runt of the family, feeble at work, too inward for sports, he knew Sharn's dislike went beyond that. She wasn't staring at him now, but he looked away just in case.

She seemed to know, to guess at least, that he hadn't changed at all in the past few months, that though the look was gone from his eyes he was still restless, a threat.

Not only did she distrust him—she could make life hard for him, since she ran the household, arranging the meals and the daily chores. While old Cromarty was the elder of the family, she—and not her father—was its guardian, more of a hard wife than a daughter. The father had no wife.

Jeo pilfered a shred of fish before she could see him—then suddenly he remembered how late it was and got up from the bench. It was already night and there was something he wanted to do. He tried to show no haste in getting up.

"Where are you going?" asked his sister, frowning.

"Get some more charcoal," he said evenly. "You told me to get some earlier."

"So why didn't you get it? Why wait till now?"

"We've been out working all day," he answered. "I didn't have time."

"You can always make time."

"They wouldn't let me leave the field."

"Why do you want to go right now?"

"Leave him alone, girl." Her father sounded almost weary saying it.

"Answer me," she kept on. "Why do you want to go now?"

Jeo shrugged his arms. "It gets very cold later," he explained. "I can hardly carry anything, my fingers get so cold."

"Let him go, Sharn," groaned a brother. "We need the stuff."

"Yeh, let him go. What do you want to keep him here for?"

Her lips pinched together. She turned to the food on her dish. "Alright, get on with it," she said. "Don't take all night—and bring enough to last the week. I've got other things for you to do, next few nights."

"Can I take the basket?"

"No. I need it."

"If I go without it, the guardsmen won't believe I'm going for charcoal. They'll stop me."

"Good."

"They'll send me back," he pressed her. "They won't let me go to the forest and we won't have any charcoal."

"Let him take it," said their father, and Sharn didn't argue. She waved Jeo away and he took a basket from beside a wall, emptied it, and left the room. They heard his footsteps fade in the passageway, his bare feet patting on the boards.

The father bit into a wedge of goat cheese and wiped his beard. "You're too hard on the boy sometimes," he said without passion.

"I don't trust him," said Sharn. "He's been too quiet this past winter. Something's going on in him."

"No," said her eldest brother. "We been working with him every day and we haven't noticed anything. He's a useless little bastard but he don't mean no harm."

"Yeh," said the next. "He's only a misery because he's tired all the time."

The father nodded. "Don't worry about him, girl. He's mending. Might be better if you didn't treat him quite so stern."

"I'll do what I like to him," she said, and her face flushed. "I'm older than he is."

"Aye, well," he sighed. "That's true enough. You're in your rights. Do what you want with him, I suppose. But you're not older than *me*—so you don't answer me back, and you don't forget what to call me."

"Yes, Senior." She picked at her food. He finished his mug of beer and pushed his chair back from the head of the table.

"I'm off," he announced. "Going to hear old Shibolleth tell some of his stories. Get some sleep early tonight—you'll be working for meat tomorrow. And put the fire out. We don't have charcoal to waste."

"No, Senior."

"Senior."

"—Senior."

He closed the door behind him and moved along the corridor, peering a little in the sudden darkness. At the far end, he stopped by the corner of two splintered walls and stood still for a while as he probed in the big pockets of his wool tunic. He found a small hide pouch and rolled himself a stick of tobacco, holding it up to his face to see it. He put the pouch away and lit the tobacco from a tinderbox, throwing light in the dark on his big fleshy face, then leaned against the oak wall as he smoked. He could have done all that in the family room, but it was noisy and crowded in there and he wanted a moment to himself.

He was always looking for that: a few minutes of his own, time to do nothing. All he wanted was the quiet life. Food and drink and a sleep in the afternoon. He liked the pleasures: drinking and storytelling and playing dice, hunting badgers and chasing women; he liked things to be easy. So it bothered him that his daughter should ill-treat his youngest son. It caused unrest, a bit of bad blood he could do without. He blew out a gust of smoke in a sigh. He didn't like Jeo very much—but he didn't hate him at all. He didn't think about him one way or the other. He was just his son, that was all. She was just his daughter. Why couldn't they live quietly together?

He pinched the last nip of tobacco between forefinger and thumb and held it with difficulty to his mouth to suck the last smoke out of it, then flicked away what was left. He did another of his sighs. He would be glad to be rid of his family some day, when he was old enough to go and live in a cottage of his own, when he could have anything he wanted. It was still a long way off, many years yet. He stretched his arms, yawned and went bluntly on his way through the inland of the tenement, daydreaming of unrationed beer and malt spirits and little girls two or three at a time.

The same night, later. Dusk, and grey light in the sky. A cross-grained summer wind and its speckles of niggling rain. A short, grizzly shepherd trudging back to his hillside croft, pushing open the low gate to the yard.

The collie dog trotted ahead of him. When he turned to push the gate shut behind him, the dog was already at the door, slapping it with a paw. Gara narrowed his eyes as he looked through the drizzle at the roof of the building.

No more than a hut, though big. The usual rubblestone walls and the deep thatched roof, now black with rain. A thickset chimney stack. He saw smoke rolling from the stack and was pleased. He opened the door and followed the dog inside.

Instantly there was heat and strong warm light. No low charcoal burners here—it was an elder's cottage. The wall on the right of the door was almost all fireplace, cut deep and high in the stonework. The fire bustling in it had no charcoal. Thick logs of fresh wood. The smell of the wood and the smell of new ash. In front of the fire, a stone hearth was almost hidden under the spread of a single wolfskin, grey and splayed and headless. Against the facing wall, a heavy blockish trestle-table, all dark brown oak, stood circled by large wood stools each with its cushion of white wool. Bulky carving knives and copper pots, hanging from a rack on the wall beside the door, gleamed in the firelight. The shepherd kicked the door shut and crossed the room to stand in front of the fire.

The collie was already there, motionless as it sat facing the blaze, as if tranced by the swaying flames. He bent to brusquely pat its head, then cursed and stood upright, hands hard on hips, pressing with his fingers as he arched his back. Pains in the lower spine, around the hips. The cold and the wet and the hard walking had brought them back. He didn't move for a time, waiting till the aching eased, then cursed some more and pulled his damp tunic over his head and dropped his kilt and threw them on the hearth rug.

The shadows on his body showed its lines in bold relief: the thin hard fibrous muscles, the bones too clearly defined, the skin loose in places. The padding of youthful fat had begun to waste, showing more of the body beneath, showing its age—though the old man was still strong and cussedly fit. There were very small rows of wrinkles on his belly and above the knees, the hair more white than grey on his breastbone. He found a dry housecoat and put it on.

He sat on one of the stools at the table, in front of the iron dish and cutlery already laid out, and pulled off his boots. His feet were still cold and he wanted to go back to the fire but he was tired and his joints were in pain and he couldn't be bothered. He rubbed his toes together, then left them to warm at their own pace.

It was while he was rolling a fat stick of tobacco that the door
to the other room opened. He looked up straight ahead and saw
the tousle-haired girl in the doorway. He licked the tobacco and
didn't say anything as she gave him a look and crossed to the fire,
where a small brown pot hung from the spit over the flames. The
bright glow highlighted the heather purple in her hair as it stumbled around her shoulders when she bent to lift the pot—and as
she bent, the short, thin tunic was clinging to her big hips and
upper legs. The shepherd turned away to finish rolling his tobacco
as she came away from the hearth and dumped the full pot on the
table. He glanced at her but still didn't speak while she sat down
and began to ladle a thick stew onto his dish. She pushed the dish
closer to him, served herself, and began to eat without looking up.
He left the thumb of tobacco on the table.

"Where have you been?" he asked, eating. "Sleeping, I
shouldn't wonder."

She raised her head and nodded it. He looked back at his
plate.

"Aye, well, no doubt you needed it."

He said no more for a while and finished his stew. Lamb,
again—better than the old mutton and turnips which the tenement
dwellers might eat once in a month. They worked like dogs to earn
it, too. He bit deep into the pieces of good meat. He was glad, in
some ways, to be old.

Rhosarran refilled his dish and he watched her. He couldn't
see why she aroused him. He'd never been able to understand it.
But she did. She was exciting. Her hair was full and wild and an
outlandish colour. Her face was big and odd but compelling. Her
silence had its own fascination. He could see her eyes were still a
little swollen with sleeping. He moved his hand to touch her but
she sat back and he put his hand on his spoon.

The meal went on in its usual silence, neither of them looking
at the other. The shepherd drank his mug of wine and left it by
his plate, took his tobacco and went to sit crosslegged by the fire.

Rhosarran fed the collie with the waste of the stew and came to sit beside him, a small distance away. He smoked.

"All day out on the south hill," he said. The dog came and lay beside him, on the other side of him, away from the girl. "All day I was out there, dawn to dusk in the sodding rain. All day, and you know what I saw?"

Yes, she knew. He saw the same every day.

"Not a thing." He made a show of shaking his head. "Same as yesterday, day before that. Not a damned thing." He put his hand absently on the collie's neck and it looked up. "Nothing to speak of out there," he was still saying. "Nothing I could tell the captains. Every night I see them, and most times all I can say is nothing to report. Good thing too. But there's times I think there must be something else besides all this. Another way to live."

Another of their long, isolated silences. The old man looked to the adjacent wall, where highland flowers brightened the stonework. Oxlips and pink willowherb in small baskets pegged in the wall, a dog rose in a cup of earth—like mountain flowers growing from cracks in a cliff face. Rhosarran had set them there, splatters of colour against the drabness. He was glad she had. He would never have thought of it.

He moved his feet as they warmed, blew smoke to the ceiling, glanced at her. "I don't see much of that boy any more," he lied. "That friend of yours, Jeo. Keeps well out of sight nowadays."

She looked at him with just a faint crease of her brow.

"I've not seen him since last autumn," he went on. "Have you?"

When he looked at her she shrugged heavily and shook her head, her frown darker. He kept his eyes on her.

"Never?" He threw his tobacco in the fire. "You've not seen him any place, all these months?"

She made a face to tell him she'd seen him, of course she'd seen him, but it didn't mean anything. She mimed the use of a spade digging.

"Aye, you've seen him in the fields. We all have. But no-where else, you say? Not in the hills, by the river some time? Never?"

She shook her head hard.

"I don't know," he muttered, looking away again. "I can't be sure about you and him."

She leaned and touched him. He turned and saw a very slight smile on her face, a shade of something tender in it. He didn't believe the smile. He didn't believe her touch of his arm. But he softened all the same.

"Aye," he said, staring at the burning logs. His face was hot so he moved back a space. The dog had a hot face too, and put its paws on its muzzle, rubbing its nose with them. But it stayed where it was.

"Have a care," said Gara. She frowned, to herself this time. "The guardsmen still watch that boy. Not as close as they did, but they do watch him. If they should see him do anything wayward, the slightest thing, they'll have him. They'll put him away in the castle or take him to their brochs. And if they see you with him, even if you meet by chance, they'll take you too. I don't want that."

He didn't look at her as he said this. She didn't want to hear any of it. She had to go now. She stood up and he turned round. The collie lifted its head and stared at her.

"What are you doing?" he questioned. She pointed at the wicker basket beside the hearth. He saw it was almost empty.

"You want to fetch wood—now? On a bloody night like this? Wait till morning, girl."

She shook her head and pointed at the fire. It was low. She hugged herself and shook as if very cold, then pointed harder at the basket. His face shrugged.

"Maybe you're right," he said. "But I don't want you to go." He stood up and moved to her, took her shoulders in his hands and pushed some of her bunching hair from her brow.

"I want you to stay here," he said, gently as he could, and

held her to him, his arms urgent around her, his cheek against hers. She kept her arms by her sides. She smelled his tobacco and his old-man smell, and her body was rigid in his grip. He held her tighter but she did nothing. He pushed her away.

"Go, then," he snapped. "I don't want you here anyway, you cold little slut. Get out and fetch your filthy wood—but be back in an hour or I'll have the guardsmen set their dogs after you."

She stood and looked at him and thought about trying to placate him. She wanted to be away more than an hour—

"Get out, damn you. Get away before I beat all the skin off you."

She left the door open behind her.

The old man wondered bitterly why it was always like this. She'd lived in his house for almost two years. Still she hated him. He kept her by force and she hated him for it. He didn't want to keep her against her will—he knew it could never make her want him. But he didn't know what else to do. He wanted her. He couldn't let her go. And only by using his right as an elder could he have her. If he gave her any freedom to choose, she wouldn't choose *him*. He was too old.

An anger grew in him and he kicked the door shut. He wasn't old. Why couldn't she see that? He wasn't feeble and soft in the head like the old men and women in the glen. He was hard and strong and quick-witted. He was young for his age. He was young. He kicked the door again when it was shut, over and over till the pain in his bare feet brought him to his senses. He kicked the door in silence but when he stopped he fell into a fit of coughing and the collie dog got up from the fire and watched him.

While he sobbed, Rhosarran ran away down the hill, holding a short axe she'd taken from the woodshed in the yard. Black night now, but she knew the stretch of hillside well and ran quickly across it.

There were moments, like this, when she almost felt a pity for the shepherd. She knew what he felt for her. She felt his anguish that she didn't return his feelings. She knew that for all his high standing and comforts as a glen elder, she was all he had.

But none of that was her fault. She hadn't asked him to want her. And his want was only that of an old man for a young girl, nothing deeper. He didn't want her for who she was. He was taken by her youth, the firmness of her body, the shine in her eyes—and he was allured, she knew, by her muteness, which only made her more aware of the affliction. She didn't feel pity very long or very much. She hated him profoundly, as much as Jeo hated his grandmother. She was repulsed by his touch, his smell, the very sight of him. She hated him even when he was good to her. He was old and could hold her captive because he was old.

On her way down through the blackness of the valley she looked around and listened hard for any movement on the open hill. The guardsmen didn't watch her closely any more, but she would never feel completely safe.

She was in a hurry so she ran fast—and stumbled, just once, which made her gasp. She was glad she couldn't cry out. Otherwise her silence was always a hard load. It either repelled—most thought of her as backward and were afraid of her as they were afraid of the blind and the deaf and cripples—or enticed, with some obscure sense of mystery, a promise of hidden depth. Either way, an extreme. She didn't want that. She wished she were like everyone else—but only Jeo treated her that way. She lengthened her stride down the long slope and slanted away to one of the great oakwoods. She passed a shrine in a hill wall but didn't go in to give homage.

Near the top of the valley hill, on the south side of the river, a young girl lay on her back and stared up at the night sky, looking for stars. She was a slim girl and her hair was fair, quite white in the moonlight. She was pretty in a grubby way. Her tunic was still around her waist and her legs were bare. She didn't feel the cold.

She turned her head to one side and watched the boy next

to her, who was sitting up now, knees drawn to his chin as he hugged his legs. In the pale light, she could see the side of his face, with its blunt nose and many freckles and shape like a wedge, like a lizard. He seemed to be staring into space down into the glen, and he kept a stem of oat-grass clamped in the corner of his mouth, like a man with a nub of tobacco, after lovemaking.

There was no expression on his face, none that she recognised, and she wondered about him. She didn't know him. She didn't like his face or his body. He was her junior, the first time she'd been with anyone younger than herself. He was just a boy—yet she was out there beside him. Perhaps there was something compelling in his coldness, or the skill of his touch, or just that he was a cub guardsman. She didn't know. Nor did the other girls he'd been with. She rolled onto her belly to warm the front of her thighs on the rug.

Kyrie wasn't staring at nothing. Someone was running across the slope of the hill below him, alone and carrying what looked like a bucket or a bag. Someone small and pale skinned, running in the grass, not along one of the dirt paths. He squinted and saw it was Jeo with a basket in his hand.

The lizard-faced boy smiled inside, grimly, though nothing happened on his face. He remembered the evening in the nettle-field, weeks back, the mute girl throwing stones, the pain when she struck him. He recalled, more than that, Jeo's flinching little bravery as he'd stood there with the nettles in his arms, not running away. The boy seemed to have courage—and spirit, so it was said. He had speed too, as Kyrie now saw. He was a thin boy, puny, but there was something useful about him.

Kyrie watched him disappear over a wall. Where was he going with that basket? To collect charcoal or mushrooms, most probably. Running fast because he didn't want to be late getting back, for fear of a beating. No cause for Kyrie to follow him, this time.

"I'm going back now."

He gave a glance. The girl was on her feet, tugging her tunic down. Her hair was on her face and she pushed it aside. He looked back into the valley, just to look away from her.

"I got to go back," she said, still holding her hair. "I'm late. You coming too?"

"Why?" he asked.

"It's raining," she said.

It was. The start of a firm drizzle. He hadn't noticed it before.

"No," he said. "I'm staying here. You go back."

She stood and looked at him. In the moonlight his hair was like ash.

"I could be having a baby," she said, louder. He didn't turn round.

"Tell that to your older brother," he said.

She took her hands from her hair and walked heavily away, leaving him to wrap himself in the rug and sit in the lee of the sheep wall as the rain came down, chewing a fresh slip of grass.

He was glad to have seen Jeo again. It put thoughts in his mind. He might have a use for the boy one day. He hadn't expected to see him that night. It was a chance sighting—but the kind of chance he was always likely to come across. He liked to put himself in positions where he could see and hear things, where a chance happening might come to his notice. Even when he went out on the hill with a girl, he chose a spot where he could see the whole of the glen.

When Jeo hurried out of his tenement he cursed his luck. The moon was fat and bright and he could see much of the valley all around him—which meant he too was clearly visible. On any other night he wouldn't have cared. But now, intent on a forbidden act, he wanted total darkness.

He ran creeping across the broad flats by the river towards one of the intense oakwoods nearer the sea. He glanced this way and that as he went, looking over his shoulder more than once. But he did it out of habit, not for any good reason. Moon or not, it was night and he couldn't expect to see very much.

He kept on his toes as he ran, as light on his feet as possible, wincing when he trod on anything that made any sound. The sounds were always small, almost nothing at all, but they seemed to him to echo round the entire glen. He was sure the whiteness of his limbs could be seen for miles.

For all that, he reached the forest without interference, just as the first drizzle began to come down. At the edge of the wood he stopped to catch his breath and have another look around.

The giant tree in front of him was no more than a black outline and its brimming crown of branches reminded him of the antlers of some colossal stag. He pushed through the bushes below and made his way through the bracken fields towards the innards of the forest.

The undergrowth was piled high and close. Mostly grass and heavy ferns. A few remaining cuckoo-pint, snapping succulently underfoot. Brittle leaf litter, very dense. Jeo waded through it knee-deep. He felt the dampness of the humus beneath as it reached up over his ankles—but generally the forest floor was dry. The rain would never touch it.

Progress was slow. He climbed a number of huge old logs lying dead on their sides, the wood crumbling under his heel. Halfway into the weald he passed the giant granite head of an old figure in a hood, almost hidden in a high grassbank, ivy and roots smothering the face, cracking the ancient stone. He couldn't see it in the dark but he knew it was there and he moved away from it.

He paused in a small clearing and filled the basket with cold charcoal from a large iron brazier—then on, quickly, till he reached the place he wanted and had to sit to rest his legs.

He listened but there was no one there and he put the basket down and settled himself against a tree at the foot of an earthbank, sitting with his back against the trunk and his legs straight out ahead of him so the lower half of his body was buried in dead leaves and only his head and torso would have been visible.

Even in the total blackness, he knew exactly where he was. To his right, beyond the earthbank, a small empty glade, one of the few without a charcoal burner in it. On his left, at the top of the bank, the landmark of a broken oak on its flank, the tendrils of its tap roots hanging out over the slope like a hundred rat tails. Otherwise, all around, nothing but trees and undergrowth, invisible.

His thoughts wandered. Ever since his last walk on the moors, the day he killed the stag, he'd merged back into the life of the glen. Throughout the long months, he'd carried out his daily tasks without so much as a gesture of complaint. Hedging and ditching and cleaning out stables in winter. Ploughing and cutting young grass in the spring. In early summer digging out new root crops, hoeing, gathering nuts. Never alone. Always with his brothers or other youths. Always under the eye of a guardsman. He did the work quickly and well. He remembered to call his elders Senior and kept his face quiet. He stopped going for walks in the hills and generally did all he could to make himself unnoticed.

He was still watched and he knew it. He saw Meagher's men looking—and some of the older peasants. They'd seen the change in his ways but were still watching.

But the change was of course no real change at all. He still hated the same things, as much as ever. And having to stay stifled in the great wooden slum made him frantic.

So sometimes he had to get out of the place. The hills and open spaces were out of the question—so the big forests, at night, were his only resort.

Here, hidden from the prying eyes of daylight, he could sit and do nothing with only his knife for company. Here at least, in this one clearing, he could get away from the stench of charcoal. Tonight he was in the forest *not* to be alone.

He opened his eyes. Still the same gaping blackness. Then, in the mash of ferns ahead, a single tiny jab of light. Then two of

them. They came closer, then disappeared. Just a passing firefly and
its mate. He closed his eyes again to listen. Any number of faint
woodland noises. The distant flitter of a nightcap or some other
small bird. The tapping of a deathwatch beetle somewhere in the
tree above him. The fall of a twig. A kind of underlying forest
hum, nothing he could distinguish. He was impatient to hear
something else—someone else. He didn't have much free time,
most of it was gone, and he didn't want to be kept waiting. He
tried to stay calm. He crossed his arms and leaned back on the tree
—to rest. It had been another hard, dull day in the fields, another
soon to follow. He took in the greenwood smells in long, slow
breaths.

Something, suddenly, touched his arm—and for just a moment he was stiff with fright. His mouth opened and he yelled like
a rabbit but no sound came out. A hand covered his mouth quickly
and firmly and held him back against the treetrunk. Almost immediately he wasn't afraid any more.

The hand left his mouth. From the heavy rustling in the
leaves beside him, he knew someone was sitting very close. He
turned to look. Still too dark to see. A strong, familiar body smell.

"You frightened me," he said in a fierce but very low whisper. "I wish we could meet somewhere else. Not in the dark."

A hand patted his shoulder. A face pressed against his cheek
and he edged away from it. The face didn't insist. It drew back
from him and the hand left his shoulder.

"I wish we could meet in the day," he went on. There was
no reply but he didn't expect one. There was silence for a while,
one of the many they had to have. Jeo looked towards her again.
"I'm glad you're here," he said awkwardly. He inched out his hand
and touched her. Before he could pull his hand back she grasped
it in her own fingers and held it firm. Her grip surprised him. He
hadn't known how strong she was. He hadn't really expected her
to touch him at all.

She rubbed his arm with her other hand, to show she was glad
to be with him. He smiled at her foolishly in the dark.

"I can't stay long," he whispered. "They let me out to get some coal. Did he make you work hard today?"

She made a single noise with her throat and Jeo gave a soft growl. He enlarged every sound he made, so she'd understand his exact meaning in the darkness.

"I hate him," he said about Gara. "He hurt me that time in the hills—you remember? Did he beat you today?"

She clicked her tongue to say no. Jeo growled anyway.

"He treats you like one of his sheep," he said. "He treats his dog better. They all do that. They think we're no better than animals. Just because we're young."

Rhosarran moved in the dry leaves and put her body closer to his. She kept hold of his hand. Jeo stayed stiffly where he was.

"Even the way they talk makes old sound better than young," he said, his thoughts off at a tangent. "They say I'm fourteen years old. But fourteen is young. I don't want to be called old. Why do they always talk about the good old days when today's older than yesterday? It's all wrong."

There was no answer, of course. He almost felt he was talking to himself, especially in the dark where he could see none of her expressions. But he was glad enough of the chance to put what he was thinking into words. Though she was older, he was sure she thought the same things. So he was speaking for both of them.

"Why are things called old-fashioned but everything new is new-fangled? It makes new things sound not as good. And I have to call Cromarty grandmother. She's not grand. She's just old. They always talk about her being a great age. What's great about it? I think they just mean a big age, with lots of years. So why don't they call it that? They twist everything. I hate them."

She put her arm across his waist and rubbed his side in a calming gesture. But she made gruff sounds in her mouth and it was clear she shared his anger. He felt there was no more to say for a while. They both understood. He lay and did nothing, content to just spend time with her before he had to go back. She had other ideas.

His hand and his other arm were still in her grasp and she was stronger than him, so he couldn't draw away. She reached and put a kiss on his face, and he was very surprised. No one had ever kissed him before. He was bold enough to return the kiss—he turned his head to find her cheek, but she felt him turn and pushed her mouth against his, covering his lips.

It was all very strange to Jeo. She didn't breathe into his mouth and she tasted of nothing. He couldn't see a thing in the dark, so her every touch was a surprise. She released his hand and held both his shoulders instead, and pulled him round, predictably enough, to lie along her as she settled back in the soft leaf litter at the foot of the earthbank, away from his basket of coal and her own hatchet. He didn't resist.

She kissed him again, the same way. This time his lips moved. Her mouth stayed on his and she did things with her tongue and he did them too. It was still very strange but he was excited too. She felt his heart beat on her chest and was glad.

They kissed for what seemed a long time to Jeo, all one kiss, before he moved his mouth away—not because he didn't like what they were doing but to kiss the rest of her face and down to her neck. He bit her and she smiled and pulled his hair and bit him back. His laugh was a gasp and very brief. His lips pushed on her skin and his hands began to hold her.

She took one of his hands and spread it over one of her breasts, moving his fingers for him. He felt his pulse in his ears, and his head was hot. He gripped the breast. It was firm as muscle. His face went to it and mouthed it through her tunic. Rhosarran wanted to take the tunic off, at least to pull it up to her neck—but they had so little time.

He was very bold now, already. He moved down the length of her to her belly. She was happily surprised and made a soft humming noise. He lifted the hem of her tunic and searched in her groin with his face. Her smell was different here, something he'd never smelled before, as strong as the rest of her. His tongue worked willingly in her mat of harsh hair, but she took his shoulders and drew him up along her, her smile broader but not unkind.

She kissed his mouth again, then pushed him easily off her and rolled him onto his back deep in the oak leaves. They were faintly damp against the back of his legs but he didn't notice that for long. He was lying rather tensed on the ground, staring wide-eyed in the darkness and wondering what she was going to do next —and he caught his breath in a kind of sob when she reached up under his tunic and took his penis in both her hands.

His whole body was tight and she'd heard his intake of breath. She made soothing sounds in her throat, and her touch was very light. She was more than ready to use her mouth, but there was no need. The penis, thin and very straight, was desperately hard, the hardness of the very young. She moved her hands on it, then knelt astride him and ducted it inside her.

Jeo didn't breathe. He couldn't really believe it was all about to happen. No girl had so much as touched him before. He was too young for most of them. Now he could feel nothing but the grasp of her hands and his bloodbeat aching through all his body.

She didn't need to do anything very much, very long. It took very little time. He didn't feel her movements around his penis. He was too excited. It was the *idea* of being inside her that aroused him. He didn't know how to control himself, and a single short cry, a gasp in the dark, told her it was all finished, almost at once, all achieved.

She bent from the waist and kissed him again, on the cheek and chin. His arms went round the small of her back and held on with all his fierce little strength. She made her humming sounds again and he kissed her face. All he could think of saying was thank you and she swamped it with her mouth on his. She didn't want him to thank her. It was a release for her too. She wanted to thank him.

They lay like that for a very few short minutes. Jeo began to hear sounds again. The faintest rustle of a rodent, the cackle of the rain high in the treetops.

He wasn't thinking of anything at all, but for the first time in his small life he felt strong, absurdly invulnerable. He didn't think he felt any older, but he felt young like a young man, not a little boy. She'd given him that, in full spite of the glen and its laws, and he hugged her harder to him.

She broke from his clasp and went away to an edge of the glade. To clean herself, he guessed, so the old shepherd wouldn't know. He cleaned himself too, with grass and leaves as he knelt, then went up the bank to find his basket, scrabbling in the dark. She joined him and picked up her axe.

"I'll be here again, the night before the rest day," he said, standing close in front of her. "They'll let me out for more charcoal then. Will you be here?"

She put her face against his cheek so he could feel her nod, and gave him a last strong kiss before she left. He wanted to return the kiss, but she went quickly away to cut firewood, and he ran from the clearing without watching her go, moving in an opposite direction.

Outside, out of the closed forest, the moon was still showing —but now it was cluttered by clouds, so the light was not so good. The rain was still only a drizzle, but naggingly constant. Jeo took off his tunic to cover the charcoal and keep it dry, then ran naked across the open grass.

His penis had been in a girl's body, but he didn't feel proud or anything like that, not yet. He was glad it had happened and was buoyed by it, but he was quick to put it out of his mind. He could dwell on it later. Just now, his first and only thought was to get back to the tenement as soon as possible, and he ran hard through the soaking fields. The black spires of a rank of poplars reared ahead of him and he followed them along the riverbank. Halfway across the last broad pasture, a man from his own shanty saw him running but noted the basket in his hand and thought nothing of it. The boy's nudity was in itself unremarkable.

Jeo was very nearly back at the shanty block—only yards from one of the high wooden stairways leading to the upper storeys—when a noise, somewhere close ahead, made him stand and look. He used his free hand to wipe rainwater from his mouth and watched as a lone horse and rider came slowly into view from around the nearest corner of the block.

Jeo didn't move, the horse came to a halt only when it was close beside him, and for a moment there was silence between them as the soldier in helmet and chain mail looked down on the skinny naked boy with the basket in his hand. Jeo's body was sallow and oily bright in the rain. The Guardian was a black shape.

"Out on your own, Jeo." A simple statement in the usual soft voice, any accusation thickly veiled. Jeo stared up at him and the rain hit his face and he blinked.

"I've been to one of the forests, Senior. To get charcoal." He held up the basket for a moment. "My father sent me."

The Guardian made no sort of move or a sound. He saw the shabby tunic covering the load of charcoal. So the boy had given up his clothing to keep the family fuel dry. Perhaps he really had changed after all. The soldier looked in his eyes. Nothing there but rain.

"What else is in the basket?" He asked it quietly, almost politely.

"Nothing, Senior. Just charcoal."

"Show me."

He lifted his tunic aside. The knife moved in its pouch but thankfully couldn't fall out. He watched the Guardian looking in the basket. Raindrops went down the man's face into his short beard.

"Empty it," he said.

Jeo turned the basket upside-down. Pieces of charred wood fell everywhere. The Guardian looked at them in silence. Jeo was starting to feel the cold.

"Good," said the Guardian. "But next time you go for charcoal, go in the day, in the light when others can see you— not like a thief in the dark."

"No, Senior."

"Go home now."

"Yes, Senior."

He waited till the guardsman rode away before gathering the lumps of coal back in the basket. They were all damp now. His pains had been wasted.

He was a little shaken, though nothing could have disturbed his new feeling of strength. A timber owl hooted high overhead in the tenement as he scaled the crude shanty ladder and bolted into the wooden tower block at one of its highest levels.

The Guardian had made him late and the coal was wet, so his sister beat him with the broom and in the morning he was sent to work in the fields with nothing to eat.

The Grandmother

IT WAS EARLY AUTUMN and Jeo was nearly fifteen when his father died. He came back through the tenement very late one night and made the drunken mistake of climbing one of the old disused stairways, which simply collapsed under him. They didn't find the body for a week, then took it away and his family watched as it was burnt in a shallow pit and the ashes were thrown in a wind. Land was too valuable to be clogged with corpses. Only an elder could be buried in soil.

Jeo had hated his father, so he didn't feel any sadness at the death. But he wished the man were still alive, because now his day-to-day life took an abrupt turn for the worse. His sister took charge of the family, and she and the old grandmother made things very hard for the boy. They loaded his every waking hour with obscure and difficult jobs of work, so he never had a minute to himself. He ran errands till he could hardly walk, and didn't see Rhosarran for weeks at a time.

Cromarty was sitting up in her bed, bent forward from the waist as her granddaughter tended her hair. She used a heavy quill brush and a wooden comb and it took her an hour or more, the hair being so long and tangled. It was something Jeo would never have been ordered to do. He could help his grandmother to her slop bucket but he couldn't touch her hair.

The candle was close to the bed, above their heads so Sharn

could see the lengths of hair easily. She saw much of the face too, and she could tell from the face that Cromarty, that night, was well. It wasn't always so. The old woman's condition fluctuated from day to day, from deep muttering feeble-mindedness to bouts of clear sight when she was coherent for a while, before her thoughts turned dark and she sank into a fearsome depression that could last for days. Tonight she was well and Sharn could talk to her. In the quiet of the room, she listened for sounds from the room below—but her brothers were making no noises and she assumed they were going about their chores.

"Tell me how long it's been since your father died."

"Nearly three months," said Sharn.

"And the boy, in three months, is he changed? Have we changed him, all this hard work?"

"No. I don't trust him."

"Aye, I think you're right." Cromarty made a fitful movement of her shoulders. The girl waited till it subsided before putting the comb back in the gush of white hair.

"That look in his eye," said the old woman. "That's what it is. Take the look from his eye and he'll be right. We got to work it out of him, however long it takes. He'll never survive otherwise."

"He don't have the look any more," said Sharn.

"He always had it."

"Not now. He looks like everyone else his age. Others think he's alright now—but not me. The guardsmen mostly let him alone."

"Guardsmen," said Cromarty. "What do they bloody know? They can't see no look in his eye, but it's there. One day they'll see it too and he'll be in deepest trouble."

There was no sense in arguing. Sharn combed the hair back behind her grandmother's ears, showing the thread veins on the neck, showing all the face, emphasising the nose. She saw an impatient look come to the face.

"I can't understand it," said Cromarty. "I don't know why he don't change. How long since he was stopped going out on the hills?"

"Year or more."

"A year. All that time—such a long time for a boy his age —and still he's the same inside. All the work and the beatings, still he don't change. Why can't he learn? It's for his good."

Sharn put the comb down and used the brush, moving it down through the tresses in long soothing sweeps. "He wants everything *now*," she said simply.

"Everybody of his years wants that. I did, once. We all grow out of it."

"Not him."

"Ah, he's a poor stupid boy."

Sharn saw the faintest touch of disappointment, a kind of wry sadness, in her grandmother's very harsh features. She frowned herself. She couldn't understand why the old woman persisted in seeing Jeo as just a kind of little boy lost, who could be brought back into line by a few hard knocks and a stint of hard work. He was more dangerous than that, she was sure of it. Why did nobody else see it?

"He might never grow out of it," she said.

"He will. Everybody does, soon or later."

"He don't think like everybody else. He hates everything old."

"He's not so wrong," muttered Cromarty. Sharn put on another frown.

"You can't mean that, Senior."

"I can mean what I want to," said the grandmother. "Put that brush away and leave me alone. I've had enough of your brushing, same thing all the time. Come round here where I can see you. Sit. Now look at me and tell me—how old am I, Sharn?"

The girl looked at her face. The big long nose and sharp chin, the malign angles of the eyebrow arches. The eyes were steady for once. She looked away.

"I can't say, Senior."

"Well, never mind how many years I got. I look very old, don't I?"

"Yes, Senior."

Was it a smile on the hard old face? "Poor girl," she said softly. "You think it's good I look old, don't you? You think I want to hear it. You don't know how it is. I'm not as old as I look. If I was, I'd have my own cottage hut by now, wouldn't I?—not still lying here in this box of wood. I just look older, that's all. And I hate it, Sharn. I hate it like nothing else. I was beautiful once. You can't see that now."

Sharn had to look at her. There was nothing good to look at in the face. It hadn't aged well.

"It's age done this to me," said Cromarty, still in her low voice. "I've not been well, I know—but it's mostly just getting older that's made my skin look like this, my flesh go soft, my hair all white. It makes my mind go too, doesn't it?" Sharn couldn't answer but it didn't matter. "That's the worst thing—when I talk all day and can't remember the last thing I said. It happens when you start to get old."

"But it's good, too," said Sharn. "You can do more what you want when you get older. That's worth having, must be."

"Aye, must be." The old woman frowned bitterly. Her face looked terrifying when she frowned, worse in the candlelight. "It's worth having because it's better than nothing. But what does it mean—what use is it to me as I am? A bit of meat with my soup, a small room to myself. Not very much after a life of work, is it?"

"But you have power," said the girl. "We have to do what you say. You stopped me being wed."

Cromarty stared at her, a gentle look. "You still feel bad about that? You know we needed you here. Couldn't let you be a wife someplace else."

"Yes, I know."

"You still feel bad?"

"You're an elder. You had every right."

"But how do you feel?"

Sharn looked at her. "Different now," she said. "I know it was for the best. I was too young to be wed."

Her face told Cromarty nothing. The old woman shrugged.

"So I stopped you leaving here. So that's power, is it? While you have to do as I say, what am I doing myself? I'm old so I get tired. I can't get around on my own. I can't do the things I used to. And as I get older it gets worse. What's the good of having my own cottage if all I can do is hobble round it—if I'm too old to care any more? Cottages, they're just houses for old people. And all the power you say I have, when can I ever use it? The guardsmen have power. They live as good as elders, and they do it while they're young. That's power, girl."

"You can tell a guardsman what to do."

"Only when it's not important. I can't tell him to do something that really matters. Anyway, that's the same as telling *you* what to do. I still can't do much myself. I've become an outsider, like everyone else who's old. They put us in cottages and look after us and we're not useful any more. We don't do anything. We can't work. We're not part of the glen." Sharn shook her head to say it wasn't true but her grandmother wasn't looking. "I'm alone in this room when you all go out to work. I wish I was your age. I know more now, but what use is that when all there is to know is this glen and the guardsmen and my illness, then dying? I knew nothing when I was a girl, and I worked hard and had to do what I was told—but I was beautiful and I had my health. I wish I was all those years younger."

Sharn was surprised by all this. Her grandmother had never talked to her this way before. She didn't know old people ever thought like that.

"I don't think you should be talking like this, Senior."

Cromarty showed her teeth in what might have been a smile. "Don't misunderstand me, girl. I don't want anything to change now. Nobody my age wants that. We all been through the hard times of being young, so we want what we've earned for our old age. I don't want anyone younger to have more than me. That wouldn't be right."

Sharn nodded in thought. She was uncomfortable. "I'd best go downstairs," she said. "Got to give Jeo his job for tonight. Is your hair alright now?"

"Aye, you done very good with it. I still got beautiful hair, haven't I?"

"Yes, Senior."

Cromarty took her hair from behind her back and fingered it in front of her. It was white as a bloodless face in the candlelight.

"Beautiful." She almost whispered it. "I was beautiful too. Your grandfather he still thinks I am."

As soon as she talked about her old husband like that, as though he were still living, Sharn knew she was fast going into one of her dark confusions. The girl left the bed and crossed to the one oak bench where she found a long stone jar of nettle wine which she brought back with her, leaving it standing on the floorboards beside the bed head. She went away, leaving the brush and comb and the candle. She lifted the trapdoor.

"You're a good lass, Sharn."

She glanced across. Cromarty had a smile but through the fault of her face it looked malicious. Sharn smiled back but she was disturbed to see her grandmother like this. It made her question whether it was really so good to grow old, seeing a mind wander so easily. It seemed a hard price for a few added privileges. The old woman already had the stone wine jar in her hands. Sharn went down.

Behind her, Cromarty coughed and her body shook as she coughed. She'd wanted to cough before, but while Sharn was in the room she didn't. She didn't want her grandchildren to know how ill she was. Sharn closed the trapdoor.

Jeo and two of his brothers were sitting at the table, shadowy in the red brazier light. Jeo had barely started on his soup when his sister seized his hair and plucked him from the bench. She thrust an iron bucket in his hand.

"Fish," she ordered. "Don't come back till it's full."

Jeo looked unhappily at the bucket. He indicated one of his brothers with a nod of his head. "That's his job, not mine—"

Sharn hit him on the side of the face, stingingly with the flat of her hand. There was no need for her to say anything. Jeo went out of the room and didn't rub his face till he was in the passageway. His brothers chuckled and began to fight for his soup and bread. Their sister wasn't hungry so she left them to it.

Sunset outside, big and red, a dramatic skyscape in the west. The light was crimson on the sweated limbs of peasants leaving the eastern fields, pink on the faces of guardsmen on the upper slopes, their chain mail and the leashes of their dogs glazing like red lead. It was the light of a winter sunset, so it would flare only briefly, then die fast. Until it faded it would be bright as an ember before everything returned to black, cold as soot.

The evening itself wasn't very cold. The winter was mild. Jeo ran across the top slope of the southern hill with no shoes on his feet.

As he ran he was seen from the shadow of a shrine in a drystone wall by a young guardsman in a cloak who watched him with no kind of expression on his tight freckled face. There was a stem of grass in his teeth and he worked it with his tongue.

Kyrie was alone this time. There was no girl with him. And he was watching Jeo in particular, not just keeping his eyes open in general. He often kept a few hours' vigil outside the boy's tenement—and sometimes, as now, he saw him leave the wooden block on some errand or other. He did no more than that, just watched, but he listened to things about Jeo, and learned, and bided his time.

He now knew something of the boy's hardships. His lack of friends, the constant surveillance and interference from guardsmen, the need to keep silent and appear respectful, despite what seemed to be a hidden hatred of all things old. He knew about the longer working hours and the beatings under the hard rule of his sister and grandmother. Family pressures. Kyrie had no family.

Knowing all this about Jeo, he had an idea something was going to happen. He was sure Jeo couldn't cope with the strain very much longer.

Kyrie had no thoughts of adding to the strain himself. He would watch and wait. He'd learned it was the best way to track any quarry. On some of his long walks beyond the hills, towards the cold heights of the east, he'd seen a number of small wolf packs, far from the threat of man. He'd studied them from a distance as they went about their various migrations, and he'd watched them kill. He saw that the way of the wolves was to catch as much prey as they could with as little loss of blood and stamina as necessary. They never chased the leader of a herd. Not for them the tiring sprint across the wastes in pursuit of fast able game. They just followed, and waited till the weaker members of a herd or flock fell behind or collapsed to die in the deep snows—then killed and ate at their leisure. This was the way Kyrie had learned to hunt. Now, as he watched Jeo hurry along the ridge of the hill, he didn't give chase. The boy might see him, and be wary of him from then on. He stayed where he was. He doubted whether Jeo was going anywhere interesting with his bucket. He didn't seem about to do anything drastic. There was time yet for that—and if he ever did erupt under the tensions, Kyrie would be the first to know, and to profit. He knew ways of using the boy.

He drew his cloak tighter, spat the nick of grass from his mouth, and went away from the stone shrine, down to the valley floor, to cross the river and see if he might catch a look at the mute shepherd girl bringing her sheep to their fold on the low slope.

The Sea

JEO WALKED ALONG THE CREST of the slope, along the top of the valley. All the great forests were down to his right. On this side of the glen they were just dark masses below him, but across the river they had shapes in the low red light, pressed together like huge clumps of black broccoli. Their branches didn't move.

He was hungry. He'd had no supper. Perhaps he could eat some fish when he reached the sea. He didn't know how to get any fish. No one had told him and he hadn't wanted to ask. He couldn't catch any. He was ignorant enough to think the fish might be lying about on the rocks, ready for him to pick up. He knew there were fishermen who lived by the sea. He supposed he'd have to ask them.

Far away, the curfew bell clanged in the castle behind him. He turned to look, to see if the stronghold was visible from that long distance. It was. It was small but he could see all of it. So perhaps the castle could see all of him.

The thought made him weary. He was tired of being watched. Tired too of working all day and half the night, sick of the beatings and the gratuitous passing blows. He was finding it increasingly hard to hide what he really felt. The punishments were intended to bring him to heel—but his hatred was growing. He thought more and more of things like the giant stag he'd killed, of his knife, the heather-haired girl and what might lie beyond the moors. He wanted to break out in some way. He wanted it intensely. But he didn't know how to do it, so he did nothing at all. He went to the sea with his bucket.

Up in the air and on the rocks all over the coast and just above the surface of the water far out to sea, gangs of seagulls hunted, their high skirling cries slashing across the yells of all other birds.

From a high, flat vantage point, Jeo stood and was absorbed. He'd never been to the sea before and he found it overwhelming in its sights and sounds and strong smells. He looked out across the ocean, along its dark back to where it met the vast sky at its distant horizon. How far away? He had no way of telling. He tried to imagine what might lie beyond it all, where the sea had to stop.

The birds were the only living things he could see. The place was thrillingly empty. He found a way down from the clifftop, a trodden path, and jumped onto the first flat ledge below. The wet bare rock was very cold underfoot but he didn't care. He picked his way down from ledge to ledge until he was at the water's rim, standing in a rock puddle with the very last stretch of the cold tide dribbling over his ankles, the sea reaching for him with its fingertips. He would have gone on, further into the water, but the sudden acres of black mussels pestered his feet so he stopped where he was.

The wind was full of salt and strange high smells and he filled himself with it. There was seaweed on his feet. This was an astounding part of the world. He couldn't understand why his brother was reluctant to come here. A boy could lose himself in a place like this.

He didn't feel hungry any more. He didn't feel anything he could explain. The dark coast didn't make him sad or wistful or lonely or in any way joyful. It was just the moody feeling of being at the sea.

He looked in the bucket. He didn't know where to go to fill it. He stopped staring out over the barraging sea and looked instead for a sign of any stray fish. He looked back—a small stone landed on the rock beside him before jumping ahead into the water. He turned quickly. Another stone, thrown just as hard, hit his arm and he gave a cry, as much in surprise as anything.

Above him, on the top of the cliff behind, was the single figure of a man. What was left of the sun's reddish light came in over the sea and was on the man's face and front and showed an ordinary peasant's tunic, shoes with thongs crossed over the shins. The face was sparsely bearded and would have been quite red even in another light. Even though he was far away, Jeo saw it was a boy, not a man, the big fat boy Ouse. Another stone struck the rocks nearby. Another hit his bucket and it rang in his hand.

He was forced to step back to move out of range, out quickly onto the spread of mussels that jagged against the soles of his feet. He flinched and stepped even further back, edging to the right to move off the sharp shells.

The boy saw him and stopped throwing stones. He went down the rocks—and Jeo bolted, dashing further to the right, leaping off the mussel bed onto smooth rock, from there onto the beach itself. He ran fast over the hard wet sand, hurling loose black boulders and patches of cloying seaweed.

He was very quick and he was afraid and he would have run far away from the fat boy if it hadn't been for the bucket. It weighed him down. He couldn't drop it and leave it behind. His sister would flog him senseless if he returned without it. He might even have escaped, bucket and all, if the sand cove hadn't been surrounded on all three sides by cliff walls. He ran towards them, away from the water's edge, climbed them—but with the unwieldy pail he couldn't climb very fast. And the chasing youth, though overweight, wasn't as slow as Jeo had hoped. Yet another stone hit him on the back of the knee and he jumped around to face his pursuer, the bucket held in front of him like a breastplate.

Ouse was below him on the sand, no more than twenty paces away, only ten feet below. He had a big stone in each hand, having taken them not from the beach but from the pouch at his waist. He'd obviously come prepared. His back was now to the setting sun so Jeo couldn't see anything of his face. He was a junior guardsman now.

"We're all alone here, little piss," he said, his voice shuddering slightly, with exertion and a kind of excitement. "That dumb girl isn't here to look after you now. You can't hide behind nobody's skirts this time. I can throw all the stones I want, this time."

When he threw his next piece of flint, he missed. The second too went wildly astray. But he was too close to go on missing for long. A flat pebble hit Jeo on the shin, cutting the skin, and he couldn't restrain a shout of pain. He couldn't help lowering the shielding pail, and another stone cracked into his chest, hurting through his tunic. He clung to the bucket as he'd clung to the clutch of nettles, months before—but this time he was trapped. The pain of the stones was the same, no worse, but in the nettlefield he'd had the chance to run away. Here there were high cliffs all around him. He bent to crouch behind the bucket and heard the fat boy laugh.

"You can't hide behind that thing, little piss. You're not *that* small. Makes no difference—I'll knock holes in it. I'll get you anyway."

Jeo hadn't dropped into the crouch just to avoid being hit. When he jumped back to his full height he left the pail on the ledge. He'd seen stones near his feet, and now he threw them down one by one as missiles of his own. Ouse was struck on the face and put up his hands to cover his head. Jeo heard him curse. He aimed at the rest of the fat body and didn't miss. He'd often hit small crows at that range.

The big boy stepped back some paces. Then, as Jeo bent to pick more stones, he gave a loud shout and ran up the rocks, hands still in front of his face. Jeo threw a last small handful of shingle then snatched up the bucket and darted off across the jawline of the cliff. He turned immediately downhill and Ouse chased him out over the sand along the waterline.

The light, dropping fast below the horizon, was bad now, a grey red, the outline of the two figures not so sharp. From the clifftop they would have been hard to see. There was no one there to watch them. In all that outspread rocky place there were only two boys running, just the birds to see them locked in the circling rocks and the tide.

A gang of gulls, standing around in the shallows, took to the air as Jeo ran towards them, their squeals and the huff of their wings soon lost in the wind. Jeo wasn't aware of them at all. His mind was fixed on the far end of the bay, where the structure of the rocks would act as a set of stepping stones to the top of the cliff.

He was grunting for breath now, but his legs were still strong and he was confident of outrunning the fat boy. He was close to the rock steps, running over stones in the sand, when the bucket (which had been a hindrance all along) betrayed him completely. He was struggling to hold it up clear of the rocks as he jumped over them—and as he let it hang, the base hit a boulder and the bucket was knocked from his grip. Worse, it fell behind him and rolled back along the beach—and Jeo, with an empty feeling in his belly, stopped and turned round. He had to. He couldn't leave the thing behind. It was more than his skin was worth. He turned though he expected to get the beating of his life, because of a bucket.

He'd made Ouse even angrier now, and it showed on his piggish face as he stood with his foot on the pail, staring at the small boy in front of him. Jeo saw that the bucket had rolled into the water and was almost submerged. Its mouth gaped at him. Even in the poor light he could see signs of sweat on the other's face.

"Come here, you little piss." A pause for breath. "Come and get your bucket. I'm not bringing it to you."

There was nothing else Jeo could do. He walked the few steps over the sand, and it seemed the longest walk of his life. He noticed silly irrelevant things like the sea spluttering over his feet, the sound of distant surf hissing up from a rock. He stood close to the fat boy and smelled his body.

Ouse didn't hit him. He quietly took the younger boy's neck in both hands and pressed slowly with his fingers, mostly his thumbs. He had big meat hands. They seemed to wrap all of Jeo's neck.

His mouth opened at once and he couldn't breathe. His face went hot and his lips seemed to puff with blood. He clutched at the big boy's hands with his own little fingers. Soon he was ready to pass out, his eyes were pouting—Ouse slacked his grip and simply held him, still by the neck, as Jeo stood unsteadily in the shadows. The lardy face came close to his own.

"Call me Senior."

"Senior." Jeo said it at once. Ouse shook his head.

"You said it too fast. I don't think you meant it. Say it again."

"Senior—"

The thumbs pushed into his throat again, harder if anything, staunching his breath which came as a croak. His head began to pound and he couldn't feel his legs. The grip laxed again.

"Let me hear it again."

"Senior." It was a groan.

"No," said the placid voice. The face was just a black patch. "You're only saying it because you're afraid. Say it because you mean it."

His fingers were tight on Jeo's neck and the boy couldn't say anything at all. He shook his head.

"Say it, little piss."

Still he couldn't. Ouse dragged him sideways, further out into the sea. When the waves were chest-high to Jeo, he loosed his hold.

"Now," he said firmly. "Say it again—and say it with feeling, not because you know I want to hear it."

Jeo took a big breath. "Senior," he said, and tensed himself for the next crush on his windpipe. It didn't happen.

"Not bad," said Ouse, mock-reflectively. "I think we're getting somewhere. Try it one more time."

"Senior."

"Again."

"Senior—"

The hands, hard once more on his neck, pressed downwards this time, and Jeo had no strength to resist as he was forced under the water.

Again his hands went reflexively to the other boy's wrists, but they did no good there. His eyes were wide open but everything was rushing dark. His nose and mouth were full of water. He could taste the salt in it. Thoughts, out of place here, came to mind. Memories. He was suddenly light-headed. The fat boy held him under so long he was about to take water in his lungs, but the stranglehold was too tight to let anything in. The hands pulled him up and held him upright, same as before.

"I didn't hear you last time. Must be the wind in my ears. Sorry."

Jeo was choking and couldn't speak. Ouse gave him time to recover.

"Senior," he gasped.

"And again."

"Senior—" a cough of water—"Senior."

By now, Jeo didn't know why he was saying the word. He felt too weak and sick to be afraid any more. He could hardly hear himself talk. The bigger boy's voice seemed padded and far away.

"Again, little piss."

"Senior."

"Not quite. We'll try again in a minute."

He pushed Jeo down a second time. Now, amid all the distress and the sound of roaring water, something in Jeo's mind told him to use his knife.

It was in his pouch at his hip as always. He still had enough strength to fumble for it and jut the blade in the round belly close to his face. It wouldn't be difficult. But he let the thought pass. He wasn't so desperate yet. The older boy surely wouldn't kill him—the laws were on his side, for once—and he was afraid of what would happen afterwards, if the fat corpse was found. He couldn't hold his breath any more and he let water into his body.

A darkness filled his head, a bizarre sense of peace. Ouse heaved him up and he spluttered violently for breath.

"Let's start at the beginning, shall we?" The same thing all over again. The same cycle. The inflicted pain followed by the victim saying the same word followed by more pain. Repetitions of the expert torturer.

"You'll get it right in the end. Say it again."

Jeo thought he'd vomit soon. "Senior," he said yet again. Ouse held him up, on the points of his feet, their faces very close.

"You ought to be in the castle and not let out." The tone was harsher. "If I had my way, you'd be in a Shrieking Pit tomorrow. There's something very wrong with you."

Jeo looked weakly at him. They had turned in the water, so now the other boy was facing out to sea. The last dreg of sunset light was in his face and Jeo could see his expression, the heavy frown. He saw something else too. A slice of blood on the cheekbone, the skin already swollen around it, a black gash in the purpling light. One of Jeo's stones had crushed the flesh, and his eyes grinned when he saw it. He remembered how he'd killed the stag, such a very long time ago. He felt the same defiant pride now.

Ouse pushed him under again, without a word. Sea foam splashed around his elbows. He saw bubbles on the surface but still he held the boy down. When he finally lifted him out, the legs had sagged and the head was lolling, its long black hair flattened all over the face. He had to use much of his strength to heft the body out. Jeo couldn't help. He'd fainted.

Ouse dragged him backwards out of the water and dropped him on the wet sand halfway up the shore. For a moment he stood over him, breathing hard. Skinny little boy, but quick and defiant and oddly brave. He was lying there senseless but he was still untamed. Ouse kicked him awake.

He let him lie there on his back as he bent and looked down at him. "That's just for a start," he said. "Next time I'll hurt you. Better change your way of thinking, little piss."

And that was enough. He stepped over the boy and marched

back up the beach towards the black rocks. He passed the iron bucket and kicked a dent in it with his boot.

Jeo rolled over and lay on his belly as he looked across the sand. "I'll get you, Ouse," he shouted, then heaved for breath. "I'll kill you when I'm older."

The fat boy turned. "No, you won't," he called back. "You'll never get the chance. I'll always be older than you, so you can't touch me. I'll always be your elder. That's the way it is."

He was lost in the shadows of the cliff. Jeo put his head back on the sand and wept as the tension began to leave his body, leaving him shaking. He wept with anger and cried himself into a helpless sleep as the tide began to cruise in behind him, slicking over lone rocks and washing away the fat boy's bootprints in the sand. Night fell like a black blind and there was no more mauve light.

It was the cold that woke him. The night air chilled the seawater that came over his legs and lower body and shivered him awake.

His legs were weak when he stood and he had to walk a few steps to sit on a rock to rest them. He was a hardy boy, but this was rare cold and he shivered in it. His toes were close to freezing.

His breathing, however, was almost back to normal. There was no more spluttering. He left the rock and moved unsteadily over the sand to where the bucket lay on its side in a splay of sea couch. He picked it up and the metal was ice-cold to his touch. In the vague light of moon and stars, he saw the dent in it and scowled. It was still empty. There were no fish. He didn't know what to do.

He couldn't stay standing where he was, so he carried the pail back up the beach. When he looked at the cliffs to find a way up, he saw the outline of a man watching him from a low ledge close to the shore.

He stood still. He thought Ouse had come back. The black

figure was standing hands on hips. Neither of them did anything.

"Don't stay there, boy. You'll freeze to death. Come to me."

A clear voice, strong—as if accustomed to making itself heard above the noise of breaking waves. Not a young man's voice.

Jeo did what he was told. He climbed the low rocks and reached the ledge. His last long step was difficult—he slithered on the slippery rock and might have fallen back, but the man caught his arm in two firm hands and pulled him upright. They stood close together for a moment. It was a narrow ledge.

"What's the bucket for? Building sandcastles, were you?"

There was humour in the tone, but none of the ridicule Jeo was used to. He tried to answer but his teeth were knocking and his lips too cold to form the words.

"Fish," he said at last.

"I see," said the man. "Come with me, then. I'll give you fish. And a fire too. You could use some warming, by the looks of you."

He turned and Jeo followed him—and as he turned, the boy had a glimpse of white or grey hair and a beard on the face he couldn't really see.

The rocks were all very cold to his feet, colder than the sand, but he was cheered by the promise of a fire. He stayed close behind the man, who walked in a crouch, long arms swinging like an ape.

He led Jeo to a point near the top of the cliff onto another much wider ledge where the rocks were dry.

Here, the walls of even the tough basalt cliff had been cracked in places by the relentless attack of the sea, forming a great many wide clefts in the rock. Most of these were horizontal, following the formation of the basalt itself. But where the pounding had been very severe, they were vertical and high. They came to one of these scissures and Jeo followed the crouching man inside.

He guessed at once that the gap had not been formed entirely by the sea. For one thing, it was far wider than any of the others he'd seen—and rather neatly cut. The marks left by iron implements were still on the stonework. And it was high above the waterline, so the sea couldn't have caused such a broad gap. Only a freak storm could reach it.

They crept in along a very short, narrow passageway, basalt black and straight—and immediately the smells were different. Outside, the wind had been high with the tang of crustaceans and seaweeds. Here the smell of gutted fish and smoke and damp textile. Already they were out of the cold and the stone floor was warmer under Jeo's feet. At the end of the passage, a curtain of nets hung from the ceiling to the rock floor. They pushed it aside.

The cave behind was small and square. A driftwood fire gave it light and a thick heat. Some way above the fire, half-hidden by smoke, clutches of herring and sand eels hung from poles attached to iron hooks in the top of the wall. The smoke went out through a gap in the low ceiling.

The fire was alone in a small space near one of the corners. The rest of the cave was cluttered with big sacks and clay jars and gourds, lobster pots and tin buckets and fishing sticks. Nets hung like arras screens on the black walls, root vegetables in string bags from the ceiling.

Jeo saw all this very quickly. What he noticed most of all was the man in front of him. At first all he saw was the bent back, then the man went to a heap of thin furs close to the fire and sat there crosslegged, facing Jeo but not looking at him. He took up a hammock and carried on where he'd left off, stitching it with a length of oiled twine.

Jeo stood and watched as the other went about his task as if oblivious to him. The man's head was bent over his work and his face was hidden. But the fire's light, jumping around the room, showed the rest of him clearly. Jeo saw there were no sleeves on his sealskin shirt. His arms, like his bony legs, were bare. A sacking loincloth and thin leather sandals were his only other clothes, though the rest of his body was hung with decorations. A thick wide strap of seaweed served as a belt round his middle, seaweed thongs at both wrists and around each ankle. Even his hair looked something like seaweed. Down on his chest, a necklace of shells —at the centre, on his breastbone, a queen scallop, blood-crimson as the sunset sky, was flanked by needle shells and tortoiseshells and dog whelks sheening in the firelight. With his long spindly arms and legs and his rags, he looked like some strange breed of spider monkey that lives only by the sea, the fingers and toes curled, the thumb thick and prominent. He started humming to himself, but stopped when he looked up at Jeo.

"You're going to stand there all night, are you?" he said. "It's warmer by the fire. Wrap yourself in a fur if you want it." And he went back to his stitching, lowering his head again.

In that short glance, Jeo had seen all the man's face. It was round and flat, with a crushed nose, and it was very old. The eyebrows were pure white, as was the beard that circled the face from temple to temple, round under the thin chin like a layer of dried sea salt. His hair, when his face was turned up, fell to his shoulders, wild and ragged and grey and white. Now, as he bent over his needle, some of it hung over his face. His skin was weathered and dark.

Jeo stayed stupidly where he was. The old man raised his head again, eyebrows up. He looked the boy over, then tossed the hammock away somewhere beside him, put his hands on his thighs and a deliberate smile on his mouth.

"Sit, will you? I don't bite young boys."

The smile and the tone of his voice. Jeo was more than surprised. An elder was being kind to him. He wondered why. He didn't take up the offer of a fur as a cloak but he sat, crosslegged too, in front of the fire and held out his hands to it. The sudden warmth on his palms made his spine flinch. The old man scratched himself.

"Name?" he wanted to know. "You've got one, I suppose?"

"Jeo." His teeth had stopped chattering.

"Jeo," said the elder. "I've heard about you. Not much, but some. They say maybe you're not to be trusted." He looked emptily at the fire. "Do you know who I am?"

Jeo just looked at him.

"They call me Sligo. They call me worse things than that, sometimes. They say I'm also not to be trusted."

"They say you're mad," said Jeo. The old man looked sharply at him, but he wasn't angry. There was another smile, almost a grin.

"Well now, you're a bold young boy, speaking your mind to an elder. But tell me—who says I'm mad?"

"The elders. The guardsmen." Jeo shrugged. "Everybody."

The old man stared at him. "They would say that, I suppose. They could hardly tell anyone the truth." He toyed with his shell necklace.

Jeo put his feet closer to the fire. "What is the truth?" he asked. Sligo was still looking at him, but didn't answer for a moment. He appeared to be still thinking. He gave a quick breath.

"First things first," he said. "You're hungry, I expect. Don't get much to eat at the best of times, from the look of you. If I give you food, you'll eat it, no doubt."

"Yes," said Jeo. No doubt.

The man left the fireside and went to a corner of the cave. Jeo watched. The stone walls were like bronze in the firelight.

"How did you get that blood on your leg?" asked Sligo.

Jeo looked down. One of the fat boy's stones had cut his shin. Sand had caulked the wound. He flicked the sand away. The flesh was sore but there was no bleeding. The old man came back to the fire with a small brown pot which he simply pressed into the embers.

"It's already cooked," he said. "I'll just heat it some more. It won't take long." He gave Jeo a bowl and sat down opposite him, crosslegged as before, same place.

"Well? The blood on your leg?"

"I cut it on a rock," said the boy.

"Did you now? And what were you doing lying in the sand where I found you? Having a snooze, were you? Been out for a midnight swim?"

Jeo didn't look at him. "I fell off the rock where I cut myself. Knocked myself out."

Sligo stirred the contents of the pot with a wood spoon. "Do I look like an idiot, master Jeo?" The boy lifted his head. "I know you haven't known me more than a few minutes, but in that time have you decided I'm soft in the head?"

"No—"

"No. You know better than that. Then you should also know better than to tell me you fell off a damned rock. The only rocks by the sea are smaller than you are, not much of a fall—not enough to knock you out. If you must lie to me, boy, lie well. I'm sure you know how."

Jeo took his admonishment with a nod of the head. He was beginning to like the old man.

"So," said Sligo, after a peer in the pot. "Someone's been knocking you about. I didn't see who it was. I only saw you when you were getting up. Guardsman, was it?"

Jeo hesitated. He was wary of everyone and trusted nothing he heard. And yet, though with his family he was incommunicative as an autist, he felt he could tell this man things.

"Sort of guardsman," he said. "Not much older than me."

"Name?"

"Ouse."

"Never heard of him. Why did he harm you?"

"He doesn't trust me. Says I don't believe in the elders. I think Kyrie sent him."

Sligo didn't know who Kyrie was either, but he wasn't thinking about that. He looked at the skinny boy across the fire, saw him push his sodden hair back off his face. A boy who didn't believe in the elders. If that was true, he was a rare thing.

"Is that right?" he asked. "You don't believe—you don't like the glen to be ruled by its old people?"

A small frown from Jeo. Surely the old man didn't expect him to answer that? He couldn't say yes it was true he hated the elders. The man was an elder himself. He sensed danger here.

"I haven.'t done anything wrong," he said again.

"I understand," said Sligo. "You're afraid to tell me. I don't blame you. I'm old, after all—and you see the old as your enemies, don't you?"

He couldn't expect Jeo to answer that either. He stirred the pot. It was making liquid noises now. The boy could smell something—fish but not quite fish—and he felt his hunger again.

"Maybe you won't be afraid if I tell you something first— if I tell you why I have to live here by the sea instead of in the glen. That's what you wanted to know. The truth." He put his hands on his knees like an old storyteller in the valley and wetted his lips with his tongue. He thought of spitting in the fire but didn't.

"I'm not mad, boy, whatever you've heard. I'm not like other people maybe, but my mind's all there. I've been sent here because I think the wrong things. I think like you do, that the glen shouldn't be ruled by elders and guardsmen alone. It's not right. I'm not the first to think that, but I was one of the few to say it openly."

"They beat anyone who talks like that," said Jeo.

"Only the young. I was already an elder when I spoke out, so they couldn't touch me."

Jeo moved back from the fire. His face and feet were hot. "Why didn't you speak out before, when you were younger? Were you afraid?"

"I would have been, no doubt. As afraid as you or the next man. But I didn't even think like that when I was young. I was no different from anyone else. I changed my way of thinking late in life. Now I'm more of a troublemaker than you are." He didn't resist a quick wink.

"But why?" asked Jeo as the old man looked again in the simmering pot. "Why did you suddenly think like that, the way I do? You were an elder. Things were good for you."

"Good?"

"Better than being young. You can do what you like when you're old."

"Aye, mostly—and some of the other elders are glad they're not young any more. But the way I think it, growing old is a disease. A long wasting illness. Maybe other elders would tell you the same, if you were allowed to speak so personal to them. Old age eats you, boy. It blinds and deafens, and rots your limbs and your brain. And there's nothing to be done against it. As you say, being old means doing what you like—that makes it bearable. But there were things I was thinking, so I had to say them. Since then, I *can't* do what I like—so I feel nothing but the disease. Be glad you're young, Jeo. In spite of all the hardships, be glad of it."

Jeo shrugged. "I am," he said. "But at least being old means you know more."

"Does it?"

"Doesn't it?"

The fisherman was smiling again. He lifted the pot from the embers. "Remember when you were a small boy? When you were ten years or less? Everyone who was just a few years older, they all seemed to know everything, didn't they? Everything worth knowing."

Jeo nodded.

"Aye. And now *you're* those few years older, you find you don't know so much after all. Now anyone of, say, twenty years seems to know more. Am I right?"

"Yes."

"Well, so it goes on, lad. You reach twenty, then thirty years —and still your elders seem to be your betters. You know the truth? When you reach my sort of age, when there's not too many older, it strikes you that since *you* don't know everything, nobody does. Nobody can. I know a little more than you do, Jeo—but very little."

He reached to take Jeo's bowl, filled it from the pot, put a spoon in it, passed it back to the boy, who began to eat at once. The fisherman watched him.

"Good, is it? There's more here when you're finished."

"Very good," said Jeo, mouth full. "What is it?"

"Crab soup," said Sligo. "There's other things in it. Onions, few mussels, bits of lobster and crossfish. Mostly crab."

"Very good." The taste was unusual but he liked it. And the soup was thick and full and hot and there was more in the pot. He ate quickly, as if afraid it would all vanish in the smoky air. He'd never eaten so well.

He stared into the bowl and listened as the old man went on talking, as much to himself as to his guest, as if glad to talk at all, the flamelight tinting his grave colobus face as he looked in the fire.

"They talk about the good old days, don't they? Well, they were good *young* days, when the body was lithe and quick and the fires were hot inside it. *That* was the time to do what you liked, to have power—when the mind and body were strong enough to make use of it, young enough to have time to savour it."

He stopped and wiped hair from his face. It clung to his cheeks like wrack.

"I know a little more now than when I was young. I understand a few things. In that way, it's better to be older, maybe. But I wish I was a young man again. Friends of your own age, they die as you get old. So do your loved ones. You get ill—and only the old get ill in the glen, so you get edged out of everyday life, put in a cottage or the castle—and the guardsmen rule in your name. Like I said, I began to understand that, and I began to speak out about it. And that made me very dangerous, it seems. So the guardsmen and my dear fellow elders sent me here, to this forsaken place. To hunt turtles and spurdog for the glen. Place where the dampness curls my bones. I'm not as young as I was, Jeo. I can't move as well as I did. My fault for living so long. Time's short now—but then you know that, you in your hurry to be something more than a ploughboy."

Jeo didn't want to talk about himself. "Do you have to do all the work here?" he asked.

"No, not all. There's other fishers along this stretch of coast.

And most families from the glen come here once in a time. They all have piscary rights to free fish."

"My brother comes here some weeks."

"He's probably one of those who take my fish from my nets, never catches any himself. That's his right too. I catch for all the glen."

"Not on your own."

"No. I have helpers, time to time."

"Hake helps you."

"You know about him? Aye, he helps. He's good, too. Very strong. Strong body because his mind's weak."

"They say you're both mad, that's why you work together."

A grin from the fisherman, like some old ocean devil in the firelight. He rubbed his feet with his fingers. "Neither of us is mad, Jeo. I'm an odd-man-out and he's a bit simple. But not insane, either of us. The rest of the glen is insane."

"Why is he called Hake? That's a fish."

"Yes, a fish. He's been simple all his life, so nobody wanted him. So nobody gave him a name. I called him Hake. A hake is a very simple fish."

"Where is he now?"

"I won't let him stay here every night. He's not the best of company and I need to be alone most times. He sleeps rough in the glen, wherever he does his odd jobs."

"He said you're alright."

"Told you that, did he? Well, no one but me is kind to him. He does me some good too. Hauls in the fish, takes the weight off my hands. It's hard work all the same."

"If it's so bad, why don't you go away?"

"I've told you, lad—I'm forced to stay here. Where can I go away?"

Jeo held out his bowl for Sligo to refill it. He spoke between mouthfuls. "Isn't there somewhere beyond the sea?"

The old man picked his beard with both hands. "The sea? It's

as wide as the sky, young master—as far as the rainbow. How
should I know what lies at the end of it? I know this bit of water
like my own piss. But beyond that? Nothing, I should say. Nothing at all."

"Another place?"

"I doubt it."

Jeo looked at the fire, at the sticks and small planks in it.
"Where does that firewood come from? There must be somewhere
else out there. Boats from another place—"

"No no." The old man shook his head. "That wood's not
from the sea coming in. It's brought by the river going out.
Driftwood from the glen, Jeo. From the housing blocks and the
forests. Not from another place at all."

Jeo put the empty bowl down.

"More? There's plenty."

"No. I can't eat any more." He added thanks.

"You ask a lot of questions," said Sligo.

"Nobody answered them before."

"I'm not surprised. Keep asking them anyway. Why do you
ask about other places?"

"There must be somewhere better than here."

Sligo prodded the embers with a flat of wood. "You know
nothing if you think like that," he said. "The glen is a garden. It
has everything. The most beautiful things grow there. Tear away
those vile wooden blocks and you have an orchard to live in."

"I thought you hated the place. Especially after what they've
done to you."

"Hate it, lad? No, not hate it, love it. It's a garden, I tell you.
What's bad is the way the people in it have to live. The rule of
the guardsmen is bad. The castle with its hidden tunnels and torture
holes, the elders. But the glen itself is nothing but good. It could
be."

Jeo had never thought of the glen as a good place to live. He
stared at the embers, which were less bright now. The old man
raked them with his piece of wood, then reached behind him for

lengths of kindling, sprinkled them on the fire. He blew on the wood and new flames rose to eat the kindling and lighten the cave. Jeo was warm all over by now. His tunic was dry. Only his hair was damp.

"All these questions," said Sligo. "Maybe it's time you answered some of mine."

"Why have you told me all these things?" asked the boy.

"Another question," smiled the fisherman. "You only want to ask, not answer, don't you? Afraid of giving yourself away, I suppose. Alright, I'll answer this one too. I've told you because you've shown interest, that's why. No one else, old or young, has ever done that. And because you do, I think you question the way things are, the way the glen is ruled. You don't have to say you hate the elders, Jeo. I think you've let me know already."

"Yes, I suppose I have."

"But I wonder—do you really hate them, or are you perhaps here because the guardsmen sent you?"

Jeo's face was full of surprise. "It was a guardsman who nearly drowned me," he protested.

"So you say." There was a calm hard look to the old man's eyes. "But I saw no guardsman. I saw no one but you lying there on the edge of the sea."

"He was there."

"Maybe I don't believe you. Maybe you're another of the guardsmen's little spies. They don't all wear chain mail and swords."

"I don't spy for the guardsmen," said Jeo. "I hate them." He realised he'd said too much and he fell quiet, but he was glad to say what he felt. It had been in him so long, with no outlet. He hadn't spoken to Rhosarran for months. He felt he had to talk to the old man, whatever the cost.

Sligo looked hard at his face, then his own expression softened. "Aye, lad, I know. If I didn't, you'd have learned nothing from me. If I was truly suspicious I'd have thrown you out without a bowl of soup. You're a very different kind of boy, Jeo." Pause.

"Maybe you should trust me. Do you really think I've lived six years in this stinking place for the slight chance of catching out little rebels like you?"

"No," said Jeo. It didn't seem likely.

The fisherman looked around for his pipe but couldn't remember where he'd left it. "So you hate the guardsmen as much as the elders?"

"Yes."

"Well, hate them if you must. I have no liking for them myself, or for any of my own age. They're too old. But I can't hate, lad. Hate destroys but it changes nothing."

"I think I hate enough to change everything, if I could."

The old man frowned. "That much?" he said. "I didn't know. You shouldn't hate that much. If you want to change things, change them because you love the glen, not because you hate those who govern in it."

"I can't love it."

"Have you tried?"

Jeo looked away, at nothing across the cave. The shadows were long on the low walls. He didn't answer.

"You've had hard times," Sligo went on. "Harder than most, from the little I know. And it's made you angry. That can be a good thing. But be angry because something you love is spoiled, not because you hate those who spoil it."

He was repeating himself. A scowl made Jeo's face ugly.

"What difference does it make?" he said. "It doesn't matter if I hate and you love. We can't change anything."

Sligo took a long breath and blew it out slowly. "The two of us, no," he agreed. "We're both being watched too closely— I by guardsmen who look down while I fish, you by everyone else. But if there were more of us, boy—what then?" He saw the wild hope in Jeo's face and shook his head at it. "No, lad—not what you think. You want to fight, don't you? You're that kind, I think. But it's not my way. As you get older, you're less willing to fight. You let things happen. All the elders are like that."

"Not just the elders," said Jeo. "Everyone's like that."

"Yes," said Sligo. "And I think they're right. Fighting's not the right way."

"What else is there?"

"For me, not much. I have to stay here. But you can go back to the glen and do something."

"Me? What can I do? I'm on my own."

"For now, yes. But you can talk to others, tell them what you think, how things might be different."

"It wouldn't change anything. There's many others my age, they all think the same. They all talk about how wrong everything is. But it's only talk. None of them wants to do anything."

"Talk to them." The voice was almost stern and Jeo stared at him. "If you say what you feel, you can start a way of thinking. That's how things change. Talk to the younger guardsmen, to anyone just above you in age."

Jeo thought of Kyrie and Ouse. How could he say anything to the guardsmen? He was their victim. "If we talk like that to anyone older, they'll beat us."

"Are you afraid?"

"Yes. It hurts."

"Better to have the pain than the fear of it. And if they beat you, let them. They can't beat you for ever, not all of you. In time, they'll see it doesn't work, and things will change. Say what you think, and bear the pain it brings. You have to suffer for what you believe."

Jeo looked the old man in the eyes, which were darker now. The fire was being left to die. "You've suffered," he said pointedly. "What good has it done you?"

Sligo looked around the cave. The rock walls were sweating. It was a grim place. The nets and mounds of cloth and the fire couldn't hide the fact. He shrugged.

"Looking at all this, the way I have to live, you might say it's done me no good at all. But I've embarrassed the elders and their guardsmen. I've shaken the order of things, in my own small way. And, more important, I've been true to myself. I've said what I believe. That means something. And I've kept my thoughts. They couldn't take them from me. I can share them with you now."

It didn't sound very much. Jeo said nothing.

"I know it's too late for me," said Sligo. "I'm too old. I can't change anything. But you still have time."

"Time," said the boy moodily. "You keep saying I can make things happen *in time*. How long is that? What can I do *now*?"

"Be patient."

"Why?"

"You can't expect to change the glen in a day."

"So how long do I have to wait and talk and take the beatings? Years and years, I suppose."

"As long as it takes."

"That doesn't mean anything. That could be all my life."

"Yes."

"I'll be too old."

"Your thoughts won't be. You're not like others, Jeo. You can lead." The boy frowned. How could the old man think that? He didn't think it himself. "You can make others follow your way. Maybe the elders and guardsmen know it too. That's why they treat you harshly. But you can live with that. You can bear the pain."

"Sometimes it gets too much."

"You can bear it. Take the pain and keep talking to those of your own age. They'll know you believe in what you say and you're ready to suffer for it. People follow that kind of man. Lead them."

The fire was dark red and Jeo was colder. He didn't like what the fisherman was telling him. He didn't want to lead anybody. He wanted things for himself. To be a leader sounded too difficult.

"I'm only a small boy," he said quietly. "And I'm on my own."

Sligo reached over the fire and lifted Jeo's chin with a finger.

The boy looked at him. He'd never seen kindness in an elder's face before.

"You won't always be small," said the old man. "And, as you said, there are many who think as you do. All they need is someone to lead them, a spokesman. Keep speaking for them and go on taking the knocks. Things will change. That's my counsel—and it's all I can do to help."

Jeo had nothing to say. He nodded. Sligo smiled.

"I can do a little more," he added. "I can send you home with a pail full of fish."

"There's no hurry," said Jeo. "My sister won't care if I stay out here all night."

"I'm not concerned with what your sister thinks, boy. Guardsmen may come. If they see you with me, all your year's good behaviour will be wasted. They'll maybe put you in the castle. And they'll not be very kind to me."

"I didn't see any guardsmen when I got here. Do they watch you at night?"

"As a rule, no. But sometimes. And I never know when our friend Hake may come by."

"But he won't tell anyone—"

"He will, I'm afraid. He's good to me and if he thinks you're my friend he'll be good to you. But he's not clever and his tongue is loose. He'll tell a guardsman about us and never know he's doing it."

"I'd better go, then."

"Yes, you'd better." He uncrossed his legs and got up. Jeo followed him across the cave to the far wall, where he filled the boy's bucket with flatfish and cod.

"Can I have some more crab?"

"No," said the fisherman. "Crab is rare food, better than your family's used to. They may ask how you came by it. You can't catch any yourself, they'll know that. The only other way is for me to give it to you—and they'll question why I should do that.

We don't want them linking us together. Your father's suspicious of everything you do, no doubt."

"He's dead."

"His next in line, then."

"Yes. She hates me."

"She fears you, lad—that's what it is. The old people and the guardsmen fear you too, for what you might be thinking. They're maybe as afraid of you as you are of them. That's power for a young boy, don't you think?"

"Yes," said Jeo, but he didn't mean it. If the soldiers were really afraid of him, they could harm him. He was afraid of them and could do nothing. He had no power at all.

He picked up the pail. Sligo had overfilled it. Fishtails and staring heads flopped out over the rim. The old man and the boy looked at each other. The light wasn't good, like the lowest sunset, and only the shells of the fisherman's collar had any glint to them.

"I won't see you any more," said Jeo.

"Probably not. It's not safe. You know your way back."

"Yes. I wish I could stay here."

"That's because you know I'm free here, in my way. You can say what you think here. This place isn't what I want, boy—but it's better than what's in the glen, and I got it because I spoke out and was ready to be shunned for it. Don't let them break you, Jeo, and don't let them shut you up. Go away now. It's late."

He touched the boy's face, just for a second, with the palm of his hand, and Jeo left the cave. When he was gone, Sligo trod the fire out and wrapped himself in a wool rug by the wall. He had a lot of thinking to do and he was worried about Jeo. But he was glad to have met him. He lay awake for an hour but when he slept he slept very well.

On his way running back through the dark, Jeo thought about what the old fisherman had told him but there was too much to take in at once. He came away with the feeling that he'd been told

there was nothing, really, he could do. Wait and bear the pain—
but the glen was already ruled on those lines. He didn't want to
go on and on waiting. He didn't want any pain.

He didn't think talking would do any good, whatever Sligo
said. It was surely better to *do* something. But he was powerless.
Nothing had changed.

And yet as he ran he felt less alone. Listening to the fisherman
had been good. He'd never once called him Senior and the old man
hadn't told him to. He ran freely through the hillside grass.

He knew his sister would see the dent in the bucket and beat
him for it. But he didn't worry. It was only a bit of pain and he
could bear it.

The Pit

AN EARLY SUMMER MORNING, a common day, and the body of an elder was found in his room. He'd died in the night. There was blood on his neck. Blood on the knife by his bed. His family were surprised and wept. Guardsmen came and went away. They took young men and girls, known malcontents, and questioned them in the torture rooms of a broch. But the young people could tell them nothing. The elder had killed himself.

The short sinewy boy ambling down one of the hillsides had no fear about being seen out in the open. He was whistling and his thumbs were in his belt. It was noon and all the workers were expected to stay in the fields to eat their mid-day meal—loitering on the slopes was of course forbidden, especially for the young— but the boy wasn't concerned by things like that. Being a guards-man, however junior, brought certain privileges, and he was taking advantage of one now.

In fact he was actively encouraged to walk the hills. One day, when he was a fully fledged soldier, he would be expected to know every square yard of the glen. So now he had to spend part of every day exploring the woods and grasslands and sometimes the high-land moors.

On his way down the hill he stopped at times and stood still, to look and see where things were, or to spit a half-chewed stem of grass from his mouth before he bent to pick a fresh one.

High on the slope he came across a shrine in one of the hill walls and took the latest piece of grass from his lips before going inside.

He spent no longer than he had to in the dry little den. And he made no sign of reverence to the broken statuette. He gave it a smile, with just his mouth, moving the freckles on his cheeks, took a step forward and patted the cowled head with his fingers. He walked back out into the sun, pausing to snap up another of his habitual shoots of grass before carrying on down the hill, aimlessly, towards a small birchwood.

A quick look to the castle hills. He was quite certain that no one from that distance could see the expressions on a face. But he could never be sure who else might be watching, nearer by—so he kept his face blank. Because he couldn't be sure, he'd followed the laws and entered the shrine. For that reason too he'd taken the grass from his mouth before going in. Showing even the slightest sign of disrespect for the Elder's image was a serious thing, especially in a youngster and more so in a cadet guardsman. And Kyrie, as usual, was careful to show nothing at all.

He went on whistling as he sauntered on down towards the valley floor. He was in a good mood, having just spent a fast half-hour in the company of a fletcher's daughter, a girl with big eyes and good teeth and the longest fair hair in the valley. Older than him, too. Very nice. He skirted the birch copse and left it behind. Then a small sound in the wood made him turn and he stopped whistling while he stood and listened.

He heard it again, then a third time. The sound of tapping on wood. A single knock followed by a short silence then the next blow, like a very tired woodpecker. Rustling noises too, in grass and leaves. Kyrie moved to the edge of the copse to hear better, but even from there he couldn't imagine what was making the noises. Animals, perhaps. Or a bird of some kind. It was unlikely. They weren't the kind of sounds he expected to hear coming from a small wood. He angled his way into it.

It was a new young wood, trees little more than saplings with wide airy spaces between them—so Kyrie had to tread slowly and

carefully to avoid discovery. There was little in the way of undergrowth so he was able to move quite freely and his approach was
quiet enough. The occasional brittle leaf crackled under his boots
but the noises ahead were now loud enough to conceal any slight
sound he might have to make.

When he saw some first signs of movement between the trees
he stretched himself flat on the grass and crawled on his belly to
the side of a long green birch. Here, hidden from view by a crisp
clump of bracken, he could see what was happening in the small
glade in front of him. And he stared wide at the sight of a small,
very thin white-skinned boy throwing a twin-blade knife at the
trees around him.

Kyrie watched and did nothing and a smile crept across his
mouth. After all these months of acting like any other youth in
the glen, here was little Jeo doing an unlawful thing, in secret, with
a weapon he was forbidden to own.

But the lizard-faced boy wasn't smiling at this discovery
alone. He was genuinely astonished by the skill and unsuspected
speed with which Jeo threw the dirk. He appeared to have a dozen
different ways of hurling it—and, as far as Kyrie could tell, he
never seemed to miss.

After each throw, Jeo would stand still and look feverishly
around, listening hard, waiting to see if anyone was near. Kyrie
noted that for all his looking around Jeo didn't see the right things.
He had no woodcraft. He hadn't realised there was someone only
a few paces away.

Kyrie tried to edge back behind his tree, so that if Jeo chose
to throw his knife at it, he might not see the freckled boy when
he came to retrieve it. But it was hopeless. The tree was very thin,
the hank of ferns far too scanty. So he stayed where he was and
hoped he wouldn't be seen until he was ready. And he watched
—and smiled. He'd been waiting for an opportunity like this.

He'd always thought of Jeo as something of a young animal.
He could be beaten into obedience but not tamed. He moved like

an animal as he threw the knife—well balanced, quick on the turn, well built in a very thin way. But if he was an animal he was now Kyrie's prey. All the long hours of watching and waiting now had their reward. He was the first to find Jeo breaking rules—and, supreme opportunist that he was, he knew how to profit from the discovery.

Jeo that day was in a very bad temper. His ear was still painful where one of his brothers had punched him for lagging too far behind the plough. Earlier in the morning his sister had kicked him bodily out of bed for oversleeping. And old Cromarty had thrown her bucket of slops at him in one of her rages. His tunic had been so badly soiled that the rest of the family had sent him down to the river to wash. What with all this and being made to work harder than usual in the field, and the clinging heat, and the flies, he was feeling even more sorry for himself than usual.

So he'd snatched a few minutes of his noon mealtime to be alone in this little scrub of woodland. Now he was throwing the knife not for practice but to vent some of his suppressed anger, to do a violent thing or burst with the frustration of it all. All these months of silence and obedience, and still he was under suspicion. His sister still beat him. He'd seen the old shepherd still spying on him. He was overworked by his family and harassed by guardsmen. He still had no friends, wasn't allowed outside on the rest day, hardly ever saw Rhosarran. His hatred of the elders and soldiers was stronger than ever, and his chances of doing anything to improve his lot were no better. He was bitterly aware of it.

Now, in his resentment, he'd lost concentration and was openly throwing his knife. He flung it harder than usual, with less accuracy, wishing each tree were someone he hated.

Soon he was tired and knew it was time to stop and go back to work. He rolled the blade in his palm and drew back his arm to throw it one last time at the nearest birch. And then everything —all his distant unformed plans and his present wretched life— fell undone like a slipknot. All the endless weeks of caution and hard labour meant nothing at all as a short, freckle-faced junior guardsman stepped out from beside the tree and stood in front of him, hands on hips, grinning like a snake.

Just for a moment, in a rush of blood, Jeo thought of throwing his knife. He would never have a better chance than this, with one of the hated cadets defenceless in front of him and no one to see the act. But he didn't throw the knife. He would be caught and they would kill him. He let both hands drop by his sides and stood with his head half-bowed as he waited for the fair-haired boy to do something.

Kyrie had yet another of his stalks of grass between his teeth and he chewed hard as he stood smiling across the clearing. He was enjoying the situation. He was sure Jeo wouldn't throw his knife. He took the bit of grass from his lips and held it to his face, rolling it between forefinger and thumb as he pretended to examine it.

"Bring me the knife, Jeo." He didn't look at the boy.

Jeo walked across the grass and held out the dagger, holding it by the nibs of the blade. Kyrie took it and turned it in his hand. He was surprised by the brightness of the blade and he'd never seen one with two points. Jeo hung his head and wished the soil would open and hide him.

"You're very good with this," said Kyrie chattily. "I never guessed you could handle a knife. Looks like you've had a lot of practice. Have you?"

"Yes," said Jeo, not bothering to lie. In his despair he forgot to say Senior but the other boy overlooked it.

"Knives aren't allowed," he went on, in the same airy tone. Jeo hated all this, though he'd expected it, all this mock friendly talk. He felt like a rat in a cat's hand and wished the freckled boy would take him to one of the brochs and have done with it.

"Knives are dangerous things," Kyrie was saying. "In the wrong hands, that is. That's why they're forbidden except for elders and guardsmen. You're not a guardsman, are you, Jeo?"

Jeo didn't look up. "No," he said—and then he gasped as the other thrust the dirk into his chest. There was a sudden dull pain and he looked down at his chest. He saw that Kyrie hadn't stabbed him, merely prodded him with the bone handle. He looked up and saw the freckled face was still smiling but without malice. The knife was held out offered to him. He didn't understand.

"Take it, then. You use it better than I do."

He took it and went on looking puzzled. Next there was a silence for a time as Kyrie stood and looked carefully around the clearing, watching the trees and listening. Apart from the filtered sunlight and the natter of small birds there was little to see or hear, and nothing caught his attention. Jeo followed his gaze but he wasn't really looking. He was waiting for the soldier boy to continue, still wondering why he'd given back the knife. Kyrie looked at him.

"You know, don't you, if I tell someone about that blade of yours, things won't be good for you."

Jeo knew only too well.

"And I might just do that," said Kyrie. "I ought to." Then his thoughts seemed to take a different direction. "I said only guardsmen are allowed to have a knife. How would you like it if *you* were allowed to?"

Jeo's face didn't move. He was finding things rather hard to take in.

Kyrie took the grass from his mouth and threw it away. "I thought you'd be surprised."

Jeo shook his head in a vague sort of way. He looked down and saw the knife in his hand—and all of a sudden he loathed the thing for having put him in this position. He didn't want to be a guardsman, as Kyrie was suggesting. He hated even the thought of it.

"Why me?" he wondered.

"Because, for a start, you've got a good chance of being accepted. The captains are wary of you, but they know you've got your uses. You're quick and you're used to hard work. They know how well you throw stones at birds in the fields, so they guess you've got a good eye. You could be guardsman material. And they won't be so suspicious of you if they find you want to join them." He smiled again. "And I can tell them you don't cry or run away when someone throws stones at you."

Deep within himself Jeo scowled. He'd never forgotten the evening in the nettlefield when the stones were thrown at him. He was glad, though, that it had made Kyrie believe he had courage. He hadn't felt very brave at the time.

He brought his thoughts back to the present and wondered if there was any way of getting out of all this. A crow let out its single raucous cry overhead and both the boys looked up, a moment's reflex.

"So you've got chances," Kyrie said. "And I've got my own reason why I want you to join." Jeo stared at him and waited. "If you want more than you've got in this place, there's only two ways open to you." He glanced around the clearing again. "You can wait till you get old, of course. But nowadays everybody seems to live longer than they used to, so you have to wait longer to become an elder. The only way to get anything when you're still young is to become a guardsman. And then, once you're in, you can get on much faster if you've got someone to help you. Someone to work for you."

He waited for some kind of reaction from Jeo but all he got was an empty face.

"It's not a bad life in the brochs," he went on. "Better food and more of it. Good places to sleep. You don't have to work in the fields and you can go where you want. And nobody hits you, no matter how old they are. Before long you'll be allowed to do the hitting. There's a few you wouldn't mind hitting, I'm sure."

Oh yes, thought Jeo as they looked at each other. Yes, some more than others.

"Yes," he said.

"That's settled then, seems to me. I'll talk to some of the captains and see what they think. What do you say?"

Nothing.

"Come on, Jeo. What's worse—being my servant or the

family slave? All you'll have to do is obey a few orders when I give them. It's got to be better than the way you're living now."

That was true and Jeo didn't deny it. Nothing could have been much worse than what he had. By joining the guardsman youths he would live better and have some kind of standing in the valley instead of being the ill-treated serf he was now. He would be able to punish his sister.

But the soldiers of the glen were part of everything he hated about the place. And the thought of becoming the lizard boy's churl revolted him. Even as he looked at the smug freckled face he knew he couldn't join him. He wouldn't, whatever happened.

"Well?"

"I don't know," he muttered, and he didn't know what else to add. There was a scowl on the other's face, hooding his eyes so he looked more of a reptile than ever.

"That's not the answer I expected, Jeo." The voice was sterner. "You want me to tell someone about this dagger of yours?"

Jeo tried to buy some time. "I need time to think," he said feebly. Kyrie stood glaring at him for a while, then gave a shrug.

"The Gathering at the Stones tomorrow night," he said. "I'll come looking for you at the end of it, before daybreak. But if you turn me down I'll tell the captains about the knife and say you were going to use it on me or someone older. You know they'll believe me, whatever you might tell them. They'll take you to the Shrieking Pits."

Jeo stared through him, his thoughts in a tangle. Guardsman or dead, the freckled boy was telling him. He had the dagger in his hand, but he didn't think of using it. It wouldn't really solve anything. And somehow the time for throwing it was gone.

"I'll look for you at the Stones then," said Kyrie. The sudden sound of a voice and they stiffened to it.

Kyrie reacted first. He took a glance in the direction of the voice—then grabbed Jeo's tunic and pulled him close.

"Get back to the fields," he said in a barking whisper. "Re-

member—I'll come and find you at the Gathering tomorrow.
Now get out of here. And keep that stupid knife hidden."

He pushed Jeo away from him and the boy scrambled away
out of the copse, down the slope away from the voices. Kyrie
winced at the amount of noise he made as he went. When Jeo was
gone, he set off in the opposite direction, walking briskly between
the trees until he came out into the open and saw three hooded
guardsmen marching downhill.

At first even Kyrie was taken aback when he saw that one
of them was Meagher himself. But his face as ever betrayed nothing and he went up the hill towards the soldiers, who stood and
waited for him.

He stopped in front of Meagher, put his feet together and
gave a stiff bow with his head. The captain stared at him.

"Kyrie." The voice was flat and said nothing.

"Senior."

"Something interesting in that little wood?"

"Jeo, Senior." There was no hesitation in the reply. Someone
might have seen Jeo leave from the other side and Kyrie couldn't
risk a lie.

"Well now," said Meagher. "Jeo. I wonder what he was
doing in there. . . . "

"Lazing about, Senior. I sent him back to the fields."

Meagher sucked his teeth and said nothing. Kyrie glanced at
the two flanking guardsmen and found their lack of expression
hostile. They each had a long black club.

"This lad Jeo," said the captain. "It's not like him to leave
his place of work like that, from what I hear. They say he's
changed, this past twelvemonth."

"I think he has, Senior."

"Do you now? And yet today he's lazing under the trees, or
so you tell me. Why's that, do you think?"

Kyrie put the very faintest shrug in his shoulder. "I'm not
sure, Senior," he said plausibly. "I think he just needed a rest. I
found one of his brothers doing the same last week."

Meagher raised his eyebrows a fraction. "His brothers are all older, aren't they? That makes a difference."

"Yes, Senior." The tone was apologetic.

"Still," the captain went on, "he's young. Can't expect him to behave himself every minute of the day, I suppose. Does he do this often?"

"Not that I know of, Senior."

"And you see a lot of him, do you?"

"Just sometimes, Senior."

Meagher nodded and didn't say anything.

"He seems to have changed for good, Senior," ventured Kyrie.

"Seems," said Meagher reflectively. "That's the word. Seems. Keep watching him, master Kyrie."

"Yes, Senior."

"Yes. I'm sure you have other things to attend to for the moment. Duties of some kind."

The boy gave a quick bow, turned on his heel and set off down the hill.

"Kyrie." He swung round. They were still standing there, almost identical in their hoods and leather jerkins.

"What were *you* doing in the wood? Just passing through?"

"Just passing *by,* Senior," he answered, rather too coolly. "I heard him in there as I went past."

"You did, did you? Well, I admire you, Kyrie. You must have excellent ears to hear someone lazing about."

The captain turned and strode away down the hillside with the others in tow. Kyrie went to his broch, walking hurriedly with a step that for him was unusually fraught.

It was midsummer's eve and all through the long stifling afternoon the people of the glen made their way up the northern slope to the circle of huge standing stones on top of the hill, leaving the day's work unfinished behind them.

They came from every corner of the valley. The thralls and bondsmen from the tenements, the villeins and the older cottars from their crofts near the sea—urged on and controlled by ranks of guardsmen from the stone forts.

As evening drew on, the robed and hooded elders came out of the castle. Almost everyone every year came to the great Gathering at the Stones, bringing their dogs and sacks of food and earthen jugs of beer. Some led ponies hauling carts laden with logs and kindling for the great central fire, or brought rows of dead geese and chickens, plucked and hanging by their ankles from long poles, or enormous single cheeses that even the strongest men had to carry on their shoulders. They came singly or in family groups, sometimes twenty or more at a time, in their hundreds, then thousands, of every age group and all professions, labourers and loaders and their overseers, old master cartwrights and young swineherds and masons and mongers and storytellers and stockmen and millers, all in the same glum tunics or thin stuff robes, grey and brown and very dirty white, all with black or fair or Celtic red hair. They laughed and talked and drank wines and beer and cursed and quarrelled in the heat, kicking their dogs and their children and struggling with their various loads.

When finally they reached the broad level plain at the top of the hill they slumped on the brown grass and took a short rest, gasping in the sun and fanning their bodies and nursing their aches and pains . . . until groups of guardsmen came and shouted at them and prodded the children with their clubs to get them back on their feet to prepare for the Gathering itself.

Around the edge of the plain, a number of megaliths formed the remains of a circle, a henge of immense stones eroded by long ages of rain and wind. Some were huge single menhirs standing alone and unattached, others fixed together in dolmens: two menhirs close together supporting a capstone lying lengthwise across the top. Each dolmen had once been the entrance to a large burial mound over an unknown number of underground tombs. The earth of each mound had long since been worn away, leaving nothing but the great stone doorway and the buried tombs. No one knew what the single stones had been.

The area was no common graveyard. Through the centuries only the bodies of the Elders and the Guardians had been brought here. It was something of a holy place.

In the very centre of the circle, the peasants built the great midsummer bonfire. They had to spend most of the afternoon stacking the logs, and by the time they finished, just before dark, the complete structure was as tall as the walls of a broch and much wider. It took several large tinderboxes to light it—and then it blazed throught the night like a beacon, ruffled by coaxing hilltop winds, so hot and fiercely bright that no one could sit within yards of it. As soon as darkness fell and the fire was the only light in the valley, the Gathering could begin in earnest.

The night was quite cold so the elders sat at the front of the ring of people, closest to the heat. The children were put at the back, where they played noisily in the shadows and bullied food from one another. Only the guardsmen didn't eat or drink or sit. They stood with lances and crossbows in their hands in a circle round the edge of the crowd, some looking in, a few facing out, keeping watch. Some stood on discarded carts for a better view. All, from time to time, hit the youngest or most boisterous of the children with the butts of their weapons.

Two of the guardsmen, the most senior of all, were on their own by one of the stone columns, Meagher standing beside the Guardian's horse. They were out of the shadows, out in the garish torchlight so everyone could see they were there.

"Quiet again," said the Guardian as usual. It was usually quiet in the glen. It was late night now, not far from dawn.

"Not like last year," said the captain. "Two killings we had then."

"I remember. You've brought in more men this time?"

"Nearly all of them. Left only a bare few in the blocks, less than I'd want. All the Lookers are here too, and all our informants."

"Good."

"I got someone watching that boy Kyrie I told you about."

"You really think there's something between him and the other one, Jeo? It doesn't seem likely."

"No. But I know they been together—"

"Just the once."

"—and I think it's best to be sure. There's something about Kyrie bothers me."

Kyrie, thought the Guardian. Small, freckled boy, fair hair. Yes, he knew him. A boy who knew what he was doing. Maybe a little too clever. The kind that soon became officers, even Guardians. Better to make guardsmen of boys like that fat one Ouse. The unquestioning type. The zealot. All guardsmen should be like that. But Kyrie and the child Jeo—it seemed an unlikely pairing.

"You're right," he told the captain. "Best to be sure. If they're seen together again—"

"Yes."

They watched the crowd for a while.

"Anything else?"

"Nothing," said Meagher.

"The thieving in the mill-house, week ago. You know who did it yet?"

"Three boys from the east-side blocks. Caught one of them day before yesterday."

"Only one?"

"Took him to one of the brochs. He told us about the others."

The Guardian's thoughts moved on. "That girl who belongs to Gara. The one who can't speak."

"Nothing to say about her. Does what she's told, does her work. None of my men seen her doing anything she shouldn't. Spends all her time with the sheep."

"Everything's in order then, you think."

"Seems so. I'm going down to the river, stay there till first light. Just to keep an eye out."

He went away and faded into the blackness of the hillside behind the pillar.

The Guardian looked at the elders around the fire. Shibolleth and Bodach Du, fat Shelagh. Odd, he thought, that such very old people should be seen as rulers. They were feeble and often ill. He had no affection for them, as he had no affection for the young, but unlike most children he didn't dislike or despise them either. They were cover for his own rule, the real dominance in the glen. He didn't need to feel anything for them.

He was still thinking about them while across on the far edge of the plain, on an ox-drawn cart, a group of youngsters sat and did what he was doing, looking at the crowd. Kyrie and his little gang, Ouse among them.

It was nearly dawn. The sky was greying between the mountain peaks. Time for Kyrie to go and find Jeo. He didn't know yet where the boy was. He hadn't seen him in the crowd.

"Where are you going?" grunted Ouse as soon as the lizard boy got to his feet.

Kyrie jumped down from the cart. "Just going to look around. Doing my job."

"I'll come with you."

"You'd follow me if I was going for a piss, Ouse."

The others laughed at the fat boy. He glowered and stayed where he was.

Kyrie slipped away into the great mob of peasants, many of whom were standing, all very close together. He saw a face in the crowd, a glimpse of a firelit head in the overall half-dark, and knew at once he was being watched. He didn't know all the informers in the valley—there were many—but he recognised this one face. Being an accomplished snooper himself, he knew another when he saw one at work. He knew too how to evade a watchful eye. In a minute he'd worked his way deep into the throng, twists and turns, losing himself from any spying sight. He moved fast. He wanted to find Jeo before daybreak, to tell him not to do anything at all. They were both being watched. Meagher had his suspicions. To do anything now would spoil all his future plans.

A picture appeared in his mind, of himself in helmet and full mail on a Guardian's horse.

Behind him, Ouse watched to see where he went, but very soon lost him in the crowd. He looked away, looked around, and saw some of the shepherds standing on the edge of the great circle, Gara and his housegirl with them. Two of the shepherds left the group and the fat boy didn't look at them. He stared at the mute girl.

Her face was turned away from him and all he saw was her mess of hair, light purple in the glow of the bonfire. The girl who'd thrown stones at him in the field of nettles. He still thought about it. She'd cut his head, made him look clumsy and helpless in front of the others.

But he'd got to Jeo in the end, despite her. He wondered if she knew about that. He hadn't told anyone about it himself. He'd lied about the cut on his cheek. He would do it again soon: if he still thought Jeo's obedience was a sham, he would punish him again. Even if it wasn't a sham he would do it. He liked it. He looked at the shepherd girl. Others found her strangely attractive, they told him. He didn't see it. She was stupid, she couldn't talk. She was Jeo's friend and he wanted to punish her too.

Rhosarran was tired of the old shepherd staring at her so she gave him a small smile, knowing it would please him and take his mind off Jeo. She turned away and he moved his hands with fumbling gentleness through her hair and her smile died.

She was anxious, as she always was, about Jeo. In all the weeks since their first time of passion in the black wood, she'd met him just twice. Neither of them had been able to get away. He'd seemed more bitter than ever. All he could talk about was running away—other places, the moors and the sea. He kept toying with his knife. She'd tried to calm him, and to a point she'd succeeded, but he was unquiet. Even his lovemaking, which should have been a new delight, seemed distracted. She wondered what was happening in his mind now, as the night moved to its close. She saw him again, a secret glance. He was alone and unnoticed and seemed to be hiding. The shepherd kissed her shoulder and though she didn't move she shuddered.

Jeo was half-buried in a pile of sacks on one of the wagons right at the back of the crowd. No one saw him sitting there. He was in one of the darkest areas of the plain and the sacks were heaped all around as well as underneath him. No one, as yet, had come looking for him. The cart was quite high so he was in a good position for looking out over the crowd and seeing who was there.

He gazed towards the ring of stones on the far side of the bonfire. They were yellow in firelight, ochre in places, black shadows wobbling on the cromlechs and upright stonework. But Jeo wasn't looking at the stones. He was watching the guardsmen, glancing from one to the next, looking for one in particular, one of the youngest cadets. He didn't recognise many of them. He looked in among the children playing and fighting around him. Still no sign of the lizard boy. So just for a while he turned away and stared at the fire and the faces in the ring around it.

He looked most of all at the elders. Some of the very oldest in the valley were there, emerged from the castle and the finest cottages. Some with their faces still hidden in shadow under the cowls of their ceremonial robes, others with the hoods pulled back. Morag was there, the oldest woman in the glen. And Shibolleth, one of the oldest men. Chacmagh and Uehag and Cailleach. And Bodach Du, the old man with the very black hair. Others whose names Jeo didn't know. Some who might have been men or women, so old he couldn't tell which. They sat in groups, like knots of old toads, or singly with their child companions, nodding and staring at the fire. If they showed any of the softer feelings in their faces—any kindness or compassion or fun, any sadness— Jeo didn't see them.

He looked away and searched the lines of guardsmen again, then looked about in the semi-darkness close to him. Still no Kyrie. Time passed and nothing happened. Jeo saw thousands of faces in the roan light. Almost everyone from the valley was there on the plain. Some, a very few, were missing. Guardsmen roaming the tenements, some keeping watch on the hillsides, a handful in the castle. The very old, who could choose to stay away if they wished. The very ill. The Elder in his fortress. And, on the harsh coastal rocks, a skinny old man with a white beard, fishing with heavy nets, watched by a guardsman from the high cliffs.

Jeo looked at the elders one by one. They were shorter than younger adults, he noticed. Their limbs and fingers seemed longer. They looked like apes, hunched and wrinkled and their thumbs curled. Shibolleth had very long white hair and rag robes, bent over like a bishop monkey. Chacmagh stabbed her last tooth in a baked apple. The old man next to her had a sour crinkled face. Another, nearby, had suffered a stroke and didn't move much. Kureagh sat scratching his legs, his blotchy piebald face daubed blue with woad, the image of a mandrill.

Jeo nibbled his lip as he watched. They were no better than animals, these old people. And yet they were the most important in the glen. They had all the power in it. He'd been thinking about what Sligo had said, and decided it must be a dreadful thing to grow old. He'd begun to notice what it did to people's bodies. He didn't want it to happen to him. The failing eyesight and the bad hearing, the wasting muscles, the teeth that fell out and the difficulties of breathing, the stiffening joints, the weak undignified bowels. They sat in their groups in front of the bonfire, looking as if they were just waiting to die, in a kind of pre-death. All that degeneration—yet to be old was to govern the entire valley. Jeo suddenly felt very small and alone in his hatred for them.

He glanced from the elders to the middle-aged. He saw the shepherds sitting all together, grim faced, some with small beards like goats. He looked at Gara and Rhosarran.

Someone blocked his line of sight. Someone looking at him, close. He drew back and tried to hide deeper among the sacks. He couldn't.

"What you doing in there, Jeo?" A very big man. A dark

shape with the firelight behind him. Jeo peered at his face, saw it was dirty with dust. He relaxed.

"Piss off, Hake," he said softly.

"You alright in there?"

"Yes, I'm alright. Now piss off. I want to be alone."

He was worried Hake's presence would lead someone to him. Kyrie perhaps. A big man talking to a pile of sacks was bound to attract curiosity, even if the man was a half-wit known to do peculiar things. Hake seemed to understand his anxiety. He sat on the cart with his back to Jeo so nobody could see the boy behind him, and talked over his shoulder.

"You're alone in there," he said. "You want to be alone sometimes."

"Yes," said Jeo, more willing to talk now there was less danger of discovery. He still wished the man would go away and leave him to think, but couldn't raise his voice and couldn't show his irritation too much. He didn't know how Hake would react.

"You want to be alone but they don't let you. They don't like you. I know."

Nothing from Jeo.

"They don't like me neither," said Hake. "They think I'm stupid. I don't like them neither. Fucking guardsmen."

Jeo moved his legs in the cramping space. A sack fell on his face and he edged it away. "I don't even want to talk about it," he said.

"They make Sligo work in the sea. They tell me I'm stupid."

"Why do you keep talking about Sligo?"

"He's my friend."

"Well, he means nothing to me. Tell someone else about him. Leave me alone."

"We could kill a guardsman," said Hake suddenly, and Jeo frowned.

"Don't talk shit, Hake. Go away."

Hake stood up. He half-turned. "You just think about it, that's all. We could kill them, me and you. You think about that."

He went away to look for scraps of food in the crowd. Jeo puffed his cheeks. Things were really bad if the only person who approached him with any kind of companionship in mind was the valley idiot.

It was the least of his worries. He stared at Rhosarran and wished he could be with her. He saw the old shepherd touch her hair and he looked away.

He put his face in his hands and closed his eyes. He knew it was nearly dawn. Very soon, Kyrie would come and find him. He looked between his fingers at the crowd.

He wouldn't do what Kyrie wanted. And so the freckled boy would tell the captains about the knife. So Jeo would die soon. He put his hands on his legs and stared at the sky. Still dark, not yet daybreak, so he still had time before Kyrie came for him. Time for what? There was something he wanted to do before he died, and there was no reason to sit and wait. He came out from the pile of sacks and moved around the edge of the Gathering.

He merged with children playing, glancing at the guardsmen as he went. He found a place where he could pass close to one of the megaliths, and he darted out into the darkness down the hill.

Rhosarran caught just a side-glimpse of his black hair and ragged tunic as he disappeared. She'd tried for so long to cool his hate and keep him calm in the hard times—but as she saw him leave she knew she hadn't done enough. He was gone from her now, and she feared for him, and for what he might do.

In the charcoal darkness of his tenement, Jeo stopped at the corner of another corridor and stood still, a pause for breath. He'd run all the way from the ancient henge, down the long hill and across the river and now back into the shanty. He could have gone anywhere else if all he'd wanted was a place to hide and somewhere to sit and think. But he'd come straight back to where he lived, for a reason.

He stood and listened very hard before moving any further. The tenement was almost totally empty and there was surely no one to see him or stand in his way—but all the same he was wary. Partly out of habit. Partly for fear of stray guardsmen.

He made his way with stealth round the corner into the next passageway. No sounds yet, though he listened hard. Not a croak of wood or the scamper of a tramp dog. And not a fleck of light —the whole place suddenly like some enormous catacomb of wood.

He found his way by memory to one of the highest floors, where he was soon standing outside his family's quarters.

He was afraid now. He hesitated before pushing his way into the small main room. He crept across to the other side, to the ladder by the wall.

He climbed it briskly and lifted the trapdoor. Like everything in the tenement, it now seemed to make no sound. He couldn't understand why. Just his imagination, probably. His mouth was parching and he licked it with all his tongue.

When he was standing in the blackness of the room above, the enormity of what he was doing made him stand still with fear. Listening through the boom of his pulse, he heard the other sound in the room—as far as he knew, the only noise in all the shanty.

He hoped he'd been wrong. He wanted to go away. But that single sound told him he was right. He hadn't seen his grandmother at the Gathering. She was here, breathing in her bed, making dry noises through her nose.

He didn't move for a while. He sniffed and the smells in the room seemed stronger—more odour of old woman, more piss in the wood, the rushes more soiled. Perhaps his senses were simply wider open. It didn't matter.

He smelled wine too, so he knew Cromarty was deeply asleep, in one of her depressive stupors. She wouldn't wake up.

He walked to the edge of the bed. A sudden noise, small in the distance, made him turn his head and he went quickly back to the trapdoor, knelt over it and listened.

Another noise, a tag of the first. Jeo glanced back to the bed, but he knew he couldn't stay in that room. He might be trapped there. He stepped softly down the ladder and crossed to the door of the passage.

The same sounds, louder. Footsteps on wood floors. From which direction? He listened. From all directions. He wasn't sure which way to run, but he had to go somewhere. He went left, running quietly on his toes, keeping close to the wall, staring in the dark, turning the corner. No one there. He hurried along the black hallway.

He was nearly out of the tenement, darting down one of the widest passages, when he saw two dark figures at the other end and stopped in his flight.

There were any number of black shapes throughout the great slum. Even now, in the creeping daylight, these two could so possibly have been a pair of wood beams leaning on the walls of the corridor, one on each side. Neither of them moved.

But Jeo knew just about every log of wood in the building. Even in his wild, breathless state he was sure he'd never seen these before. For a second or two he stood very still. Then he took a few paces backwards. As the dark shapes moved and ran towards him, he turned and bolted down the hallway to his left—a guardsman's hand reached from the shadows and held him hard.

"Where you going, you little shit? What you doing in the blocks? You should be at the Gathering."

Jeo stared at him, seeing only a tall black figure, saying nothing.

"Answer me or I'll black your eyes."

"Nothing," said Jeo.

"Nothing? What does that bloody mean? Where you going?"

"Just walking—"

"Little liar. I'll pull your filthy ears off."

He shook the boy and slapped him on the face, hard so his head was knocked sideways. Suddenly, in his pain, Jeo felt everything welling inside him. He didn't want to be struck any more. He didn't want to be watched and bullied and overworked. It was too much now. He couldn't bear the pain.

His knife was in his hand and he punched it into the guardsman's chest. He didn't know what he hit. The force of the strike jarred his wrist and forearm and he heard the soldier grunt. He pulled his knife away and ran as the man went down on one knee. The other guardsman gave chase but lost the boy in the next short passageway. Jeo heard him shouting behind him, calling for help.

He heard other soldiers in the shanty as he ran. He went down ladders and sprinted along hallways, keeping to the smallest scissures and some almost unknown gangways, moving through the tenement till he came out at last into the bright grey early dawn.

He creased his face in the sudden light. He didn't stop to look around. Turning to the right, he ran panting through the long grass and veered up the slope towards a small copse in the distance.

A shout and he glanced back. Two soldiers were running from the tenement. They dropped their lances and chased him with clubs in their hands.

Jeo hurried away towards the group of trees up the hill. The soldiers were stronger than he was, so by the time he reached the trees they were very close behind. They saw him vanish through the skirting of bushes and followed him in, smashing their way through the hawthorn with their clubs.

There were very few trees in the wood. A dozen large elms standing around a small grass clearing. A small undergrowth. No sign of the boy. The guardsmen moved to opposite sides of the glade and examined each tree quickly and thoroughly, looking all around them, behind the big buttress roots, high into the branches. Still nothing. Not a hollow to hide in. They thrashed the undergrowth with their black cudgels. One of them pointed between the trunks at the hillside beyond. They ran out up the slope towards the next line of trees.

In the scrappy bushes, his body pressed into the hole of a familiar badger set, Jeo lay and waited. When he dredged himself from the soil, his knife spilled out of its pouch. He picked it up and ran with it in his hand. He dashed out of the wood and down the slope, further to the right, west, not sure where he was going. Just looking for a place to hide.

One of the drystone walls was in his way. He scrambled over it, ran alongside it, crouching to stay hidden. Just as he was about to pass the first shrine in the stonework, someone—with ghastly timing—stepped out of it and stood in his way.

Jeo stopped and stood where he was and tried to hide his knife by his side when he saw it was a short, heavy guardsman with no helmet and a dagger in his belt. Meagher himself.

The captain flexed his fingers and said nothing for a moment as he looked the boy up and down. The suspicion of a smile reached his lips.

"Well now, Jeo, why so out of breath?" He indicated the shrine with a flick of his eyes. "In a hurry to pay respects?"

Jeo didn't speak.

"I didn't see you at the Gathering," said Meagher, matter-of-fact. "You were there, were you—somewhere?"

Jeo nodded. His knees weren't steady. "Yes, Senior."

The captain saw the knife in his other hand.

"You shouldn't have that, and you know it. What have you done?"

A noise. A shout in the distance. Meagher looked to the wood away behind the boy. Two of his guardsmen were running towards them shouting things he couldn't understand. He frowned inquiringly at the boy—but before he could say anything or move, Jeo ran past him, pushing him aside with a backhand sweep of his arm. The captain put up his hand to protect his face but was too late to baulk the lash of the small dirk as the blade sliced into his cheek and cut his lower lip in half so his face bled like a chicken's neck through his beard.

He grunted with the pain and the surprise of the boy's move, and stumbled back against the wall of the shrine. He caught one last sight of the grimy tunic and thin white limbs as Jeo disappeared into the big young forest up on the slope.

The two guardsmen rushed across and found their chief with his hand pressed against his cheek, the palm over his mouth, blood on the fingers. There was a short, awkward silence.

"Shall we get after him, Senior?"

Meagher shook his head. "No," he mumbled behind his hand. "He's like a bloody little stoat. You'll never find him, just the two of you. Go to one of the western brochs and bring everyone out here. Short swords and knives, no lances. And archers—I want thirty crossbows here first thing. One of you go tell the Guardian what's happened. Tell him it's all under control."

They gave him a clipped bow of the head then ran past him alongside the wall. Meagher scowled at the wood ahead of him as he fiddled in the pocket of his jerkin with his free hand, looking for something to stop the bleeding.

Jeo ran on and on into the forest and only stopped when he was sure no one, for the time being, was following him. He fell down and stretched himself wearily under a long bush.

When he recovered his breath he didn't think about what to do next. It made no difference what he did. He was as good as dead. Yet he smiled. He'd killed one of the guardsmen. Something he'd always longed to do.

A soldier and the stag. That was enough. Plenty. He could die pleased with that, though he wouldn't let them kill him if he could help it. He turned the dirk in his fingers as he looked at it. Like any tool of death, it had beauty—neat and clean and stream-lined like an arrow or a swordblade or the beak of a kingfisher, like the act of killing itself. Corpses were bloody and ugly, but he didn't mind. He wished he could do it again. Perhaps he would, when they came to take him. He might kill one or two before they overpowered him. He gripped the knife and allowed himself a brief sleep under the bush, still smiling. He would die soon—but that only made him feel calm, not in the least afraid. In fact he was rather pleased with himself. He'd done something, at last— and he now had some standing in the glen. He was an original.

Jeo was woken by the bark of a dog. A dreary sound, like a cough in the distance. Almost at once he was on his feet and wrestling his way out of the bush. He stood and looked to see where he was.

It was one of the huge sapling forests, perhaps the largest of all, somewhere quite high on the slope. The soil in this western end of the valley was mainly limestone, too dry for oak—so nearly every tree was a tall young beech, all spaced wide apart to allow for future growth—and their top foliage was scanty, so the sunlight gushed in through the awning of branches, flooding the forest so it was bright like a cathedral with high windows. None of the claustral darkness of the old oakwoods.

He could tell he'd been asleep for a very long hour, so it was dangerous to stay where he was. First of all he had to decide which way to go. There was a narrow forest path nearby. It would be faster than running through the threads of ivy. But he saw it was going south, further up the slope, whereas he wanted to go on west to the sea to his right.

A dog barked again. The sound reached him cleanly across the open woodland. It came from somewhere down the hill, not very far away. As soon as he heard it, Jeo set off hurriedly along the forest floor. There was nothing unusual in itself about a dog barking in a wood. The valley was full of them. But this was no ordinary morning and the boy was certain the dog had been sent into the weald. It was no stray. Another bark—the howl of a hound—confirmed his suspicion. He quickened his pace through the ivy matting, breaking into a run.

A small burn crossed his path, deep with slow brown water on its way downhill to join the big river. A simple clam bridge in the middle of it, a single boulder to be used as a stepping stone. He ignored it. He waded through the water itself and took several steps upstream in an effort to put the dogs off his scent if they ever reached the crossing. It might, he knew, make no difference—especially if they used the right kinds of dog. But every little might help.

He crossed the burn and ran on through the forest, still holding the precious knife. The woods began to thin out in front of him, the trees even further apart. He heard the sound of more dogs, this time straight ahead, and came to a halt.

Obviously they weren't the same animals he'd heard before. They simply couldn't have had the time to circle the forest. They were other dogs. The wood was being surrounded.

He stood and looked and listened. From where he was, fairly high on the hill, he could see over the tops of the trees lower on the slope—or look through their latticework of branches and catch the far side of the river in a glance. Horses in pastures, oakwoods and fallowfields. He had no time to stare at them.

A small sound turned his head and he had a glimpse of falling leaves and two brown husks of beech mast, blown by a cheap wind and landing with a little hollow noise on branches and the ground. A magpie feather floated down away to his right, past the statue of an elder in robes.

He saw these things but was only looking out for danger. He was still there, wondering what to do, when something else moved among the trees in front of him. Not, as he expected, a dog. A guardsman in chain mail and helmet, moving across his line of vision on the right, up the slope, working his way closer from tree to tree. Jeo turned and sidled quickly back the way he came, drifting slightly downhill—and then a loud fricative sound scraped the air and something nailed the thin beech beside him. He looked up and saw a short grey crossbow bolt buried to its flight in the bark of the tree.

He didn't give it a second glance. Turning back uphill he pelted up the slope as fast as he could, his back bent almost double as he tried to make himself a smaller target. Another bolt hissed through the hanging ivy and sent a qualm through a tree behind him. A third made no sound at all and seemed to simply appear, horribly sudden, as if grown out of the grass just ahead. Somewhere to his right, more guardsmen. He heard them bustling through the short undergrowth. Further away, the hue of the hounds. He ran faster still, veering to the left.

And as he ran, the slope grew steeper and his legs were soon very heavy, his breath coming in short gasps. And the higher he went, the less cover he found on the hill. Fewer trees and they were thinner. Young and green and sapid, with svelte branches no bigger than twigs, their trunks contorting to follow the line of the slope.

He was running for the top of the incline because he had no other choice. There were archers and footsoldiers and dogs behind him and to the right barring his way to the coast. There were others, no doubt, to the left—but in any case he didn't want to go that way. Most of the tenements and stone forts were in that direction. So the only thing left to him was the faint chance that even in the hour he'd been asleep they might not have had time to seal off the crown of the hill. Somewhere in his mind was the half-thought that he was being deliberately driven towards the top, but there was nothing else he could do anyway.

Nearer the peak of the hill, where rain and the angle of the slope had slipped away the topsoil, there was more open chalk underfoot. It was damp, in places smeared with slippery dark moss —so even Jeo, with his very sure feet, stumbled as he ran on it. Here, too, the slope was so steep he couldn't stand upright for fear of falling backwards. He reached for the exposed roots of young trees and used them as rungs to pull himself up.

He stopped for a very short rest. He had to. His legs were beginning to hurt and there were pains in his chest and side. He stood breathing heavily beside a tree, looking anxiously around him and wondering in his pain if it was worth the agony just to earn a few more minutes of a life that had never been happy. The idea of glorying in his defiance, of pitting himself hopelessly but magnificently alone against the might of the Elder and the entire glen—all that was gone from his head. He wanted to stay alive to avoid the pains of death, but other than that he was just very, very tired and at that moment anything seemed better than the distress of this never-ending run up the forest hill. He thought of Rhosarran, her huge ling hair and the touch of her big hands, the look in her eyes. But she was very far away now. She seemed a long time ago. . . .

His thoughts were slashed by a great threshing in the hedge of ivy to his right and he jumped round just in time to catch sight of a big snarling dog as it shrugged out of the undergrowth and rushed straight towards him.

Jeo had a glimpse of the dog's handler, a guardsman with a whip and a long knife, hurrying behind it. Another soldier further back. The dog itself was a huge mongrel mastiff, brindled and ugly and fierce as a ferret, snarling from the pit of its throat.

There was no time to run away but Jeo had a second in which he could throw his knife. He kept it in his hand. It was all he had, and he wanted it with him when he died, not to waste it on the killing of a dog.

The beast launched itself at him without breaking stride. The weight of its body threw him backwards, knocking him on his back on the ground. But Jeo had already started to fall. The teeth and front claws missed his face. As the heavy body fell on him he thrust upwards with his knife hand—a fraction late, but the effect was much the same. Instead of driving the dagger up between the brute's ribs, he struck just above the groin, puncturing something inside and jolting his wrist.

The mastiff screamed with the pain, a sound like a small dog. It didn't fight the boy when he rolled himself from under it, pulling the knife out with him. There was no time to think of finishing the animal off or to wonder if it could recover and attack again. He'd barely picked himself off the ground when the dog handler came running into the clearing.

Jeo was at the other side of the grass patch, already climbing,

sprinting away, so the man's whip was no good to him. He set off
in pursuit but Jeo had found a second wind and was too fast for
him. He dropped the whip, switched his knife to the other hand
and flung it at the boy's back. He wasn't as good with a knife as
Jeo and it was too long for throwing, so he missed. The other
soldier appeared from the left and they went up the hill without
a word, taking the whip and the long knife with them, leaving
the mastiff to twitch and whimper behind them, a back leg jerking
in the air.

Up ahead of them Jeo suddenly realised that for all his efforts
he was getting nowhere. Till then, he'd been changing direction
at almost every step. A movement in the ivy to his left would make
him edge to the right. The threat of an arrow and he would run
several steps in a crouch, weaving and dodging. In his anxiety to
escape the immediate dangers he was losing sight of his main aim
—to snatch the chance of getting to the top of the high hill before
the guardsmen encircled the forest and cut him off completely.
Remembering this, he straightened his run and dashed through the
last sparse belt of trees towards the crest of the slope.

He was a strong boy for his build but he was tired now.
Nevertheless he couldn't help noticing, absurdly, what a good day
it was.

The grass on the high open reaches of the wood was damp
to his bare feet and patterned with clusters of small bright woodland flowers. The beech trees pushed themselves out young and
green from the fossil chalk. Their ivy shawls had their own kind
of elegance. And the whole wide airy space had the smell of warm
grass and the tattle of small birds up above. It occurred to Jeo that
this wasn't a bad way to die, running through a forest of fresh
young trees with his elders in pursuit.

Even as this notion came into his head he realised the last
stretch of hillside, now not far ahead, was empty of trees. And he
brightened when he saw no one waiting there for him. He'd been
right. They'd not had time to close off the top of the wood. Once
over the hillcrest, even out in the open, there might be somewhere

to hide. In the dells of heather, perhaps. He could already see glimpses of purple on the rim of the slope.

He ran a little faster, forgetting his pain and the weakness of his legs in his keenness to reach the heath. Then a sudden noise broke out behind him to the right, making him glance back as he ran—and he couldn't hold back a grunt of dismay when he saw the small pack of dogs pounding between the trees as they followed him out of the forest.

They were big rawboned all-purpose dogs, lurchers and ridgebacks and the like, and though they themselves were tired by the chase up the hill they were naturally stronger and faster than the boy. He ran harder up the last rise, bearing left away from them. A pair of guardsmen with axes came hustling round the top of the wood, aiming to intercept him on the flat ground ahead.

He found a last kick of speed from somewhere, raced further up the slope. The gradient was even steeper here. He had to run bent double again, on all fours, pulling at the grass with one hand and using his knife like a mountain axe in the other.

The top of the slope came closer, but slowly. A crossbow bolt landed with sinister gentleness in the grass just to his right. The baying of the dogs seemed louder by the second. He heard the shouts of men. Another bolt seethed overhead. And then, abruptly, mercifully, the ground under his feet was level.

Bent over as he was, he almost fell when his feet touched the flat heath. He straightened and ran on and now the running was easier. His legs, which had been heavy as bags of blood, felt slim and light and he dashed across the heather as fast as he could, his head thrown back like a stag before the hounds.

He couldn't escape the agonies of hard running. He heard two sounds as he went: the wheeze in his chest and something like a regular groan in his throat.

The air up here was crowded with flies. He had to wave his hands in front of his face to keep them off his eyes. He lost his balance and stumbled, sought to recover, put a foot in a deep dip in the heather, fell on his side.

He was up almost at once, and ran on, round the side of a huge black hole in the ground, trying to sprint, crossing the moist humps of heather by jumping from one exposed boulder to the next, past another hole—then, out of nothing, he knew it was all a waste of time.

There was no strength in his legs. He could hardly breathe. Ahead of him there was nothing but flat open country. Far too much of it. No cover. Behind him the growl of the dogs, the tread of boots. He stopped and turned to face them, retching for breath.

He saw that the chasing dogs had been brought to heel. They were now crouched in a line, half a dozen of them, no more than twenty paces in front of him. Suddenly they weren't snarling.

Just behind them, a group of guardsmen, expressionless as the dogs, holding crossbows or swords, just standing there as they faced him. Jeo took his hand down from his eyes and squinted at them in the glare. Why didn't they aim their bows and kill him? It would be more than easy from that range. Other swordsmen and archers appeared over the crown of the hill behind. They too just came and stood and looked at him with empty faces. One or two were finding it hard to hide what they thought about him. Jeo recognised some of them. For the first time, he found he could look them in the face and not turn away.

He looked past them all, to the hillcrest beyond. Even more were coming to increase the numbers. They seemed to be arriving from every direction, bringing dogs on chain leashes, or carrying bows and quivers, some with light skirmishing shields. By the time they were all there—all the patrols sent to surround the forest— there were more than a hundred of them, lined in orderly ranks as on a parade field. All these soldiers, he was thinking—any one of them quite capable of breaking him in half. It had taken them all to bring him to bay.

It was a big thought. All through the morning he'd been surprising himself with the things he could do. Pity it was about to end.

As if in response to his thoughts, someone snapped a command and the front rank of guardsmen (all archers) knelt, lifted their crossbows to their shoulders, and pointed in his direction.

Jeo blanched. Something griped in his belly. He took two involuntary steps backwards. He would have gone further back— but suddenly the ground sloped and gave way slightly under his feet. He jumped hastily aside. His eyes were on the firing squad but he spared a glance just behind him. He was standing on the lip of one of the broad black holes in the ground. One of the Shrieking Pits.

He looked back at the phalanx of guardsmen. They had all lowered their weapons and were once again just staring at him.

So that was it, he realised. They were waiting for him to jump in the Pit and end things himself. Of course. He knew they liked whenever possible to execute young offenders in these holes, and now they were plainly trying to do things in the old accepted manner. In a way, a return to normality.

But if they really believed he was going to jump to their rituals, they were very wrong. He knew well enough they were taunting him, showing him that even though he'd flouted a cardinal law, the last action of his life would be to do what the elders wanted from him. A final act of obedience.

He wouldn't do it. He knew they could shoot him in any part of his body. He'd seen it done before. They could kill him as slowly as they wanted to. But he wouldn't do the thing they demanded. In a way it would betray his great terrible action in the tenement before dawn. He glanced again at the hole behind him, more out of curiosity than anything. He'd never been so close to a Shrieking Pit.

It was an ancient disused bell-pit mine. A single deep shaft down to a much wider chamber at the bottom, where the earth had once been veined with copper or lead or coal or tin.

No one was ever killed before being thrown down into the darkness. There was no need. They were deep shafts and the pits were bottle-shaped. There was no way to climb out. Victims were simply tossed alive into the black dungeons, to break their necks in the fall or die of hunger in the weeks that followed. Many lost their minds in the darkness before they died, and their screams could be heard from time to time in the hills, occasionally echoing in the valley. Which suited the elders and captains. It sounded a warning. Even those who didn't scream in this way would shriek as they were thrown in.

Jeo turned away from the chasm and looked again at the rows of expectant faces ranged before him. One of them, on the very end of the front row, caught his attention—and his eyes flared at the sight of the pinched, freckled face of the junior guardsman who stared at him without blinking, like a small reptile. Jeo suppressed a scowl as he judged the distance between himself and the sand-haired boy. Yes, he was quite close enough. He could hit him with his knife. But only if Kyrie stood still. And anyway he would hardly have to time to draw back his arm before any number of crossbow bolts struck him down.

So he kept his knife in his hand and went on waiting, simply being alive a few moments longer. The archers lifted their bows again. This time he didn't move. There was a sudden small commotion as the whole array of guardsmen moved aside to let someone pass between their ranks. The crossbows were lowered and the archers stood up.

A short, strong man came through and stood at the front of his men, hands characteristically on hips. Jeo was intrigued. He'd never seen Meagher in full chain mail before. He still carried no weapons apart from the usual long knife at his waist—but he was wearing a helmet for once, metal cheek flaps and long nose-piece hiding most of his face so that only the beard and the tight, hostile eyes were showing.

One thing the helmet didn't hide—and the thing Jeo noticed first—was the bulge of cloth padding under one of the cheekflaps. It was white cloth, but already stained pink—and Jeo had a feeling of pride. The padding on Meagher's face and the bandage half across his mouth were covering the wound where Jeo's knife had slashed the cheek. He remembered how he'd cut Ouse's face with a stone—but this was superior.

He held his knife up to his face and kissed it, in a gross gesture of contemptuous joy, twice on the blade.

For a second, no more, there was a ghastly collective silence as the guardsmen seemed to hold their breath. Some turned their eyes to their chief.

Meagher's face didn't move. He made a curt movement with his hand and the crossbowmen levelled their weapons at the boy.

Jeo, shocked out of his display by the imminence of his death, took a tottering step back. Just one step. The ground was treacherous around the dark hole and he lost his footing and fell. For just a moment—it was endless—he was struggling on the brink, horribly aware of what was happening. In the blackness below, he saw dull rounded shapes the colour of wax, smelled the smell of the dead. He fought with all his body to pull back from the rim, clawing at the grass and heather with his hands, even biting at it with his teeth. But his legs kicked out into nothing. Rhosarran crossed his thoughts, but only for an instant, then a picture appeared in his mind, of himself in an old man's white robes.

As the soldiers watched in silence, he fell backwards in the throat of the Shrieking Pit. He didn't cry out and the knife stayed clamped in his small fist.

In the dead of night, there was no light of any kind in the grey mountain castle. In the highest room of the keep, the oldest man of the glen pulled the hood lower on his face as he hobbled to the only window and looked down at the valley. His head was cocked on one side as he stood there leaning on the sill, as if he were listening for sounds from the Pits on the distant moor. The smile on his mouth was lost in the folds of his face.

At dawn, dark and slow over the coast, Sligo and Hake sat together on a rock and mended nets. The old man sat crosslegged as ever, head bent over his needle and twine, tongue jutting in concentration. Hake's feet dangled over the side of the rock and he whistled to himself as he worked. He whistled badly and the noise disturbed Sligo but he didn't say so.

When the whistling stopped, the old man glanced up. Hake had seen three guardsmen moving down the cliffs towards them. Sligo watched them too. They came and stood on the adjacent rock, slightly higher. They all had short spears and the black clubs. The old fisherman looked from one to the other.

"Well, pretty boys, what do you want today?" They stood and looked at him. "Oh, come on, laddies, you know how to talk. They do teach you that, don't they—as well as how to break heads with your black clubs?"

"Watch your lip, old man." There was no question of saying Senior. Hake made an angry movement but Sligo quelled it with a glance.

"I'll watch it, young master—certainly I will. But I'm watching yours too, waiting for it to move. Speak to me and don't just stand there."

"Just thought you'd like to know," said the same soldier. "One of the kids died in the glen yesterday."

"They die every day, boy."

"—died in one of the Pits, trying to run away. Boy called Jeo."

Nothing at all on Sligo's face. He made an idle gesture. "Bad lad, or so I hear. Came to an obvious end. Why tell me about it?"

The guardsmen were all smiling. "Just thought you'd like to know."

"It means nothing to me. Go tell it to someone else."

"Thing is—our captains they wonder where he was going before he got caught. Seems he was heading west. This is west."

"And your captains think he might have been on his way to me."

"Looks that way."

"A naughty young boy coming to see a naughty old man.

Well, you can go and tell your officers I know nothing about it—"

"You expect they'll believe that?"

"They can believe or disbelieve—either way, they can't know for sure. Maybe they should have asked the boy a few questions before they dropped him in the Pit. Shouldn't be in so much of a hurry. Tell them that from me."

Hake smiled. The guardsmen looked suitably grim. One of them pointed at Sligo with his club.

"You don't fool nobody, you old half-wit. We'll have you one of these days."

Hake got to his feet, but he had no weapons and the soldiers weren't frightened by him. They aimed their lances at him, then turned and went away. The big man made fists of his hands and glared after them. He looked down at Sligo but the fisherman's head was bowed again over his handful of net, hiding all his face.

The man on the horse stood and stared down into the glen, looking at nothing. His head was down. The young culprit had been trapped and was in a Pit. The law had been obeyed in blood. But a soldier was dead—the security forces had been breached—something no guardsman could explain away, something no Guardian could survive. He turned the horse round and rode into oblivion in the castle.

In the depths of a giant oakwood, in the western darkness, a rugged girl with shabby heather hair sat hunched against a tree beside one of the rare clearings without a charcoal burner, and sobbed into her hands. When she left the forest at dawn, with the trickle of tears in the sooty wood dust on her face, a short sly young man was already awake to watch her hurry across the hillside, and a pensive look passed across his freckled face.

THE YOUNG MAN

In a place where age was all-important, the very minutes seemed to take an age in passing, especially as nothing happened to disturb the overall life-cycle, nothing to quicken the pulse. There were no undercurrents. Most things didn't change. There was always an Elder—still the same Elder—in the castle, always a Guardian and the guardsmen, the peasants tilling the fields in rotation. Time seemed to move very slowly, and in a valley where everyone was impatient to advance in years and status, no one felt any older from day to day. The young boys stared in mirrors of burnished metal, searching their complexions for the first facial hair. The young men and women hunted white hairs on their temples, wrinkles around their eyes. The middle-aged yearned for their elders to die. Everything seemed to take its time, yet the minutes went by, and the days and the long dragging months, and by the time five years had passed, everyone in the glen had moved inexorably that much further up the age scale. A small boy had grown into a youth. His brother was now a man. An old woman was now an elder. Another had died. A young thrall was an adult freeman no longer bound to the soil. And a short wiry cadet with freckles on his face was now a full guardsman with a wider range of authority, though his promotion had been far slower than he could once have expected.

The Rain

IT HAD BEEN RAINING FOR nearly a week in the valley. All day and night for six days on end. It was still coming down with no sign of a break. It had started in the east, behind the range of mountains. Thin light showers fell from the gathering of high cold mare's-tail clouds that thickened and darkened and sank down on the hillsides in flat grey drizzle formations. Then on the third day the dark autumn blanket cloud came to swamp the floor of the glen itself. No winds, so it stayed where it was, soaking every inch of the valley with its tight continuous rainfall.

The sun was virtually blocked out and except at mid-day or in the depths of night every hour looked much the same as the next. The weather was bad enough to break the everyday working routines of the valley dwellers. It was a freak rainburst and they weren't prepared for it. Suddenly there were new tasks to be carried out. The livestock herds had to be brought in early from the fields, their pastures having flooded as soon as the great river burst its banks. They were lodged in their hundreds in the giant barns and byres on the lowest slopes. But by the fifth day, the water had risen to such a level that even these immense buildings were waterlogged and the animals had to be led higher up the hillsides, to be huddled in hastily built wooden shelters or in the tenements themselves.

While a great many peasants were occupied with the herds, others were taking their families onto higher floors of the shanties, out of reach of the flood. Elsewhere some were busy slaughtering and salting pigs and sheep to make room for the cattle and horses and grain stores. Others lumbered through the beechwoods and oak forests, hacking down trees and cutting the logs to make new walls and roofing and repair those structures broken by the speeding river. Some of the largest treetrunks were left uncut. The water was far too deep for teams of oxen to drag them, but the giant boles were floated to the buildings that needed them most—sometimes to shore up an entire tenement block.

Almost every building in the glen was undermined by the deluge and its swelling of the river. Even the few not made entirely of wood were flooded out or buckled by the pressure of rushing water, their thatched roofing broken down, their food-stores spoilt.

But of course it was in the vast shanties that the effects of the flood were felt at their worst. There was no time to build enough new shelters to house the people who swarmed up away from the lower levels, so within just a few days there was severe overcrowding as the refugees struggled to find what space they could for themselves and their families, their poultry and foodstuffs.

There was plenty of food in the granaries and warehouses. The harvests were only just over. But it could only be moved with difficulty. There wasn't enough to go round. Some of the youngest children had to be left to starve.

Soon fighting broke out on every floor of all the tenements—in places, at times, bad enough to need the intervention of guardsmen. And before the sudden headlong week was out, the great wooden boxes were overspilling with archers and patrols of lancers and sundry footsoldiers in riot helmets. From outside, on the empty hillsides or the overcast moors, the whole dark sprawling valley seemed as it ever was. But in all its buildings, inside away from the rain, the glen was running around like a hen with its head cut off. And there was no telling when the rains might stop.

Out of the tenements, high on the open hill, a young man sat under the meagre shelter of a tree, huddling under a blanket, limbs drawn in under it. There was a small buff beard on his closed reptilian face and it was sparse and grew slowly. He chewed on a long stick of wet grass as his eyes, hooded at the outer corners, looked around at what he could see of the slope below him, peering through the rain as it fell in lumps from the low ceiling of cloud. He was twenty years old but looked older.

He was a guardsman, which was why he was keeping watch out in the hills—though from the way he looked around it was clear he was doing more than just keeping an eye on things. He seemed to be looking out for someone. While his gaze scuttled about the gloomed valley he brooded on other things.

The five years had passed and he was now a full guardsman, an officer. And yet things weren't happening as fast or as well as he wanted. Ever since the night Jeo killed the guardsman all those years before, the freckled boy had been carefully, almost imperceptibly, always within the laws of the valley, held back. His superiors had never forgotten his claim that Jeo had changed, that he'd been no longer dangerous. So the events of that one fraught, bloodsplashed night had made Kyrie's opinion, his ranking in the hierarchy of things, something to be seriously doubted. He was almost suspected of some kind of distant collusion with the killer boy— and was now entrusted with only the most menial duties that someone of his rank could be made to carry out. All in all, his advance—which before that single faraway night had been so brisk and sure—had taken a jolting step backwards. And he could see no path to recovery.

He was still in command of a small patrol—but it had never grown in number. He'd moved into better quarters in his broch —but he was the last of his age to do so. He was accorded the absolute minimum of privilege and was always, every minute of his life, aware that his every most banal activity was under scrutiny.

In that time, in the wave of anger after Jeo killed the guardsman, the glen had become a harsher place. There was a new Guardian, an older man, whose grip was crushing. The age-old curfew had been extended by an hour. Movement was more restricted. The young were forbidden to go about in groups, even to help during the flood. Penalties for any offence were out of all proportion, seemingly vindictive, as if the valley were venging itself on its youth. New Shrieking Pits had to be dug.

Resentment welled among the youngsters in the tenements. It had always been there, in a mild form—now it was stronger. But there was little hope of changing things, less than ever. There were more guardsmen and they were a sterner breed. Meagher had shouldered some of the blame for the guardsman's killing. He was still a captain, but reduced to lesser duties, and he would never advance. New, harder men had command. The fat boy Ouse, for one, was now a sergeant, and he delighted in his duties and in his superiority over others—especially the lizard boy, once his leader.

Kyrie squinted through the downpour. There were no co-lours in the valley. Heavy grey and patches of black, the river far below winking very white like a river in a watercolour. There was no movement he could see. After a time he got up and walked the hill, the blanket tugged around him reaching to his knees. Below it, his legs were clothed in a thick wool hose tied with crossed string thongs. His boots were thick but the rain had still managed to soak through the hide and his feet were damp.

He walked more than a mile on the top of the hill and saw nothing, either in the valley or to his left where the first tract of moorland was indistinct in the rain, like something through a translucent window.

The way he now had to live was a continual reminder of how he'd misunderstood Jeo. The boy should have been easy meat, but Kyrie hadn't realised just how unstable he'd been—dangerously so, unpredictable and ultimately violent as a beast at bay. A huge mistake by the freckled boy, and he'd never recovered from it.

Now he was in the same position Jeo had been in. He managed a wry smile at the thought. He too was cornered, under continuous watch, his advancement stunted. For five years he'd endured the pressures and the various privations, the abuse from

Ouse and his captains, the cold shoulder of all the glen—and, though he was far more patient and forbearing than Jeo, he was now feeling the strain—and he knew he would soon want to break out in some way. To do that, to do anything at all, he needed an ally.

Something a long way down the slope moved through the rain. He stood very still and watched and as suddenly as it started, the movement was gone. For a moment, Kyrie thought it was just a wile of the rain. He set his lips and went on looking, just in case.

It moved again, whatever it was. Further away ahead of him, moving quickly across the flank of the hill. As soon as he saw it he set off down the slope.

The movement was that of an animal, brisk and surefooted as a goat—but it was too big, too tall, for a goat, too far down in the valley to be a stag or a wild horse. It had to be human. Kyrie quickened his stride down the hill.

The figure ahead of him seemed to be in a hurry. It drew rapidly away and he lost sight of it more than once. He broke into a run and gained on it for a while. But the waterlogged ground offered no sort of foothold. He had to slow to save himself from slipping at every step.

The dark figure appeared to have no such troubles. It skipped across the slope like the wraith of a deer. Before long, before it reached the blackness of the last great forest before the sea, it was gone from view in the blanket of rain.

Kyrie stopped for a moment. He scanned the grizzled hill with eyes squeezed almost shut. Not a thing. Not a shadow in the downpour.

He wasn't the kind to waste time standing around thinking about it. There was too much rain. Seeing there was nothing left to do, he set off back to his broch.

The same figure appeared once more, away to the right, moving parallel with him downhill. He followed at once. This time he didn't run towards his quarry. He simply carried on straight down the hill. It was easier this way, quicker than running across the slope with one foot always higher than the other. He took off his blanket and carried it bunched in one hand. The rain dashed straight through his wool shirt and soaked him to the skin but he took no notice. He was wet enough as it was, and now at least he could run faster. His arms, too, were free to stretch out, to keep his balance as he sprinted down the incline.

As soon as they both reached the lower part of the valley, where it was less steep, he turned to the right and chased directly after the grey form as it went on running towards the riverbank.

This time he gained on it very quickly. Soon he was close enough to see what it was, who it was. The girl he wanted to see. She had bare legs and a thick sprawl of hair and a one-piece tunic that was more dirty brown than gorse yellow, clinging to the shapes of her strong body.

She ran like a brood mare through the long grass, as though running nowhere, for the feel of it. Kyrie didn't care where or why she was running. He wanted to reach her before she reached the lowest slopes and all the dwellings, before anyone saw him going to her.

He ran harder still. Within yards, he was close to her, maybe ten paces away. The noise of the rain on grass had muffled his footsteps behind her, but now she felt his tread and glanced back through her hat of hair—then caught him by surprise by suddenly swerving sharply away to the right, back across the hill, not down it. Kyrie tried to turn, but too fast—the marshy ground slipped his legs from under him and he fell on his side on the wet grass, the force of the fall knocking the breath out of him.

He tried to get up, again too quickly. He was winded and had to stay on his hands and knees as he looked up to see where Rhosarran was running.

She was standing looking at him, some thirty paces ahead, breathing heavily. Her purple hair was blackened, thick with water. She held it away from her face in two long sheafs, one at each shoulder. Kyrie opened his mouth to talk but couldn't. The rainwater ran in at the corners of his mouth. She had a hard look in her eyes. She turned and ran away, towards the oakwood. The rain closed behind her.

Kyrie struggled to his feet and took a number of long harsh breaths, wincing. The rain ran like tears down the sides of his face as he stared through the deluge and snatched a small sight of Rhosarran as she galloped away to the forest. One last mouthful of air and he was running after her.

He knew he had almost no chance of catching her. He was still winded and she was probably faster anyway. Soon she would be lost in the labyrinthine wood where she spent so many of her free nights. He could hunt her for a year in there and never have a glimpse.

But he couldn't allow himself to think like that. He ran hard through the boggy field, finding the strength from somewhere, grunting with the pain under his ribs.

He remembered seeing her chest heave when she was looking down at him. She must surely be tiring too. The thought was enough to push his body to greater efforts. Far ahead of him, her pace didn't slacken—but he noticed she wasn't getting any further away. He dropped his blanket and pounded across the marsh. A wind came and pushed at him and he lowered his head and ran harder. By the time Rhosarran reached the first trees of the oakwood he wasn't far behind.

He pelted head-down through the first outcrop of bushes and found himself brusquely out of the rain in the darkness of the forest. He looked all around but the ling-haired girl was nowhere to be seen. He wasn't surprised.

There was silence as well as dark in the wood, the sounds of rain muffled by the dense canopy of overhead foliage. A few gaps in the treetops left room for thin cataracts of rainwater to come trickling down from branch to branch, almost the only sound in the forest, like water in a cave.

Kyrie set about trying to track the girl in the quiet and darkness, knowing she couldn't have gone very far in any direction. She must have been as tired as he was. Surely.

He bent to search the leaf litter at his feet, thick with acorns and twigs; in the poor light it seemed a single unbroken carpet, all the same dark colour and thickness. But it *had* been broken. No footprints, of course—but Kyrie saw the signs well enough, the spots where a foot had pressed into the oakleaf matting, leaving its slight mark. He found the girl's tracks and followed them between the trees.

A deep hooded sound echoed in the branches high above his head and he shot a glance to it. Somewhere in a tall oak, a small brown owl, the colour of tree bark, would be perched blinking, staring like the ghost of itself. Kyrie didn't see it. He went on looking for the imprints, trying to follow them as fast as he could. He had no idea how deep into the forest she might have gone.

He found the tracks harder to see as he moved into the thicker darkness in the deep of the wood. A few pools of light stippled some of the very few open glades, but there was no sunshine outside trying to get in, so the pools were dim and grey. Kyrie caught the faint blue green glow of a giant honey fungus which had eaten through to the heartwood of an old oak, causing it to collapse. It lay in a hill of leaves. A moss had covered it and the fungus was still there, glowing in the dark as it fed. Kyrie trod through it as he climbed over the trunk to make his way into the undergrowth beyond.

How close was the girl? Had she heard him following her? The foot-tracks came to an unexpected end and the freckled man was left standing on the edge of a very small hemmed clearing, staring around at the trees and listening to the silence.

Something fluttered above the tangled bushwork to his right. An old-lady moth or a leaf. He walked round the clearing, eyeing the dark shades at the top of each tree. He couldn't see a thing. Shadows and shapes of branches.

Where had she gone—and how? She must surely have climbed the tree beside the last of her tracks. But it was a pollard, no branches within reach. Could she have climbed the bare trunk to the first boughs high overhead? There was no glimpse of her in the tree. He went on looking. In this thick dry place he realised for the first time how wet he was, how cold his arms and legs.

A scuffling noise above him, in the fat tree next to him. A pair of big brown horseshoe bats fluttered clumsily out of the leafwork. Kyrie jerked his gaze upwards and found himself looking behind them, to where they'd come from—and saw, to his fright and his glee, that the heather girl was there above him, squatting on a thick branch and staring down at him like a rusalka in her tree. He saw her face through a gap in the creepers and her eyes were screeching at him. She looked older than he remembered.

He wiped the wet hair off his forehead. Neither of them moved—nothing but Rhosarran's eyes, showing in the gloom as they flitted to one side, hunting a place in the next tree, somewhere to jump. Kyrie watched and stood still. Even if she managed to leap across to the nearest oak she wouldn't go very far. She'd have to come down some time. They both understood. They both waited. But Kyrie didn't have time to waste. He raised both arms and held them up, inviting her to jump down. She rearranged herself on the branch but otherwise stayed firmly where she was. He dropped his arms back to his sides.

"I haven't come to hurt you." Even in that dense padded place his voice seemed too loud. He dropped it to just above a whisper. "I only want to talk, that's all."

Nothing. Her face stayed still and hostile. He couldn't even be sure she was listening.

"I know you can hear. There are things I want to tell you. We can help each other, you and me. Like you and Jeo wanted to do."

The mention of the name brought the first reaction. Her big lips moved in a grimace, showing her teeth, and she made harsh noises in the back of her mouth. Kyrie hid a frown. He made a small waving motion with his hand.

"No, it's alright. I knew Jeo. I was his friend."

The sounds in her throat rose to a high hiss and she grinned at him with derision.

"I knew him well—" he persisted, but a shake of her head cut him short. He tried again. "I saw him at the Gathering, and the day before that. We talked together. He was going to join me—"

She shook her head again and leaned out from her branch, holding on to a thong of ivy with one hand and pointing with the other, shaking a big accusative finger at him—then ran her forefinger across her throat.

"No," said Kyrie. "I didn't kill him. I didn't have anything to do with it. Listen—think what you want about me, but Jeo's dead and you and me we can still—look, I want the same things he did, can't you understand? I want to be more than I am now, while I'm still young. I want to take from the elders. And I'll do anything to take from them—anything. I'll kill one of the old men to do it. I'll kill all of them."

She stared at him with her head slightly on one side like a bird. She was angry. This was the first time she'd been out of Gara's sight for a week, since the rainstorm started. She'd managed to snatch a quick run down the hill, just to do something fast and active for once, something of her own—only to have it interrupted by this thin young guardsman, the one who'd been there when Jeo was stoned in the nettlefield and again when he was driven into the Pit. Now he was standing below her, staring up with his freckled face, lying to her. When he talked of killing an elder, she didn't believe him.

"Think what you like about me," he repeated. "But I did share this one thing with Jeo. I still feel the same. And I need you to help me do something—I don't know what. We could kill one of the elders. We could kill Gara, you and me. The two of us could find a way to do it."

He fell silent to watch her response. She seemed far away, as if pondering. He went on talking to keep her thoughts where he wanted them.

"That could be just the start. We could kill him and maybe a few more, maybe some of the guardsmen. We could get others of our age to help us. We both know some who'd do it. We could find a place to hide in the moors and the big marshes, make raids in the glen. And then anything could happen. I've been thinking about it for years. I've got plans."

She leaned her head to him just a fraction. He shook his shoulders to throw the chill from his neck. Another owl hooted somewhere, a single morbid note. Rhosarran licked her teeth, the tip of her tongue jutting in thought. The silence went on too long and Kyrie sensed he was losing her again.

"I'll do it myself," he said in what he guessed was a desperate tone. "On my own if I have to. I know you've had the same thoughts—but if you won't help me you can go back to Gara and I'll do it alone. It's the only way left now."

She closed her mouth and that was all. He had no more words to use. If she wasn't convinced by now, he knew he couldn't talk her any closer to him.

A pause with all its tensions. The forest was very dark now, darker almost by the minute. The silence seemed deeper than ever. He heard the raindrops through the high branches, very distant. Rhosarran nodded to herself.

"You'll do it, then?" he asked. "You'll think about it for a while, maybe see me the night of the rest day?"

She nodded again, brusquely, grudgingly. Kyrie put a thin smile on his mouth.

"We'd better go," he said. "We'll both be missed before long. Come down now. You know I won't hurt you."

She worked herself into a sitting position on the branch. Her tunic was pushed up to the top of her legs and Kyrie had time to notice the muscles of her thighs before she pressed herself out of the tree and jumped heavily to the ground beside him.

She missed her footing, overbalanced, and fell on her side in a clutch of ferns. The lizard man was at her side in an instant, and though she didn't need him he helped her to her feet.

For a few seconds they stood very close. He looked at her body and her big crude face framed in its dark muddle of hair, and saw that she seemed to be made entirely out of lumps—her shoulders and breasts and upper arms, all her features. She was big and unlovely—and yet, standing so close, Kyrie felt a throe in his belly. She looked like some kind of tree nymph, but a nymph that was full of flesh. He wanted to push his mouth against hers, not so much to kiss her as to bite her lips.

"We're each other's last chance," he said. "We should be closer—" He broke off and the rest of his sentence was stopped in his throat when she punched him high in the stomach with both fists, quashing the breath from his chest and knocking him down in a compost of leaves.

She was gone before he got up. He could hear her hurdling the undergrowth away to the left. He picked himself up and set off in pursuit—though again he had little chance of catching her. The forest was dark as charcoal and he didn't know any short cuts. By sheer persistence he stumbled his way out onto the open hillside, back into the rain.

He stood for a moment and tried to catch his breath as he looked to see where he was. Rhosarran was running up the long wet slope, more than halfway to the top, running strongly. There was no point chasing after her. He stood and stared at her, then turned away down the hill towards the river, then in the direction of his broch. He ran in the knowledge that he'd failed, once and for all—and when the girl betrayed him he would be as good as dead. He was going back to the fort to collect things, not to stay the night. He had no more time and there were only desperate actions ahead of him.

Rhosarran reached the top of the hill and turned to see if Kyrie was following her. No. She slowed to a walk and went along the ridge, taking no notice of the rain which was still pelting down. She tossed her hair over her shoulders and it clung to her back.

A small piece of thunder muttered far away in the east. She looked ahead and saw the old shepherd waiting for her not far ahead. He had a cap on his head and a grey wool cloak around his body. Beside him, the border collie got up off its haunches and looked at her.

She went up to Gara and stood in front of him. He used his fists to squeeze rain from his hair, his eyes almost shut as he looked at her.

"I saw that Kyrie with you," he said. "What did he want with you—and in the forest of all places."

She didn't let him know what the freckled man had said—not out of loyalty to Kyrie but because she hid everything from the old man whenever she could. She lied to him with her hands, running them across her breasts and belly and touching her mouth with her fingers. It was better Gara should believe Kyrie had touched her body than know of his rebellious thoughts.

The shepherd scowled. "I'll have the skin off his back," he said. "Encourage him, did you? Made him feel welcome?"

She shook her head but he pulled her to him with his crook and held her very close and searched her eyes but all they showed was the usual everyday hatred so he released her.

"Go home," he said. "Build the fire and warm the bed—and hope I don't find you've been lying to me. Go now."

He cuffed her with his crook and she ran away along the hillcrest, losing herself in the rain. The shepherd faced the distant forest and pulled his cloak tighter under his neck.

He was troubled. He wondered if it was all happening again, his girl and some outcast boy. First Jeo, now this failed guardsman youth. He knew he ought to go and tell one of the captains, but if he did, they might take Rhosarran from him. He would tell them nothing. He went to see his sheep. The dog followed a few paces behind and sneezed.

Rhosarran jogged through the darkness and blew the rain from her mouth as it ran down her face. She was thinking of the lizard-faced man. She had no intention of seeing him on the night of the rest day. She didn't believe him. He would never be so desperate, enough to kill an elder. Jeo, yes—she'd always believed he could do it. He was that kind. But a soulless little schemer like Kyrie? She ran on to the stone hut, the thought of someone killing old Gara uppermost in her mind.

The distant thunder went another way and didn't reach the valley. So the only sound in the night was the relentless drivel of the rain. It ran down the sides of the castle keep and the old man in robes coughed as he limped away from the window ledge.

The Body

THE RAIN WAS REMORSELESS AS EVER, but patches of dim light had appeared in the mass of cloud, so the valley was brightened, slightly, in places. It was still gloomy overall, and the dark horse on the top of the hill was almost invisible in the rain and dun light.

The horse stood without moving its feet on the crest of the southern slope. Sometimes it turned its head or snorted rainwater from its nostrils or worked the bit with the back of its mouth. Otherwise nothing.

It was facing downhill, so its rider could look over its head into the glen. He too was motionless, hands at rest on the pommel, the reins loose in his fingers, shifting only his head as he stared down through the drizzle at the highest tenements far below.

He was in light armour and his beard was grey. He was several years older than his predecessor as Guardian. There were big lines under his eyes. His eyes were on one of the hillside forts below him as he tried to piece a few things together in his mind. He was thinking about the short young guardsman with the freckled face, the one who'd recently disappeared. Why had he vanished —and where?

They'd searched for him, of course—at once, as soon as he failed to report for his duties one morning. Patrols of soldiers had walked the hills and woods and picked their way through the tenements. But there were so many places to hide and the young man hadn't been found. It was only a question of time, the Guardian knew that—but what preyed on his mind was the reason for it. Why had he run away? Was he dead somewhere, killed, the body buried? Certainly no one in the valley had any love for him. But who would murder a sworn guardsman out of banal dislike? The penalty was too great. No, he was in hiding—that much was certain. But, again, why?

He'd last been seen with the mute sheepgirl. Gara had seen them together. So what did she have to do with it? The boy had touched her body. Or so Gara said. So the girl had told him. Had he gone underground because of that, out of fear that the girl would tell and have him punished? No, it seemed unlikely. For touching an elder's woman, Kyrie would have been beaten and deprived of food and shelter for a time. But that wasn't enough of a threat to make him run. He was used to such treatment. And now, when found, his punishment would be harsher for having dared to try and avoid it. But then the freckled man would know all that. He would realise the reprisal could only be worse. He was no fool. So why hide? Where was the sense in it?

The Guardian moved his feet in their stirrups. There was something more to all this—his every instinct told him so—some larger crime against the glen and its tenets. The boy and the girl . . . what had they been speaking of, this dark horse of a lass and the young man who'd once had words with the dead traitor Jeo? There had to be some link between the three. He couldn't see it.

He was certain, however, there was something between the last two of them. Something against the order of things, a hint of sedition. He would have to stamp it out.

With hindsight he knew Jeo should have been executed sooner, at the slightest suspicion, the first look in his eye. The last Guardian should have been more vigilant. But, there again, all children had a look in their eye at some time in their life—they couldn't all be slaughtered for it. And Jeo had seemed so insignificant then. Now the Guardian saw it differently. Now it would make sense to have the shepherd girl thrown in a Pit, housegirl of an elder though she was. And the runaway youth too, when they found him.

But he couldn't be sure these were the only two youngsters

involved. How many others might be feeling the same pulse of revolt? He couldn't know—and because of that, he knew he couldn't have the girl killed until the boy had been taken. Then they would both be put to the question—and if others were implicated they would all die.

First, of course, Kyrie had to be found. It rankled with the Guardian that he was in hiding at all. In the years since Jeo murdered the guardsman, security in the glen had become crushingly tight—for the young especially, for Kyrie perhaps above all —and yet he'd slipped away unseen and had yet to be caught. It made a mockery of the guardsmen and their methods, the kind of thing that impaired the authority of a Guardian.

Still, the boy would be unearthed, that much was certain. The Guardian rubbed the horse's neck and looked up to the top of the hillside across the river. The forests and moors had been searched yard by yard. They were empty. Only the tenements were left. When the flood ebbed, an intensive hunt would take place. There would be no escape for the renegade. The Guardian lifted his head back to look at the sky. Small dim black shapes were shooting through the clouds. Hawks. Because he could see them, he knew the clouds were thinning. That was good. They would find Kyrie soon. The rains couldn't go on forever.

Winds came at long last and lifted the cloud cover and the valley began the long process of drying itself out. While the commoners set about the tasks of rebuilding and rehousing, the army of the glen formed itself into small detachments and delved through every floor of the shanties in search of the lizard man.

Almost every guardsman in the valley was occupied with the search, far more than the number who'd pursued Jeo five years back. The repairs and restoration and drainage needed little military supervision. All day and night the guardsmen ranged through the tenements like a plague of soldier ants.

They worked in small bands, patrols of no more than half a

dozen, led by a sergeant and accompanied by a pack of tracker dogs.

One of these groups, roaming the lower storeys of the most westerly block, came to a halt at the junction of three dim passageways. They stood, the five of them, and peered into the darkness of each tunnel, the two torchbearers holding their firebrands high over their heads. The bumptious light made the shadows jump, but nothing else moved and there wasn't much sound except the continuous noise of water dripping on wet wood. Two of the other guardsmen led dogs on leashes, a pair of animals each—four brindled bull terriers, all shoulders and chest and no neck. Their handlers didn't so much lead as hold them back. They were young beasts, only half-trained, and they heaved on their leashes as they sniffed the darkness, scrabbling with their short front feet. One of the handlers cursed and hit his leading dog with the flat of his sword. He went on cursing as the dog insisted on its tugging—but then the patrol leader held up a hand and he fell silent.

The sergeant was a tall heavy man with red hair and a rust beard, a young man in his early twenties, though he looked much older. As a boy, he'd been fat. Now he was more solid and muscular, though his eyes were still pinched by the swell of his cheeks, like those of a pig. Under one of his eyes, his cheek was still marred by a small thin scar, no more than a nick in the skin, where one of Jeo's stones had cut him, one night by the sea.

Like the rest of his group—who were all very young, the merest cadets—he wore chain mail to his knees and leather leggings below, and a light iron helmet with noseguard and cheekflaps. He stood and listened very hard and peeked with his little eyes into each of the tunnels, which were no more than wells of black, despite the stark light of the torches.

Ouse looked down the passage on his left. It was very narrow and rather spick, quite empty. The one ahead was much wider, cluttered with leaning planks and soggy beams and pieces of rotted wall. The floor was thick with mud, more than ankle-deep in river silt, the whole place smelling strongly and fustily of very wet old timber. The third corridor—Ouse didn't look in the third corridor. He'd made up his mind.

"This way, straight ahead. He's got more places to hide down there."

The dog handlers led the way, the light-bearers close behind or alongside where possible, their torches held higher than before. The sergeant brought up the rear. He did most of the looking around, squinting ahead to where the lamplights uncovered a thousand recesses in the dark wooden cloister. At times, he glanced back, or searched the rafters above—the small, grim places where a short young man might hide with a weapon in his hand.

As they moved through the dark, drenched passage, they passed any number of shanty dwellers leaving to look for refuge on the upper floors, carrying their belongings in sacks. They bowed to the elders, cuffed the running children, held up their torches to scan the faces of young men. The torch flames guttered in strange internal gusts that howled in the distance as though the tenement were some huge broken woodwind. There were flies everywhere and the smell of charcoal had been overcovered by the smells of damp.

"They're real keen, Senior. I can hardly hold them back. May well be they seen something. Shall we let them run on ahead?"

"No," said Ouse. "Hold them a while longer. There's still hundreds of people down here. There's no knowing who these bloody animals might go for. The mood they're in, they might even attack an elder. Keep them at bay for now."

Something moved up ahead. A very black, very vague shape. The light from the torches reached just far enough to catch it. Immediately, Ouse sent two of the dogs, their handler and a torch-bearer running into the passageway. They turned the corner into another hall, Ouse and the other two close behind. The sergeant tugged his sword from its sheath. He grinned as he ran, thinking it was apt he should be here, hunting the sand-haired man to his death. He himself was a believer. He believed in the sanctity of old age and its rule in law. The freckled man, once his superior, did not. If he, Ouse, could be the one to kill him, promotion would follow as sure as a night.

He turned the corner and looked down the long passageway. He looked beyond the guardsmen just in front of him, to where the others were running ahead. By the torchlight of the latter two, he could just make out—some distance further on—a short black figure sprinting deeper into the dark at the far end of the gallery.

"Let the dogs go," he called. "Head him off towards the river end."

As the others ran on ahead of him, a muffled noise made him turn, towards the place where the dark figure had first appeared. He held his sword in front of him at waist level in both hands. Another, softer noise. He stepped carefully towards it. He couldn't see very well—his eyes had grown used to the light of torches and here he was in pure darkness. He groped with his feet, listening for the sound, hoping to follow it—but it was gone, leaving the usual patter of raindrops, his own breathing, the distant sounds of the chase.

Soon he could distinguish shapes and shadows, but he was nonetheless grateful for the tonsil of drab light that inched into the corridor through a slit in the wall. It brought a grey cobweb to life, spangled with drops of water—and, on the floor, something else. A spreadeagled shape near a door of planks.

He dropped to one knee and looked closely at the supine thing, and bit his mouth with shock. A fresh corpse. The throat had been cut, slashed deeply and thoroughly just above the collar. The neck and chest and clothes and floor, most of the face—they were black, with blood not in shadow. It was the body of an old man, a tenement elder. Ouse stood up and glanced around in the dark. He felt soiled and somehow accused just by being there. He ran away down the long gallery to rejoin his patrol.

There was nothing he could do about the act of sacrilege— it was done—but he could bring punishment to the murderer. His soldiers would have seized the freckle-faced man by now. They would be holding him for their sergeant to come and cut his throat. Fleet though he might be, he could never outrun the terrier dogs.

They never caught the lizard youth. When the dogs were found, three of them were barking at the foot of an old wood ladder leading to a trapdoor slammed shut in the ceiling of a deserted room. The other dog was lying on its side, dead as mutton, its head almost carved from its body by a single slash from a long knife.

The Knife

THE SECOND BODY WAS FOUND two days later. At first light, the menfolk of a family quartered high in one of the southern tenements stumbled yawning from their room. At the end of the passageway they came upon a small child weeping beside the body of her grandfather. The old man's dust-yellow robes were russet where blood had blurted from his knife wounds.

They came and took the body away. The child sat all day in a room and cried into her hands. There was blood on her arm where the assassin had brushed her with his knife. But he'd left her alive. The soldiers asked her why. She didn't know. She didn't understand much of what had happened. It had all been so savage and quick. The old man had been leaning on her shoulder as she helped him along the corridor, his other hand holding a small flametorch, which had been struck from his hand as someone sprang at him from a gap in the wall—and punched him, so it seemed, in the chest, many times, as he lay on the floor. The child had thrown herself across her grandfather's body, but the attacker had torn her away with one hand as he hit the body again.

What troubled the captains and the elders was the fact that the two murders had taken place in separate shanties, one on each bank of the glen. The river and all the land on either side was patrolled by men and dogs, yet the killer had found a way past. The patrols were doubled, reinforced by cavalry and more crossbowmen. Every one of the tenements was sealed at its base, ringed by a hundred men. At night each block was circled by an unbroken line of soldiers, each with a burning lantern. Within two days the

net had tightened to the point where no one could move in or out
of the townships without being seen. The traitor youth had to have
a den of some kind, a place to hide in the day before roaming the
warrens at night. Since he could no longer move from one tenement to another, his escape routes were now surely limited. Hundreds of men were poured into each of the blocks to flush him out.

Inside, the valley dwellers went in fear of their lives. They
barred their ramshackle doors at night, left the two strongest men
at home during the day to guard the eldest member of the family.
It was clear the murderer sought only the old as his prey, but even
so the youngsters stayed inside, terrorised like the rest. The corridors were empty. Even the small wild dogs seemed to sense the
unease and hid in their holes. A fearful tension came to the tenements and people huddled as they waited for this one single
maverick boy to be caught.

The guardsmen, for their part, were in a way grimly satisfied.
Their duty was being seen to be done. The townships were sealed
and filled with troops. Though they had no idea where he was,
the killer youth was at their mercy. Now if he killed so much as
a mouse or stole the smallest scrap of bread they would know in
which block he was confined and could concentrate all their efforts
in that one place.

Another elder had died, and that was a hard blow to the
army, to the Guardian above all—his position, like that of his
precursor, was very unsteady now—but if they could seize Kyrie
before he did any more damage, they might redeem themselves.
And it was still just a matter of time, of waiting. The boy had to
eat and drink. He would have to show his hand again soon.

The rains had gone. The sky was white. The end of the day had
a good clean autumn chill to it. The air was slightly warmer on
the flat river basin, but high on the slopes there were sharp winds.
The shepherds pulled their cloaks tightly around them.

One of them, Rhosarran, had no cloak at all. The wind blew

her grubby tunic against her back and waved her piles of hair in front of her face, so she had to turn and face the breeze to let her hair flee behind her, then pull it back and plait it in a single heavy mare's tail which bounced between her shoulderblades when she turned and walked on. There was no need for a leather strap or piece of twine. She used some of the hair itself to make the knot.

She was walking to join old Gara, to accompany him to the assembly of elders that was to take place later that evening among the megaliths on the plain across the river. And she was walking with a jaunt in her step. She couldn't hide it though she tried to.

Kyrie had killed. As he'd said he would. Two old men. And she was proud of him, of his daring and the very fact of his revolt. She wished she'd believed him, that time in the forest. She hadn't believed because there was no look in his eye, nothing of the glint she'd seen in Jeo. And yet he'd killed. She hadn't thought she could be so wrong. She should have gone with him. She wished she had. She wished she had his courage.

As she walked, she glanced to the right to see if she was being watched, then to the left at the expanse of moorland, staring to see the horizon lost in the murky light. How far did the moors reach? Did they ever come to an end, she wondered—and was there somewhere else out there, out of sight? Perhaps one day she would find out. It was something Jeo had often talked of doing.

Her thoughts were interrupted by the appearance of the border collie. In fact it had been there for some time, on the hillcrest, but she hadn't seen it while staring out over the heath. She came quite close to it. It sat still on the rough grass and looked back at her. She hated the dog. It seemed to have Gara's eyes on her when he was away. She bulged her eyes at it and showed her teeth, growling from the back of her throat. The collie curled its mouth very slightly, just for a moment—then nothing, no reaction. It knew she wouldn't harm it.

Rhosarran looked away. The old shepherd had told her to meet him where she found his dog. Now he was late—and that was unlike him. Perhaps, she hoped, he was unwell after all the days of rain, or lying injured somewhere, having slipped on the steep wet slopes. She allowed herself to think that perhaps Kyrie had somehow escaped from the tenements and found the shepherd out in the hills. She remembered what he'd said. We could kill Gara, you and me. She hadn't believed him at the time.

Half an hour went by and her hopes rose. The collie got up and walked to the top of the slope to stare into the valley. A small noise came from its throat.

She glanced straight along the ridge and wasn't surprised to see the shepherd hurrying towards her, using his crook as a walking stick, his cloak flapping as he tried to keep it close with his other hand. The collie waved its tail a little, then sat down.

Gara was swearing when he reached her, muttering something about a ewe with its back legs broken. She didn't listen. His hircine smell was strong.

"Damned bloody bastard animals. I ought to throw the lot of them down the Pits. They're nothing but trouble. Come on, girl —the damned meeting's at sundown and there's no time to stand here admiring the bloody view."

He set off down the slope and the collie dog scampered after him. Rhosarran tried to keep her distance as she followed, but her natural step was quicker and the shepherd was tired, so before long she was keeping pace with him down the hill, striding alongside.

By the time they reached the river the light was bad and Gara was more agitated. He was in danger of being late. They crossed the river on a wide stone bridge. Before they reached the other side, the riverbanks echoed to a number of shouted commands. Then the growing darkness of the valley was shattered by the sudden almost simultaneous striking of a thousand tinderboxes and the lighting of tall firesticks around the foot of every tenement.

The old man and the girl stood for a moment and watched it all. The whole valley seemed to be on fire, the shanty towns about to burn, the river itself feverishly alight. The glen on fire. Rhosarran wished it were true. Burn it to the ground. The firelight made her eyes glow.

"They've got him now," said Gara. "Look at it. Every one of the blocks surrounded. Even a rat couldn't get out of there. The same brat who put his hands on you—they'll catch him before long. Pleased, aren't you?"

Yes, she nodded. Yes, pleased. It showed on her face. She was pleased for what the freckled man had done. The shepherd hurried across the bridge and she followed with an open smile on her mouth.

They passed a number of the towering blocks on their way up the other slope. Rhosarran looked at the lines of guardsmen beside their rows of torches tied to tall stakes in the ground and spluttering in the wind. She saw the groups of archers and the captains shouting, the mastiffs and their handlers, the horsemen. The tenements rose high overhead, greasy bright at the base, the upper storeys lost in the falling dusk.

It was already dark by the time they gained the very top of the hill. At the circle of standing stones no one noticed their late arrival.

From a distance, the stones appeared to be glowing. At close range, within the henge itself, the scene was much the same as around each of the tenements far below. The amber glow came from a score of torches held by young guardsmen standing in a ring, watching over a group of elders in formal robes.

Gara led the way through the circle of troops and stood in silence at the edge of the huddle of old people, his head bowed, Rhosarran just behind him.

From there, she could look over his shoulder and see what was going on. The soldiers were holding their torches on long pikes above their heads, so while their faces and those of the elders were lurid in the lights, their lower garments and feet were patched with deep shadow. There was a wind and the evening was cold, so the old people wore their thickest robes, some with the white hoods drawn over their faces.

Rhosarran looked around. The great stones were bright in the light, blotted with shadows. Away across the flat ground, beyond

the ring of torches, she could make out just the outline of the
farthest pillars. They were very dark, like pieces of the night itself.
She was apprehensive about this place. It was cold and archaic,
where only the chief soldiers and the very eldest rulers were taken
after death. The things she hated about the glen were there now
—old people, old things, the guardsmen.

Nothing happened in that strange circle. No one said anything. Rhosarran began to wonder why they were all gathered
there. She knew they were meeting to talk about the killings—
but no one was talking. She looked around again. The elders
seemed to be taking no active interest in anything, not even in one
another. They stood and stared. One was nodding his head, another
smiling to herself. There were other youngsters there, like herself
companions of the old—wrapping cloaks around them, wiping
their mouths, holding them upright. She was thankful that at least
her old man wasn't yet so feeble as to need this kind of ministry.
She knew the time would come and the thought revolted her.

She recognised some of the guardsmen though she didn't
know all their names. Most were big and bearded. She saw Ouse
yawn as he leaned on his torch-staff like a pig on a post. Another
was very tall and ashen and had no beard, though he was older than
some, a man called Ure. Meagher was there, half-hidden in the
gloom just outside the circle of torchbearers. Rhosarran couldn't
help smiling to herself whenever she looked at him. The glow of
the flames lit his face and made a black line of the scar that his beard
couldn't hide. His lower lip was cut in two, a pair of flaps. Jeo was
dead but he'd left his mark.

Four of the guardsmen broke ranks and went to the far side
of the henge, where they divided into pairs and stood at each pillar
of a dolmen, their torches lighting the heavy capstone above. They
stood stiffly upright, a guard of honour. The rest of the gathering
turned to face the stone arch.

A sound of hooves. It grew louder. There were clearly two
animals approaching, one much heavier than the other yet somehow lighter on its feet.

Rhosarran glanced at Gara beside her. She was surprised to see him with his head bowed, not looking up at all, hands clasped below his waist, in an attitude of reverence she'd never seen from him before. The other elders were doing the same, their eyes averted from the archway.

All the guardsmen stood to attention, their eyes on the elders as though keeping watch. The young attendants kept their heads bowed like their old masters—but Rhosarran, who'd never been to such an assembly before, stood and watched the dolmen to see what was happening. Gara punched her breast and pulled her tunic to make her bow her head. She did, but she kept her eyes on the arch, looking up from under her brow. She rubbed her palm over her breast and soon the pain went away.

The snort of a beast broke above the mutter of hooves. Then the pitch darkness of the opening between the stones was burst by the torchlights flashing on a powerful brown horse that came trotting heavily into the enclosure with a man in full armour on its back.

Still the elders kept their heads bowed. Rhosarran stared at the rider, the Guardian. The cross-stone above was like a low lintel to him and he had to lower his head as he rode in. He wore a bulky war helmet and a breastplate, iron leggings and a shield, and there were two swords on the horse's flanks. The armour was burnished bright and sheened in the torchlight as if he were a god of flame. All very dramatic, but she'd seen the Guardian often enough, so she wasn't impressed.

He pulled at the reins and led the horse away to one side, to another dolmen, where he stayed, in the shadows, the horse stationary and silent. Rhosarran looked for a moment, then turned back to the archway.

The sound of the second, smaller animal was closer. The gateway stones framed another figure, and the girl raised her eyebrows at what she saw.

A tiny huddled man in big white robes and hood was bent over the neck of his mount, a black mule. The beast was short and squat. It had a very wide back, which was just as well, because the rider looked distinctly unsteady in the saddle, swaying precariously as the mule shambled disinterestedly into the compound.

There was movement in the crowd and Rhosarran looked around, lifting her head. Every head was now bared. Even the Guardian and his soldiers had removed their helmets. All hands were clasped. Rhosarran did the same.

She'd never seen the tiny figure this close before, though she knew who he was. He hadn't ventured out from the castle for years —now here he was, the oldest man in the valley, sacrosanct and all-powerful, perched on a mule in front of her.

Two of the elders moved out of the crowd towards their overlord. The Guardian put his helmet back on and the other guardsmen did the same.

The two elders stood together on one side of the mule. They held up their arms and the wide sleeves fell down to their elbows. They helped the Elder down from the saddle and stood him on the ground. One of them led the mule away and left it beside one of the menhirs, where it idly chewed at a crop of heather.

The Elder made no attempt to join the assembly. They came to him. They stood in the centre of the clearing and muttered in small, soft voices.

Rhosarran had to stay where she was, in a group with the other youngsters, watching while the talking went on. She tried to catch a sight of the Elder's face but it was hidden by his cowl.

She saw Ouse and an old captain move across and stand beside the neck of the horse, where they talked with the Guardian. She saw the other guardsmen looking around the henge, watching the dark spaces between the stones.

And she saw something else, though just for a moment. A brief black shape on the capstone of the highest dolmen. A huge raven, perhaps—though it didn't look like a bird. But anyway it was gone in an instant. The outline of a distant cloud or just a joke of the light and shade. She looked away at the flock of elders.

She knew they were discussing the double killing in the

tenements, though the real talking was done by the Guardian and his two subordinates. She thought again how the entire valley was up in arms, disturbed to its foundations by one youth with a knife.

Something moved again on one of the stone pillars—a different pillar, though the black shape was the same. Again only Rhosarran saw it. At that moment, the Elder slipped weakly to one knee despite the attentions of his supporters. Just as he did so, something flickered in the torchlight as it shot down from the top of the column.

It sped like a shining pebble, too quick for anyone to catch more than a quick bright glimpse, and struck the old woman closest to the Elder, hitting her just beside the breastbone. She fell like a clump of rags, without a cry. Rhosarran, taken aback like everyone else, glanced to the top of the monolith, but the black figure was gone.

Pandemonium. The guardsmen were running everywhere, round the stones and into the night, clustering round the old people, holding up shields, drawing their clubs. Some of the elders fell to their knees, clutching at each other, shouting. Children shouted too and the stones echoed the noise.

It was a new kind of terror. They realised that even here, in their most hallowed place, they weren't safe.

Ouse moved to where the old woman lay on her back and knelt beside the body. Chacmagh's one long tooth poked from its jaw, the eyes in the baboon face open and staring. He looked at her chest. The handle of a skean jutted from the white sackcloth—a small, neat highland dagger, standard issue for a guardsman.

Ouse ignored the panic all around him. He looked to the Guardian still poised on his horse. The man returned his gaze but with vacant eyes. The killing of a third elder, and he had failed to prevent it. He was finished as Guardian. He looked away to watch the heather-haired girl in the group of youngsters across the clearing. She was caught, the whole of her heavy body, in the glare

of torchlight, as he stared hard at her face—but she put absolutely
no expression on it.

A thick valley fog reached high up the slopes on both sides of the
river. It made the afternoon look like evening.

The elders had been moved out of harm's way, into the castle,
where even the most intrepid young killer couldn't reach them. As
for the young homicide himself, he had the new Guardian and his
captains deeply shaken. They couldn't understand how he'd escaped from the tenements. There were no underground tunnels, the
cordon of soldiers had been very tight, he couldn't fly. How then?
The area around the standing stones had been thoroughly searched
and nothing had been found. The Guardian was at a loss. While
he pondered, his guardsmen swarmed deeper into the dark slum
blocks and went back to the long thankless work of scouring the
hills and forests, the moors and even the seashore, where they
questioned the old fisherman Sligo and found out nothing.

Gara had been left behind when the elders were led off into
the fortress—left at his own wish. He was the youngest of the
ancients, he didn't think he was one of them, and he felt hale
enough to carry on his daily tasks out on the hillsides. Not that
he was ever left alone out there. A pair of guardsmen stood by and
kept watch while the old man and his housegirl spent the afternoon
repairing one of the drystone walls on the northern slope.

Rhosarran lifted the flat grey stones one after the other and
placed them in and on the wall as the shepherd directed. He wasn't
strong enough to lift them himself anymore, and she was too
young to place them without instruction. She laboured tirelessly
through the day, heaving the rocks with her hard muscles, obeying
Gara's commands without ever fully listening to him. Her mind
was on the events of the night before.

Somewhere on another slope they were burying old Chacmagh in an oak box, with wild flowers and long monotonous

laments and a retinue of children. Rhosarran was thinking of the knife that killed the old woman, and the dark figure moving along the top of the pillars.

She glanced about as she went on with her work. Gara was on the other side of the wall, kneeling to inspect the masonry, muttering to himself as he now often did. The two guardsmen were standing beyond him, not far, both full-grown crossbowmen with heavy beards. The fog was thick. They were armed but uneasy. Against an unseen enemy who knew how to throw a knife they felt strangely unprotected.

As if in answer to their fears, an armed figure came running up the hill towards them. They held their crossbows ready but it was an unnecessary gesture. They could see the newcomer was another guardsman.

He stopped in front of the old shepherd and bowed with his head. "Beg to inform you, Senior, one of the sergeants thinks he seen the killer down by the watermill."

Gara got to his feet and eyed the man. "Good," he nodded. "But why come all this way to tell me that? I can't do anything about it, and you're away from your post."

"Captain says we need all the men we can find this side of the river. Including your two here, Senior."

The old man scowled. "Where does that leave me then, boy? I'm supposed to stay out here on my own, am I? What if the sergeant saw nothing but his own shadow? I have to take on the murderous young bastard alone if he turns up, is that it? Has your precious captain thought of that? Does he want the blood of an elder on his hands?"

"Beg please to inform, Senior—captain says if you'll come with us first to our broch, you'll be safe there—"

"No, damn it. I've got this wall to finish."

"Captain says—"

"I'm not leaving this wall till it's done, boy. Tell your captain that."

The guardsman moved his shoulders in a gesture of helplessness. "I have to take your guard with me, Senior," he said quietly.

Gara gave him a sour look. "Take them, then. Keep them, for all I care. Go away, all of you, and leave me to my work."

The soldiers hesitated, but not very long. They ran down the hill and dissolved in the smoke of fog.

Gara turned back to the wall and spat on it. Rhosarran was doing nothing on the other side, waiting for his orders. He knelt behind the wall to check the condition of the stones. He was sure the fair-haired killer would find him before long. He was the only elder left out in the open. But he was ready. The thin iron breastplate under his cloak would be protection enough against a thrown dagger, and as soon as the weapon was thrown, one shout from him would bring a dozen guardsmen to his side out of the fog. All he had to do was keep his eyes open and wait. He shifted his fingers along the wall and listened for any small noises behind him.

Rhosarran followed him along the wall, still on the other side. She looked down and saw the old border collie looking up at her. She frowned. What was it doing there, on her side of the wall? It usually stayed close to the shepherd. Perhaps it had come back from chasing a hare across the slope and found itself on this side. Not that it mattered.

She snarled silently at the dog. It looked back at her but didn't move. She turned to resume work on the wall. The collie turned to go away. She took one of the big flat topstones and flung it down on the dog.

She aimed for its head but the rock was so broad it crushed the collie's neck as well, killing it without much sound.

Gara got up off his knees, to stretch his legs and tell Rhosarran how to build up the next section of wall. As soon as he was upright, she hit him in the face with a small heavy rock and he fell back on the grass.

She vaulted the wall with the stone in her hand. The old man was getting up. He was on his knees again, cursing in confusion. There was blood on his face and she aimed for the blood, smashing

the rock into his cheek and flattening him to the ground. He fell
and lay with all his limbs splayed and didn't move again. The girl
knelt briefly on his chest and hit his head with the rock again,
twice, harder than before, then dropped the piece of stone and ran
away down the hill.

Down in the bowl of the valley, the fog was thicker. She
could hardly see the ground in front of her as she ran. The floods
had made a marsh of all the grasslands, quagmires of the land close
to the river. She slipped and she fell and her tunic became dirtier
than ever and her knees were padded with mud. Things loomed
out of the fog—walls and fence posts and hedges, trees damp with
fog-drip, a small herd of cows—and they all frightened her.
Because she didn't see them till they were very close and because
they were vague in the mist, any of them might have been a sentry
or an informer.

She ran through the swamp meadows of the valley floor and
finally reached one of the smaller bridges across the river. She
listened before crossing it, heard nothing but the water lapping the
bank. She sprinted over the bridge, down the stone steps at the far
end, and on, through the reed beds beside a mudded cart track.

In the reeds the ground was slower than anywhere else, the
water reaching almost to her knees—but she couldn't stay on
the road for fear of meeting someone. So she waded through to
the end of the marsh, brushing aside the heads of the bullrushes
with her forearms.

A noise in the swamp scared her, the sound of something
crashing through the water. She squatted in the mud, hidden by
reeds, and watched as a bulky shape moved in the fog in front of
her. A horse, small and riderless. A stray dale pony. She waited for
it to pass before she moved on.

Once out of the reed bed she was on firmer ground, the mud
thicker but drier on the first slope of the hill. It was a struggle to
reach the top but she pushed with her strong legs and clutched at
the grass with her hands and at last she had the long incline behind
her and was standing on level ground overlooking the valley.

She stopped to catch some breath and stared down into the glen to see if anyone was following her. She could hardly see a thing. Just the grey density of mist, with a pale white fogbow arching over it. The glen might have been many miles below her for all she could see, the tenements in another world altogether. If there was a sun, it was invisible.

Tall dark figures appeared in the mist ahead. The great standing stones. She meant to go on past them, on across the moor. Instead she went towards them.

They were long high humps of bluestone, thinned and rounded at the top, grizzly in the fog, like skinny giants in hooded robes. She stood at the foot of the first monolith and stared up the height of its grey flank.

The stonework was pocked all over its surface with what might have been the remains of runic inscriptions or the marks left by ancient hammers. Most of the dents were small and shallow, mere nicks in the rock, but in a few places they were deeper, big enough to fit a small fist. She put her head to one side to look at them. Yes, the high stone could be climbed. It was just possible.

Something moved above her, dark and very quick. It skimmed the top of a cromlech—and on, out of sight. Just a moorland bird on its way back. Rhosarran walked away towards the open moors.

A small rock came down from the height of a sarsen and bounced into a nest of fern grass. She glanced at it, then looked sharply up at the top of the column. Did pieces simply fall off like that, through wind or rain or old age? There was no rubble in the enclosure, scarcely a pebble.

Another rock landed behind her, close by, and she turned quickly, searching the capstones. Nothing. Not a shadow in the fog. She stood her ground and waited but there were no more falling rocks.

High above her, behind her back, on top of the lowest pillar, a short black figure appeared and crouched on the stone with the pale moon at its back. It stayed there without moving until the

girl turned to look behind her. Then it stood up and showed itself
to her, hands firmly on hips.

Rhosarran stared. The silence was like something about to
burst. She took a few steps across the grass and stood under the
high stone, looking up at the self-important figure. He looked
thinner after the furtive days in hiding, more tensile. His hair
seemed to have grown very quickly. It was a mane around his head,
down to his shoulders. He didn't speak to her.

She held up both her arms to him, her hands spread open. He
just looked at her. She moved sideways around the pillar to see his
face in the moonlight. The light touched his face and she dropped
her arms to her sides.

It wasn't the lizard boy at all. The face was very white, the
overgrown hair far too dark. And the look in the eyes was very
different. There were no freckles.

For a moment, Jeo stood in a gloating silence. Then he
laughed, like a young beast with blood in its mouth. Then Rhosarran felt very weak. She was strong, but the killing of the shepherd
and the long run in the fog and now the sudden surprise had all
tapped her strength. She couldn't feel her legs and her eyes saw
nothing but mist and she fell almost gratefully into a heavy faint
on the fog-damp grass with the laughter of the Pictish youth
chanting through her head.

The Tombs

BLACKNESS LIKE TAR AND COAL and the deepest earth. Outside, a moon in the night, stars, a thousand torches in the valley. But inside the hill, underground, black as blindness.

On the hilltop plain, two squat stones supported a capstone, forming the entrance to what had once been a beehive burial mound of soil and turf, long since eroded. The stones and the mound were never tombs in themselves. The tombs were still there, under the earth.

A cleft in the ground was hidden by a mess of fern grass and nettles, thick as a bush. Down in the hole, narrow stone steps led to one of the tunnels of a labyrinth, the ceiling low so a tall man would have to stoop along it. The walls were like the ceiling, of stone. There were alcoves in the walls, twenty along the length of each, with a single stone coffin inside. The lids of the coffins had been lifted, the graves plundered—and the reek of ancient death was still there in the cramped air, blotting the smells of damp and soil.

There was no light in the labyrinth. A man would have to feel his way with his fingers on the wall. He would have to step with care—the soil had crumbled from around one of the pillars supporting the ceiling, and the stone slab lay flat across the passage-way.

The tunnel went straight for half its length, then turned abruptly and continued left, again straight, with more tombs in the walls—to a square chamber of rock from which another five corridors radiated to the blackness.

This was the central cave of the funeral catacombs. And here, suddenly, there was heat and light—a small fire bristling on the floor, the flames launching shadows up the walls, up to the high ceiling: a cantilever vault of overlapping horizontal stone slabs, firelight grimacing in the gloom. In a castle or a broch, this roof space—six times the height of a man—would have been a den for bats and rooks and a black rat. But not here in a place of the dead.

Yet there *were* living things in the room, in one of its corners, on a bed of furs over a splay of heather. Two young bodies lay one across the other, the boy's head on the girl's bare belly as he faced the vault overhead, her hand idle on his shoulder, her own hair sprawled on the moss as if the heather itself had strayed onto the pillow.

They'd made a fierce love once Rhosarran had recovered from her faint, with all the hunger of the five absent years, with no need for words. He wasn't the only man in all that time, but he was the only one she'd wanted—and he was another thing entirely from the harsh old shepherd. She'd always recoiled from the old man's rough desperate touch. She was glad to kill him. And she was different with Jeo, a different animal. They grasped and pressed and sucked the strength from each other and had small blood and bruises on their bodies, and lay in the warmth of the fire in silence. For a very short time, the valley was a long way away and they weren't hunted.

She had many things to ask him with her dumb-show gestures, but he didn't wait to be asked. When he talked, he was like someone who hadn't spoken a word for years, and she only had to lie there and listen.

First he told her about his fall in the Pit and the horrors inside it. The shapes he saw as he fell, they were bodies in a giant pile, a long way down. The corpses of children. He'd fallen almost to the bottom of the Pit. Flies filled his ears and mouth and he caught them in his eyelids when he blinked. The smell of meat made him vomit. The bodies lay all around him in shadows, their limbs yellow and slack and some of the eyes wide open. As he writhed in the ghastly heap, their faces fell close to his and their arms dropped around his neck. He vomited again.

"Some of them were just babies, Rhos." He shook his head. "Half my size. I can't understand what they were doing there. What laws could they have broken?" The memory angered him and she pressed her fingers on his shoulder.

There was food beside the heather bed, and a pot of rainwater. He offered her a pair of buckwheat cakes he'd stolen, and the thigh of a hen. She took a cake but the chicken was raw and she left it for him.

He told her little of what had happened, nothing about the way he escaped from the Pit, almost nothing of the years that followed. He learned to kill for food, with or without his knife, learned fast because he had to. He had to eat everything with no fire. When the first winter came, he needed clothing so he hunted larger prey and pulled away the skins to wear.

He told her nothing of the lands he saw or the people he might have met, and she didn't ask. She didn't care. He was back and that was everything. There was another silence between them, fractured by the crackling of the fire.

He told her he found nothing to the south of the valley, though he travelled that way for two years—so he came back. At first, he meant to cross the glen on his way to find what lay to the far north—but he'd been away a very long time and he was tired of it all. And—he shrugged as he said it—the glen was his own kith, the only country he'd ever known. There were things he might be able to do there.

It was darker in the stone chamber, the fire was low. He rolled himself from her body and went to another corner for more brushwood, dropped it on the embers and kindled it with his breath. He went back to her and sat beside her. She leaned on her elbow and watched his face in the firelight as he stared through the little flames.

He said the underground tombs were the one place he could live in. No one would have thought of looking for him there, even if they'd known he was alive. He'd gladly desecrated the stone graves, plundering the weapons and implements he found there. The ancient Elders and Guardians had been buried with goods for an after-life: swords and shields and many knives, iron cups and plates—linen and leather belts, now rotting. He'd moved easily among the corpses.

He told her he was aiming for the Elder when he threw his knife from the megalith. If the old man hadn't stumbled he'd be dead now, in place of the old woman. He wondered who she was. Rhosarran opened her mouth and held a finger against one of her upper teeth.

"Chacmagh," he said. "Well, that's better than no one at all. Still, it should have been the Elder. If only he hadn't fallen over. In a way, he's still alive because he's old. If he wasn't so weak he wouldn't have fallen and I would have had him. Funny, that."

She smiled at the thought. So did he. The amusement died away as they looked at each other and felt strong again. Suddenly a frown on his face.

"Wait," he said. "What are *you* doing here? Your old man will follow you." She shook her head and ran a finger across her throat.

"How?" he said. She jabbed the finger at her breast.

"You? You killed Gara?"

She nodded and he gave a little whoop of surprise and triumph and she laughed noiselessly with him. There was no need to say any more, not for a while. He was still smiling as he uncoiled himself and lengthened his body alongside her. She lay back on the rug of fur and took his head in her hands, seizing it and pulling down so their bodies were tightly together. Her first kiss was like the bite of a beast but her eyes were very soft. She looked at him and noticed how his growth of beard had been cut with a knife, most of it gone. She saw how his wide feral face had quietened. His shoulders, like the rest of him, had grown tensely strong, the muscles hard like rope, but no longer taut when she spread her big fingers on them.

Above them, out on the dark plain, the long grass was shuffled by the wind and by grey crouching figures moving with stealth among the sarsen stones.

As Jeo and Rhosarran slept, the fire began to burn itself out. Soon only the last embers were left and the walls of the chamber were more black than blood red. The fire had stopped its noises and the place was quiet—but it wasn't the usual silence. Something was different.

Whether that was what woke Jeo or whether he woke first, then sensed the change, he didn't know. But something was wrong and he knew it at once. His eyes and ears were on edge in the darkness.

He shook Rhosarran hard, knowing she couldn't make any noise when he startled her awake. She woke very quickly and saw from the way he crouched that something was awry. She made no move at all for fear of crackling the dry heather beneath her.

She couldn't hear a thing and everything in the cavern looked the same as ever—but Jeo seemed to know differently. He picked up his old twin-blade knife and inched himself to his feet and stepped back slowly off the bed, beckoning her to do the same.

They went along the wall to the nearest tunnel and hid in the dark of its mouth. She felt something touch her hand, reached, took an iron javelin from him and held it pointing ahead of her as she crouched beside him. Jeo had found a second small dagger. He held them by the blade, one in each hand.

Again Rhosarran stared around and still she saw nothing. Then, away to the right, a noise from one of the six passageways. Only a small sound, but the stonework carried its echo into the chamber.

Another noise, closer. They both saw something move. They waited, poised, and two men stalked warily into the half-lit room with weapons in their hands. The sounds in the tunnel had been made by their military boots.

Jeo hesitated before throwing his knives but one of his arms was raised and drawn back ready. Rhosarran did nothing at all.

From what they could make out in the dark red glow, the two men were both young and fair-haired, one tall, the other short and thin. Their clothing was identical—chain-mail hauberk, cape, leather cap. Jeo turned to the girl and held a knife to her neck. He jabbed it away at the intruders then back to her throat, questioned her with a scowl. She shook her head and her face pleaded innocence. She hadn't led them to him. He took the knife away and suddenly stepped out of the deep shadows and stood in front of the two soldiers in the centre of the room. Rhosarran followed and stood beside him.

The two men were taken aback, though they'd come expecting to find him. It was a shock to see him standing naked in the low firelight. They were surprised to see Rhosarran at all.

They had weapons of their own, swords in their hands—but when they saw the others, they put them back in their belts and stood empty-handed near the wall. The tall man dropped the sack he was carrying.

A last piece of wood spit-crackled in the ashes. It threw a little more light in the room, enough for Jeo to see the freckles on the shorter man's face.

"You," he said. "I should have killed you first, all those years ago. You started everything."

Kyrie saw the daggers in Jeo's hands. He'd seen his prowess with a knife. He bit the stick of grass in his mouth and nodded, something like a small bow.

"It's good to see you, Jeo." The voice was steady. The scowl deepened on Jeo's face.

"Let's see you take the piss with a knife in your ribs, Kyrie. You and your tall friend here."

"No piss-taking, Jeo, I swear. We've come to be with you. Ask Rhos. She knows what I mean."

Jeo turned his head a fraction, not enough to take his eyes

off the men while he looked for confirmation in Rhosarran's face
—his movement in itself was a demand for her comment.

She touched his knife hand and he lowered it. She'd changed
her mind, again, about Kyrie when she realised he hadn't killed any
elders at all. Now she was as suspicious of him as ever—she knew
he'd only come to the tombs because Jeo was his one chance of
escaping torture and the Pits. Still, it had taken courage for him
to come here, and she wanted to hear what he had to say. She
frowned at him, tapped her lips, pointed her finger at him, urging
him to explain further.

Kyrie threw her a glance then spoke to Jeo. "I've been hiding
out in one of the eastern blocks," he said. "I'd only been there two
days when I heard rumours through the walls, stories of an elder
being killed—then another. I couldn't understand who could have
done it, though I heard people say it was me. Next thing I know,
there are guardsmen surrounding all the blocks and it's me they're
looking for. But I can't handle a knife like that. There's only one
person I knew who could. After the first two killings I wasn't sure
—anyone can stab at close range. Then I heard about a knife being
thrown and killing old Chacmagh, and I knew for certain—
though it didn't seem possible. You were dead as far as anyone
knew, but no one else could throw a knife so well. So I thought
you must be still alive somehow—and I knew you couldn't be
hiding in the blocks because they're all sealed off. So I thought
about other places and this seemed the only likely one. So I took
a chance and came here."

"How did you get out of the block if it's sealed off?"

Kyrie indicated his companion with a flick of his hand. "He
helped me."

"And who's he?"

"My name's Ure," said the tall man.

"Guardsman?"

"Yes, till now. But I've always hated it."

"So why do it?"

"Same reason as anyone else. Better than slaving in the cowsheds. Only way to get anything if you're young. You can trust me, Jeo."

"About as far as I can spit," said Jeo. "I think I ought to kill you both. I've heard what you've got to say and I don't believe it. The quicker I kill you the safer it is."

"We won't let you—" began Ure, but the lizard man put a silencing hand on his arm.

"Don't listen to him, Jeo. He doesn't know."

"I can kill you both before you pull those swords from your belts."

"I know that," said Kyrie. "We can't fight you, Jeo. Anyway, we don't want to. We want to do the things you're doing. I told Rhos days ago."

The girl looked at Jeo. "No," he said. "I don't want either of you with me. I don't trust you. I'll kill you both."

But Kyrie had come a long way through the night and was undeterred. "Look—before we came here, there were just the two of you on your own. Now we're four of us with weapons and a place to hide for a while. There could be more tomorrow. I understand why you don't trust me—but if I wanted you dead, I'd have brought other guardsmen with me, a hundred of them. You must see, Jeo—they're after me too. And anyway, we're better than no one at all. If you're going to do anything at all, you'll need help. We know some others who might join us. We're all you've got."

A silence. Jeo glanced at Rhosarran and she moved her eyes to him. He turned away. The others watched his face and had no expression on their own.

"What's in the sack?" said Jeo.

The tall man bent to reach it. "Food," he said. "Didn't know if you had any."

He emptied the sack on the floor. The body of a saddleback piglet fell out, pink and black and headless. Oatmeal cakes and a skin of milk.

Jeo looked again at Rhosarran. "Alright," he said without conviction. "We'll see. You stay here tonight, in that corner together. But you leave your weapons with us."

Kyrie nodded and the girl went forward to take their swords. He kept his eyes from her body.

"You sleep on the floor. There's no spare bedding."

"That's alright," said Kyrie, with a grim little smile. "I'm used to it."

"One more thing."

Kyrie was unbuckling his belt. He looked up. Jeo punched him in the face, a blow fast as an oxwhip. It knocked the lizard man over and left him slumped on the floor with his back against a wall. Ure made some sort of movement but there was nothing he could do. He stood and watched.

Kyrie lifted himself slowly to his feet, using the wall for support and feeling in his mouth with his fingers. His lips had been crushed and were bleeding on each other.

"That's for the past five years," said Jeo. "And for throwing stones at me in the nettlepatch."

If Kyrie felt any resentment he kept it hidden. "Alright," he said through his fingers. "Call it the price I pay for joining you."

Jeo took the oatcakes and the pig and went back to the bed. Rhosarran took her place beside him. The fire died out. Ure and the freckled man lay on their cloaks in another corner. For a while, they were all awake, eyes wide in the dark. Then, one after the other, they fell into uneasy sleep, the runaway soldiers with their backs to each other, the black-haired youth at the other side of the room, his arm round the girl's neck and his other hand furled round the handle of a long iron knife.

The two elders walking unsteadily through the upper reaches of a northern shanty had left the sanctuary of the castle to come and see some of their families in the glen. They were there against the advice of the captains. The killer youth was still at large, together with the cadet Ure, the wild shepherd girl, and a scattering of other children. Gara had been killed. There was danger in the tenements. But the old men had insisted and couldn't be gainsaid.

Now, as night closed in, they were helped up a long flight of splintering stairs onto yet another charcoal landing, leaning on the shoulders of two little girls under the eye of three armed guardsmen.

The corridors were largely empty, but a number of peasants passed the small group on their way down the passages. A farm-hand and her family crossed their path from one of the adjoining galleries and touched their foreheads in greeting. A lost child was moved on. A band of youngsters came rustling towards them.

The youths stopped and stood still as the elders approached. There were six of them half-hidden in the long shadows, five boys and a skinny girl. One of the boys had a sack across his shoulder. They all bowed to the elders. The leading guardsman, a corporal with only one ear, tapped the nearest boy with his black club.

"You know there's a curfew," he said.

"Yes, Senior. But we been sent out. We got orders."

"Orders? Looting, more like. What's in the bag—and whose orders?"

The boy was short, squat, and totally bald. "Elder, Senior," he said. "Elder's orders."

One of the old men came forward and stood between two of the soldiers. He was Bodach Du, hair still black as soot. He leaned on a small stick.

"Elder?" he said. "Which elder? Who are you, boy?"

"I know him," said a guardsman. "He's Taw, carpenter's boy."

"That's right, Senior," nodded the youth. He gave another hasty bow, then straightened and thrust a fat-bladed knife in the corporal's belly.

As the officer doubled with the shock of the blow, the other youngsters attacked the two remaining soldiers. One was stunned by the butt of a staff driven into his face, then stabbed dead when he fell on the floor. The old men gasped with fear and clung to the little girls, one of whom yelled in the darkness. The third guardsman was struck down by the skinny girl with an oak club with a nail in the end.

The little girl's screaming brought a number of tenement men out of their quarters further along the corridor. Two of the boys stabbed one of the elders. They left the children to sob by one of the walls.

"Come on, Taw, for fucksake. They'll be all over us in a minute."

The bald boy had Bodach Du in front of him, the old man on his knees with terror. He drew back his knife—then changed his mind and punched the elder with his fist, an uppercut that swung under the brittle old chin and snapped the head back. The body slumped to the floor. The other youths had pulled the helmets from the guardsmen's heads, taken their black clubs. They were leaping down the nearest ladder, hurling the heavy sack before them.

"Taw!"

Just before he ran to join them, the boy knelt quickly beside the old body, made a cut just below the hairline and tore the hair and scalp from the head.

"You're too old to have hair black as this," he whispered. "It's not right."

He was on his feet in an instant and jumped down the ladder. Within seconds the passageway was full of people with weapons. They set off down the ladder—but the youngsters were gone, vanished like a skelter of lizards in the wet depths of the tenement.

The fire in the underground burial chamber was still glowing, faintly. In the thick of the night, only Jeo was awake, sitting as ever on his quilt of fur with his back against a wall as he looked around the chamber and eyed the black galleries leading off it.

The stone room was full, its every yard of space taken up by sacks of food and earthenware jars, weapons leaning on walls, heather bedding tied into ricks, piles of kindling and bundles of cloth and hide—above all, bodies asleep, the sprawled figures of young men and boys and girls.

Only three days had passed since Kyrie had descended into the catacombs—and, true to his word, he and Ure had found others to join them, most escaping from the tenements, a few from the small forts. Others had been killed by guardsmen as they tried to leave the warrens, but those who got out made their way to the standing stones and the safety of the tombs. There were about twenty of them crowded into the main vault, the same number outside sleeping in the tunnels. More than Jeo had expected.

He lay awake with his thoughts, looking around at the sleep-twisted bodies. There were too many for his liking. He really wanted to do things on his own, or with Rhosarran alone. Though he knew Kyrie was right about strength in numbers, he wasn't easy with so many around him. For one thing, they were all so young —small and underfed and he couldn't trust their strength. He himself was different. He'd grown strong in the five years, his senses were better, he had no more fear. But his new pack of followers, they were just children. He didn't want them with him.

And then there was the question of what to do next, where to go when the catacombs were full. The other tombs around the hilltop were sealed with stone, impregnable. He puffed his cheeks in the red darkness.

There was another thing too. He was the leader of this child gang—they all said he was—yet he felt it really belonged to the freckled man. Kyrie had gathered it together. He knew everyone in it. He was the organiser, the contriver behind the scenes. Why did he want so many around him—what was he planning? Jeo didn't trust him. He would never trust him. He didn't trust Ure. He heard a small rough sound from one of the passageways and cocked his head to it.

Nothing. The sound was gone. He looked at Rhosarran beside him, and for a moment his thoughts were gentle. There was a second noise, in the same tunnel, louder than the first, and he stood up off the bed. He heard the scrape of iron on stone as he peered into the dark. More noises in another passage. He thrust his knife in his belt, snatched up another—and a short sword which he held very tight. Rhosarran was awake, scrabbling for the spear beside the bed.

"Wake yourselves!" Jeo shouted. "Wake up, all of you! They're here! Get up!"

Almost at once there was uproar in the chamber, youngsters leaping and rolling from their beds, the noises of metal, shouts and a confusion of shadows. Jeo strode across the room.

"You, you did this." The length of his swordblade was pressed against Kyrie's throat, his hand gripping the naked shoulder. "One of your little friends led them here."

"No—" The blade cut his skin. "For fucksake, Jeo, it's no one's fault. They were bound to find us soon—"

"Liar. They'd never think of this place. Why should they?"

"They've probably looked everywhere else. There's no time for this, Jeo—"

A yell from one of the girls around them. A crossbow bolt nuzzled in her belly and she stared at it in disbelief. Jeo pushed the freckled boy aside and ran for one of the corridors, Rhosarran just behind him.

Two guardsmen burst out of the blackness, their weapons red in the firelight. Jeo jagged to one side, to the next passageway.

The air was cut by shouts and screaming and the noise of crossbows unleashing, suddenly the snarling of dogs. More guardsmen poured into the chamber with short lances in their hands.

Jeo jumped over the body of a boy and pushed another aside. He caught sight of Ure swinging a short axe. The crossbows were silent now. Lancers and swordsmen were racing butchering into the vault—but none came out of the tunnel just ahead. Jeo slashed with his sword and swept a guardsman out of his way. Another came at him from the right but he stabbed the man's face and left the sword in it. Then he was out of the chamber into the gallery, the sounds of fighting behind him. He ran into the darkness as fast as he could, one hand on the wall. He wasn't alone, though he didn't know it. Rhosarran ran a few paces behind—then another youngster, a few more further back, then the first of the pursuing soldiers.

Noises and a light ahead of him, round the sharp bend of the tunnel. Too much noise. Too many guardsmen. Jeo felt a gap in the wall, one of the coffin alcoves. He darted in. Rhosarran followed, and the boy behind her. The next wave of stormtroops came rushing along the corridor, brandishing torches, wolfhounds off the leash. They met the small group of youths running from the chamber and killed them all. While they were doing so, Jeo and the other two left the stone gap and ran on, unseen for the moment, along the tunnel and round the last corner.

Another mad sprint through the darkness brought them to a set of stone steps. Light at the top of the stairway—yet it was dark night outside. It had to be torchlight. Every way out was obviously guarded, staunched by soldiers.

Jeo had no intention of using the steps. Enough light glazed in from above to light the walls on either side. In the wall on the right was the doorway of yet another alcove, a gap narrower than any of the others, just a fissure in the rock. He slipped inside and the others again followed.

It was a false cell, with no coffin inside. Just a long thin passage with a stone floor. They ran along it in a straight line and reached another slight opening at the far end. Over the centuries it had become clogged with drifts of soil and rock—but Jeo had cleared it with his own hands weeks before. Now, hidden by a bank of overgrown nettles, the opening gave onto the slope of the hill.

In the light of a big glacid moon, Jeo could see that the hillside dipped away to the right, down to the valley. The plain and its henge of stones were a little higher, on the left. He could see the place was creeping with soldiers. The menhirs gleamed with torchlight and the firebrands were smoking in the cold air. He saw archers and lancers everywhere, horsemen and army dogs. He heard the captains shouting their orders, the sound of men running, the bluster of the horses.

He glanced behind him. Rhosarran's eyes were wide but not with fear. The boy beside her was Taw, his bald head showing in the gloom. Jeo crept downhill through the undergrowth, ignoring the rasp of the nettles.

Out in the open, some way down the slope, they were in heavy darkness, invisible from the hillcrest. They ran away across the hill, not down into the glen.

Footsteps behind made them turn with their small weapons ready, but there were no guardsmen. Three of the other youngsters had fought their way out, though Jeo couldn't understand how. He wasn't pleased to see Kyrie among them. Ure ran beside him, with Taw's skinny sister. The lizard man's arm was hanging loose and the sleeve was pasted with blood. Jeo turned and ran on.

"No," said Kyrie. Jeo saw him pointing with his uninjured arm. "The marshes," he said breathlessly. "Only place to hide. Marshland."

Jeo faltered, but very briefly. He followed the line of the freckled arm and led the last of his underground army up the rise towards the moors.

Beside him, he saw Rhosarran strip off her tunic and run naked over the hill. She wrapped the piece of clothing round the lizard man's arm to block the bleeding. She would have done that for anyone, he knew—but Kyrie leaned on her more than he had to, put an arm around her neck and looked at her body. Jeo ran on, the others with him. Taw and his sister hand in hand. Just the six of them, while the rest lay dead in the burial chambers or were dragged away wounded to the torture cellars of the hillside forts.

As dawn broke over the giant scarps, a big red-bearded captain rode alone among the megaliths. The bodies had been counted. Kyrie and Ure and the shepherd girl were still missing. Ouse looked up the side of the highest stone. How could the freckled man have climbed one of these things? And when had he learned to throw a knife so well? There was something about all this he didn't understand. He walked the horse away onto the fringe of the moor.

The Fen

WHILE EVENING DREW IN, the heron went on and on with its work. It stood perfectly still in the watery shadows cast by a bank of rushes across one of the thousand channels of the marshland, poising with its feet in the shallows. In the low light, its grey-and-green striped body matched the line of rushes and was obscured. It didn't move its legs in the water, nor in fact the rest of its body, as it leaned with its beak just a foot from the surface and stared into the turgid water—and waited, something it was very, very good at.

To some eyes it might have looked dignified, in its own sombre way, a stately bird. To Jeo, spying from a clump of tall cordgrass on the other side of the channel, it was nothing of the kind. Like Kyrie behind him, he saw it differently. He admired the way it was constructed—the long legs to keep it high above the water, the slim stabbing beak, the streamlined body with its coat of varied colours that camouflaged it from the eye of a fish. It was a cold, beautifully equipped, skilful and patient killer, and Jeo could have spent all day watching and learning from it. Just now, he didn't have the time.

The rest of his small band, the few who'd escaped from the tombs, were crouched just behind him. When he put out his hand, the bald boy put a stone in it.

Jeo had already looked around at this part of the fenland, checking its contours. He did it again to be sure. Without moving out of his crouch he drew back his arm and held it cocked behind him. The heron didn't move. A shower of waterflies skimmed the

surface a few yards from its beak but it took no notice. Taw looked
at Jeo. A squadron of wild geese flapped quite low overhead, in
V formation, on their way beyond the valley. Ure glanced and saw
the leading bird drop back as another took its place at the front.

Jeo didn't look up. His eyes were on the heron. Only he and
Kyrie could tell from the smudges of mud on its head and neck
that it had been dredging eels in the slime of a creek. Still it made
no move. Jeo threw the stone.

He hurled it flat and carefully. It landed a yard away from
the tall bird, splashing it with water. The heron gave a single
hoarse cry and jumped in the air. Once forced out of its deadly
motionless pose, its movements were ungainly, but quick enough.
The big bully wings lifted it up and away across the fen, to a
gaggle of buckthorn trees in the distance. The watching youths
rose from the reeds.

"Missed," muttered Taw. "Bloody missed."

"He meant to," said Kyrie.

Jeo was already across the creek and moving through the
marsh. The others went after him, briskly over a stretch of wet
grassland split by more of the same shallow canals, ahead of them
nothing but reeds and rushes and swamp grass, a few wiry trees
framed on the oil-blue skyline.

They stopped when they reached the buckthorn copse, and
the others now realised why he'd missed the heron with his stone.
It had gone straight back to its nest, leading them there. There were
several other nests up in the heronry and the youngsters threw
sticks and stones at them.

The adult birds fled in a panic of wings and flew high away
to the north, to be lost in the glum light. Jeo's gang went on
throwing till they hit all the nests and overturned them, spilling
their contents down through the trees in a spray of long twigs and
grass, to land on the mud at the young people's feet. Twigs and
grass and early heron eggs—more to eat than a single adult bird.
The youngsters caught them as they fell and put them in their
tunics. Jeo would have liked the birds too, but these would do.

"See," said the skinny girl to her brother. "He missed because he wanted to." And the bald boy smiled.

It was late evening now. The eastern sky was blue grey, then darker. In that very flat country, it reached right down to the grass and reeds, which stood like giant quills, black against the empty background. Through and above the grass, the six youths moved in silhouette, in single file, quiet because they were tired. They crossed the broad flats of grassland and splashed through endless dull channels of water. After an hour's trek, they reached an area where the countryside changed. It was still a marsh, but deeper in mud and water, the rushes fatter and much higher, taller than men, clotted together in clumps as big as fields, divided by deep canals and long lakes. The ground underfoot was swamped with water, there were no firm footholds, and slim snakes rippled through the underwater reeds.

Kyrie saw Taw adjusting Bodach Du's black hair on his bald head. The boy's sister smilingly shook her head at him.

"Why don't you get rid of that thing?" said Kyrie.

"I'm sick of looking like an old man," said Taw half seriously.

"Bloody liar," said his sister. "You've always done well having no hair. I remember. Everyone thought you was older. You could lie about your age and get more food, do less work—"

"I'd have been a fool not to," said Taw. "But I hate looking like this. I look younger with this hair."

"You look a complete idiot," said Kyrie.

Taw grinned. "At least I'm complete. I feel unfinished without it."

He went on fiddling with the thing as they all shared a laugh and moved on. They were still in single file, and Ure, at the rear, found that Jeo had dropped back to walk alongside him. They were twenty paces behind the others.

"I don't know you," said Jeo quietly. The tall man looked at him. "I've never seen you before you came to the tomb place. That worries me."

"You've been away five years."

"You're trying to be funny?"

"No—"

"Then don't tell me I've been away. I know I've been away."

"Yes. I didn't mean anything."

"We'll start again. Before I went away, I never saw you anywhere. Why not?"

"I was there. You can't see everyone in the glen. It's a big place."

"I saw every guardsman. I never saw you."

"I wasn't a guardsman till after you were gone. I was a cowherd before that, all my life. I didn't see you either."

"I don't believe you," said Jeo. "Tell me how you knew where to find Kyrie when all the glen was looking for him."

"We used to meet," said Ure. "I was the only guardsman who'd talk to him. All the rest hated him. We seemed to think the same things about the glen. We used to meet, some nights— always the same place, an old store-room in a block. When he went into hiding, I looked there and found him."

"I don't believe that either. How old are you, Ure?"

"I don't know for sure. Look, if you don't believe me, why have you let me stay?"

Jeo looked at him for the first time, and Ure watched his face. All those years in the open wilderness and the face was still very pale, almost white, as if it had never seen any sun.

"If I get rid of everyone I don't trust," said Jeo, "I'll never have anyone around me. I let you stay because I need numbers. I can't do much on my own. You were a guardsman, I know you can fight and teach others to fight. You'll be useful for a while. Then we'll see."

Ure gave a small nod in reply. Jeo looked straight ahead again.

"I don't know you," he said again. "I don't know why you're here or what you're thinking. But think this—if you're dangerous to me, I'll find out. And when I do, I won't ask you any more questions. I'll kill you without a word."

"Yes," said Ure. "I won't forget."

That was all. They quickened their step and rejoined the others. Kyrie, who'd seen them talking together, exchanged looks with the tall man as they moved on.

They pushed through a high reed patch and stepped out of it into the first reaches of yet another wide creek. It was night now and the sky was black like oil. A slice of moon in it but not enough to light the way.

They were about to cross the water when they saw something in the phalanx of reeds ahead and stood still. It was the light of a flame, tiny and tremulous and almost hidden in the heavy vegetation, but clear as a candle. They stared at it without moving, Jeo and Rhosarran already out in the shallows, the others on the edge of the bank, Ure to one side and Kyrie at the back looking over the thin girl's shoulder, his arm in a rag sling.

The light glowed a little brighter as it came nearer. The damp spines of the reeds glistened around it. The skinny girl moved next to Jeo.

"What's that?" she whispered. He shook his head.

"Swamp gas catching fire," said Kyrie.

Jeo looked hard at the light. It wavered in the reeds. "It's not swamp gas," he said. "It's burning too evenly."

"There's two of them," said Taw.

Jeo stepped back among the rushes, pulling the two girls in with him. They all crouched and hid and looked across the creek in silence.

Another, similar light had appeared, a small distance behind the other. For the first time, they heard the reeds rustling, then the noise of plants crushed underfoot. A third, more distant light showed itself, away to the left. The noises grew louder. Something was moving through the reed bank in numbers.

Jeo glanced behind him. Kyrie returned his look and his face was grim. The others were wide eyed in the dark. They all had weapons, but small ones—knives and willow clubs. No bows, not even a sling and stones.

Kyrie saw Jeo let go of Rhosarran's arm as he stared at the far bank. One of the lights burst out from the forest of reeds and glowed above the creek, splaying light over the water and across to the other side. A dozen dark figures stepped out into the water behind the lantern.

"Bloody guardsmen," whispered the thin girl Abhail, saying what they were all thinking. The manhunt had finally started.

The second lantern was carried out of the high reeds. The unknown figures began to tread across the channel, speaking in very low voices. As they approached and reached halfway across the creek, it became clear from the height at which the lanterns were carried that all the figures were short. The lamplights illuminated their lower bodies and showed their knees to be bare. Below that, their legs were under water.

Jeo listened hard and heard no sound of armour. He saw no glint of chain mail. The third lantern came burning out of the reed forest, then more of the dark figures. Soon they were almost across the canal. Jeo turned the dagger in his hand and held it by the blade. Rhosarran saw him do it. She grasped his other wrist and shook her head at him. There was no fear in her face. He frowned inquiringly at her.

A loud splash in the channel. Someone had fallen in the water and was struggling to get up. One of the lanterns swayed. The group came to a halt. Voices broke the half-quiet.

"Mind your feet, Gael." It was a hard whisper. "How can you expect to fight if you can't even stand up?" Someone else muffled a laugh.

The column moved on in relative quiet. It was nearly at the other bank. Then it stopped, abruptly, as a thin pale young man stepped out of the bullrushes at the water's edge and stood stooped in front of them, the blade of the knife in his hand clear in the lights.

The leader with the lantern took some steps back and the others fell silent as they stared past him at the threatening figure. The lights shivered on Jeo's body, his naked arms. He didn't speak—but he knew it was safe to emerge from the rushes. These weren't guardsmen, or a search group of peasants. They were children.

The leading boy raised his lantern higher, saw Jeo's face and recoiled. "Jeo," he breathed. "So it's true."

"Clearly," said Jeo.

"We got away, Jeo. We've come to join you. We want to fight the elders too."

"Who are you?"

"My name's Caldy," said the boy. "From the western farms. And there's twenty others from the blocks."

"I know him," came a voice at Jeo's shoulder. The tall man stepped out into the lights.

"Ure," scowled the boy with the lamp. "You've got guardsmen with you, Jeo?"

"I'm not a guardsman any more," said Ure.

"Nor me." Kyrie came out from the rushes, Rhosarran and the two others just behind. Caldy went on scowling.

"Well," he said slowly, "if they're really not guardsmen no more and they're with you, suppose that's alright. Anyway, we're here now." And he was quiet and waited.

Jeo looked at the assortment of shadows and lights in front of him. He walked through the water.

"Give me your light." Caldy held out the lantern. Jeo walked away behind him, past the other newcomers, holding the light over his head to look into the line of faces with their wide-eyed expressions. He saw how very young most of them were.

"You," he said. A young man with red hair came out of the shadows in the group. "Who are you? What's your name?"

"Cairns, Senior," said the man. "Ru Cairns, from the eastern blocks—"

"I don't care where you come from. You're too old. I don't want you here."

"I'm not yet twenty-five, Senior."

"He's alright," said Caldy, splashing through the creek. "I'll speak for him myself."

"That means nothing to me," said Jeo. "I don't know you from the next man. This one's too old. I don't want him here."

"Let me stay, Senior. I can fight good."

"Maybe. But it makes no difference."

"They'll kill me if I go back."

"I won't let you live here."

"For pity's sake," said Caldy. "He's come to be with you, Jeo —given up everything to do it—and you want to send him back to get himself killed. That's not why we came to join you."

Others voiced their agreement. Rhosarran heard the sound of weapons and her hand went to her second knife. Some of the children moved towards Jeo but he didn't step back. He spoke quietly and they had to be silent to listen.

"If you've come to join me, you've come to do as I say." He paused for nothing. "You don't have to stay with me. You can go your own way, fight the elders any way you know how— though it only takes one look to see none of you has any idea how to fight, or even how to stay alive for a week out here. The guardsmen will come and slaughter you like pigs. You're looking for someone to lead you, and I'm here. But you'll do what I want, without question, whatever I tell you—or find somewhere else. And there's only room for one leader. Am I right, Caldy?"

The boy gave him no more than a quick look before nodding. "Yes," he said. Then he glanced to his left. "Cairns goes back."

"No!" The red-haired man stepped to one side, out on his own in the creek.

"There's no other way," said Caldy. "It's you or all of us."

"They'll tear me apart in the brochs if I go."

"You don't have to go back to the glen," said Jeo evenly. "Hide in the forests or the moors. But you can't stay here."

"You can't send me away just because I'm older than you. I won't go back."

"I'll kill you if you try to stay."

"No! I'm staying. Who do you think you are—" he was waving a fist when Jeo, with just a backhand flick of the hand, flung one of his knives into the side of the man's neck. It struck him just under the jawbone and stabbed up through his throat, cutting the words from his mouth and dropping him like a scarecrow in the shallow water.

In the horror-struck silence that followed, Jeo went to the body and took out his knife, washed it, wiped it on the man's tat tunic, then held high the lantern and eyed the children, none of whom dared move as he looked at them. He looked at their faces, greasy in the lamplight—some of them dark, others ruddy or very pale, but all of them very young, some no more than ten years old. Hopelessly young, he couldn't help thinking. He lowered the lantern and held it down by his side and his face was in darkness as he spoke.

"We've found a place to hide," he said, as if nothing much had happened. "About an hour's walk from here. Anyone who wants to come with us comes now." He turned to go. "One more thing. No one here calls anyone Senior."

He walked past them all to the bank from which he'd come, and disappeared into the high rushes, only his lantern showing. All the children followed him, Caldy melting into the middle of the pack. As they trudged off through the creek, some of them gave the body of Ru Cairns a quick sideways look.

The red hair showed like a patch of rust in the lights. Then, when the lanterns moved away, it lost all its colour and became as dark and nondescript as everything else in the marsh, as lank as the lowest reeds.

Jeo had set up camp on a little jut of land in one of the wide upland lochs. He led the children there.

It would have been an island but for a thin strip of ground attached to the shore of the lake. At first thought, it seemed a poor choice for a hideaway. It could only be reached by that one narrow pathway, which meant it seemed to have only one escape route, easily cut off. But it was a deceptive place. The connecting piece of land wasn't the only way to the shore. There were ways to ford the lake that only Jeo and his followers could know. Besides, the narrow causeway was almost completely hidden by reeds and high grasses which spread in a wide area on either side of it, thick as bushes. Even after close survey, a scout would have decided there was no firm ground under all those acres of reeds. It seemed a place for moor fowl and water rats, not an outlaw force.

Jeo and the rest wrapped themselves in old blankets brought by the children, and sat in groups around three small fires built very low so the reeds hid their light from the shore.

They shared the handful of fish which Kyrie and Rhosarran had caught, and the roasted heron eggs, the breads and cheese and mutton brought by the others. Jeo sat by the smallest fire, with Rhosarran, Kyrie and Taw, and a girl with no name, eating very little and talking about what had been happening in the glen since the attack on the tombs some two weeks past. For the young of the valley, it had been a fortnight of horrors.

"They're killing kids every day, Jeo." The unnamed girl shook her head at the memory. "Not one or two but many. Twenty or more every day. Some of them are only nine or ten." She stopped again but Jeo didn't speak. "It's the guardsmen doing it. They throw twelve in the Pits every night. But it's more than that. There's fathers killing their kids in secret. The elders are getting afraid of the young."

Jeo blinked into the tiny flames of the fire, his brows moving in a frown. "Why? Why so *many* deaths?"

The girl shrugged. "Because of you," she said simply. "They're trying to get out someone to tell where you are, what you're going to do next."

"So," said Jeo, as if only to himself, "they know. The guardsmen know I'm alive."

"Yes, they do. Some of the kids they tortured must have said they heard you was back. You can't blame them." She paused and made a gesture. "No one could believe it at first. Everyone thought you was dead in the Pit. But then I hear the guardsmen start thinking if you been alive all these years, someone must have known about it. People must have been hiding you. So they put everyone to the question."

Jeo pursed his mouth. Rhosarran saw his face was impassive. "How many have they killed?" he asked.

"Hard to tell," said the girl. "I only know for sure about the twelve that goes to the Pits at night. That's about two hundred all told. But there's many taken to the brochs and not come out. And nobody knows how many's killed in the blocks, out of sight."

"Has anyone told them anything?"

"Apart from saying you're alive—no, nothing. Like I say, nobody knows anything to tell. There's a few tried giving lies to the guardsmen, to save themselves, but they were found out, so they went to the Pits all the same. But none of this is doing the elders any good."

"What do you mean?"

"The more they kill, the more we all hate them. Two guardsmen were found dead in one of the southern blocks. And for every one of us who's killed a guardsman or run away, there must be a hundred who want to. They just need someone to take charge —a chief."

Jeo glanced at her then looked back to the fire. "Tell me about the killings. Who's in charge of them?"

"The top guardsmen," said the girl. "Neagh and Creoch and the new Guardian himself. And some new captain, a fat one with a red face, killing kids not much younger than himself. Don't know his name."

"Ouse," said Kyrie, but Jeo didn't need to be told. He looked away from the fire, which was nearly dead. The other fires had been stamped out and the small encampment was mostly asleep, the children hunched together in stuff blankets. A small water bird made its sounds on the lake.

"Two hundred dead," said Jeo, in the mask of a voice.

"Yes, at least." The girl did some mournful nodding.

"And the others just need someone to take charge," said Kyrie. Jeo glanced at him but the sand-haired man seemed to be talking to himself.

Dawn over the giant fenlands. Bright grey and cold. A big mist clouding the bullrush walls. On a space of flat ground beside one of the countless streams, Jeo squatted on his haunches by the water's edge, beheading eels with his bone-handled knife and rinsing them in the water, washing the mud off his arms.

He finished the task and got to his feet, bundled the eels in a shallow sack. He was alone. Rhosarran was away hunting fish. Around him, nothing but the same gross tangles of reeds, swamped in fog, a few skinny trees flinching in a cold breeze that prefaced the onset of winter. The mist and the waters were very cold, the ground in places still dusted with frost. Jeo wore a sleeveless fur jerkin to his hips, thick green wool hose below. He had boots, for once, but his arms were bare. He carried knives in his belt and sporran, in both his boots. He stretched his arms and legs and yawned, slung the eel bag on his shoulder.

Out here, the glen seemed so far away he could almost forget it. He couldn't see the castle, though the mountains were just visible to the far left. There was something unreal about the marshland. It wasn't part of the glen so it was nowhere at all. It had a sense of peace but a peace Jeo didn't believe.

Figures moved in the distance, in groups, and he watched them dispassionately. The fens were full of them, more than he could see at the moment—scores of children and young adults, looking for frogs and firewood and keeping watch.

There were perhaps a hundred of them by now, at the hidden base camp, well armed for close-quarter fighting—though Jeo knew they needed more crossbows—and they were being trained to fight, by Jeo himself, by Kyrie, Ure, and another runaway cadet.

It was a slow business. They were still no sort of an army—small and weak and in truth far too young. They knew next to nothing about fighting with weapons. But it was a start. As the freckled man said, better than nothing.

Still, as he walked across the marsh, Jeo couldn't quell a sense of anxiety. Winter was still some weeks away, but that was too close. He knew from experience that the fenland was a harsh place to live at that time of year. There was no natural shelter from the freezing winds, it seemed to rain for weeks on end, often the entire marsh was covered in snow, the waters froze over and it was impossible to fish, the birds flew away. Few among his child army were hardy enough to survive such conditions.

But there again he knew of no other place to go, nothing else they could do. He didn't want to go away again and there was no possibility yet of storming the glen. He could only wait and hope for more additions to his forces, before the really cold weather set in. Then, with perhaps two hundred at his beck, he might be in a position to act.

He looked to one side and saw the freckle-faced man standing looking at him on the other bank of a stream, hands on hips and smiling quizzically. In place of the sling, there was a thread of crusted blood on his arm, where the freckles were the size of big flat pebbles.

Jeo gave him a quick frown. He was irked by the way Kyrie would often just appear like that, of a sudden, making no noise through the reed beds, with one of those insufferable grasses in his lips. He put his knife back in its boot, picked up the sack of eels, and crossed the creek.

"I've been thinking," said Kyrie. "We can't stay out here till spring. I can make another two raids tonight and tomorrow. After that I don't know. It gets harder every time. Taw knows where he can find maybe thirty more to join us, from that small block near the mill. Most of them a bit older."

"Good."

They walked on in silence. A band of children moved away

ahead of them in the fog, spiked fishing sticks in their hands. A blue frog jumped out of their reach as they waded across a broad channel. Apart from the noise of their feet in the wet, there was a thick sense of quiet in the great fenland, as if everything were drowned in the wide shallows or muffled by the mist.

"You've done well," said Kyrie. "You've marshalled the whole thing well, all these kids. I didn't think you could. All those years ago, I wouldn't have believed it. You're stronger now, and you know things. You're harder."

"You've helped," said Jeo, grudging the words. "You've brought everyone here from the glen, helped to train them. You've done well too."

"I know," said Kyrie lightly. "But you still don't trust me, do you?"

"No," said Jeo. He thought again of the evening in the nettlefield, and the day when Kyrie had tried to make him a guardsman. "But I need you for what you can do."

"For now."

"Yes, for now."

They walked on. Kyrie bent to snap up a stick of sweet-grass and put it between two teeth. He gave Jeo a glance, then another, before speaking again.

"A couple of things I've always wanted to know," he ventured. Jeo looked straight ahead. "What happened in that Shrieking Pit?"

"I fell down a pile of bodies."

"And?"

"And?"

"How did you get out? What happened afterwards, all those years?"

"Why do you want to know? Does it make any difference?"

"No, I suppose not."

"I'm here, that's what matters. That's all. What else did you want to ask?"

"Simply why you're doing all this. Why the rebellion in the first place?"

"You pushed me to it." The voice was only faintly harsh. "You would have forced me to be a guardsman."

"I was coming to tell you things had changed, that night at the Gathering—to say you didn't have to be a guardsman."

"I couldn't know that, could I? Anyway, you would have tried again, when you thought the time was right."

"We could have done well as guardsmen, you and me—without all this blood and trouble."

"I wanted more than that, something the glen doesn't give. I couldn't get it through being a guardsman. Guardsmen are just part of the glen—and with your arrangement you would have given the orders, not me."

"Yes, strange how it's worked out. I wanted you as my helping hand. Instead, I'm yours."

"Yes," said Jeo. "I don't want to obey any more. I've had my fill of it. That's why the elders have to be killed, like the old stags in a herd of deer. They have to die so the strong young stags can take their places and keep the herd healthy. We have to cull the elders."

"To make way for a young stag called Jeo?"

"Yes. And any others he trusts to follow him."

"And just how important is the rest of the herd?" said Kyrie. Jeo turned on him but didn't speak. He looked away and they went on towards the peninsular camp far away.

They went another mile, taking it in turns to carry the sack, which was heavy with water as well as eels. Suddenly, from the distance behind them to their right, from the south, a small flock of swallowtail butterflies rose from one of the enormous crops of giant milk parsley that littered the swamp, rose and climbed the fog. The young men turned to look at them and stood still as they watched the butterflies on their hectic flight away to the west. They stared at the mist from which the creatures had risen.

"Some of the kids," said Kyrie. "Blundering about as usual."

Jeo nodded, but he didn't take his eyes from the mist or move away. The freckled man followed his gaze. Nothing appeared to happen. Then, as the butterflies vanished in the mist, they heard something. A high-pitched sound, a thin wail rising above the mist, a noise Jeo only half remembered but which Kyrie recognised at once.

"Battle pipes," he said flatly, and his face was pale. Jeo took a breath.

"Well," he said. "They're here. What took them so long?"

"We'd better get back and tell everyone," said Kyrie. Jeo disagreed.

"Not yet. They're still a way off, by the sound of it. I want to see how many they are. We need a closer look."

Kyrie wasn't keen, but he followed Jeo briskly towards the sound of the pipes. They kept their heads quite low as they ran, kept to the firmer ground wherever they could.

Soon the wailing noises were louder and they heard other sounds—the booming of a bass drum, then another, then the scattered calls of men, the grunting of dogs and the tread of feet through shallow water. The two youths reached a thick wedge of bogrushes and crawled through on hands and knees. At the far end, they lay on their bellies in the marsh mud and pushed a gap in the heavy rushes to look out over the grass flats beyond. For a while, they said nothing as they watched, but their faces were grim.

An army was moving through the great marsh. The numbers reached back to the horizon. At the head, some two hundred paces in front of the hiding youths, twenty pipers led the way, a single rank spread across the front of the force. Like the rest of the army, they wore chain mail and light helmets. They played a brisk marching tune but it was stern not jaunty.

Behind and in among the pipers, a hundred wolfhounds, thick leather coats on their backs, leather masks on their long faces, wide studded collars, obedient beside their handlers.

After the dogs, the lancers and crossbowmen and whip-soldiers. Behind these, the cavalry, some sixty strong, with drummers on the flanks, and a hundred skirmishers with small square shields and thin swords. They came striding through the fog, and their numbers and the noise they made brought a chill to Jeo's stomach.

"How many?" he asked quietly.

"Can't say." Kyrie slowly shook his head. "Three hundred, maybe. More. What does it matter? Too many. They must have left enough to control the glen, but otherwise they all seem to be here. The Guardian's with them."

Jeo followed the line of his brief nod. The man on the big horse was in full armour. Jeo didn't know him.

"There's Ouse," said Kyrie. The pig man rode just behind the Guardian, to his left, the red face bulging in its helmet. Jeo made a small wry noise.

The whole army was very close by now, most of it visible in the clearing mist. For some reason, it came to a collective halt. The bagpipes fell silent and their last echoes fainted in the thin air. The horses stood in groups, ankle-deep in mud, snorting their clouds of breath. Steam rose from the soldiers as they stood and waited.

One of the big carts was pulled to the front. Four men— carpenters without armour—began to unload it. They lifted long trunks of wood from it, each as big as a roof beam. They dug a hole in the mud with long sharp shovels.

"What are they doing?" asked Jeo.

"Don't know. Looks like some kind of siege weapon, but it can't be. I don't understand it."

The carpenters hammered at the blocks of wood while the rest of the army did nothing much. When the task was finished, they lifted the thing they'd made, hauling it upright with ropes, then set it in place in the deep hole.

"Oh, very clever," breathed Kyrie, while Jeo clammed his teeth. "A nice touch."

It was a set of gallows, stark and black against the light

horizon. A rope was thrown over the cross-beam and left there to dangle as the army of guardsmen moved on past it. The pipes played and the drums pounded and the two young men backed out of the thicket of rushes. They ran away towards their lakeside camp. Some of the other youngsters had also heard the drums and pipes, and they too were making their way back, running like startled bucks through the last dregs of mist.

Another evening, and Jeo ran bent double through the canal beside a wall of spike reeds, knife in hand. Behind him, also bent over as they ran, Rhosarran and Taw in single file.

The boy's bald head was smirched with blood from a skin wound, the left side of his face running red—but he splashed on regardless, holding a stunted claymore in his fist. The scalp of Bodach Du still hung on his sporran, flapping as he went. Rhosarran ran with her javelin in her hand and a small hunting bow across her back, three short arrows left in her belt. Her ear was cut, the blood was dry and brown, one of the big bronze earrings was lost.

The watery camp was quite close now. The guardsmen hadn't found it. If the three of them could avoid being seen over the last mile, they were safe for the time being.

They stopped at the end of the reed bank and crouched as they looked round the side of it, searching the landscape. While they were running, they heard only the wind in their ears. Now, as they caught their breath, the air was stinging with the sounds of battle, most of them distant.

Men were shouting somewhere beyond the rushes to the left. From behind them, a scream, the barking of dogs. In every direction, the splatter of water as men and boys and horses blustered through it. The usual sounds, none of them close. Jeo ran on across the open spread of bogland into the rush bushes at the far side.

The fighting had now lasted three days. Jeo's plan had been to divide his forces into small groups, about twenty in all, each of no more than four or five children led by one of the older youths. There was no thought of a pitched battle. The odds were laughable. All they could hope to do was set off from the encampment at random times of the day and especially the night, and inflict what damage they could.

As Jeo realised, the whole thing could only end one way. Already his numbers had been halved. There were ten sets of gallows around the fen, and every beam grunted under the weight of hanging children. Some had died in the fighting and their bodies were hauled up and left there as on a gibbet. Others were taken alive, questioned, and killed by the rope. Elsewhere, for all their small victories, the young moss-troopers were being butchered. The guardsmen weren't very skilled in battle—they'd been trained to police, not to fight a war—but against children they were good enough. In hand-to-hand combat it was men against callow boys and girls, strong men who knew how to use their weapons against half-grown youths with sticks and little knives.

It was the crossbowmen who did most of the harm. There was no way to fight them as they moved in patrols of ten or twelve and fired volleys of their deadly bolts. They were expert and they seemed to be everywhere. The child army had found bows of their own, but pitifully few. The crossbows were fast turning the tide of battle—and there was very little the young enemy could do about it.

While he ran across another perilously open flat of bog grass, Jeo put the overall strategic worries aside. His only thought was to get back to the lake camp in one piece.

They passed a dead wolfhound in a patch of reeds, lost under a hail of flies. Rhosarran tugged the arrow from its side and pushed it in her belt. They heard the noises of men just ahead, beyond the next jungle of rushes—and cut away to their left—then, after a hundred yards, back to the right—and on, round a growth of purple reeds.

As they forded the next stream, two bodies bobbed in the shallows among the rushes. Children, face down in the water in a pond of blood. A boy, and a girl still holding one of her arms.

It had been severed just below the shoulder and she'd been carrying it senselessly back to the camp. Jeo crossed to the far bank.

A sudden moan behind him. Taw was kneeling in the blood water beside one of the bodies, pulling it round to face upwards. Jeo frowned. Another groan from the boy as he looked into his dead sister's face. He touched the stump of her arm and held the waterlogged head to his chest and sobbed. Rhosarran put a hand on his shoulder but he shrugged it away.

Jeo walked back into the water and took hold of the boy's arm. He struggled but Jeo held on and wrenched him to his feet. For a moment, there was something aimed at Jeo from the eyes in the bald head—but Jeo shook his head and Taw lowered his gaze. They ran together towards the nearby loch and the shelter of the camp. Rhosarran followed fast on their heels.

She was sick of the sight of blood. She wanted an end to all the killing. She wanted time to be with Jeo, to run away over the moors, away from the valley and all the death—but it wasn't what Jeo wanted any more.

She looked at him. He was moving intently through the next block of reeds. She sensed no fear in him now. He was no longer a frightened boy to be protected—and he seemed older than his years, though she could never tell him that. He had more awareness now than she'd guessed was in him, more cunning and savagery —but no fear. He didn't seem to feel anything at all.

As he ran, as he realised how hopeless everything was, Jeo wondered again if there was anything more he could do, anything different—and some of old Sligo's words came to mind, something the fisherman had said about the castle, five years before.

Out of his sight and sound, away on a vast dome of mud, a man on a horse took off his helmet as he talked to his chief captain standing alongside. He was a young man, no more than thirty, as nameless and faceless as every previous Guardian. The captain had a red face and beard.

They scanned the countryside but did nothing to direct operations. It wasn't that kind of fight. They were watching, really just waiting, till all the outlaw children were killed.

But the new Guardian was impatient. They'd left the valley still in turmoil behind them, its buildings ruined by the recent flood, its people killing one another in secret. He'd been appointed to put a quick end to these swamp children, and he didn't have time to waste.

"All those kids taken alive," he said. "Some of them must have said something."

Ouse shook his head. "Not a bloody word out of any of them. Maybe there isn't a base."

"I don't believe that. There must be somewhere they can all run to, one place they can defend together."

The Guardian shook his helmet to cool it. None of the children had said anything about their camp, nor where Jeo could be found. They chose to die instead. He frowned at the fact. No one, not the Elder or any Guardian, could command that degree of loyalty. Ouse held up a linen cloth. The Guardian took it, wiped his face and all his neck and gave it back.

"I want all this over and done with, and soon," he said. "The glen's in a bleeding mess and winter's about to break. We can't waste time spanking unruly children."

"Be easy once Jeo's taken."

"*If* he's taken," said the Guardian. "If we ever get anywhere near him. He's like a rat under the boards. He fights like the best of our men and he uses the right tactics for this place. Yet he's had no training. An old head on young shoulders if ever I knew one."

Ouse grunted.

"What I can't understand," the Guardian went on, "is why he's still alive. He fell down the Pit, didn't he?"

"Everybody saw him. I can't understand it either. No one could have pulled him out."

Another silence as both men let their thoughts wander.

"How long do you think we'll be out here?"

Ouse shrugged. "A week," he guessed. "More, maybe. Ten or twelve days."

"That's what I think too. Too long. We need to do something more."

The captain nodded, but his face was blank.

"Take thirty archers into the south section of the swamp," said the Guardian. "That's the one area we haven't covered. If they have a camp, that's where we'll find it."

He put his helmet back on while Ouse went to look for his horse.

Early night. The darkness settled on the strip of land, out in a lake, where Jeo and the left-overs of his little army sat in groups and licked their wounds. No fires, through lack of wood. Almost no food, broken weapons, soiled dressings for the wounded, nothing for the dying. Children crying—then silence, except on the very tip of the piece of land, where Jeo and some of his auxilliaries were talking in low voices.

Ure was there, and Kyrie and Taw, Rhosarran, no one else. The usual. The loch was placid, not a sound from the faraway reeds. The moon reflected itself sharply on the surface. Kyrie glanced around at the rest of the camp.

"Look at them," he said. "Bloody impressive, aren't they? Half-starved, bleeding to death, no weapons. A few of us can still get away, Jeo."

Jeo nodded. "When there's no chance left, we can run. Then it's everyone on their own. But maybe there's still something we can do."

"There's nothing."

Jeo looked at him from under his brow. "You can leave any time you want to, Kyrie." The freckled man shrugged and looked at the lake.

But he was right. Jeo knew it too. They were only waiting to die.

Jeo raged at the thought. He hadn't come back after five years to die like a rat in a dirty creek.

"Ure," he said, and the tall man came and sat closer. "You were a guardsman. Did you ever go inside the castle?"

"Yes, once."

"Does it have any other way in?"

"Only the main gate," said Ure.

"No tunnels, no secret doors?"

"Not that I know of."

"What are you thinking, Jeo?" asked Kyrie.

"I'm not sure. Maybe there's another way into the castle, a way most people don't know about. If there is, we might be able to use it."

"Someone's told you there's another way in?"

"Not in so many words. It was just something I heard. It might mean nothing."

"Where did you hear it?" asked Ure.

"From an elder."

"An elder?" frowned Taw. "You've not been talking to the old people, Jeo?"

"I heard it years back."

"You can't believe what an elder tells you," said the boy.

"I know," said Jeo. "That's why I'm not sure about it. But if there's any elder I might trust, it's Sligo."

"The old fisherman?" said Ure. "They say he's mad."

"They say wrong."

"I've heard nothing about him for more than a year," said Kyrie. "Maybe he's dead by now."

"Yes, I've thought of that. But maybe he's alive."

"I think he must be," said Taw. "That big idiot Hake would have told everybody if Sligo was dead." Ure agreed.

"And he told you about another gate in the castle?" said Kyrie.

"In a way. He talked about the castle and its hidden tunnels. That's all. Hidden tunnels."

"That could mean anything," said Ure.

"I know that too. But why are the tunnels hidden unless they lead out of the place? There may be something to it—and it may be all we've got left."

Rhosarran frowned. Jeo hadn't told her about the tunnels.

"That's it, is it?" said Ure. "That's our chance of not getting cut to pieces? A couple of words that most likely don't mean a thing, from an elder that can't be trusted, an old man who may or may not be soft in the head? You're grabbing at straws, Jeo."

"What are you grabbing at, Ure?" asked the lizard man, and Jeo looked at him. "What can you offer instead?"

"I say we run. That's what you say too."

"Yes," said Kyrie. "But if there's any chance of taking the glen, I agree we should take it."

"It's no chance at all."

"Maybe not," said Jeo. "I already know that. But I've been five years away. Why do you think I came back? There's nowhere else. Now I'm here, I've got to take the whole glen or be killed. Maybe old Sligo knows a way to help."

"I don't believe he knows anything," said Ure. "I believe if we run we stay alive."

"Then do it." Jeo was severe. "Take your weapons and run, find somewhere else if you can. Take anyone who wants to go with you. I'm going to Sligo."

"This is all well and good," said Kyrie. "But tell us what you expect to do."

Jeo shrugged. "First we have to find a way through the guardsmen's lines to the sea."

"Simple," said Ure.

"Shut it," said Kyrie.

"If we can do that, we have to hope Sligo does know another way in."

"If he does, why should he tell us?" asked Kyrie. "He's an elder. We've killed elders."

"He's not like the others," said Jeo. "He thinks more like we do."

"Maybe. Maybe he used to. But is he the only one who knows about these tunnels, if they exist? Do the other elders and the guardsmen know?"

"If we get to Sligo we'll ask him."

"And if we do get into the castle, what then?"

"We kill the Elder."

"And after that?"

"What we've done so far, it's already turned the glen against the guardsmen. The kids have seen they've got leaders and they've come to join us. So far, the guardsmen are holding the glen—but they're not finding it easy. If the Elder dies, they'll find it impossible. They'll have no figurehead. The whole glen will be turned upside-down."

Kyrie pouted. He wasn't convinced, but it sounded plausible. Very hard to achieve, but just possible. "You *are* reaching for straws," he said. Ure made no comment. Taw looked worried. Rhosarran looked at Jeo.

"What else can I do?" he said. "We're cornered here, finished. Sligo may be worth nothing to us, but he's all I can think of."

A silence. A long one. Nobody liked the thought of relying on an elder, and he was a ludicrously thin hope—but they had no choices.

"It's something to go for, I suppose," said Kyrie. "Better than nothing."

"I thought you'd say that," said Jeo.

"Who goes to Sligo?"

"Me," said Taw.

"No," said Jeo. "Two will have to go, in case one doesn't get through."

"You and me then, Jeo."

"No, you stay here."

"Why?"

"I'll do it," said Ure innocently. "Me and Kyrie can go."

"I'm not letting either of you leave camp," said Jeo. "I'll go. I'll take Rhos with me."

"Oh, yes?" said the tall man.

"Yes. For one thing, I don't trust anyone else. And if we're caught, she can't tell them anything. Anyway, if they take me, they may not bother with the rest of you."

"Very noble," Ure said archly. "And of course you'll both be away from the fighting for a while. Maybe for good."

Jeo's expression was poisonous. "I may have to face more guardsmen, there and back, than you do in a week's fighting. As for not coming back—I've had five years away, remember? I don't want that again. But think what you want, so long as you keep the fight going while we're gone."

"When do you go?" said Kyrie.

Jeo glanced around, out across the loch, over the deep rush beds on every side. The skyline was very dark.

"Now," he said. "No use waiting. It's probably a wild goose chase, but either way I want to get it done as quick as I can. Another night may be too late."

When Ure looked round, Jeo and Rhosarran were nowhere to be seen. He glanced at Kyrie and they exchanged looks before moving off to the centre of the camp to see the wounded. Taw stood watching the lake for a time, then he too moved away from the shore.

The Tunnel

JEO HATED THE MOON. It was always there when he didn't want it. Big and off-white and low in the sky and much too bright, and he needed darkness to move through the guardsman army to the sea. The swampland was well lit, the miles of shadow sliced by streaks of vertical white where the moonlight touched the edge of a billion reed stems. The streams and thin lakes were bright as mirrors.

Jeo and Rhosarran had to stop and hide after every short dash over the marsh. If a moon could have been bled of its light by a knife, Jeo would have done it at once.

They were facing west. The valley was miles away to their left, nothing but more fen to the right, the sea somewhere ahead. They were already in among the army lines, though there were no lines as such. Groups of guardsmen were all over the marsh, some moving at random through the night, most asleep in camps. Jeo touched Rhosarran's arm and she followed him across the next low channel of water.

Into another medley of reeds and rushes. From here they looked out over a big flat of swampland, all grass and dwarf bushes, no waterways, no cover, bright as a day. The outline of a guardsman would have been black and clear on it, but there were no soldiers. The place was empty, and Rhosarran wanted to risk a straight run across it. She nodded to Jeo but he didn't agree.

"Too easy to see us," he whispered. "And if they know we're going west, they'll follow, cut off the sea."

He glanced around then moved away to the left, aiming for

the nearest shelter of reeds, taking the safer long way round. Rhosarran ran alongside and the moonlight made a white stick of her bronze javelin.

They stopped again in the reed bed and saw a patrol of crossbowmen striding through a creek further to the left, their chain mail winking in the light. They passed out of sight and the youngsters moved on.

Jeo knew as well as anyone how stupid it all was, chasing a hope that was nearly nothing—but he had his reasons for it. He had to take the whole glen, nothing less, if he wanted to survive —and if Sligo was the last chance of doing it, he had to see him, simple as that. Anything else was death, or the half-death of exile again.

He led Rhosarran along a thin mudbank and they worked their way through the black and white darkness. They filtered between the teams of guardsmen and reached the sea without being seen and without killing anyone.

The moon was still bright and the rocks and seawater were black and grey and gloomy white. In the cordgrass on the roof of a low cliff overhanging the beach, Jeo and Rhosarran lay on their bellies and watched the shore.

She'd never been here before and thought it an awesome place. Jeo had seen it all before. He searched the shoreline for soldiers and fishermen, but the area was deserted at night. He led her down the rocks, over the rock pools, onto a high dry ledge, and from there into the flank of the cliff itself, in along a very dark passage where the smells of the sea didn't go.

He went slowly along the rock floor, his knife tight in his hand. Rhosarran didn't like being in the tunnel. It was tight and closed and she was a girl of open spaces. She glanced over her shoulder as they went.

In front of them, now so close they touched it, the drape of fishing nets covered the access to the cave beyond. Jeo stopped here, but only to edge the netting aside and look in. Rhosarran's pulse was big. When Jeo brusquely pushed his way into the cavern, she followed close behind him.

The usual firelight in the place, with all its shadows, and the old fisherman lifting a bunch of flatfish onto a hook in the wall. He had his back to the net curtain. When he heard sounds behind him he quickly turned, and when he saw Jeo his face stretched in surprise.

The young man nodded at him and would have said something, a greeting—but Sligo took two steps away to the back of the cave, where he turned to face them with a short iron spike in his hands. He stood crouched in the light of the flames, and his look of amazement was replaced by something stony.

"So it's me you want now," he said. "You've killed other elders, I know. You won't find me so easy."

Jeo didn't say anything. He was looking. The fisherman's face was as he remembered—it had already been too old to change much in five years—but the clothes were very different. No shell collar, no more seaweed thongs. He was wearing an untailored grey sack, holes torn in each corner for his arms and legs, and small flat sandals, nothing else. His hair and beard were longer.

"Put that thing down, old man, before I come and take it from you."

"You can try, boy. There's two of you, so you stand a chance."

Jeo flipped the dagger in his hand and flung it across the cave. It fled through Sligo's hair just beside his neck and buried itself in the wood crab pot behind him. In an instant another knife was poised in the same hand. The old man put his harpoon away in a corner and stood facing them, hands down by his sides.

"I should have known I can't fight you," he said. "Well, if you want me dead, do it and be quick. You don't have time to waste gaping at me."

Jeo shifted the knife in his fingers. "What makes you think we want to kill you?"

"Don't waste time talking, either. You kill elders and guards-men, you and your mob of cut-throats—so you'll kill me. Though why you've come all this way to slit *my* belly, I don't know."

Jeo put the dirk in his belt. "We haven't come to kill you." He jerked a hand towards the doorway. Rhosarran, who'd been staring hard at the fisherman, moved across and stood looking out, holding the nets aside.

"No need for that," said Sligo. "We won't be disturbed. No one comes in here except Hake, you know that—and I've sent him out to mind the lobster pots. He won't be back for a time."

"If he comes in before I'm ready, I'll kill him."

"Mighty ready with that knife, aren't you? I didn't know you could use one." He sat by the fire, motioned for Jeo to join him. The young man hesitated, then crossed the cave and picked his knife out of the wooden pot. He came and sat down facing the fisherman. He kept the dagger in his hand and stayed back from the fire. Rhosarran stayed by the doorway.

"Is that your answer to everything now, that little blade of yours?"

"It's usually the right answer," said Jeo drily.

"Aye, well maybe it is, the trouble you're in. What are things like up in the marsh? Very hard times, I should think."

"You know about that?"

"Boy, I know more than most. Hake brings me news, and if not him then one of the other fishing folk. And when the whole glen's falling apart, it's not something that can be kept quiet. I hear the marsh is awash with guardsmen. How do you fight them?"

Jeo licked his lower lip. "There are ways," he said with a shrug in his voice. "It's not easy."

"That it's not. The army of the glen against a gang of children. I wish you well, young man."

"Do you?"

Sligo leaned earnestly forward. "You hope I do. That's why you're here—you think I'll help if I can. Why else would you be here? You say you don't want to kill me."

Jeo nodded. "If you can't help, we'll all be killed. No one else can do anything for us."

"Who do you mean by *us?* You and your friend here?"

"And a few others back in the marsh. We're all that's left."

"What are you called, girl?"

Rhosarran was looking into the black corridor. She turned and stared at the fisherman and he waited.

"Her name's Rhosarran," said Jeo. "She used to live in Gara's place."

"Then she's the one who killed him. Seems you're well matched, the two of you. But why didn't you say so, lass? Can't you speak for yourself?"

"No," said Jeo. "She can't speak at all."

"I see," said Sligo. "We all have our pains to bear. I thought you were dead, boy."

"I'm not."

"No," said Sligo. "You're alive and killing. You didn't try what I said. You didn't talk first—"

"No. It's a waste of time."

"And this isn't? The bodies in the swamp are not a waste of time and blood? Children are dying—more children than elders or guardsmen."

"I know. That's why I'm here. I told you—we need your help."

The fisherman made a big gesture with his hands. "What can I do, boy?" he frowned. "I can't fight with you, even if I wanted to. What can you ask from me?"

Jeo waited before answering. "When I was here before, you said the castle has tunnels. Hidden tunnels, you said."

"Did I?"

"Do any of them lead outside?"

"A secret gateway or such like, is that what you mean?"

"Give me a straight answer, old man. You said yourself there's not much time."

The fisherman looked hard at him. Rhosarran turned to listen. "No," he said. "They don't lead outside. They're all internal."

Jeo felt himself sink inside. "Liar," he said, though he didn't know for sure. Sligo frowned.

"There are tunnels but no gateways," he said. "Only the centre door."

"I don't believe you."

"So you've said. Why should I lie?"

"Because you're afraid. You don't like the killing I've started. You're afraid of what I can do if I get inside the castle and take the glen."

"There are no other ways in."

"There must be. Why should tunnels be built if they don't lead out?"

"They join the underground dungeons, that's all."

"No. That's too easy an answer. You're lying."

A very small, grim smile from the old man. "If I'm not, you're all finished, aren't you? Without a way into the old fortress, you have nowhere to go."

"That's right. I've got to believe there's another gateway. I do believe it. You've got to tell me where it is."

"Why? You know what I think of the things you've done. Why should I tell you?"

"I'll kill you if you don't."

Sligo knew he was in command. "Kill me and you'll learn nothing," he said. "You'll never breach the castle walls and the guardsmen will garotte you in the swamps. What's more, I don't care very much if you jab me with your little knife. I've had a long life and I'm not desperate to hang on to its last breath. I'm ill, Jeo. My breathing's bad. I won't live long now. You'll be doing me no disservice if you take this life from me. You need a better reason than that."

Rhosarran looked at Jeo as he stared at the fisherman. The youth's face, straw coloured in the firelight, seemed to have lost all hope.

"If we don't get into the castle, the guardsmen will kill us."

"You could run away, some other place. You don't talk about other places any more."

"No."

"Did you find any, the years you were away?"

"All I want is here."

"Then you'll die, as you say. But you're just a few more bodies now. Hundreds have been slaughtered already. When the last of you is dead, it will all be finished."

"It will all be wasted," said Jeo. "All the deaths, all the children you seem to worry about, they'll mean nothing."

"And what will they all mean if I help you, if any of the tunnels do lead out of the castle?"

"The Elder's rule will be broken. No more guardsmen and Shrieking Pits. All the deaths will lead to the changes we talked about before—have you forgotten?"

"You're talking dreams, boy."

"And what are you talking? You're saying there's nothing we can do, so we shouldn't try. You're a pessimist, like all old people."

"You're just a killer. All you've got is a blood lust."

"You're wrong," said Jeo, suddenly very softly. "I want to make things better."

"No." The old man made a show of shaking his head. "There will be more deaths, that's all. Old men and women and the captains. Who knows how many? This way, when your little band is gone, no one else will die."

"How can you talk like that?" said Jeo, his voice raised for the first time. Sligo frowned at the glare in his eyes. "If we all die, everything is back to how it was. Children will die in the Pits as before—maybe hundreds more, as punishment or just as a warning. There will be more guardsmen than ever, and they'll kill people for even looking at an elder. The glen will be a worse place to live—because you won't tell me how to get into the castle."

"No, because you started the fighting."

"I had to, can't you see? Nothing can be changed by just talking. I had to *do* something. And do you think anyone would have helped me if they didn't want to? The whole glen believes in the need for a change—that's why so many have joined me. Talking wouldn't have been enough, so I had to act. You've never done anything but talk—and you've never helped anyone that way, not a single child. Now before it's too late you can help make the changes you know the glen needs. I can turn it into the garden you say it is. You can return to it, away from this place. For once in your life, make your talking mean something. Tell me about the tunnels."

The fisherman looked away from him, stared at a wall, at his own knees, anywhere he didn't meet Jeo's stare. For a time he did nothing but think, both youngsters eyeing him in the brassy light. In the quiet, Jeo heard the fire for the first time, sizzling very softly, and the drip of condensation from a neck of overhead rock, a small regular patter of sound. It had always been there, even when he'd been in the cave years before. He hadn't noticed it before. He started counting the drips. When at last Sligo spoke again, his voice was low, as if weighted.

"Yes. There is another way into the castle. You already know that."

Jeo closed his eyes. A picture appeared in his mind, of himself in an old man's white robes.

"But what good can it do you?" said Sligo. "What will you do if you ever get inside?"

"Just tell me about the way in. How do we reach it?"

Sligo looked through the fire as he talked quickly and gravely. "There's only one way in," he told. "And it's not a gateway as such. You have to go on past the swamp. Miles beyond it, on that same side of the glen. There the land goes up and around to the right and rises into the same foothills where the castle stands. It rises steep and hard, cliffs and the like. The only way up there, if you're not an eagle, is a narrow dirt path at the end of a frozen gully path. They used to call it a goat track, though no goat would ever risk it. Very steep and difficult it is, more of a climb than a hike. At the top of the path, you find yourself back in open hill country, approaching the castle from the side. Close to the fortress walls, there are small holes in the ground rock, hid by great stones. You go down and walk—"

"Go down which hole?"

"Any. They all lead to an ancient tunnel. Walk through the tunnel for maybe a mile, then you come to a place where the roof is broken by age. Pull away the one loose stone above your head, and you come out into daylight—not out on the hill outside the castle but just inside the great wall."

"Who else knows about it?"

"Few. One or two captains, some elders. It's a secret place. Maybe even the Guardian doesn't know of it. He's new."

"It may be guarded."

"Aye, it may be. It should be. But it's a very old, forgotten tunnel, not been used for years on end. Anyway, they're fighting you in the swamps, they must know there's few of you left—they can't think you'll go to the castle. How would you know about any secret way? The garrison won't be expecting an attack from a handful of children." He shrugged. "There again, maybe the tunnel has been filled by rock over the years."

Jeo stood and walked the cave. Rhosarran couldn't catch his eye.

"Don't stay here thinking about it. Go back to the marshes and think about it there if you have to, if the guardsmen don't cut you down on the way. I don't want you here. I don't know that I've done the right thing, but I've told you what I know, all of it, and all you're doing now is wasting your little time—unless you're deciding if you should kill me, lest I tell others of your visit."

Jeo looked at him. Rhosarran suddenly backed from the doorway nets. Footsteps on the rock of the corridor outside. The old man spat in the fire.

"It's only Hake," he said. "Have no fear of him. He'll do what I tell him. Don't harm him with your knife."

Jeo took a second dirk from his belt. The nets parted and

Hake pushed his way into the cave. He had a full sack in one hand, a black trident in the other, and he was bare to the waist, nothing but a twill loincloth below, sandals on his feet. He stared at Jeo and Rhosarran and his blank eyes narrowed. Jeo held one of his knives by the hilt, the other by the blade. Rhosarran pointed her javelin at him. He lifted the trident.

"No, put it down," said Sligo quietly. "They haven't come to do any harm."

Hake frowned. "They been killing old people," he said.

"They won't kill me. Put it down."

He lowered the trident and stared at Jeo. "You were dead," he said. No reply, so he turned to Sligo. "Guardsmen outside," he said simply.

"Where?" said Jeo. "Did you bring them here?" He squeezed his knives. Hake glared at him.

"Me, no, I didn't. I hate them. Maybe you bring them here, they follow you."

"They didn't."

"Maybe they did and you don't know—"

"Where are they?" Sligo asked urgently. "How many of them?"

"Ten, I think. Not here yet. Walking across the sand."

"Go," said Sligo, but Jeo and Rhosarran were already at the net door. The youth and the old fisherman looked at each other but neither spoke as the big man stood aside to let the youngsters run past. They disappeared into the dark of the passage and left the old man to stare blinking into his fire while his giant companion went to put the sack of crayfish against a wall.

The Fisherman

IN THE SHORT TIME they'd spent in Sligo's cave, nothing had happened to the light outside. The moon was still strong and Jeo, edging out of the cliff wall, could see the entire shoreline easily enough. A cluster of black figures were moving along the sand. Some were already scaling the lower rocks towards him. He wondered if they were coming to see Sligo, and what they wanted with him. He led Rhosarran to the right along the ledge, keeping to the widest shadows, and they crept a hidden way to the top of the cliff. A shout from a guardsman below, but they didn't look back. They quickened the pace of their climb and the soldiers didn't give chase. The shout hadn't been a cry of discovery or any kind of command. It was nothing. Jeo and Rhosarran ran unseen from the roof of the shore across leagues of grass before reaching the first range of fenland.

Back to the slow motion of creeping from one bank of rushes to the next. As he stooped in a soaking undergrowth, Jeo felt the silence of the vast place. It was quiet for miles. All night birds had long left, fleeing the carnage. There were no small stealing animals making their noises. There was no zither of insects, not a wind, not so much as the blub of a toad.

It was strange but it was good. There were no distracting sounds. If any guardsmen moved within a hundred paces, Jeo would hear them before they heard him.

It took two hours of painstaking movement to cross just the first few miles. Then, soon after reaching the deeper marshes, they had to stop and lie flat on their bellies in the cold water at the feet of a broad reed patch as a detachment of guardsmen chose the same spot for a place to take a quick rest.

For half an hour they stood around and chattered, wishing they were back in their brochs, boasting of the children they'd killed, drinking beer from long skins. Jeo smelled the tobacco they were chewing. And then they went away.

Rhosarran led for a while, along the bank of a long, straight canal, flanked by high rushes so they could run upright. They crossed a span of open grass and were briefly caught in the stark moonlight and a man followed them at a furtive distance with a spear in his hand.

Another crop of reeds, then another—and on, in a long twisting route towards the distant loch. They passed bodies in the swamp, six in all, looted of weapons—a guardsman in mud, children in other places. A girl's head lay trapped by roots in the shallows at the edge of a rushbank, the upturned face chill white under the moon, eyes in shadow, mouth open, like the face of a naiad coming up to taste the air. Jeo imagined a body under the face, underwater. But there was no body at all.

They shuffled through a hash of bullrushes and looked out. More open land, cut by a stream. The lakeside camp was barely an hour ahead. To the left, they saw nests of low reeds—and above them, a flat mile away, the landmark of a gallows, overhung with carrion, moonlit but mostly black.

They were both on hands and knees. They stood up. The giant dark figure of a man rose silently from the rushes behind them and moved quickly over the grass. They were facing away and didn't see him.

Then, as he closed on them, his feet slithered and made a brusque movement on the wet grass. The sound was a very small one, negligible, but Jeo glanced round—and had time for one shocking glimpse of the huge shape before the man brought his spear thrusting down with both hands.

Jeo jerked aside. The lance came down—and again, as he slipped and fell and was on his back. Again it missed, this time spiking the ground, as Jeo rolled away and jumped up, knife in hand.

The man didn't speak as he turned to face the youth, jutting again with the spear. Rhosarran made to throw her javelin and the giant shirked it, and Jeo used that moment to throw himself forward, knocking the man down. Quick as an ape he was on top, kneeling astride the other's chest, one hand over the bearded mouth. He had his knife against the big neck, ready to stab down through the throat, when he looked at the face, pale against the grey grass. The man's weapon lay near his head and Jeo saw it wasn't a lance but a trident.

"Hake," he said quietly, taking his hand from the fisherman's mouth. Rhosarran stood close by, her javelin held ready. They made a bizarre tableau.

"Why are you following us? You tried to kill me."

Hake lay still under the point of the dagger. There were bruises on his cheeks, one on the forehead. His eyes were big with malice.

"You killed Sligo," he said.

"Not so fucking loud," Jeo whispered savagely. "You'll bring guardsmen round us like flies. What do you mean—I killed Sligo? He was alive when we left you."

"You killed him. You bring guardsmen to him. Now they killed him."

"They didn't follow us. We saw them on the beach. They came from the direction of the glen. Sligo told me something to help me fight them."

"What did he tell you?" snapped Hake. "Nothing he didn't tell you. Sligo didn't know things to tell. Just a fishing man. He was my friend."

Rhosarran pushed Jeo's shoulder and he looked at her. She urged him to do something quickly. They were exposed out there with no cover. He nodded and looked down at the big man.

"I ought to kill you and finish," he whispered.

"Do it." The voice was flat. "I don't care now. My friend

is dead and everybody fighting. The guardsmen will kill me if you don't."

Jeo had no time to waste, but he hesitated. His dirk was a thumb-length from the giant's neck. A single plunge and he could leave the body behind and run on. He wanted to kill the fisherman. It would make sense. It was his better instinct. But he was thinking how small his band of followers was, how it could use some more muscle, someone whose hatred of guardsmen matched his strength. He remembered how Hake had approached him years before, the night of the Gathering at the Stones, saying they could kill soldiers together. He stood up from the big man's chest and allowed him to rise.

A quick look in all directions. "What are you going to do now?"

"Don't know," said Hake. "Can't go back nowhere. Hide and kill guardsmen before they kill me, I think."

Jeo looked at him and afforded himself a moment's thought. "Come with us," he said. Rhosarran was already running to the nearest reed cover and they followed. They hid in among the tall stems and looked out along the length of yet another skinny creek.

"Why did they kill Sligo?" asked Jeo.

"Don't know. They said time he was dead, he was trouble. Then they beat him with their sticks."

"Why didn't they kill you too?"

"They tried. They cut me." Jeo saw the welts on his face and the drying blood on his forearm. "I killed two and run away. I knew you can't be far away, you got to move careful, not fast, so I follow and I know I'd find you. Everybody knows you fighting in the marsh. I wanted to find you and kill you."

"You still want to?"

"No." The giant bowed his head. "Sligo said you're his friend. You could have killed me just now. You let me get up."

"Come with us. We can use you."

"Yes." The big face looked almost cheerful in the reed-stripe shadows. "I'm strong. I can help you."

Rhosarran began to edge out of the reeds. She had Hake's trident in her hand and he reached for it.

"Give me that," he said. She didn't.

"Not yet," said Jeo. He went out onto the mud and across the creek and disappeared into a thicket of high white grass. Hake followed, Rhosarran behind him.

Not a cloud in the sky as dawn crept up on the marshes, but the light was grey. On the shores of a lake, the mass of reed stems was black on the grey. They spread over the lake and hid the causeway of land that edged out into the water. On the bank, hidden in sweet-grass, a tall man and thin boy and a girl looked out for signs of life.

"Nothing," said Jeo in his lowest voice. "No one at all. They've left the place unguarded. I'll kill Kyrie—"

Rhosarran touched him and pointed across the loch. He saw a figure moving, very slightly, among the causeway reeds. The girl was about to get up and walk across to the encampment. He was ready to follow. Then he looked again at the dark figure and suddenly grasped her arm to keep her low. She stared and saw that the outline of the head was rounded by a guardsman's helmet.

"I don't believe it," whispered Jeo. "They can't have found us so soon." He stared at the sentry. There was only one. "I've got to find out what's happened," he said.

"I'll go," said Hake, but Jeo wouldn't let him.

"You'll make too much noise, and you'll probably kill him before I can ask him anything."

He made very little noise as he waded with practised care through the shallows. The guard turned only his head as he stood watching the shore. Jeo saw the line of his profile, then the back of his head, then sprang out of the reeds and dragged him to the ground, the grip of his hand across the throat cutting off any cry of surprise. He held a knife blade to the face.

"No noise," he said, and then frowned. The helmet was

askew and the face was round and small and very young. "Taw," he breathed. "What's happening here?" He jabbed the dirk back in his belt and stood away to let the boy get up.

"Just guard duty, Jeo," he said breathlessly.

"Is that what you call it? Didn't see me coming, did you? Might as well have no guards at all if they can't see when we're under attack." Taw looked sheepish. "And why are you wearing that helmet, and the chain mail?"

Noises to one side, from the direction of the camp. A group of armed boys and girls came out of the reeds, some in helmets and mail, the lizard man at the head.

"Jeo," he said. "We thought you weren't coming back."

"No doubt," said Jeo. "What's all this armour for? Where did you get it?"

"From the guardsmen," said Kyrie. "Where else could we get it? Took it from their bodies. Did you get anything from the old man? Is there another way into the castle?"

"Let's get back to the camp," said Jeo. "It's getting light and we may be seen out here."

"Hake," said Kyrie, as Rhosarran and the fisherman came into view. "What's he doing here, Jeo? He's a simpleton."

"You talk to me like that, I'll kill you," said Hake.

"He's no better than a child. Get rid of him, Jeo." Some of the others agreed.

"He stays," said Jeo. "We need his strength. He's already killed guardsmen. They killed Sligo after we left. They tried to kill him too, that's why he's wounded. He can help us fight them."

"How did he find you?" Kyrie asked.

"Tracked us in the marsh," said Jeo. "He thought we led the guardsmen to Sligo, so he followed—"

"What? He thought you caused Sligo's death? And you want to let him stay?"

"We need any help we can find," said Jeo. "He hates the guardsmen as much as anyone. And he knows how to use that three-prong spear."

"He didn't use it on you, by the look of things."

Jeo set his teeth. "You've had your say and he stays. We can use him. And I trust him as much as I trust you."

He turned away before any more could be said, and went to the camp. The others followed. They trooped along the strip of marshy ground and reached the encampment itself. All the others were there, the rest of the pocket army, scattered in twos and threes, some still asleep. Some stood when they saw Jeo. He noticed how few were left.

"Is this all?" he said in no tone of voice. "Nobody else? Nobody out hunting?"

"No," said Kyrie. "This is all that's left."

Jeo looked around. There were twenty in the camp. Hardly any weapons. No sign of any food. "How many wounded?"

"All of us," shrugged Kyrie. "But only three badly hurt. The guardsmen kill us rather than wound us. Kelpie's going to die."

Jeo didn't speak. He looked blankly out over the loch. Rhosarran went to the wounded.

"What did Sligo say?" asked Kyrie.

"There's another way in," said Jeo. "Now we have to try and get to it."

The freckled man nodded. "Leave it for a day or two," he suggested. "We might still get some more kids joining us from the glen."

Jeo moved away to the far side of the camp. The small boy Kelpie caught his eye and he knelt to talk to him.

The Captain

DAYBREAK OVER THE BROAD lakelands came with a mist that went away and left the sky clear and poison blue with just a veil of cloud. The light was good—and Jeo, standing on the shore of one of the lakes, could see for miles in every direction. The land was flat and the reedbanks short. An upright guardsman would have been easy to see above them.

There were no men at all. No soldiers. No sign of the youngsters in his dwindled army who were scattered in pairs around the marsh, hunting food. Jeo looked out across the lake itself.

It was small and narrow, no more than a simple highland tarn, shallow and clean and garnished with muddles of rushes and fox-tail grass. Jeo filled his chest with the air, which was thin and sharp, and caught the scent of bog myrtle from across the lake.

In the water near the far bank, Rhosarran swam aimlessly away from him, her hair slick and dark, spreading on the surface. He kicked off his boots and untied his rope belt just as a small genial rain began to fall, spottling the surface of the lake like the marks of small fish biting the water for flies. He left his clothes and knives among the rushes behind him and walked into the water. Very soon it was deep and he had to swim. It was chill but he was used to it and didn't gasp when his body was immersed.

He knew he should have stayed on the bank, waiting for Rhosarran to finish her bathe. Now they were both unsafe, naked in the water. But just now, just for a while, he didn't care. He took the few small free minutes to lose himself, almost lose himself, in the peaceful silence and coldness of the little lake. For a time, at least, he had the chance to be clean.

He swam underwater like a white bonefish and broke the surface close to the far side. The water had flattened his hair down over his face and he wiped it aside with his palm. He looked up and saw that Rhosarran was moving out of the lake. There was no slope on this shore and she had to lift herself out with her arms. He watched the movement of her buttocks and the single swing of her hips. As her feet touched dry land, he reached and held one of her ankles.

She made a sound like a chuckle and turned to face him. He tugged at her ankle and she lost some of her balance and let herself fall on the grass. He pulled her towards him till she was sitting on the edge of the bank facing him with her feet in the water. Thinking he wanted her to join him, she moved off the bank— but he put his hand on her belly to stop her, then pushed her so she lay on her back on the bank. She took her heavy breasts in her hands and closed her eyes at the sky.

Her legs were already apart but he moved them further. He stood in the lake with the water level just below his hips and moved his face high between her inner thighs.

She had no taste. The flesh was simply wet and cold and he warmed it with his mouth. He moved his tongue very simply, up and down, alternating long strokes with the short fast flickers he knew she liked, sometimes kissing in her lips. He felt her leg muscles harden as she pointed her toes, and listened for her different gasps.

She opened her eyes very wide and didn't see anything and neither of them felt the rain as it dropped on their bodies and on the lake and among the reeds across the water, where Kyrie watched them for a while with a tight-lipped expression.

He heard Jeo laugh, a sound he didn't associate with him. A laugh with no triumph or derision or cruelty. A sound rarely heard in the glen. He listened and watched and finally moved away through the reeds and disappeared.

Soon Rhosarran slid back into the water and washed herself
and Jeo climbed out and stood dripping on the bank. He looked
back across the tarn and saw nothing out of the ordinary. Rhosarran was swimming to the other side, to where her clothes and
weapon lay with his in the rushes. It was time to go back to the
camp. A sound in the long grasses behind him.

He turned. Something moved, big and brusque, in the grass.
Jeo took some steps back to the waterside, his body in a crouch
and his face with a wide-eyed scowl, hands reaching for weapons
he didn't have.

There were no animals or wading birds to be making such
a noise in the swamp. He listened and stared at the wall of grass
and nothing seemed to be happening. He turned to his right and
walked around the lake. Rhosarran climbed the opposite shore and
turned to look for him. She wiped water from her eyes and nose.
The tall grass parted across the lake and she saw two bearded
guardsmen come out almost delicately onto the open bank. They
had shields and short swords.

Jeo wasn't looking at her and she couldn't shout to him. She
kicked one of her feet in the water—and when he glanced to the
noise, pointed urgently behind him. He turned and faced the
soldiers and for a moment he didn't move.

They seemed to have stumbled upon him. Certainly they
stopped in their tracks when they saw him. One of them gave a
short grunt of surprise. They seemed taken aback to find him, and
to find him naked. Then they raised their shields and came at him,
hesitant though he was unarmed, like men who'd been hunting a
young, wild killer beast and now found him almost thrillingly in
front of them. They moved on him cautiously, as though they
knew that cornered as he was, he might be at his most dangerous.
From his crouch and the look of his face, they almost expected him
to leap at them with claws and teeth.

Jeo saw at once that neither had a crossbow or a throwing
weapon, so he turned without hesitation and sprinted away around

the bank, hugging the shoreline. The soldiers chased him through the drizzle.

Rhosarran wasted no time in jumping to the nearby reeds and snatching up two short knives from the heap of clothing. Jeo was still some way away and she ran to him with the dirks.

The soldiers saw they had little chance of overtaking them. They had no clothes or iron to weigh them down. One of the guardsmen gave a shout and it was answered by similar calls in the distance ahead. Jeo, glancing, saw several vague figures moving towards him through the high cross-reeds on the right.

He ran faster still, round the lake, and waved Rhosarran on ahead of him. They dashed away from the tarn with the soldiers in pursuit, crossed another of the shallow marsh canals, and soon lost themselves in the sodden undergrowth on the other side.

There, for the time being, they squatted and caught their breath and hid as best they could. Rhosarran held out his twin-blade knife and he took it.

For a few moments, nothing. Then the noise of heavy movement through the rushbank, from two directions at once. Jeo rose to his feet and listened hard as he stared into the forest of stems. The noises grew louder, a soldier shouted something. Jeo slapped Rhosarran's shoulder and pushed her away in one direction while he moved off in another, running in a low stoop with the dirk held out in front of him. His feet made noises in the water and the squelching rushes, but he couldn't help that.

He forgot about the girl and sidled away to the right, in an arc that took him back, not forward, to one corner of the rushbank. He stepped cautiously out into the next broad channel, glanced both ways along it, then crossed over and ran along the thin grass strip on the other side, following the line of the creek in a roughly northern direction, towards the region where his own forces were dispersed.

After a hundred yards or more, the tall bullrushes came to their end and he was back in flat empty country with miles of bogland ahead of him. He looked back along the length of the canal and saw there was no pursuit, then ran on. The last patch of rushes was just ahead on his left and he was almost beyond it, the open waste in front of him, when two more figures burst out of the undergrowth and stood in his way.

They were only lightly armed, and for a moment he thought they were two of his own. But they were guardsmen with javelins and small riot shields. Jeo stopped quite still and clenched his knife. He saw to his dismay that one of them had a chalk-white scar on his face under the light iron helmet. The lower lip was cut in two pieces. There was a big grin in the captain's eyes, though the face didn't move at all.

A cold thrill in Meagher's belly. This was the first time he'd seen the man-boy since the day at the Pit, the first time in five years and more. He could hardly believe Jeo was alive. He wasn't afraid, but he couldn't help being halted by the difference in him. The black hair was wilder and much longer, the skin still pale but with a harder look to it, the tension of an animal in the spare body. There were muscles now, like creepers twined round the thin bones. Hardly the same boy at all. A look was still there in those eyes, but it was harshly different.

Jeo clenched his lips and held the knife further in front of him, but otherwise made no move. The two men had their javelins. They stepped apart from each other and came in at him from two angles. Meagher stared at his face and watched him closely, and still didn't speak.

Jeo surprised them by lunging forward with his knife, and they thrust out their spears to halt him. As they did so, he dashed away to one side and crashed his way into the bank of tall reeds before they could twist their javelins into a throwing position.

They didn't follow him into the reeds. The captain pointed with his spear and the other soldier ran round to the left, round the reedbank, while Meagher moved off to the right. It was a small patch of plants and the boy couldn't hide in them. He would have to emerge almost at once. When the two guardsmen met round the other side of the bank, they saw him sprinting wildly away ahead of them.

Meagher spent a few seconds looking around ahead. There was only open land, acres of it, nowhere to hide. In the distance, a straggle of figures in helmets and armour, away to the left. They moved towards the fleeing youth and he veered away from them, his tense white body shining with rain against the grey background sky. There was nothing else to look at. The captain set off to give chase, the other guardsman alongside, and though Jeo ran like a small deer they gained on him strongly.

It seemed to him, as he careered over the empty heathland, that he'd been through all this before, all those years ago. The same frantic escape bid over the open wastes, the same captain chasing, the familiar pains of running, the same fear and despair. He longed for an end to it.

He was moving fast, he knew. He was some way ahead of the two guardsmen. But he also knew they only had to run within throwing distance to kill him. And the other armed figures he'd just seen, coming in at him from the far left, they too had lances. He ran faster but he was tiring. Even in the drizzle, he heard the two soldiers gaining on him. He was quick but they were older and stronger.

A noise—and a javelin thrashed through the air close to his shoulder and stabbed the grass just ahead. He angled sharply away, further to the right. Again he felt he'd seen all this before, the lance or the crossbow bolt shooting past. Even the knife in his hand was the same. Naked as he was, it was once again the last thing he had.

Ahead of him, a huddle of white birch trees. He dashed towards them, though he knew they were no shelter. It was just somewhere to run.

He brushed past the trees, ran on beyond them, then came to a halt. He was tired and there was nothing ahead of him, no point in running any more. Just as he did all those years before among the Shrieking Pits, he stopped and turned, knife in hand, to face his enemies.

He was just in time to see the captain and the other man coming out between the trees. In the distance behind them, far away, the impression of others running to join them, shadowy in the rain.

Again the two soldiers moved away from each other. Whichever of them had thrown the javelin had retrieved it, and they now both stood facing him with spears at the ready.

Again Jeo made some sort of move towards them. But this time they raised their shields and drew their weapons back to throw. He had very little time to think. Meagher was to his right, and he wanted to spend his knife on the captain, but the second guardsman was much closer on his left, close enough to strike— and he had to act quickly.

He feinted a throw to the man's abdomen. The shield came down. He threw his knife into the crux of the man's neck and the soldier fell, as though dead before he hit the ground.

Jeo knew it was his last throw. He was grimly glad it had been a good one. Even as he made a half-turn to face the captain, he had some last satisfaction in his despair.

Meagher moved a step closer. For the first time he could remember, Jeo saw a grin on the captain's face. It twisted his scar and made a mess of his lip. There was no need now for him to hide anything. The boy who'd cut his face and laughed at him in full view of his own men, the cause of his shame and demotion —the same youth was standing in front of him, naked and un- armed and helpless.

But Jeo felt no wretchedness as he stood there. He wasn't sure he felt anything at all. He stared at the captain's face. In the very few seconds he looked at it, he saw how much it had aged, even in just a few years. More lines under the eyes, the skin looser on the cheekbones, the hair all grey. It was older, but he didn't hate it for that. He despised it because it had grown softer, frail, hardly the face of a soldier at all.

Meagher had many things to say, too much to speak. He didn't say anything because his split lip made him lisp and he didn't want Jeo to hear it. He drew back his javelin. Jeo stared at him.

The first of the other armed men came running in from behind the captain. Jeo glanced. Meagher, who felt no need to hurry, turned idly to look.

The colour seeped from his face and he stepped aside in disbelief as he saw that the newcomer wasn't one of his guardsmen but a hulking figure in oilskin rags with a helmet tight on his head and an iron trident grabbed in both hands.

The captain's eyes were wide in almost excessive surprise. He seemed utterly stricken by the arrival of the big man, who now held the trident high above his head. Meagher made a small move to protect himself, but it was too late. The trident blurted through his chain-mail coat and crushed its way through his chest in a single heavy thrust.

The captain fell back and was dead on the soaking ground. Jeo looked breathlessly at Hake. The big bearded face was almost smiling. Jeo crossed to the corpse of the other soldier and took out his knife. Hake pulled out his trident from Meagher's ribs. The other figures ran in towards them. Taw and Ure and three others, all in guardsman mail. One threw him a wool cloak and he put it round himself.

As they left the copse, Jeo passed the captain's body and gave it a look. The face was upturned and the bristle of rain fell on it, on the bloodless scar and on the eyes still wide open, still more in surprise than terror.

Jeo, folded in a stiff blanket, stood with his back to the others, staring out across the darkness of the windbeaten moor.

Meagher was dead but it made no difference. The Guardian and the other captains were still out there. The lakeside camp had been discovered and destroyed. There were archers all over the moors, swordsmen in the swamps. Most of the child army had been killed or taken to the valley. Only nine were left, now jumbled round a small ember fire in the half-shelter of a stone mound out on the eastern heath, some in plundered chain mail, some in rags. They would have to move on before first light, before the soldiers came. They didn't know where to go. No more children had come from the valley to join them.

Rhosarran watched Jeo from the darkness around the fire. She looked at some of the others, thinking nothing about Ure and Hake and turning away when she saw Kyrie staring at her. She knew something of the way he thought about her—the way he glanced at her body, the way he looked when Jeo touched her. She didn't know if he was interested in her because she was a girl—she knew he liked girls—or for who she was, because she was mute or because she was unattainable. Whatever it was, she couldn't do much about it, and in the circumstances, it didn't matter much. There were more serious things to think about.

She watched as Jeo turned back to the others and sat on the cold earth. He looked at them one by one in the dull firelight, then stared at the ground. "No one's going to help us," he said. "No one can get through the guardsmen—so there's only the castle left. We'll have to see if Sligo's hole in the ground is guarded or not."

Some of the others nodded. Not Kyrie.

"Not yet," he said. Jeo looked at him from under his brow. The freckled man shrugged with his hands. "There's guardsmen all over the place," he went on. "Chances are we won't get past them. Even if we do, if we get all the way to the castle without being killed, even if Sligo's other way in is open, even then we can't do anything."

"We can find our way to the Elder himself," said Jeo.

"But what then?" said Kyrie. "Even if we're all still alive, even if by some huge chance we take the whole bloody castle by killing the old man, where does that leave us?"

"It leaves us in command of everything. The whole glen is ruled from the castle."

"Only because the Elder's in it. Even if we somehow kill him, and everyone else in the place, we'd still be the same outcasts, still hunted. They'd starve us out in the end—the glen people, not just the guardsmen, because they'd hate us."

"So," said Jeo, "we have to find a way of making the people turn against the elders and the guardsmen."

"That's right," said Kyrie.

In the short pause, they heard the wind running away through the heather. It blew on the embers and they were brighter but no warmer. Jeo moved the blanket on his shoulders.

Someone moved away from the fire and came to him. He turned and saw Rhosarran and gave her a drab smile—then frowned questioningly. He could see all the colour of her hair because she carried a small red-smouldering twig in her fingers, plucked from the fire, and it cast a glow on her head and upper body.

She thrust the burning twig at him and he recoiled. But he saw how fervid bright her eyes were, how very eager. She had a memory in mind but he didn't know that—all he saw was the hot stick. But he could guess what she was thinking.

She held the twig to him and he looked at it, then back at her. She nodded fiercely and there were small smiles in the shadows on their faces, the same look in their eyes. Kyrie and the others watched from the half-dark. Rhosarran waved her hand and the tiny fire went out. The darkness was back and all Jeo could see was the smoke.

Astride the river, on one of its bridges, Rhosarran stood and stared, and though her face was covered with dark ash and sweat, she gleamed at the sights around her. Once before, she'd stood on the same bridge, with her old shepherd keeper, and looked at the torchlights reflected on the water and thought of seeing the glen in flames. Now here she was again, smiling again, and this time it was happening. The tenement blocks were burning. They were black against the greying night sky; some had small winking flame-lights in them, some were draped in bulging clouds of pale smoke.

And the giant hovels weren't the only places burning. The barns and bartons were ablaze, the grain houses, the huge sty and the byres. In the firelights, Rhosarran saw Kyrie and some of the others running away, still with torches in their hands, their work done. They were all in looted guardsman uniforms and helmets and the valley dwellers would believe the soldiers had burned the glen.

Even the river was on fire, the wind blowing long flags of flame along the oils and fats that spilled onto the water. It looked beautiful burning. Rhosarran heard noises on the riverbank and ran off the bridge up the slope.

THE OLD MAN

The Charcoal

HIGH ON THE NORTHWEST SLOPE, in the fringe of a beechwood, Hake sat on a log and stared down at the valley.

He had his elbows on his knees, his chin in his hands, and he was pouting. There was very little in his eyes. A touch of disbelief.

The glen was spread out before him, and the greens of the grass were smirched with acres of black, the seared remains of the great tenements. Rain had slaked the miles of wood, but it hadn't dampened the tart smell of burning which still rose from the wreckage. Hake, high on the hill, could smell it from where he was.

The blocks had burnt so very quickly, he remembered, the fires jumping from one to the next, blown by haphazard winds. The whole glen, and most of its people, burnt to the ground in two days. It was charcoal now.

The huge gnarled cinders had smouldered for days. Then a rain came and put out the last of the fires and ended the smoke.

And after the rain, ash. The great fires had hurled their volumes of smoke high in the sky. When the smoke cooled, it turned to ash that fell out of the air in a relentless thin powder that no one could see. Anyone who stayed out on the open land was tainted and had to wash the grey dust from limbs and face. Jeo's band stayed well out of sight, under cover, and were not sullied. All the grass and nettles were dirty green and the few remaining livestock coughed as they trudged in the fields.

There were no guardsmen in the brochs, no elders in the valley. When the news of the burning reached the commanders in the swamps, they brought the army back to the glen. There had been no more sign of the outlaw youths. They were assumed dead or more likely fled over the moor. So the soldiers came back.

When their captains saw what had happened, the glen was evacuated. Every remaining wain and cart had been seized, and loaded with the last of the unspoiled foodstuffs. Then the food and the bales of winter clothing and the guardsmen and the elders went to the castle, leaving the glen and its people to fend for themselves. It had all happened very quickly, to some long-ordained strategy. There had been no time for much protest, and what protest there was had been brushed, murderously, aside. All the guardsmen were gone, though it was said some of their informers had been abandoned in the glen.

Hake wasn't thinking about informers. He was grieving, slightly, for the valley, for the dead and the utterly destroyed. No one in the glen had ever loved him, but it was all he'd ever known. Strange, sickening, to see it in black ruins.

He was wondering, too, why he and Jeo and the others were still in hiding, still waiting. No one had told Hake what was going on, so he didn't understand. But then there seemed to be many things he didn't understand. His face itched and he wiped it and saw that it left soot on his hand.

No rain for a week. The sun came out but it wasn't hot.

Some ten days after the fire, a band of armed figures came out of a beechwood and settled high on the northern hillside, where they stayed for the rest of the day. They were seen at once but no one went towards them. Without the guardsmen to tell them, no one was sure what to do. They knew who these newcomers were. They saw Jeo and they saw the young crossbowmen at his side and they were afraid.

"He wants us to go to him," said a young girl. Her father turned to her. He was an anonymous man with a white face and small beard. She had red hair.

"What are you talking about, girl?"

"He's waiting for us to go up," she said. She was twelve years old.

"How can you tell?"

She shrugged. The man looked up the hill and shook his head. "We can't go up there," he frowned. "He's the cause of all this."

"We have to. He's all that's left."

He glared at her but she wasn't afraid of him any more. She turned and walked away.

"Didn't you hear me, girl? I said we won't go up there."

She turned to look at him and her head was tilted back a fraction. "Haven't you learned anything?" she said quietly. "Don't you know it's not for you to say?" She went away. A boy, older than her, laughed and followed her up the slope.

So, towards evening, the people of the valley, led by their young, began to make their way up the hillside. Before nightfall, the slope was crowded. Nearly all the survivors were there, in groups in the cold, waiting for Jeo to speak to them. Those who'd known him saw how much he'd changed. It was strange to see him alive.

There were some forty others around him, the numbers swollen in the days after the fire, by young men and girls running from the tenements. His own little group of arsonists was there too. Having started the fires that slaughtered the thousands, they now came out of the wood in their guise of saviours to pick up the spoils. They were all armed, though their guardsmen uniforms had long been discarded and they were in strong warm rags.

Jeo stepped away from the others and stood lower on the slope in front of the crowd below him. He smelled the burnt grass and the charcoal buildings.

There were very few old people in the crowd. Most of the elders were in the castle, though many had died in the fires, died because they were too weak and slow to get out in time. Survival had been for the strong and the quick. Survival, for the most part, of the young.

They stared up at Jeo in silence, standing in their various groups, divided by age. He looked over their heads at the stricken valley and threw out a dramatic hand. "Who did all this?" he asked. His voice sounded grim.

Silence. It went on so long he was about to repeat himself, then a young voice said simply "Guardsmen."

"That's right," said another. "I saw one myself. Guardsmen with flame torches."

Jeo nodded. "And now they've gone into the castle."

"Aye, and taken everything in with them," grunted a voice. Others muttered.

"As you say, taken everything with them." Jeo stared towards the distant fortress as though lost in thought. He faced the crowd again.

"It's almost winter." He said it quietly, making them listen hard. "And they've taken everything. The barns are burnt, most of the livestock dead. We can't feed ourselves. We've got no shelter when the snow comes. We can't last till spring."

He paused for effect and pointed to the mountains. "That's the only place with any food," he said. "It's your food and it's in the castle. If you want to live, you have to go in and get it. Simple as that."

"Oh aye," said a man blinded in the fire. "Simple as that." Others laughed with him.

"What do we do, boy?" said a woman. "Walk up to the caer door and knock?"

More laughter. Higher on the hill, Kyrie bowed his head to hide a smile. Jeo scowled.

"There's another way in," he said. "A small group can maybe find its way in without being seen—then, if and when the main door is opened, you can go in, all of you, kill the guardsmen and take the food, the castle, and all the glen."

"That's all very well," someone said. "You make it sound nice and easy. But we got no weapons and the caer is full of guardsmen. They'll cut us up like sheep. We wouldn't have no chance."

"That's right," said a girl. Jeo shrugged.

"What else can we do?" he said. "It's the only place to go. And there are more of us, we outnumber the guardsmen twenty to one. You say there's no weapons. Make them. Take wood from the burnt blocks, from the forests, iron from the farmsheds. Search for hammers and shears and knives, anything you can lay hands on." He made a fierce gesture with his fist. "You should *want* to fight. The guardsmen burnt the blocks and left you out here to starve."

Talk in the crowd, some nodding. A thin young woman stepped to the front and looked him in the face. "Why you?" she said. "Why should we do what *you* say? You started all this. Where were *you* when the fires were burning? Why should we follow you?"

Jeo moved his gaze among them. "I saw what they were really like, the elders. I saw it when I was a child and I've tried to do something about it—which is more than any of you did. That's where I was when the burning started—out in the marshes fighting. All these fires and thieving, they're not my doing. All I've done is kill the ones who were bleeding us." He looked again at the outspoken girl. "Who's going to blame me for that?"

The girl looked away. The crowd looked to him. Kyrie, impressed, lifted his eyebrows a fraction.

"And if by a miracle we take the caer, master—what then?" A middle-aged man, greying in his beard, moved to the front of the crowd. "You're to be the new Elder, I suppose?" He smirked and narrowed his eyes.

Jeo's face was unmoved. "No one will be called that any more. But if we do take the castle, we'll have to rebuild the glen next. We'll need someone to take charge of that—and after everything I've done, I won't follow anyone else." The man nodded knowingly. "Anyway," Jeo added, "I can't be the Elder. I'm too young."

Scattered laughs. Jeo pointed among them with his knife, stopping any amusement. "Talking of age," he said, "I won't live in the glen with anyone who's old. No more elders. They caused all this. If you follow me and do what I say, I want no old people. Before we move on the castle, I want them all thrown in the Pits, where they wanted to throw me."

"Old people?" queried the same middle-aged man. "How old, chief? Older than yourself?"

Jeo leaned down towards him. "Old as you," he said quietly.

"That's all?" said Kyrie, with a frown. "Just five of us? You're sure that's enough?"

Jeo buckled his belt. "Plenty. Any more is too many. More chance of being seen."

"Alright—but is it the right five? Maybe you should stay here. Keep an eye on things. You'd be safer."

Jeo gave him a half-amused frown. "And leave you to get into the castle without me?"

A resigned shrug from Kyrie.

"Anyway, I have to go," said Jeo. "I'm the only one who knows the other way in. And I'm not telling you about it."

"Maybe we should take Taw with us."

"No, five is enough. I'll leave him in charge here."

"We might need him. He's quick and clever and he fights well."

"No."

"Why not?"

"No, he's too young. He stays here and we leave as soon as it's dark. Make sure we've got enough arrows. We might be more than a week in the mountains."

"You're gambling, aren't you?" said Kyrie. "You're staking everything on Sligo's tunnel being unguarded."

"Yes."

"What are the odds?"

"About the same as getting through the guardsmen to Sligo —and we did that. About the same as finding out there was a tunnel at all."

"Long, in other words."

"Yes, but not impossible. Anyway, if the place is guarded, we can still survive out there."

"With no food or shelter?"

"I did it for five years. There are ways, for the five of us."

"And you'd leave all the others back here to starve? They trust you."

Jeo's scowl was more impatient than angry. "Think of yourself first, Kyrie. You always do."

He went to fetch more warm clothing. Kyrie frowned as he packed his own sack, thinking his own thoughts.

He faced along the length of the valley to the mountains. The northern slope was to his right. Above and beyond it, the giant swamps. The five of them would have to walk for miles along the ridge of the slope, going directly east—then, after passing the marshland, climb the first foothills and go to the right towards the higher mountains, to approach the castle from its northern flank. It was a long hard way.

The Soldier

AFTER THE BURNING OF the tenements, the Guardian was dismissed
and Ouse took his place and supervised the evacuation of the elders
and stores and livestock into the castle.

It should have been a proud time for him. He'd reached the
high point of his ambitions. But it was a hollow advancement,
based on the mistakes of former Guardians and on the complete
destruction of the glen. It wasn't what he wanted.

He didn't refuse the appointment. He ushered the elders into
the stronghold and shut its big door and manned its battlements.
He'd never been in the castle before.

The keep was impressive. It towered high above everything
else as he stood with his soldiers in the great sloping courtyard,
staring up. There were no other outbuildings. All the rooms in the
castle were set in the massive outer walls. The whole place was
austere, even chilling, and he was glad of that. It had a domineering
quality which he respected, and it was old, the oldest structure in
the glen.

But though he admired the construction, the masonry itself,
he was dismayed by its habitants. He'd half expected to find
assemblies of white-robed elders, delicate and wise and aloof, in
great stone halls with furs on the floor and big fires in the hearth
and a garrison of hand-picked soldiers at the door. He found a
scattering of old women, a few old men, shivering in cold rooms
or talking to themselves in the cloisters under the ramparts. The
garrison was a rabble and Ouse replaced it with his own men.

He housed the elders in the stone chambers, many in the keep, and billeted the guardsmen and livestock herds in big tents in the courtyard, filling all the cobbled space. Fires were built and maintained in the chambers, and the elders were well fed. Sentries were posted on the walls and at the base of the keep. After that, the new Guardian did nothing but wait.

"How long we got to stay here, Senior?"

"Long as it takes," said Ouse.

The captain didn't understand. "Till spring, Senior?"

They were on the rampart of the front wall, looking out from the battlements. The valley was far below them and Ouse could see very little in it. It was a cusp of green with the line of the river in it, the greens blemished black where the tenements once stood. The sun was out, a high wind.

"Yes, till spring," said Ouse. "Till the glen sorts itself out."

"You mean till they all die in the winter."

"Till enough of them is dead and we can go out and retake the place."

"Who do you think put fire to the blocks?"

"Kids."

The captain spat over the wall. They were so high above the ground and the wind was so strong his spit floated and he didn't see it land.

Footsteps on the stonework and they turned and saw two other guardsmen approaching—one of the fat Guardian's own, holding a lance upright, and one from the castle garrison who walked with his head down. He was the other man's prisoner and had no weapons or helmet. His hair straggled onto his face.

The man with the lance gave a salute. "Beg to inform, Senior —this man been caught stealing food from an elder."

A short pause as Ouse looked at the prisoner. The man was thin and slovenly. He didn't look much like a guardsman. He didn't smell like one.

"Lift your bloody head up," said the fat man. "I know you from somewhere."

"You should," said the man, sullenly. "I was the Guardian once, few years back."

Ouse was quiet again, with surprise this time. It was almost eerie to see his old superior like this. "Why are you here?" he asked. He almost said Senior.

"You know why. I was sent to work here when that brat Jeo killed one of my men. Been here since. I'm not the only one. There's other Guardians here, since Jeo came back. We wash the floors now, carry the Elder's shit bucket. Fine way to live."

"Way of the glen."

The man wiped hair from his face. The wind blew it back.

"You been stealing from an elder," said Ouse. "You could die for that."

"You're not serious, Ouse—"

"Senior."

"Senior, then. But guardsmen don't die because of an old woman. We're the ones who rule the place, more than ever now."

"The elders rule," said the Guardian. "Same as always. Guardsman or not, you can't take from them. I'll have you flogged."

"You could have the glen for yourself—we could all rule it —and all you think about is flogging a man for eating a slice of beef."

Ouse came and stood close to him, smelled the unwashed body. The other two soldiers went on watching and saying nothing.

"The glen's not mine," he said. "It don't belong to any guardsman. When we get back there, we'll make it like it was, an elder's place."

The prisoner looked him in the eyes and his own face was scornful. But his voice was almost gentle. "I always knew you were a fanatic, Ouse. I didn't know just how much. You're like Jeo, in your own way—"

The Guardian used his knee to hit him very hard just above the groin. The man fell gasping and couldn't get up. The other two lifted him to his feet. Ouse hit him a second time, same place, and he fell again. The guardsmen picked him up.

"Take the bastard away. Strangle him somewhere."

Ouse wiped his red hog face with his palm as he looked out over the valley. He couldn't help wondering where Jeo might be. If he'd escaped beyond the marshes, he might perhaps come back, as he'd done before. But if he did return, what could he do? The Guardian had the castle, the upper hand. He looked to the right towards the swampland. He couldn't see it. He rubbed his teeth on his big lip and went to pay his respects to the Elder.

The Mountains

THE FIVE TRAVELLERS WALKED with their heads down in the teeth of a fast iced wind. Light sliced through the sky, above the mountains, and Jeo raised his head in time to see a skinny leader-stroke of lightning fork its way down to the hills—then, almost in the same instant, a return stroke, just as savage, back up to the sky, where it lit the underside of the entire cloudpatch. He looked away and cursed the downpour. Rhosarran gripped his hand and he gave her a brittle smile before glancing to his left, where he saw the lizard man pointing the way ahead as the rain splashed on the hood of his canvas coat.

They'd been walking for three days and were now far to the east. The vast marshland was somewhere to the left but mostly behind them. The mountains were more to the right than straight ahead. Even at this closer range they were still very dark, black with granite and gabbro and shrouded in thick cloud. The castle was almost lost from sight, though Jeo could always see it, dimly, where it stood in silence on its high gibbous hills.

They were quite close to the stronghold now. Another two nights of walking. They always moved by night (unless the day's weather was dark) to go unseen from the castle windows. Always in the dark or half-dark, always in the cold and wet. Jeo had no liking for all this, but he was accustomed to it and he did it because it was safer than travelling in the light. Nonetheless he was aggravated, not by the conditions but because they were taking so long to reach the castle. He was impatient to be in there stalking the Elder. And he didn't like leaving the valley for long.

Up here on the heights, the heather was shorter, stunted, a twiggy carpet kept short by freezing winds and poor soils, patched with clumps of tough sedge, a few short vulpine trees. The beasts of the region were different too. Goats and grey stoats and dotterels, the occasional eagle freewheeling around the high craigs in the distance, alpine butterflies. They'd shot and eaten a mountain hare and heard the peevish night cry of a wild cat somewhere in the black hills. Now, after three days and nights, the mountains were very close, almost overhead.

It was on the fourth day that Ure disappeared. They were moving along a high ridge, with the sparse moorland back to the left and a steep narrow gully on the right—and the tall man was suddenly gone.

"Who saw him last?" said Jeo, turning his back to the east wind. The others tried to keep their heads bowed to shield their faces. "Who saw him?" he said again, shouting in the gale. Kyrie shrugged at him.

"We all did. He was walking alongside, then he dropped back."

Jeo stared into the evening darkness around him. He didn't expect to see much. Even when he stood precariously close to the rim of the gully and looked down, he saw nothing clearly. It was dark and it was a long way down. Kyrie appeared at his side and he stepped back from the edge.

"He might be down there," said the lizard man.

"No," said Jeo loudly. His words were losing themselves in the wind. "We'd have heard him. He'd have made a sound, shouted as he fell."

Kyrie looked him in the face. "Not if he was thrown down."

"What are you talking about?"

"If he was hit and pushed, he might have made no sound. The shock could have kept him quiet."

"It's possible—"

"It's fucking likely." The freckled face was scowling. He spat the slip of hill grass from his mouth.

Jeo frowned back at him. "You think I did it?"

"You never trusted him."

"I don't trust you. You're still here. Anyway, I could have killed him any time. Why now?"

"You tell me why."

"I didn't kill him." It was nearly a snarl. "Who's to say anyone killed him?"

"You could have stabbed him without anybody knowing it."

"I didn't touch him." Jeo searched in his belt. "Look, here's my knife. You saw me getting ready. You know it's the only one I brought with me. Do you think I've had time to stab him and clean it without anyone seeing anything?"

"You didn't need the knife," shouted Kyrie. "You could have hit him and pushed him."

"I didn't."

"He wouldn't just fall—"

"He might have. The rocks are wet."

"He wouldn't, not Ure. Someone pushed him." His voice was very loud. Jeo grabbed his coat in his fist. Rhosarran frowned anxiously at them.

"If I'd killed him, you would have bloody seen me. I was never far away. And most of the time I was walking ahead of you."

"Most of the time."

"I didn't kill the tall streak of piss. I was nowhere near him."

Kyrie leaned back from Jeo's grip and pointed with his arm. "Even if you didn't do it yourself, you could have had him killed. She might have done it. Or that big ox you insisted on bringing along."

Jeo released him and shook his head in a show of helplessness.

"This is all a waste of time," he said. "Ure's gone and that's that. Whatever happened to him, we've got to keep moving."

"We should stay and look for him," said Kyrie. The rain ran down his face. "He might be lying injured somewhere."

"There's no time. We move on. Anyway, he may not be dead or hurt."

"What does that mean?"

"He's gone, that's all we know. He might be out there listening to us even now. He might have disappeared for his own reasons." He walked away up the slope.

"What reasons?" shouted the lizard man.

Jeo paused to give him a hard look. "You'd know more about that than I would," he said.

He pushed on into the wind. Hake and Rhosarran followed. And Kyrie too, after a short hesitation, after glancing into the darkness behind him. There was nothing much to see in the bad light, nothing more than the wind to be heard.

They saw no soldiers in the hills. The garrison clearly didn't want to waste men in guarding an area where they could expect no threat. Perhaps, too, the hidden tunnel wasn't guarded, perhaps not heavily.

They found a place to rest, a breach in a hillside, something like a small cave. They put their outer clothes on the rock floor and lay down, but sleep wasn't easy. The disappearance of the tall man had unnerved them all, in their different ways, and they lay and watched one another.

When darkness came, they left the cave and went on over the hills. They walked through the night and on through the cold of the next morning. The land sloped steeper up and they followed it round in a long arc to the right, to the foothills. They went down a long slope and found themselves in a strange deep gulch angling away further to the right.

It was a steep-sided crowberry pass. Tall cliffs on both sides. But no berries, no living plants. The place was utterly white. Crystalline frost on the heather underfoot, frost and tuffets of snow on stone ledges, a fleece of frost on every rock. And icicles everywhere, pointing from every overhanging jut of rock, from the underside of small arches, in holes in the gully walls. There was a brittle splendour about the place. It seemed gealed in time, frozen like no other area around it. They might have been the first living things to set foot in it.

Jeo didn't care about that. He was in a hurry to reach the other end. They scuffed through the crunching frost, followed the curve of the pass, then came to a complete halt. In front of them, rising almost sheer above their heads, a cliff of iced granite, hundreds of yards high. They turned their faces up and stared at it, shivering, all thinking the same thing.

"Can't never get up there," muttered Hake, and Kyrie gave a rueful sniff.

"So this is it," he said. "The start of old Sligo's other way in. Look at it."

"Look for a path," said Jeo. "A goat track, anything. Anything that looks like a pathway."

Kyrie gave a derisive laugh, but he scanned the cliff face all the same. They leaned back and looked.

"Nothing," said the lizard man. "It's a wall. We'll never climb it." Hake shook his head in agreement.

Rhosarran gripped Jeo's arm. With her other hand she was pointing up the wall. He watched her finger trace a path, slow and tortuous, to the top. He grinned and squeezed her hand.

"There," he said. "See, where that patch of frozen grass starts to go up the side. That's the way up. Follow my finger."

"That?" said Kyrie. "You must be out of your mind. That's hardly a cut in the rock, never mind a footpath. A snake couldn't get up there."

"Sligo said it would be just a goat track. More of a climb than a walk."

"The whole thing is covered in ice. It won't hold our weight."

"It will. Try it, Hake."

The big man looked at him, licked his mouth, then set off. He stopped at the base of the cliff, set the trident in the back of his belt, and clambered up onto the first thin, frosted ledge. From there, he began to haul himself very carefully up the wall. Rhosarran followed him.

"Are you going to stay behind?" asked Jeo.

"You go first," said Kyrie.

It was a long hard climb, hazardous with ice and snow—but easier than it looked. The cliff wasn't so much sheer as steeply angled. For the most part, they were able to move on all fours, quite briskly, though in places the rock was unsafe, frozen and cracked and liable to fall away in the hand. Once, a plump snowy owl flapped irascibly past the fisherman's head and Rhosarran turned for a moment to watch it sweep down and vanish in the white gully below.

It was cold, of course, on the ice wall. Their hands and faces and feet were numbed, almost frozen, while the sheer white cliff gave them a kind of brief snowblindness. But they couldn't stop. They went on, and after dark they reached the top.

They lay on the ground for some time, waiting for breath. Jeo got to his feet and looked around to see where they were.

From the top of a flat hill, they looked down across a spread of plain, itself the plateau of a hill, on which he saw the northern side-wall of the grey castle itself, several leagues away. The mountains towered overhead on the left, ten times as high as the cliff they'd just climbed. Below the castle, tumbling down the steep hillside to the right, the icy sheen of the valley spring went into the river.

"We'll rest here half the night," said Jeo. "Too tired to carry on. We'll get there before dawn, before the place wakes up."

Kyrie nodded. He too was close to exhaustion. Even the giant and the rugged girl were very weary.

"Wish we could make a fire," remarked the lizard man. "Have some hot food."

"We can't," said Jeo. "Someone might see the smoke."

"Yes, I know," said Kyrie testily. He found a place to sit

behind a rock, close to the edge of the white cliff. He was shuddering cold and pulled his long coat all around him.

Nothing moved in the dark in the mountain hills. Some nocturnal
bird might have wafted away on a freezing downdraught, back to
its arid nesting place—but if it did, it belonged to a different place
altogether and didn't pass into the world below. There were no
ground animals on the frozen surfaces, no insects, scarcely a plant.
Only the gelid winds blundering through canyons and rounding
the hilltops, shrieking like banshees in the high passes and raven
gullies, blowing a small rain against a million rocks, then blowing
it away, drying the cliff walls and the ground.

Very close to the top of the rockface they'd climbed, Jeo and
Kyrie sat side by side against a boulder. The wind groaned over
their heads. They were wrapped in their clothes, one in a coat, Jeo
in a wool sheet, sitting with their knees drawn up to their chins.

The countryside sprawling beneath them was in darkness, the
distant hillocks black but blurred, vague as sin. Even the whiteness
at the foot of the cliff was dim grey. There was nothing to look
at, to fill the eyes as they talked.

Jeo rubbed his beard. The wind made his fingers cold and he
kept his hands under the woollen cloak. He glanced round to
where Hake and Rhosarran were sleeping under blankets, quite
close together. He couldn't see them, of course. He turned back,
glanced at Kyrie.

"You knew what would happen after the fire, didn't you? It
was part of your thinking."

The other turned his head to him, though he couldn't see in
the dark. "*My* thinking? The fire was Rhosarran's idea."

"Yes, I know," said Jeo. "But you knew how it would
change things. You knew the guardsmen would take everything
into the castle and keep the elders safe there."

"It was one of the first things I was taught as a guardsman.
The elders come first. Any kind of danger and they're to be taken

to the castle first thing. It's happened before, years ago, in times of drought and crop failure. Good for us it happened this time."

"Yes. The glen's on our side, for once. If we get into the castle at all, if we can kill the old man—"

"You'll be the new Elder."

"In everything but name," said Jeo.

"That's alright with me," said Kyrie. "I don't want to rule this place. I never did. I wanted to be more than I was, more than just a kid guardsman waiting to be old enough for better things. But that's as far as it went."

Jeo was frowning to himself. "You expect me to believe that? You've been using me to get this far."

Kyrie chuckled. "Yes, I have," he said. "I've settled in behind you while you've played the part of leader, something I could never do myself. But all I want is a share in the kill, not all of it." He pouted. "Anyway, you've made use of me too. I collected your army for you, killed guardsmen with you, done some of your thinking—most of your thinking. We've used each other."

"Yes," said Jeo. "And now?"

"Now?"

"If we get past the sentries and the glen is ours, what then? You've said yourself you collected my army. What if they're really *your* army and do what *you* decide, without listening to me?"

Kyrie huddled deeper into his coat. "You don't seem to understand," he said. "There's nothing left of the army I put together. Just a handful, maybe. The rest died in the swamps. All the people who survived the fires, that's the army now—and it's yours. I didn't collect them."

Jeo didn't speak but he did some thinking.

"You've got nothing to fear from anyone," Kyrie went on. "Unless Hake still wants to kill you for what happened to Sligo."

"Or unless Ure wants to kill me."

"I still say you killed Ure."

"He's still alive, said Jeo. "Unless *you* killed him."

"You don't believe that. He helped me away from the blocks. I was closer to him than anyone, for what that's worth."

Jeo made no reply and was quiet for a time and they sat and didn't do anything. The wind seemed to have died. The small hours grew less dark. Jeo stared down towards the distant valley, then looked away.

"I'm glad to be away from the glen," he confided. Kyrie looked at him and saw the very faint outline of his head. The dawn was just beginning.

"I'm glad to get away from everyone down there."

"You'd rather be on your own?" said Kyrie.

"It's what I'm used to."

"You don't have any liking for anybody down there—"

"Hardly surprising."

"It's true they weren't good to you, once. But they've never been good to me either, and I can't feel the same as you. They're my kin, after all. They're yours, too."

"I don't feel part of them. They wanted me dead."

"They were led to think like that. They didn't know any better. They welcome you now. They already think of you as their chief."

"I don't trust them," said Jeo. "I don't feel they're my kin. I think I hate them."

"Only the older ones, surely?"

"Old or young. They've done nothing for me."

Kyrie looked at him, looked for a facial expression in the dark. "Why are you telling me these things?" he asked.

"It's what I think."

Another pause before Kyrie stretched his arms above his head. He didn't yawn. He put his arms down. "I know why you tell me," he said. "You think of me as your brother."

Jeo said nothing. He didn't expect the lizard man to leave it at that.

"You had brothers of your own, I know. But they were all

older, so you were never close to them. Me, I'm the same age as you, the nearest thing to a brother you've had."

"I suppose that's right. I never explained it to myself that way. Am I your brother too?"

"Yes. I never had a family."

Jeo looked up and around. "It's getting light, just about. We'd better wake the others."

They got up. The rogue winds had gone and there was a hard silence on the hilltop. They passed the edge of the cliff and Jeo punched the lizard man fiercely above the belly, stopping the breath in his chest and butting him backwards off the clifftop without a cry. His small grunt of surprise and horror was lost in his throat and he fell and died in the ice-white gully below. The last piece of grass gasped from his mouth.

Jeo stood on the edge and looked down. He couldn't see Kyrie's body on the valley floor. It was too far away. But he didn't expect to.

Jeo went back to where the others were sleeping and woke them. "Kyrie's gone," he shouted. "I can't find him anywhere."

They stumbled to their feet. "Gone?" mumbled Hake. "Gone where?"

"He's just disappeared in the dark," snapped Jeo. "He was next to me, talking, then I fell asleep and he wasn't there when I woke up."

"Never seen him," said Hake—but Jeo grabbed his jerkin in both fists.

"You, you big bastard. Have *you* done something to him? Have you? I know you hated him."

The big man couldn't see much of Jeo's face in the half-dark, certainly not his expression—but the grip was fierce enough. "Never touched him, Jeo," he pleaded. "I didn't like him but he was with you so I never hurt him. I never went near him tonight, I been asleep. Didn't kill Ure neither."

Jeo pulled him closer, then abruptly released him. He glanced at Rhosarran, but she wasn't looking at him.

"Maybe he's just gone, then," he said. "Gone to join Ure. But why didn't he kill us in our sleep when he had the chance?" He shook his head.

He saw Rhosarran standing at the rim of the cliff staring down. "Do you think I haven't looked down there?" he called. "It's the first place I tried. He's not there. I couldn't see him."

She went on peering down into the gully, but in the deep greyness she couldn't see anything much. The canyon floor was a long way down. She turned away. He couldn't see the frown in the poor light, but the way she was standing told him things.

He made an impatient move of his arm. "No, not me. I wish I did."

She worked her lip with her teeth. Jeo looked around at the sky. "It's getting light fast," he noticed. "We've got to be at the castle wall before daybreak. We'd better move. And keep your eyes open. They may both be out there."

He picked up his sack and moved away over the hilltop, down the slope. The big man followed a few paces behind. Rhosarran came and walked alongside Jeo and put her hand in his. But there was still some frown on her face.

They moved briskly down the hill, onto the plain, and away towards the castle. Jeo was glad to have killed Kyrie, but he was still troubled by the disappearance of Ure. He glanced at shadows as he went.

The Castle

IT WAS VERY NEARLY DAWN. In the highest room of the castle keep, the Elder went to his due place at the window.

He no longer spent an hour every night looking down over the glen. He was older and too frail to stand for long. And now there was less to look at in the valley, even if his eyes were strong enough to see that far down. Only the charred remains of a hundred tenements.

As the light improved, the old man turned his head and looked straight down, to a point on the hilltop directly below, where—not far from the front wall of the castle—a crowd of glen peasants had gathered in a single swarming unit. They had weapons and there were many hundreds of them, almost the entire population of the valley, a rustic army of young men and women and children, collected there for two nights and a day.

They seemed to be just waiting, just out of range of arrows, too many to be attacked in a sortie. Waiting for what? If the Elder was troubled by their presence he didn't show it. From his face, hidden as it was under his cowl, it was hard to know if he could even see them.

He turned to look up for a second, to the grey sky blacked with clouds—then drooped his head as if the movement had tired him. He stared down again, but this time at the sill.

There were no middle-aged peasants in the waiting army. They were all dead, killed by their young. They weren't the only ones to die. Any children known to have approved of the old order were thrown in the Shrieking Pits on top of their elders. Some old scores were settled. After a day and a night of executions, the young people had moved through the foothills to present themselves at the castle with their crude weapons and their dogs and their very few provisions, to wait and hope Jeo would somehow open the door.

Within another day, they had no food left—and the soldiers in the castle knew it.

One of them tossed a beefbone over the battlements and it fell on the stone plain close to the wall. The young peasants watched and did nothing. Another bone was dropped from the heights. They heard a sentry's laugh. One of the dogs, a tall thin hound of some kind, ran out from the crowd and threw itself on the bones. The soldiers fired crossbow bolts at it. Some missed, some punched into the dog's back and killed it. More laughter from the ramparts. The youngsters made no sound.

Then a tall sharp-faced girl walked out to the front of the throng, faced the castle, and searched in the black sack she was holding. She pulled a head out by its grey hair, the head of the oast-house keeper, fifty years old, a man known to everyone in the glen. She held it above her head and the army behind her roared and the castle walls and hills reflected the noise. In their anger and revulsion, the guardsmen shot more bolts, but they were far out of range.

A wind had risen at the ebb of the night. Hake lowered his head as it crashed against him. Jeo and Rhosarran followed close behind him, using his huge body as a windbreak. They trudged along a last goat fell, went down the far slope, and stopped on the rock-strewn plain, where they huddled behind a boulder.

Jeo half closed his eyes in the wind to look over the boulder at the castle itself. It was only now, when he was so close, that he realised just how enormous it was. The grey massif walls stretched to the pied sky, the dark keep reaching even higher. There was no sign of life in the walls—no faces among the northern battlements, no crossbows at the window slits, not so much as a bird swirling around the stones—but in that swarthy light it had a monstrous presence of its own.

Jeo looked at it all and wondered. He glanced around the plain, then moved from behind the big rock to look for a hole in the ground.

"What's that?" said a guardsman on the ramparts. Another came and looked down over the edge.

"What? There's nothing there."

"I saw something. There was more than one. They disappeared at the bottom of that rock pile."

Again the other looked, longer this time. "No, it's just a lot of old stones."

"I know that. But I saw something near it."

"Shadows."

"Crap."

"Dogs, then. Or fucking goats. What else is there up here?"

"I saw something. Somebody."

"The light's playing with your eyes, Uist. Wait till the sun comes up before seeing things. Anyway, if you want to worry about what's down there, worry about that army of scum under the west wall. That's the real danger."

As they left the north wall, Uist cast a last quick look down and didn't see anyone. Below the surface of the plain, Jeo and his two companions moved cautiously along a dark tunnel.

A long curving passage. Judging from the hew of the walls, it was a natural thing, not cut by men. The walls were smooth, eroded by some ancient underground river long dried and forgotten. In places, the stonework was marked with sharp, jagged fissures where water had once frozen, cracking the walls.

There was no water here now, not a patch of mud or even a damp smell. They heard the rumble of the valley spring through the rock.

They could see something of the walls around them, and the ceiling, and each other, because an obscure light found its way into the tunnel at the far end. They went towards it, to where there had to be an opening in the rock. They moved with their weapons ready, but there were no sentries.

Sligo had called it a hole in the ground. It was certainly a tight place. Hake had to walk with his back bent and his big chin on his chest, looking ahead from under his beetle forehead.

They followed the tunnel towards the light, which brightened as they went, and reached an area where the floor rose very sharply and stopped, the way out blocked not by any mound of fallen rocks but by a single stone slab overhead. Beneath it, to one side, reared the statue of an old figure in robes, higher than a man.

Hake eyed the overhead slab. "Too big," he said.

"Keep your voice down," said Jeo. "If Sligo was right, we must be under the castle now—and maybe there's someone just above our heads. Try moving the stone."

Hake settled himself directly under the slab. He put the palms of his big hands on it and heaved with all his body. Nothing. He took his hands away and pressed against the stone with his shoulders, pushing with his legs. No difference. He stepped aside and shook his head.

"Maybe it takes a pack of guardsmen to shift it," said Jeo. "Or maybe they've sealed it. Sligo didn't say anything about that."

They stared around at the ceiling. Jeo could see no way out. Hake hardly seemed to be looking at all. Rhosarran took Jeo's arm and pulled him towards her. He looked above her head and saw, just to one side of the main flagstone, a smaller rock, deep in shadow, higher than the big slab, out of reach. Jeo gave it a fierce little smile.

"Right," he said to the big man, "you lift me up there. I'll get that stone out of the way and climb out. Then you do the same with Rhos. After that we'll pull you out together."

Hake didn't like the sound of that. "Why not I go first and pull you both out?" he said.

"Do what I tell you," said Jeo.

The giant scowled but didn't argue. He held Jeo by the hips and lifted him as though he weighed nothing.

"Higher," said Jeo, reaching with his fingers. "That's it. I've got it." He pushed and twisted the rock and levered it away from its resting place. At last, with a tug, he wrenched it up out of its hole and grey light dropped into the tunnel. Jeo craned his neck and looked outside. He saw nothing that worried him. He heaved himself up and out. Rhosarran saw his legs disappear and she took his place under the gap.

One by one they came out of the tunnel. Hake held up his trident and they took it. They strained to pull him out. Jeo had never known anyone, anything, so heavy. His own arms felt thin and ludicrously feeble as he leaned back and pushed with his feet. Somehow, with Rhosarran's help, he helped the giant squeeze his bulk through the gap.

Once he was out, Jeo left him and turned to see if they were threatened. No one there. They were inside the great burg itself and no sentries were in sight. The garrison was concerned with the child army outside, and Ure clearly hadn't alerted them. Where *was* Ure?

They were in the very shadow of the castle wall, close to a dark corner, the junction of the north wall and the west, deeply hidden in wall ivy and nettles.

They crouched in this undergrowth and Jeo glanced around at everything. He saw they were in a shaded cloister which ran the length of the north wall to the left, the ceiling being the floor of the rampart, supported by enormous pillars. The west wall, to the right, was much the same. Set in both walls were the oak doors of storerooms and armouries and latrines—and on either side of each door, statues of elders in robes, identical giants, their backs against the granite wall and their cowled heads hidden in the dark vault of the ceiling.

Everywhere, in the walls and the great stone columns and the statues, the hard ancient stone was split and ruined, in places rudely patched, mostly crumbled and pocked and furred with red moss. Nettles and mountain grass grew hip-high in cracks between heaving floorstones.

Jeo looked across the courtyard in front of him and saw the place was one great shanty town. The broad cobbled motte was overcrowded with tents and makeshift canvas stables and store-houses, all erected to house the sudden influx of guardsmen and animals. A new tenement, out of the glen.

In the darkness of early dawn, Jeo could see that the camp was stirring itself. Soldiers stepped yawning from their tents. Some carried balls of hay and couchgrass for the livestock. He heard the scattered calls of men and the tread of boots on stone.

Some of the tents and shelters were quite close, across a small space of paving stones, but the nearest soldiers were some distance away. Jeo looked beyond them, over the shanty camp, to the keep, up its high grey side to the upper windows—the half-whisper of a voice broke through his thoughts and sent his pulse punching in his chest.

"You can put your knife away now, boy. It's all finished."

He threw glances along both sides of the cloister, out across the yard, and saw no one. Then he turned, with swelling fear, and the small dirk fluctuated in his hand.

Hake was holding Rhosarran against his body, forcing her to lean back and almost lifting her off her feet by pressing his huge forearm on her throat. In his other hand he held the trident, its teeth against her cheek. They were framed in ivy, nettles to their waists. The expression in the big man's face was something Jeo had never seen there before. The dullness was gone from the eyes.

"Yes," said Hake. "I killed Ure. Threw him off the moun-tainside like I suppose you did to Kyrie. I was going to kill them both, but you saved me half the trouble. I killed Sligo too, of course—but he never told me what he'd said to you. So I've had to stay with you to find out where this tunnel was. See, none of the captains knows of it—it's been forgotten over the years."

Jeo didn't speak. It was all very clear now. Hake was an informant. He'd been in the pay of the captains for years. Simple as that. There was no need for words.

There was no time, either. The big man would soon call out to the garrison. Jeo looked at Rhosarran. She was the only thing in the valley he didn't hate. She was staring at him with hunted eyes. There was nothing he could do.

Then, even as the big man was about to speak again, Jeo noticed that because the girl's head was pushed to one side, a space was left open, and part of the informer's ribs were exposed. But it was a very small space and his chances of striking it were negligible. He'd already turned the knife in his hand, holding the blade horizontal so it would pass between ribs. Hake smiled. Jeo threw the knife.

The blade went precisely where he meant it to go. Hake gave a short gasp of surprise, glanced down, and loosened his grip on the girl, whose eyes were hugely wide as she stared at the hilt of the dirk now protruding from just below her breast, the yellow cloth staining brown at once. She lifted her head to Jeo, looked at him, then fell limp and soon dead in the giant's arm.

Hake stared in astonishment. Instead of a shield, the girl's body was now a thing of burden. He struggled to hold the dead weight upright. He had to let it fall, jumping aside and holding the trident ahead of him with both hands. He put a smile back on his mouth, but he was far less sure of himself.

"Well, well," he said. "You really want this little glen, don't you? I never knew just how much. In the end, nothing else matters to you."

"No, nothing," said Jeo in a dead voice.

"Nothing except me, boy. I matter. I'll show you just how much."

He stepped forward from the nettles and stems of ivy, the trident held at waist level. Jeo edged away. The giant came closer. He backed further away and reached in the back of his belt, under the flap of his doublet. The big man had just started to draw back the trident when he saw the second knife in Jeo's hand.

His face wavered with fear. He was close enough to lunge with his spear, and he jabbed it forward, but the distance was just out. Jeo stepped aside and his arm was drawn back. He held it there, tauntingly.

"You only brought one knife," said Hake limply. "I heard you tell Kyrie."

"Did you think I'd tell him the truth?" asked Jeo in his cold voice.

In a last desperate move, the informer changed his grip on the iron shaft and held it in one hand to throw it. He tried a single final shout of warning to the garrison, but it came as a screech of terror, strange in such a huge man. Jeo lashed the dagger at him, grunting with the effort, and it struck the huge body in the chest.

Hake fell heavily and began to die. Jeo crouched and listened and heard the distant sounds of running between the buildings in the courtyard, the tread of feet somewhere along the western cloister roof. He should have run away to be sure of escape, but he didn't want anyone to know the fortress had been penetrated. If that happened, he would have no hope of reaching the keep.

The castle was huge and he was in one of its remote sections, so he had a little time. He took Rhosarran's corpse by the arms and heaved it through the nettles. He tugged the twin-nibbed knife from her chest without looking at her face, then forced the body down the hole. He did the same, with difficulty, with the big man's body. He replaced the flat stone, then ran away from the overgrown place, frantic along the west cloister, to hide behind one of the great statues as guardsmen came running in from the shanty.

"No," said one. "Just a shout, not an alarm."

"Aye, I heard it clear enough. Like a horse screaming."

The Guardian scowled. "Why should a horse scream? You, see to the horses in the nearest compound. See if they're restless." The man ran to a corner of the courtyard.

"I think it was a man, Senior, not a beast."

"Aye, that's what I think," said Ouse. "Where could he be around here? Was it you up there?"

"No, Senior." Four guardsmen looked down from the rampart. "We only just got here."

The Guardian stood looking around for a moment, as did the others. He stared at the nettlepatch, the ivy wall—and away, moving his little pig eyes to scan the length of each cloister, even the vaulted ceiling. He didn't see anything much, and there were no more shouts.

"Check the storerooms and search across the whole motte. Anything different, I want to know about it. I doubt we'll bloody find anything."

"What about all this ivy, Senior? Might be somebody hiding. It's like a wood in there."

"No," said Ouse. "Not enough room for a rat to hide in there. Search it anyway. Look through the nettles." He moved away along one of the walkways and out of view in the dirty light.

They found nothing in the undergrowth and they went away and Jeo was safe to move to find a better hiding place.

But he didn't move from where he was. Not straight away. He looked along the dark cloister and saw there was nowhere he could hide in it. He edged round the stone robe of the statue and looked again across the teeming courtyard, across to the keep.

He couldn't see the door to the tower. There were too many tents and shacks in the way. But he knew it must be well guarded. He looked up along the flank of the keep and saw that the stone was broken and pitted like the statues and the castle walls. For someone who could scale the great monoliths, it wouldn't be impossible to climb. And there were slit windows in the wall.

So it could, just possibly, be scaled. He could perhaps reach the highest window without going inside. But the daylight was brighter now. He could see the details of buildings instead of just the outlines. The camp was awake. Men were moving between the crammed tents. There was no hope at all of reaching the keep. Not yet.

He needed, first of all, somewhere else to hide. The longer he looked, the more he realised there was nowhere really safe. He couldn't go into the encampment, he couldn't open any of the doors in the cloister wall, he couldn't move far from his present place without being seen. There again, he couldn't stay where he was. The soldiers hadn't seen him in the bad light, but that couldn't last.

He looked up and saw that the high barrel vault of the cloister ceiling was still dark, nearly black. He stared at it for a few moments, then glanced around before clambering his way up the back of the statue.

He used the broken masonry and the folds of the granite robes to haul himself up the height of the giant figure, and soon he was settled in the dark space behind the hooded head, his neck bent under the curve of the vault and his pale, thin limbs huddled in to his body like a peeled ape.

From there, he could see very little. But no one could see him. And he wasn't really interested in looking any more. He had to keep out of sight, nothing more, till dark. Close though he might be to that last room in the glen, he knew any kind of haste would be fatal. So he simply settled back on the elder's stone shoulders to do nothing and wait, with all the patience of a preying heron, though it meant wasting another day.

His thoughts eddied. He tried to put Rhosarran out of his mind but couldn't. His sense of sadness was cold. He felt little remorse. He remembered the look in her eyes and wondered why it meant nothing to him.

"They're all dead," said the tall young woman, looking at the castle. Taw, standing beside her, leaned on his oak spear and watched the battlements, looking over the heads of the peasant army. He saw sentries in the high sun, but they didn't move. There had been no sign of Jeo and the others.

"We don't know they're dead," he said.

She looked at him. "He said he'd have the gate opened today if at all. Early this morning, at dawn. He said."

"He said he'd try."

"They never had a real chance. They're dead, almost certain."

"Maybe."

She turned away again. High in its nest of behemoth rocks, the castle looked more impregnable than ever. She'd never realised just how massive it was. They were all fools to think they could breach it.

"How much longer do we stay out here?" she asked. "What happens if the guardsmen come out to fight?"

"They won't," Taw said. "We outnumber them too much. They'll just wait to see what we do." A half-smile. "They must be wondering what we're doing out here."

"I wonder too," she said. "We'll freeze to death or starve. Even if he does get the gate open, we'll die in the fight."

She sniffed. Someone came past with food, an older man with a last urn of soup. They drank hastily from the ladle and he went away.

"Are you afraid to fight?" asked Taw.

"Afraid to die," she answered. "I want to go on living."

"And grow old?" he said slyly.

"We'd all stay young forever if we could. Let's hope he opens the gate. Otherwise we'll none of us grow old." She blew on her hands. "How much longer do we wait?"

"I'm not sure yet," said Taw.

"Why should you be the one to decide? Why not any of us? Why not me?"

"Because he left me in charge, not you. Because I'm younger, I suppose."

She glanced at the black wig on his head and thought, again, how absurd it looked. "My respects, Junior," she said, with a small mock bow. While he chuckled and went away, she glared at the castle, at the top window in the dark distant keep.

The night came down over the castle shanty and quietened it. An hour of darkness passed, more than an hour, and still Jeo stayed where he was, listening more than watching. The stone of the statue was cold on his legs but it didn't matter.

A patrol of crossbowmen marched in silence along the flag-stone pathway below. When they were gone, he waited, then took off his boots and left them forever on the stone head. He looked at his jerkin. The sheepskin was brown, not white, not too visible in the dark. He didn't take it off. He stretched out from his hideout and worked his nimble way to the ground, where he squatted at the foot of the effigy and stared out across the cluttered yard.

A few isolated lights showed in the dark, but otherwise, with the moon for once smothered in cloud, it was all black and greys. Not silent but quite still. Jeo jumped across the stone floor and pressed himself against one of the great pillars. He glanced left and right and saw and heard nothing.

He moved warily but as fast as he could, mostly between closed tents, or stooped behind a row of fodder bales, keeping his eyes moving and staying well away from anything that moved.

There were sentries everywhere, watching the wagons and livestock tents, but Jeo saw them and changed his directions to keep out of sight.

It took him half an hour to cross the encampment—and then he was pressing himself against a small canvas shelter in the very lee of the keep, staring up the side of the high stonework, tilting his head back so his mouth gaped. His eyes sought the lowest window and found it. Like all the openings in the building, it was unlit, so he guessed the room inside would be empty of people. He stood for a long time and examined the wall, looking for footholds, judging a climbing angle. He looked around him. Soldiers moved in the near distance but didn't see where he was. A horse snuffled somewhere nearby. He looked round the side of the keep.

A big firebrand, perched in an iron clasp some twenty feet above the only door, spluttered smokily in a wind and sent its light shivering on the ground and on the batch of sentries at the door.

Jeo saw them very clearly. He knew that to them he was in

deep darkness and couldn't be seen. He moved stealthily up the last yards of cobbled slope and threw himself without a pause up the sheer face of the bastion wall. He was no more than a dozen paces from the armed men but they had no way of knowing. They talked and sometimes chuckled and cursed the cold, while their most insidious enemy was working his way above them.

His fingers and feet found immediate purchase and he clawed up the stone flank with abnormal speed, finding the nooks in the weatherbroken surface with his strong hands and big, almost prehensile toes, pushing with his legs. The dark granite was harshly cold to the touch and his breath froze in clouds.

He reached the first arrow-slit window and looked quickly inside. He didn't see anyone so he glanced down behind him and thinly inched his way in.

The chamber had a high ceiling and was dark, and empty but for bales of white sackcloth piled along a wall. Elder's robes, he thought, and touched the cloth with his fingers as he crossed the room. If the door was locked, he would go back to the window and climb further up.

It was locked and he retraced his steps. He was about to swing back over the sill when he looked down and saw two of the sentries moving round the curve of the wall. They stopped almost directly under his window. He drew back and waited, then glanced out again.

The two men were facing the wall, standing close to it as they talked. At first, Jeo thought they might have had a glimpse of his climb or his run to the wall. But neither of them looked up, and Jeo slid out to continue his climb.

The next room was also empty. He went to the door and his knife was ready for any sentry outside. The iron latch moved to his touch and he drew the door back, no more than a hand's width.

Light outside, on the stairs, but it was pale and cheerless. Jeo held his breath as he looked for soldiers in all the shadows. None. There was a deep silence in the huge tower, the chilled echoing silence of stone, with just the faint drip of water from a sweating wall. Jeo stepped out of the room. His every breath seemed to hang and climb the stairwell to the black heights of the keep.

He was standing on the curve of the stairway and he saw that the whole building was just an enormous hollow cylinder with simple stone steps jutting from the wall, each held in place by the one above, spiralling to the top. No bannisters and a sheer drop.

He stared up the walls and saw no sentinels, so he began his run up the stairs, his bare feet patting on the cold stones, his hands reaching at the steps above as he ran like a beast, half-man, half-dog, towards the highest level of the place. Where he passed any of the high oak doors in the wall, he ran quickly on his toes to get out of the torchlight above the lintel.

Even as he ran, thinking only of reaching the top, he was aware of the stillness around him. The tower seemed to be a dead place, without so much as a flapping bat or a patch of lichen, not a small breeze to move the torch flames. It was a huge stone lung but it didn't breathe.

For some reason, the thought made him fearful and he ran even faster up the long stairway—till at last the steps came to an end and he was standing on a long thin ledge leading to a final, stunted door in the wall.

Here, in the big darkness, he stopped and sank to his knees to recover his breath. From his kneeling position, he could see over the edge of the narrow platform, down into the bowel of the stairwell. He saw nothing but stone, ill lit in patches, blackness down beyond the lights. No guardsmen, no old people in robes. For the time being, nothing to fear.

He began to breathe more freely and got to his feet. He moved to the last door of the keep and took the iron ring-handle in both hands. The latch was feather light and lifted very very easily. The door seemed to weigh nothing at all as he pushed it all the way open. In two small paces, he was standing inside the highest room of the glen, his knife tight in his hand. He shut the door behind him.

Some of the grey darkness of the night came in through the only window, so the room wasn't as black as the ledge outside. A single glance showed Jeo everything in it—just the burnished mirror. Nothing, no one else. The place was emptied. Jeo scowled and didn't understand. He stared at the walls. Then suddenly a wild incongruous grin came to his face and he stuffed the dirk back in his belt. He moved across to the window, chuckling and shaking his head. Of course the Elder wasn't there. They'd moved him to a place no one would think of, just to be sure.

He looked down from the window. There was no way out. Only guardsmen below.

The Elder was out of his reach and soon he would be taken and killed. He looked around at the room and realised that this was all—this was the pinnacle of everything, this one small cramped space of stone. All his suffering and exile and running battles, all the blood, led to nothing but this. The highest point of the glen, the most it had to offer, was just a small bare room with no way out, dark and very empty.

But he loved the room. He thrilled at its emptiness. The mirror had only *his* reflection. He stared at all the stones in the walls. He had no need to feel them. He knew they'd be cold, and clean, as if untouched. He had time to touch them, later, with his fingertips and cheek. They were his now. He was glad no one was there to share them—Kyrie, Hake, any of the others, even Rhosarran. At the very last, after all the struggles, the horrors, he'd found the one place in all the glen where he could be alone.

He stood at the window and looked out. The peasant army was there beyond the walls, just a spread of blackness with few camp-fire lights dithering. It was the first time he'd given them a thought.

There were lights in the shanty camp too, figures moving. He realised now that from such a height no one could see or hear much of what happened in the glen. It was very far away. His fear, as a young boy, that the Elder could see his every misdeed was ridiculous now. He stood for a while, and sharpened his knife on the stone sill—not to keep it keen so he could use it when the soldiers came for him, but to keep it looking its best.

Under the castle, in a stone tunnel blocked by overhead flagstones, the body of a bearded giant lay face down across the corpse of a big girl with a bronze earring and a small wound in her chest, their limbs crooked and stiffening in death. In the dark of the place, her eyes had no lustre and the colour was gone from her tunic and her tousle of hair.

At the foot of a cold white cliff, a young man lay spreadeagled in snow, his back broken in places, his body arched and already sprinkled with frost that covered his sand-coloured hair and all the freckles on his face.

Somewhere in the lower mountain slopes, a tall young man lay dead in the pit of a ravine. Already the big hawks had found him and made a raw muddle of his face and abdomen. Soon they would take all his flesh back to their young in their nests, leaving only a skeleton that no man would ever see.

Bodies still in the swamps. Old soldiers and children and horses in the shallow water and the bullrush forests. The smell of death was chilled by the upland air. Moorland birds came and perched on the gibbets and pecked at eyes and livers and genitals. Horseflies fed on waterlogged corpses, and robber flies fed on horseflies as they swarmed on the faces of a young girl still clutching her severed arm and a tall man with rust-red hair. On a marshy field, an unknown soldier lay close to his captain, whose mouth was still slack with astonishment, his eyes full of flies.

Further back towards the valley, beyond the hillside corpses of old stags, the Shrieking Pits were shallow, some almost filled, with children from the torture cells of the brochs, and peasants with their throats sliced, bearded men, mothers taken from their babies, thrown down on Jeo's command.

Among the scorched ruins of the tenements, black cindered bodies with no faces or limbs. Among them, somewhere, Jeo's sister and brothers and his grandmother, together in anonymous death. Thousands of bodies, smothered in smoke, then burnt by fire, burnt so deeply that even the bones had taken flame, and the chemical stench had drifted in the valley till it was overwhelmed by the one great smell of the tenements. The smell of charcoal was back.

A small sound turned Jeo's gaze back across the chamber. A soft noise, noise of cloth—and the slow gentle rub of wood on stone. Someone was opening the door.

He stepped away from the window and stood against the opposite wall, where—to his left—the door crept open. He held the knife by the tips of the blade. As the door swung in, a wild thought came to him. He suddenly knew this was no guardsman entering. There was so little noise. And he remembered, all in a moment, that the Elder had always appeared at his window only at dawn. Perhaps, then, he spent the rest of the night away from the keep, or in one of its lower warmer rooms, returning only to look over the valley when the sun came up, to order the opening of the castle door.

He clenched his knife. The door opened fully. The dwarf in

off-white robes came limping into the stone room. There was no one with him. He struggled to push the door shut behind him. He turned, looked to the window . . . then slowly to the right, where he saw the young man facing him from the dark corner, dagger in hand.

Neither of them moved and in the massive silence Jeo held his breath so his pulse sounded in his head. He stared at the Elder and was suddenly afraid.

Nothing—not his moment at the Shrieking Pit or his last meeting with Meagher, not the daily threat of death in the swamps —had ever given him this kind of nameless fear. He couldn't understand it.

If the old man had any fear himself, it didn't show. He made no sound, but took a few tiny steps closer to the youth, who stood where he was and didn't do anything. He wanted to move back, but the wall was there, and he didn't think of using his knife.

The Elder lifted his hands and peeled the cowl back from his head.

What light there was, was on the old man's face. The eyes were half-closed by drooping eyelids, the mouth pursed by wrinkles, and the lower lip had sagged and turned out, exposing the gums. No teeth, of course. The inside of the lip was black.

He was exposing his face, Jeo knew, like a man showing credentials. He was telling the youth that this, he, was what the glen stood for.

He was wrong. Jeo had won. His fear was just a childish thing and it didn't last. In its place, anger that the old man should be in the room. It didn't belong to him any more. Jeo stepped forward from the corner.

He didn't use his knife. He didn't want to waste it in such a squalid shrunken body. As the Elder stood and shivered a little and otherwise did nothing, he took the wrinkled neck in one hand and pressed with just his thumb till there was no more breath. The body fell quietly to the floor and lay like a curious white rag doll, with lolling arms and no expression.

When the man in white robes appeared at the high window and motioned for the castle door to be opened, the guardsmen were horror stricken.

"What's happening, Senior? Why's he opening the door?"

The Guardian raised his red face to the heights of the keep and slowly shook his head. "Don't know," he said. "But open it. Elder's word."

"There's that whole bloody army still outside, Senior. Too many of them. They'll pull us to pieces."

"Must be a plan, maybe," said Ouse, but he was sweating. "He maybe wants to talk to them." He gave a forced shrug. "Elder's word."

The giant door was opened and the forces outside came shrieking into the courtyard. The guardsmen had the weapons and the training to use them, and they killed many, but they were outnumbered. Before very long, the waves of young peasants overwhelmed them and were free to tear them apart.

They killed everything in the castle, all the soldiers and the old men and women, even the animals, with their sticks and stones and knives, some with their bare hands and teeth. They maimed the corpses and loaded them on wagons and moved them to the Shrieking Pits.

Jeo watched it all from the tower. He didn't go down to fight. There was no need, and he'd had enough of it. Let others do it now.

The Garden

IN THE HOUR AFTER DAWN, the master of the glen looked down from the castle keep into the mist of the distant valley. The morning was cold and he pulled the collar of his jerkin up to his ears.

The glen was thick with fog and drizzle now, but it was spring—and under the fog, the hills were in flower and the trees in heavy blossom, like an orchard.

The crops were back in the fields, the livestock multiplying. There were no tenements—they hadn't been rebuilt. There were fewer people and they lived in huts on vast farms. Without the shanty blocks, the place had a more rural look. The river was fast with spring rain. There were no statues of figures in robes.

There were no guardsmen, only armed men and women, some of them young, watching the communal work in the fields. There was no one called Senior, just overseers to be obeyed. There were no Shrieking Pits, just gallows brought in from the fen. There was no rest day.

The castle's hidden tunnel had been filled with rubble and charred wood and would never be used again.

The castle was still there. The man moved back from the window in the tower and went to his long thin mirror, leaned forward to examine the reflected face.

The hair was still dense and black but cut short, the beard dark and thickening. Tiny nets of wrinkles had appeared around the eyes, some lines across the thin throat, a few white hairs. He wasn't the oldest man in the glen, but in any other sense he was its Elder. He didn't have an old man's white robes, but he had everything else.

He adjusted his jerkin and the small knife in his rope belt and left the room. His bare feet made sounds on the stone ledge, then nothing.

Outside, very far below, the mist began to clear. A cockerel yelled in a farmyard till someone beat it quiet.

A NOTE ON THE TYPE

The text of this book was set in a digitized version of Bembo, a well-known Monotype face. Named for Pietro Bembo, the celebrated Renaissance writer and humanist scholar who was made a cardinal and served as secretary to Pope Leo X, the original cutting of Bembo was made by Francesco Griffo of Bologna only a few years after Columbus discovered America.

Sturdy, well balanced, and finely proportioned, Bembo is a face of rare beauty, extremely legible in all its sizes.

Composed by
The Haddon Craftsmen, Inc.,
Scranton, Pennsylvania

Printed and bound by
The Maple-Vail Book Manufacturing Group,
York, Pennsylvania

Typography and binding design by
Tasha Hall